CHAPEL
STREET

SEAN PAUL MURPHY

D1153628

TouchPoint Pre
Relax. Read. Repea..

CHAPEL STREET
By Sean Paul Murphy
Published by TouchPoint Press
Brookland, AR 72417
www.touchpointpress.com

ISBN-13: 978-1-946920-97-3

Editor: Kimberly Coghlan
Cover Design: Colbie Myles
Front Cover Image: Chapel and road at Mount Olivet Cemetery in Frederick, Maryland by jonbilous, Adobe Stock; art-portrait-human-old-antique, SarahRichterArt, Pixabay
Author Photo: J. Bryan Barnes

Visit the author's website at http://seanpaulmurphyville.blogspot.com/

First Edition

Printed in the United States of America.

For my brother, Mark.

I grew up in a haunted house, and, much like hero of this book, lived through a cluster of suicides in my family. My mother inspired this novel when she asked one day whether I thought the entity in the house was responsible in part for deaths of my sister Laura and my brother Mark. That was a possibility I had long considered. This novel is my attempt to explore the implications of my mother's question in a highly fictional manner.

I also want to take this time to thank my lovely wife Deborah. I could have never written this novel without her undying love and support. I am also indebted to my trusty editor and friend Trish Schweers, who always manages to hammer my work into shape against all odds. My beta readers, Patty Gehret and Beth White Werrell, also contributed heavily to this book with their red ink. I would also like to thank my editor Kimberly Coghlan, who managed to pull me across the finish line. I am also grateful to my fellow authors and media professionals, including K.A. Hitchens, Krista Wagner, Kenji Gallo, Jamie Hope, Sydnye White, and John Molli, for their advice and kind words.

In the end, I also want to thank Sheri Williams and the folks at TouchPoint Press. Sheri showed a lot of faith in me when she published my oddball memoir *The Promise, or the Pros and Cons of Talking with God*. She is showing equal faith with this book. I hope it is rewarded.

"For we do not wrestle against flesh and blood, but against the rulers, against the authorities, against the cosmic powers over this present darkness, against the spiritual forces of evil in the heavenly places."
Ephesians 6:12

Prologue: My Mother

My name is Rick Bakos, and my story began on September 27, 2011.

I arrived home at St. Helens Street at midnight. The drafty five-bedroom Victorian house was nearly a hundred years old. Sheltered by oak trees, it sat on the second highest hill in northeast Baltimore. You could see everything from the skyscrapers in the Inner Harbor to the smokestacks of the steel mills at distant Sparrows Point from the upstairs windows. We moved into the house when I was three years old, which was a considerable upgrade from my maternal grandparents' basement. To me, it was a veritable castle with plenty of nooks and crannies to explore. Now, however, its size seemed to mock the diminished state of our family.

Lights still illuminated my mother's front bedroom as I pulled into the driveway. No voice greeted me when I stepped inside, but I heard her television playing. I called to her, but she didn't answer. I went to the door and gently knocked. Once again, no response.

I announced myself before quietly opening the door. I didn't want to wake her up if she was already asleep. In that case, I would just turn off her lights and television as I frequently did. Her doctors proscribed a dizzying array of drugs since her battle with lymphoma began a couple of months earlier. Her nighttime dosage often sent her on a peaceful night's sleep, provided her television didn't wake her back up.

As expected, I saw my mother, Alice Bakos, lying in bed. Her head was cocked toward her nightstand. Her eyes were open. I assumed she was awake.

"Hi," I said.

No response. Nothing. She didn't even turn to me. Now I was worried.

I crept forward. A thick comforter and more blankets than the mild fall night demanded covered her. Her head and shoulders were exposed. She wore red, plaid flannel pajamas. One of her arms hung stiffly off the side of the bed. It was motionless. In fact, there was no motion anywhere. The blankets were not rising and falling with her breath. Nothing was.

I turned to her brown eyes as I walked forward. They were wide open, and they appeared dry. Sticky, even. They didn't blink. Not once. A little pinpoint somewhere deep in my mind registered the truth: she was dead. The rest of me couldn't accept it. My mother was fighting a losing battle against lymphoma with chemo. I knew that much, but the doctors assured me she still had months to live. She couldn't be dead. Not now.

Her mouth was wide open, too. Crookedly. There was a dry, white substance around her lips. It wasn't vomit. It was like she had been foaming at her mouth in her last moments.

Now I was close enough to touch her. Her neck was exposed. I reached out to check for a pulse, but I couldn't bring myself to touch her white skin. I had a sudden, overpowering thought that it would be deathly cold and that the cold would never leave my fingers. I hated myself as I pulled back my hand.

What if she was still alive? What if she was just unconscious?

What could I do anyway? I wasn't a doctor.

I had to call nine-one-one.

I took out my cellphone. As I dialed, my eyes went to the nightstand. All of her yellow pill bottles were on their sides. My first thought was that she knocked them over while she was dying, but where were the pills? They should have spilled all over the place, but I didn't see a single one. Some the bottles should have been full. I refilled two of the prescriptions on my way home from work that very evening.

The truth flooded into my brain: she killed herself.

I dropped my phone as I staggered backwards out of her bedroom. I couldn't believe she actually did it. My older brother Lenny killed himself a year earlier by jumping off a sixth floor balcony at a hotel in the resort town of Ocean City, Maryland. His death wasn't a surprise. He suffered from bipolar disorder and schizophrenia for nearly his entire adult life. Still, his suicide crushed our family emotionally. My mother most of all. She was never the same afterwards.

And now she decided to inflict the same pain on us again herself.

How could she?

I couldn't go back into her bedroom and retrieve my cellphone. I went downstairs and called nine-one-one on the ground line in the kitchen. Afraid they wouldn't consider it an emergency if I reported her dead, I told them I thought she was in a coma. Then I called my kid sister Janet and gave her the news. I dreaded that call. Janet and I were not close. I resented her decision to escape to college in California, leaving my mother and me to deal with Lenny. Still, there was no one else left to call her. It was my responsibility. When I got her, I told Janet that Mom was dead, but I didn't mention suicide. I didn't want to freak her out completely. She was always the emotional one in the family, and I couldn't handle that now. Not alone.

Next, I called my girlfriend, Gina Holt. She rushed over from her comfy downtown apartment, where I had spent the evening. She arrived after the ambulance, but thankfully before my sister. Gina was perfect. She stayed glued to my side the entire time, always keeping a supportive hand on my shoulder, back, or arm. Gina seemed genuinely upset about my mother's death, despite the fact that my mom had tried every trick in her considerable playbook to ruin our relationship.

My sister arrived right before the paramedics came downstairs to give us the bad news. They also noticed the bottles. Apparently, when a person dies of natural causes, the paramedics have you call the funeral home to remove the body. However, since they now suspected suicide, they were taking my mother to the hospital for an autopsy. Just as I feared, Janet became hysterical, alternating almost equally between mournful moaning and angry rants. After they removed my mother's body, the three of us sat up all night and drank every ounce of alcohol in the house. Janet left at dawn. I left, too. I couldn't stay at the house. I went back with Gina to her apartment.

I took the week off from work to take care of the funeral arrangements. Gina took off the week, too. For the next month, I rarely returned to the family home. For the first time in our nearly five-year relationship, Gina and I actually lived together. I assumed it was a preamble to the marriage both Gina and I wanted, but from the beginning, our life together was marred by vivid nightmares. Each night, I imagined waking up to find Gina dead beside me. Sometimes, it was present day. Sometimes, it was in the distant future. It didn't matter when. The truth was undeniable. If Gina and I stayed together, the day would come when one of us would awaken to find the other one dead.

I couldn't face that prospect. Claiming I needed space to mourn, I moved out of her apartment and got my own place in a high-rise in Towson. The dreams stopped, but with them the relationship fizzled out too. I was heartbroken, but I let it happen anyway. Call me a coward, but I knew if I stayed alone, I could limit my future pain.

Gina deserved better.

Ironically, my mother won. The sight of her dead in bed ultimately shattered the relationship she had long desired to destroy.

Chapter One: RestingPlace.com

June 2016.

I am a cemetery junkie.

My obsession was an outgrowth of genealogy. As a bachelor with no children of my own, I turned my eyes backwards toward my ancestors. I traced all of my familial lines back at least a couple of centuries. In the process, I talked to hundreds of cousins while compiling my extensive family tree. They tended to be elderly women happy to share the stories that their own children and grandchildren had grown bored of hearing. As the years passed, I found myself attending their funerals out of gratitude for the stories and photos they shared with me.

Perhaps because of all of the funerals I attended, I developed a desire to visit the graves of all of my ancestors. I would visit the overgrown cemeteries, thorns and stickers tearing at my khaki pants and tennis shoes. I often felt an acute, practically supernatural, sense of connection to my kin as I stood upon their graves looking down at their weathered monuments. I knew they were all once just like me. They lived. They loved. They fought. They laughed. They worked. Then they died. But part of them remained—me. Did they imagine when they bought their little oblong plots that a hundred and twenty years later, a great-great-great grandson would stand above them in respect? Were they looking down at me from heaven? Or up from hell? Was there even a heaven or hell? Or did we, as I suspected, just disappear into nothingness? It was maddening to think we lived in vain.

How many people in this world truly achieve a legacy that outlives them? None of my ancestors; that's for sure. They were just worker bees, living in little houses and toiling endlessly at jobs to fulfill the dreams of men who the world considered greater and more important than they. What did they have to show for their labors in the end, aside from generations of progeny they would never know and who would never know them? A tombstone. That was it. A slab of granite or marble with their names etched into it.

In theory, those stones could last for centuries, far longer than the once living bones beneath them. That was encouraging, but what did it really say about them? Occasionally, a short poem or Bible verse had been inscribed into the cold stone. That was better than nothing. Most of their markers only recorded their names and the dates of their birth and death. I hated seeing my ancestors, whom I had painstakingly researched over the years, reduced to a mere string of facts. A human being is more than the sum of their name and dates. I wanted the world to get a taste of their individual humanity: their personalities, their struggles, and even their small triumphs, as insignificant as they might have been in the overall scheme of human history.

I found the perfect place to honor my family at RestingPlace.com, a vast online database of millions of graves slowly compiled by thousands of volunteers around the world. I began building online memorials to all of my relatives. I wrote short biographies of them and included plenty of photographs. The website even allowed me to link them all together by familial relationship. A person could easily click through my entire family tree, person by person. Now my ancestors were no longer simply names and dates carved in stone. You could look into their eyes and get a sense of their identity.

In my own way, I granted my family cyber-immortality, which was probably the only actual form available. I couldn't bring myself to accept any sort of spiritual continuance, despite my nominally religious background. My parents were both Catholics. They were not necessarily weekly churchgoers, but they took their faith seriously enough to send my brother Lenny and me to St. Dominic Elementary School.

After my father Stan's death in an automobile accident, my mother took us out of the Catholic school and unceremoniously dropped us in the Baltimore City public school system. It was probably an economic decision, but I suspect it was also her way of rejecting the cruel God who prematurely stole her loving husband. She attended church much less frequently as the years passed. In the end, she only went for weddings and funerals and the occasional Christmas when she was feeling sentimental. Still, my mother didn't reject all spirituality. She believed in signs and omens and became obsessed with charlatans and fortunetellers who played her like a violin.

My religious beliefs also changed with the death of my father. I stopped believing in a loving God who took a personal interest in the lives of his people. It wasn't until college that I pretty much closed the door on the very concept of God itself. I wasn't an atheist. Atheism was too intellectually arrogant for me. I accepted a limit to human knowledge. I could concede that an entity we could define as God could possibly exist somewhere in some unknown dimension. However, for all practical purposes, I believed we human beings were on our own. When we died, we just blinked out of existence. That reality fired my resolve concerning Resting Place. In the absence of God, I would provide the human race what little measure of immortality I could muster.

I began documenting the graves of strangers when I ran out of my own relatives, starting with a small Methodist cemetery a few blocks away from my apartment. One sunny Saturday afternoon, I walked through it and photographed every tombstone. I spent the rest of the weekend uploading the photos and documenting the graves on the website. Whenever I came upon a name I found particularly interesting, I would research the individual on various genealogical websites and include the information I found.

I found it a very rewarding hobby, much more interesting than my day job as an accountant at Johns Hopkins Hospital. My primary responsibility consisted of checking physical inventories throughout the hospital: counting all the essential implements of modern medicine. The doctors and nurses got the glory. I got the clipboard. By the time I finished my rounds, it was time to start walking those same corridors again. At least I got some fresh air when I documented the graves, and people really appreciated my genealogical efforts. Every week I got emails from happy people thanking me for finding the graves of their relatives. No doctor ever thanked me for ensuring that rubber gloves were nearby when he needed one. No patient did either for that matter.

I also made it a habit to fulfill photo requests that people submitted to the website. I would drive out to the cemetery and get the location of the requested grave from the office. Sometimes the cemetery had no record of the loved one in question. In that case, I would send the submitter an email saying so. If I found their loved one, I would photograph the grave and upload the picture to the website for them. They were generally very grateful. In a world defined by death and sorrow, it felt great to do something nice for strangers.

Chapter Two: Elisabetta

Saturday.

I got up late, around eleven. Usually, I didn't allow myself that indulgence, but I'd been out late the night before. I was a regular at the weekly Friday Night Swing Dance at the American Legion Hall. After Gina, I accepted the fact I would never marry or have a long-term romantic relationship with a woman. Still, the dances gave me a chance to enjoy the company of women. The organizers offered a free lesson before each dance, and I had developed some finesse on my feet over time. Some of the ladies seemed interested in me. Straight, unmarried men my age, unencumbered by crippling child-support payments, are apparently rare. I was tempted to ask out some of them, but I could never pull the trigger. If I couldn't make it work with Gina, what made me think it could work with them? What if the nightmares came back?

No, I was better off alone.

After completing my morning grooming rituals, I had a light breakfast at my computer. I went to the webpage of the Baltimore Sunpapers to check the death notices. I checked every day for my cousins. My family appeared unscathed. Then I started making memorials for the deceased on Resting Place. I was lucky today. Another local contributor, who called herself Tombstone Teri, also combed through the local death notices. If I started too late in the morning, she would memorialize the dead before I had the chance. I didn't know if she considered me a rival, but I certainly viewed her as one. Tombstone Teri was racking up some very impressive numbers. I posted about sixteen thousand memorials over the past four years. Teri was only a member for two years and was already up to nearly fifteen thousand memorials. I couldn't let down my guard for a second.

While memorializing someone buried at Eternal Faith cemetery, I noticed a new photo request. I paused. The cemetery sat about five miles from my home. It would be easy to go over and snap the picture, but I always approached the place with a heavy heart. Eternal Faith Memorial Gardens was slated to be my own final resting place. My father, Stan Bakos, bought six plots and joked that we could have them on a first come first serve basis. He snagged the first one himself a short year or two later, when I was nine-years-old. My older brother Lenny got the next one. My mother Alice followed him. Only my sister Janet and I remained on this side of the grass, and it looked like we were going to leave an empty plot unless one of us got married.

Something told me not to go to the cemetery, but fulfilling that request was a matter of pride. Tombstone Teri put up some good numbers, but she was lazy. She generated most of her memorials from Internet newspaper death notices and funeral home listings. Her fieldwork was weak. According to her profile, she only fulfilled three photo requests. I had fulfilled forty-nine more than that. I couldn't resist making it an even fifty. So I slipped on my shoes and headed out into the world.

Eternal Faith Memorial Gardens was a perfect example of the kind of cookie-cutter cemetery I had grown to despise over the years. It gave me no comfort to know I would be buried there one day myself.

To preserve the so-called natural appearance of the grounds, the management only permitted flat markers, dull rectangles of granite topped with bronze nameplates and the occasional ceramic photograph. Spare me. A person will rest under their monument for a long time. They should be entitled to choose one indicative of their personality. Throughout our lives, society forces us unceasingly into conformity. Shouldn't we have the freedom to express ourselves in death? A philosopher could argue that the cemetery policy satisfied some egalitarian impulse. The graves of the rich and the poor and the famous and the common are indistinguishable at Eternal Faith. Whatever. I suspect the real reason for the policy involved was cost. It is cheaper to cut the grass with these flat monuments.

When I turned my trusty, red Toyota Corolla into the cemetery, our family plot came into view. The graves lay near the top of a small rise about a hundred-and-fifty-yards from the service road. A sheltering willow tree stood nearby, making the spot extremely easy to find, but I averted my eyes quickly. While I often felt a mystical connection at the graves of my distant ancestors, that sensation wasn't repeated at the graves of people I actually knew in life. All I felt when I stood at their graves was their absence. And I didn't want to feel that today. It was too bright and sunny. Life was still too alluring. I preferred to think about Andrea, a girl who had asked me to dance three times the previous night. She was someone I could see myself dating, *if* I were dating. Then again, so was Rita Falstaff. At least on the days she tolerated me.

Rita was the receptionist at the cemetery office. She was about thirty-two-years old and always professionally-dressed. Her hair was blonde, but her roots made a lie of that on occasion. She possessed a friendly smile, and she always seemed relieved to talk to someone who wasn't in mourning, unless said person was a genealogist. Genealogists were the bane of her existence. Our questions always sent her to a wall of black filing cabinets in the unventilated back room. She despised rummaging through those file cabinets, complaining the whole time about her predecessor who only had a passing knowledge of the alphabet.

"No, I don't have time for you, Rick," she said, groaning audibly when I stepped through the door. "We've got three interments today."

"Only one name, Rita," I said. "Please."

"Is it a relative?"

I hesitated.

Her eyes narrowed. "Are you going to make me go back there for that stupid website?"

"I'm doing a favor for someone."

"I'm the one who's doing the favor." She sighed as she picked up her pen. "What's the name?"

"Matilda Ritter."

She didn't even bother writing it down. "She's in the mausoleum. Third tier, on the left."

Forty thousand people buried at Eternal Faith, and she knew the one I wanted right off the top of her head? I was skeptical. "Are you sending me on a wild goose chase?" I asked.

"No," she said. "Somebody was just in asking about her."

Oh, no. "Was it Tombstone Teri?"

"Who's Tombstone Teri?"

"Describe her."

"White. Mid-thirties. Kind of stiff–like a high school math teacher or librarian," Rita replied. "Is that her?"

"Don't know. I never met her."

"Then why did you ask me to describe her?" she replied, pointing to the door. "Get out, and don't come back this week."

"Thanks, I owe you."

"Damned right you do!"

I jumped into my car and drove over to the mausoleum. There weren't any cars parked out front. That meant Tombstone Teri got her picture already, but I could still beat her to the punch. If I uploaded my photo to the website before she did, I could still get the credit for fulfilling the request. I smiled. Talk about snatching victory from the jaws of defeat. The day was getting better by the moment.

I opened the heavy glass double doors of the mausoleum and stepped inside, shivering instinctively. Outside, the temperature hovered around eighty-five degrees and humid, but inside the mausoleum, it felt like sixty-five degrees. The white marble walls and floor sucked the heat right out of the air, leaving only a clammy humidity. I wrapped my arms around myself for warmth. As I did, I felt goose pimples rising on the exposed skin. I suddenly realized I was afraid, really afraid.

I couldn't believe it. My genealogical journeys have taken me into catacombs and crypts. I have seen exposed human remains on numerous occasions, but I have never been afraid. There are no such things as zombies or vampires or ghosts. The dead were simply dead. Unmoving. Uncaring. Unknowing. They were worthy of respect for who they once were, not for what they had become. The dead couldn't hurt you, aside perhaps from some living disease brewing in their decay. I know all of that, but I was still afraid. It was crazy. I had been in this mausoleum many times before, and I had never felt this way. It had to be the cold. The sudden shock to my system sought a supernatural cause where none was necessary.

The vault housing Mrs. Matilda Ritter's casket was slightly above eye level, but the camera angle wasn't too awkward. I brushed away the brittle, dead flowers in the bronze vase partially blocking her name. The flowers disintegrated as if they were a thousand years old. The tiny fragments fluttered slowly to the marble floor. That was when I noticed the other flower fragments. The floor was littered with them.

Dead stalks rose up out of the vases of the nearby vaults. Their petals lay brown and crinkly on the floor. I was surprised. This wasn't like Eternal Faith at all. The cemetery was young and viable with thousands of empty plots for sale and dozens of new burials a week. They had the money and staff to police the grounds properly. Jose Garcia, the groundskeeper, was particularly meticulous. The grass was always cut. The trees and bushes were neatly trimmed. The dead flowers were always discreetly discarded.

This was sloppy. Creepy, too.

Once again, an unnatural fear tugged at me. My heart rate increased, and my breath caught in my throat, but I immediately pushed the fear from my mind. There had to be a rational explanation. At first I theorized that the unnatural cold of the mausoleum killed the flowers, but that didn't make any sense. You refrigerated flowers to preserve their freshness. They should have thrived near the clammy marble. Nevertheless, they were dead, all of them in the building.

Well, no. Not all of them.

A veritable forest of flowers bloomed beneath a vault at the end of the building. I thought it had to be a new interment of a much beloved individual. After snapping a quick photo of the Ritter grave for the webpage, I found myself walking toward the vault, but the colorful array of flowers brought me no joy. If anything, each echoing footstep shouted a warning.

Stop.

Don't do it.

I didn't listen. If I stopped, I would be giving into superstitious fear. That was an affront to my rational mind. I kept walking, but I couldn't shake the strange feeling my steps were pre-arranged and pre-determined. I felt like a chess piece being moved into position by a force beyond my control.

A ceramic photo of the deceased was attached to the vault above her name. I smiled briefly despite my growing dread. I always appreciated when people included a photo of the deceased on their grave. A photo gives you a definite feel for the dead person. This black and white photograph revealed an attractive woman in her mid-to-late forties. Her dark hair and eyes didn't surprise me. My years of walking through cemeteries taught me that Italians, Jews, and Eastern Europeans were most likely to memorialize their loved ones with photos, so I expected her to have stereotypical dark features.

My assumptions about her ethnicity could have been confirmed by looking down at her name, but her eyes wouldn't release mine. They drew me in and pulled me forward. They were not inherently intimidating or scary. The eyes, much like the half-smile lingering beneath them, hinted at a world-weary wisdom. They shimmered with the power to seduce but lacked even a hint of love. The dark lady seemed to possess a cynical secret that empowered her, but at a terrible price. People spent centuries speculating on the meaning of the Mona Lisa's smile, but I didn't want to know the reason behind this dark woman's smile. I knew instinctively it would terrify me.

Still, I walked forward until we were practically face-to-face. Only the wall of flowers stopped me. The smell of flowers could charm me in the wild, but their scent in enclosed areas often sickened me. They brought back memories of all the funerals I dutifully attended. Now, however, I wasn't thinking of the emotionally neutral funerals of my many aged cousins who contributed mightily to my family tree. I found myself instead at Rucks Funeral Home staring down at the powdered face of my dead mother, Alice Ann Bakos, nee Sullivan. Eyes shut. Jaws wired tightly. Lips twisted into a smile she never made naturally. Blinking quickly, I travelled a year further back in time to that same room to the closed casket funeral of my poor, doomed brother Lenny where mother's mournful wailing filled my ears.

I shut my eyes, hoping the darkness would break the spell. It did. I rested in the soothing darkness for a moment, my heart calming, before finally opening my eyes. I resolved not to meet the woman's eyes again, but I was too curious to turn away. I had to know more about her. I turned to the inscription:

Elisabetta A. Kostek

September 19, 1942 – November 15, 2014

The date of death surprised me. From the abundance of flowers, I assumed she recently died, or experienced an anniversary. Perhaps it was a wedding anniversary, but no husband was listed. Vaults generally sold in pairs. The names of surviving spouses were usually listed in neat bronze letters on the marble, waiting only the inevitable date of death. If she was single, who left the flowers?

And why were her flowers still fresh when all the others were dead?

I took a step back, and then another and another. I thought I was leaving, but instead, I found myself raising my camera to photograph her grave. First, I took a wide shot, capturing the entire front of the vault. Then, with some trepidation, I zoomed in on the photograph of Elisabetta A. Kostek until her face filled my viewfinder. I half-expected her eyes to hook me again like they did earlier, but this time, she simply stared blankly. Still, call me crazy, but it seemed like the corners of her lips had crept up a little bit.

Once the camera found the proper focus, I snapped the shutter and turned away. In the back of my mind, I hoped whatever drew me to the grave would release me once the pictures were taken. That wasn't the case. I felt the dark lady's eyes boring into me as I walked. My pace was brisk at first, but my speed steadily increased. The bright sunlight just outside the glass doors seemed like oxygen to a man swimming up from the depths. I was practically running by the time I reached the doors. My heart was thumping in my ears, practically drowning out my footsteps. An irrational fear suddenly overwhelmed me that the doors wouldn't open when I pushed them, but they did. Still, I didn't slow down until I was out of the shadow of the building itself and bathed entirely in the purifying light of the sun. My heartbeat slowed as I sucked in the fresh air. Before long, the chill of the mausoleum left me. Fear left, and reason returned, but I had no explanation for what happened.

Chapter Three: The Upload

I headed straight for my car upon leaving the mausoleum.

I rarely left a cemetery with pictures of only two graves, especially Eternal Faith. With over forty thousand graves and only about three thousand memorials uploaded to Resting Place, the cemetery was practically virginal. Whenever I visited it, I always strolled up and down a few rows photographing every visible monument. It seemed like a waste of time and gasoline to leave here with only two graves to upload. However, the paranoid fear that grabbed me in the mausoleum robbed me of the sense of purpose I usually felt in the cemetery. I had to leave.

Normally, I would have gotten something to eat on my way home. My trusty Corolla, knowing my normal routine, found the slow-moving drive-thru lane of a McDonald's near my one-bedroom apartment in a Towson high-rise without much conscious assistance from me. However, the sight of the glossy pictures of the items on the menu, which usually looked more appetizing than the food itself, made me feel strangely nauseous. And I liked McDonald's food. This time, however, the hamburger meat on the menu appeared sickly grey. Dead. As if it were tough with rigor mortis. Coughing, I felt the sharp sting of some bile at the back of my throat. That was all I needed. I pulled out of the lane and headed home.

I had no firm plans for the day. The Baltimore Orioles were playing the Cleveland Indians that afternoon. I enjoyed baseball and followed it avidly. It was the only team sport my mother deemed safe enough for me to play, especially since my general lack of ability relegated me to the undemanding role of late-inning replacement right fielder. Still, I enjoyed being part of a team, and watching the games on television brought back good memories.

I planned to spend the afternoon creating dozens of memorials on Resting Place while watching the game. Since I left the cemetery with only two graves, I thought I could relax and watch the Orioles beat the Indians without distraction. I was wrong. I found myself strangely restless, shifting from my sofa to my chair. A few times, I found myself walking toward my desk, but I always stopped myself. I knew what I would do as soon as I sat down at the desk. I would take the memory card out of my camera and load it into the computer. Then I would upload the dark lady's photograph.

The thought scared me. Not just because I didn't want to look into her eyes again. No, I felt something deeper there, far beyond mere flesh and bone and even mind. I felt some inchoate fear that I was no longer in control of myself. That something, or someone, was manipulating me from shadows too deep to examine.

I tried to shake off the feeling. It was crazy. Irrational. There were no shadows lingering over me. I experienced my share of darkness—perhaps more than my share, with the deaths of my parents and my only brother by the time I was thirty-three-years-old. I certainly went through deep and profound moments of sadness, but nothing like the depression that killed my brother Lenny.

I secretly envied Lenny when we were younger. He possessed an easygoing charm equally effective with both parents and peers. Everybody liked him, especially the girls. I watched in amazement as he would walk up to pretty girls at the mall and have them smiling in no time. I, on the other hand, got better grades in school. It wasn't a fair trade. The grades got me into college, a life experience Lenny opted to ignore, much to our mother's consternation. He wanted to start living an adult life. On a whim, he became a car salesman. I have to admit, it was an excellent choice. He could sell anything when he was sane. The problem was that those sane periods became increasingly infrequent.

Lenny drifted into madness in his early twenties. We thought it was drugs at first, but after an arrest for disorderly conduct and a forced committal, we discovered the problem was in his mind. We never got his true diagnosis. Lenny never let his doctors discuss this condition with us. Lenny used the words manic depression, bipolar, paranoid, and schizophrenic to describe himself during his lucid periods, which lasted for months, provided he took his medication. When he was off his meds, Lenny quickly waded into the darkness of insanity again.

What happened to him frightened me. It was horrifying to watch a dark fluke of internal chemistry send a decent, good-natured guy with prospects spiraling into a tortuous world of his own creation, buffeted by voices and images only he could see or hear. I wouldn't have survived as long as he did. No way. The way I looked at it, we *are* our minds. Period. The human mind is our only window to the world—and our only means by which to process it. If we lose control of it, we are left with nothing but the derision or pity of those around us. I valued my dignity too much. I could never accept that fate. In the end, neither could Lenny.

One night he leapt from a six-story balcony at a hotel in Ocean City, Maryland where we had once stayed with our family as children. He landed head-first on the concrete about two and half feet away from the edge of the swimming pool. Some of Lenny's more optimistic friends chose to believe this death was a crazy stunt gone awry. They thought he was aiming for the pool, but I knew the truth. It was suicide, pure and simple. Poor Lenny was doomed. It was only a matter of time.

I shuddered with the memory of my brother, and I couldn't fathom what sent my mind reeling in that direction. I wasn't that kind of guy. Despite being half-Irish, I wasn't prone to prolonged bouts of melancholy. When Lenny died, I genuinely mourned him, but I moved on. That's what strong people did, and, in my own way, I considered myself very strong.

I knew the visit to the cemetery wasn't responsible for my strange mood either. I had visited Eternal Faith dozens of times without experiencing any inordinate sorrow. It might have been different if I actually visited the family graves, but I wasn't there to mourn my family. I was there for another family.

The dark woman, I thought.

"No," I said aloud as I immediately dismissed the thought.

It was just a strange day, I told myself. Things would improve if reliever Darren O'Day held onto the Orioles' one-run lead through the top of Cleveland's order. I got up from the sofa and headed into the kitchen for a beer. When I opened the refrigerator door, the smell of spoiled, rancid meat overwhelmed me. Cupping my nose and mouth with my hand, I quickly slammed the door shut. I was stunned. What could have gone that bad that fast?

I cautiously opened the door again. The smell was gone. I couldn't believe it. Had I just imagined it? Hearing the commercial end in the other room, I decided to grab a beer and forget about it. But, as I reached for the beer, the mere thought of drinking it made me nauseous.

What was going on? Was I going crazy? Closing the refrigerator door, I headed back to the living room to watch the game.

I headed for the sofa, but I found myself sitting down at the computer. The screensaver slowly rolled through the family photographs I had scanned during my genealogical quest. The parade of images usually calmed and reassured me of my place in the universe, but I found myself becoming unnerved instead. I didn't intend to go to the desk. Why did I? Angry, I wanted to stand up, but I became defiant instead. Walking away now would be giving into this absurd fear. It was better just to get my work out of the way now so I could enjoy the rest of the game in peace. Plus, I still had a chance to beat Tombstone Teri to the punch with the Ritter grave.

I took the memory chip from my trusty Nikon camera and plugged it into my USB adapter. I opened a browser and went to the Resting Place webpage. The photo request for Matilda Ritter was still listed. I smiled. I could still beat Tombstone Teri. I transferred the photos from my memory card to the cemetery folder on my computer. I found my photo of the Ritter grave and dropped it on the add-photo icon.

After the photo uploaded, the memorial for Matilda Ritter refreshed. The photograph looked fine, but I didn't care for the memorial itself that only listed her name and the dates of her birth and death. Not even her maiden name. If I created the memorial, I would have gone to the newspaper and copied the death notice. I would have also gone to the webpage of the funeral home, too. They often featured photographs of the deceased. Pictures of the dead gave a memorial life.

And, speaking of photographs, I still had two more to deal with.

I brought the cursor to the wide shot of the Kostek grave, but something told me to delete the Kostek files instead. Then again, another force pushed me to create a memorial for Elisabetta Kostek for the whole world to see. This conflict made no sense to me. I had posted literally thousands of photographs of graves and their inhabitants on the website, and I never before felt like I was making a moral choice. I certainly felt sad at times, but only if I was creating a memorial for a child or a suicide victim.

I clicked on the file. The image of Elisabetta Kostek's grave appeared on my computer monitor. Nothing on it should have triggered such an emotional response in me. She wasn't a child. The late Miss Kostek was seventy-two-years-old, which was more than enough time for anyone. Nothing indicated she died by her own hand either. My misgivings seemed groundless, except that there seemed to be something strange about her face.

I clicked on the next file, and the close-up of Elisabetta Kostek filled my monitor. She didn't creep me out quite as much this time. Her dark eyes looked strangely satisfied. The smile now appeared to be a tiny gloat of victory, as if she knew I would perform as instructed.

I went to the main page for Eternal Faith. I typed in her name. It didn't show up, which meant the grave was unlisted. I clicked on "add memorial" and typed in her name, then stopped. I needed more information. Was she married? If so, what was her maiden name?

I opened another tab on my browser and went to the death notices section of the Baltimore Sun. I typed in her name, but nothing came up. That was surprising. But maybe she wasn't local. I opened up Ancestry.com with the hope of finding an obituary there. No such luck. They had absolutely nothing about her. Opening another tab, I googled her name. Nothing came up—not even those find-a-person pay websites you'd get when you type any name into the search engine.

What the hell? You'd think a woman who earned such a wall of flowers two years after her death would have left some sort of Internet trail.

I returned my attention to Resting Place. The cursor blinked in the slot to add her date of birth. The fear that engulfed me in the mausoleum returned. Except this time, I knew I couldn't escape by running outside into the sun. Some wordless voice beyond the realm of logic and reason assured me that the only way to dispel the fear was to finish the memorial. Another voice, much quieter, warned me that I was making a dangerous mistake.

"*Delete the files*," said the voice.

I highlighted the two Kostek files in the folder. My finger actually went to the delete key, but I couldn't do it. Deleting those files would be giving in to superstition. I always considered myself a rationalist. I was an accountant. I lived in a world of numbers. One plus one equals two, even if a black cat walks by or someone breaks a mirror.

No. I wouldn't delete the Kostek files out of fear. That was absurd. With newfound resolve, I typed Elisabetta's dates of birth and death into Resting Place using the brass plaque as my sole source. Then I went to my photo directory and grabbed the wide shot of the Kostek grave and dropped it on the add-photo icon. I felt no misgiving as it quickly uploaded onto the webpage. That wasn't true when it came time to add the close-up of Elisabetta's face.

I grabbed the photo from the directory and held it over the add-photograph icon. Once again, I felt I was making a choice between good and evil. Once again, rationality rose up in me. There are no voices, I told myself. There are no forces. It's just a photograph. I found my logic reassuring, but not entirely convincing. It placated my concerns, but I knew deep in my heart, I was acting out of fear. I was afraid that something dark had a hold of me—and that it wouldn't release me until I put the photograph on the Internet.

I dropped the file onto the icon, and the haunting photograph of Elisabetta Kostek was added to her memorial for the world to see. I gave her one last look before I closed the browser. Her smile now seemed to reflect some happiness, as if I had freed her. And, if I did, she freed me, too. I felt better than I had all day. Hungrier, too. I was famished.

I went to the kitchen and opened the refrigerator door again. I barely remembered the horrible stench that greeted me a few minutes ago as I pulled out some containers of leftover Chinese food. I heated it up in the microwave and took it back into the living room to eat during the last few outs of the game. Happily, the Orioles won, and despite my plans to take the salsa dance lessons that night downtown on the thirteenth floor of the Belvedere Hotel, I found myself drifting off to sleep.

Chapter Four: The Kobayashi Maru

A familiar voice awakened me by softly singing the old hymn, "Rise and shine, give God the glory, glory."

The song echoed from my earliest childhood. My paternal grandmother Sadie, a very religious woman, sang it to us in the morning when we spent the night at her house. However, this wasn't my grandmother's voice. It was my older brother Lenny. He would sing it to wake me up, but without my grandmother's reverence.

I opened my eyes to find twelve-year-old Lenny crouched down beside my bed in our old shared bedroom on St. Helens Street. He stood up. "Get your bathing suit on. We're going to do a little trespassing," he said. "And whatever you do, don't wake Mom up."

I smiled. We were going pool hopping again. It was one of my favorite childhood memories with Lenny, but he never planned for me to go along.

One summer evening the year after my father died, Lenny convinced our mother to let him and two of his friends, Charlie Woods and Pete Thompson, camp out in the backyard. She was at her over-protective worst then. There was zero possibility she would let him go on a real camping trip—or even spend the night at a friend's house. I don't know how he managed to convince her to let him set up that little pup tent at the back of our yard, but he did. He didn't, however, intend to stay in the backyard all night.

He knew she would be watching, but he planned to outlast her. But what he didn't count on was me. After my mother fell asleep, I saw them sneaking out of the tent, and I went outside to join them. Lenny heard the creak of the back door and turned to me. He angrily pointed back inside, but, in a rare display of boldness, I shook my head no. He hurried over to me.

"Get inside," he whispered.

"No," I replied, "I want to go with you."

Lenny pushed me. "You go inside or I'll beat the crap out of you."

"If you do, I'll tell Mom."

That trumped his threat. Charlie and Pete wandered over. "Come on, Lenny," Charlie said. "Let's give the boy an education in trespassing."

Lenny gave Charlie a look and then turned back to me. "You say a word about this, and I will kick your ass."

With that warning, we indulged in Charlie's favorite summertime passion: pool hopping. That night we wandered throughout the neighborhood clandestinely swimming in the pools of our neighbors. By four a.m., we had swum in thirty pools. Charlie said that was the all-time neighborhood record, which would never be broken. I know I never broke it. I tried to repeat the feat with my friends, but they always chickened out. I don't think Lenny and his friends came close again either. The next summer, they discovered pot and spent most of their time getting high in Charlie's basement.

Now, in this dream, it looked like Lenny and I were finally going to get the chance to break the record.

I didn't remember getting dressed. I just found myself walking down the middle of Beechwood Avenue trailing a few steps behind Lenny. This was quite unlike our last adventure when we stayed close to the shadows out of fear of being spotted. There was no fear now. The houses lining the street were completely dark. It was very eerie, as if we were the only two people in the world.

"Must be late," I said.

"Yup," Lenny answered.

It suddenly struck me that I was still speaking in my adult voice, not my unbroken ten-year-old voice. I looked ahead at Lenny. He was taller than me, physically, so I was still my ten-year-old self in this dream.

As soon as the word dream entered my mind, I calmed down. This was only a dream, and dreams had their own logic. I had nothing to fear.

"Where are we going?" I asked Lenny.

"The Kobayashi Maru," he said as he turned and gave me a wicked smile.

The Kobayashi Maru was a Star Trek reference to an unwinnable training exercise in Star Fleet Academy. I knew immediately what Lenny meant: the Coleman Pool. We opted out of hopping in it on the night of our triumph. The pool itself wasn't much, just a four-foot circular above-ground model. The problem was the location. An unclimbable seven-foot-high wooden privacy fence surrounded the entire Coleman backyard. The only entrance to the yard was a gate between the garage and the side of the house located a few feet from the back door. That's why it was so dangerous. If you woke up the owners, you had to pass right by their back door to escape. Plus, Mr. Coleman supposedly kept a shotgun loaded with rock salt near the back door. Even the reckless Charlie balked at hopping that pool. He was the one who named it the Kobayashi Maru.

The next thing I knew we were sneaking alongside the Coleman house toward the metal gate. I should say, *I* was sneaking. Lenny walked normally. When he opened the gate, the metal clicked so loudly, it seemed to echo throughout the neighborhood. I grabbed his shirt to pull him back.

"Let's get out of here," I said.

Lenny just turned to me. "No," he said softly. "This is one thing I always regretted not doing."

I released his shirt. He turned and walked into the yard. I stood motionlessly trying to figure out what was going on. Did his words reflect his childhood perspective or his adult one? Who was this Lenny?

A soft splash interrupted my thoughts. I stepped into the yard and went to the pool. I found Lenny floating on his back with his eyes closed and a big smile on his face. He opened his eyes and turned to me.

"What are you waiting for? This is the Kobayashi Maru, and we've beat it," Lenny said, and then he laughed sharply. "I bet Charlie's rolling over in his grave."

His words scared me. Charlie died of a heroin overdose two months earlier. I went to his funeral. Everybody from the old neighborhood was there. I put up a very nice memorial for him on Resting Place that made his poor mother cry in gratitude. How did Lenny know Charlie was dead?

He was long gone before it happened. But I quickly answered the question myself. This Lenny, this person before me, was just a figment of my imagination. He knew everything I knew. That thought reassured me.

"You coming in or not?" he asked.

Why not? Nothing could hurt me. I was safe in my bed back at home. I moved closer to the pool, but I hesitated. In the darkness, the pool didn't look very inviting. The water was black as tar, and I had a strange feeling that if I got in, it would never release me.

"You're not afraid, are you?" Lenny asked. He stopped floating and straightened up in the pool, kneeling down enough to keep just his head above the water. "It's not bad in here, Ricky. Not bad at all," he said, his eyes becoming more serious. "I wish I had taken the leap earlier. I would have saved myself a lot of misery."

His words gave me a chill. I knew what leap he was talking about.

"It's not what you think, Ricky. It's very peaceful here. You'll like it." Lenny paused and then added, "The world has no pity for screwed up people like us."

"I'm not screwed up," I replied.

Lenny laughed as he moved closer. "Please! You're the boy in the plastic bubble. You don't touch anyone, and you never let them touch you," he said. "I might have been a paranoid schizophrenic, but I embraced things. I followed my feelings. I made contact."

"And what did that get you?" I answered defensively.

"Peace," Lenny replied. "Come on, Rick. I don't want to argue with you, man. We're brothers. We're supposed to love each other." Lenny swam back a little and opened his arms. "Come on in and try it out just for a minute. You'll see what I mean. I promise."

Lenny's eyes radiated sincerity. Despite my misgivings about the water, I decided to try it. After all, it was just a dream. I was safe.

I stepped forward and hoisted myself up on the rim of the pool with both arms. I threw a leg over the top, but before I even felt the water, I heard a fire engine. The sound stopped me. The siren was echoing as if it were reverberating off tall buildings. It should not have sounded like that here where the trees would have swallowed and muffled the sound.

"Don't worry about that," Lenny said. I turned to him. His eyes were anxious now, but he forced a smile. "Come on. Let's do some laps before Mr. Coleman breaks out his shotgun."

There was something wrong about him. I could see it now. Brothers were supposed to love each other, but I wasn't so sure he was my brother. Who was he? What was he?

The siren continued. I turned to it. When I did, I really opened my eyes. I could see the fire truck moving down Joppa Road ten stories below me. I watched its progress for a moment before I realized I was standing on my balcony and that I was hanging halfway over the railing.

I normally enjoyed the view from the balcony, but now it was terrifying. I froze. I had no idea how strong the rail was and whether it could hold my weight. I was afraid to move and equally afraid to stay still. Closing my eyes, I resolved to throw myself backwards in one motion. Like a frightened child, I even counted to three before I pushed myself back.

My neck hit against the seat of one of my lawn chairs as I tumbled backwards onto the hard concrete of the balcony floor. My elbow and back ached as I reached back to rub my neck. My other hand went to my skinned elbow. I slowly stood up and looked over the balcony. The fire engine was gone. All that remained immediately below was a decorative fountain in front of the building. I doubted the five inches of water in it would have done much to break my fall.

I staggered back into my apartment to find the television and lights on just as they were when I fell asleep in the afternoon. I looked to the clock. It read 3 a.m. Exactly. *That was almost my time of death*, I thought.

My eyes went to my desk. As they did, the screensaver switched to one of the pictures of my brother Lenny I used on his Resting Place memorial. He had a lazy, happy smile in it. The photograph made it easy to see why he held onto so many friends. There is no way I'd get as many people at my funeral, even if everyone brought a date.

"Lenny, are you here?" I asked, not believing the words as I said them. Of course, he wasn't here. He was dead, and dead was dead. Forever.

The screensaver image suddenly changed again, and I found myself staring at Elisabetta Kostek. Her smile was now a bemused taunt as if to say she had done this thing.

"This is crazy," I said with the voice of rationality.

I was tempted to go to the computer and move the mouse, but I was afraid Elisabetta wouldn't disappear. Instead, I retreated into my bedroom without bothering to turn off the lights in the living room and kitchen. I closed the door and locked it. It was the first time I ever locked my bedroom door in my own apartment.

Chapter Five: Gina

Sunday morning.

The bright, morning sunlight hit my face from between the curtains of my bedroom window and awakened me gently. Blinking into the warm light, the world felt reassuringly normal again. The purifying rays washed away all of the weirdness of the day before. *Maybe it was all a dream*, I thought with great relief until I moved. The residual pain in my neck and back dispelled my wishful thinking.

I crept out of the bedroom cautiously. I expected the smirking face of Elisabetta Kostek to greet me from my computer screensaver. Instead, I found a photograph of my entire family taken at my grandparents' house the Christmas before my father died. There were not many pictures of the five of us. My father died when Janet was only four-years-old. She had practically no memory of him. Sometimes I couldn't blame her for escaping to California when she had the chance. She didn't experience the good times so why should she stay and endure the madness?

As the image of my family dissolved into one of the thousands of tombstones I had photographed for Resting Place, I walked to the sliding door leading to the balcony. The overturned deck chair was further evidence that I had…

I stopped in mid-thought. What had I actually done? Really. I had a nightmare, and I walked in my sleep. That was all. I wasn't crazy. I wasn't suicidal. I wasn't like Lenny at all. Furthermore, it had nothing to do with that stupid picture. I turned back to the computer, and there she was smirking at me.

"It's just a coincidence," I said aloud.

There had to be a rational reason why Elisabetta's photo now appeared so regularly on the screensaver. While I walked toward the desk, the image of her face dissolved into the photo of her grave. That made me think. Perhaps the screensaver had some internal preset that favored the more recent photos. That made sense. People would want to see their most recent photos most often, right? The people who designed the program probably took that into account. I was just surprised I hadn't noticed it earlier.

I sat down at the computer. While I was reaching for the mouse to turn off the screensaver, the photo of the Kostek grave dissolved into a photo of my ex-girlfriend Gina Holt taken at a party the year we met. It was the first photograph of us together. She was smiling at the camera, but my face was turned slightly. Still, it was a great picture. Gina was quite fetching in it. Her hair was short, almost Tom Boy-ish, but nothing else about her was reminiscent of a guy. She wore tight stretch pants and a shirt that showed off her cleavage in a tasteful manner. Very sexy. I was always attracted to voluptuous girls. She was Rubenesque, but my mother saw things differently.

"You can do better than that fat girl," she always said. Not that my mother was into body shaming, per se. Why would she limit herself to the physical when, in her eyes, every single aspect of Gina was worthy of criticism?

Turns out I proved my mother wrong.

I had not done better since our breakup.

The party picture dissolved to another photo of Gina and me taken on Thanksgiving at her parent's house. Her family really liked me, and I liked them, too. They had even moved their Thanksgiving meal to early in the afternoon so I could share it with them. That was the only way I could have seen them. It was impossible for me to bow out of spending a holiday with my mother. Even Lenny, at the height of his madness, always found his way home on Thanksgiving, Christmas, and Easter. None of his inner demons were as formidable as our mother's wrath.

The picture changed again to one I took of Gina at an Orioles game. She was seated and looking up. Her smile captured me. She seemed so happy that day. I could see the genuine love in Gina's eyes despite the seeds of doubt my mother planted in my heart. My mother was relentless. She even got spiritual ammunition from a fortune-teller friend, who predicted doom for our relationship.

I couldn't blame my mother, despite the heartache she caused. I understood what motivated her. Having tragically lost her husband, she wasn't about to lose another man in her family. Still, knowing my mother's motives didn't prevent her words from poisoning me. I could see that now. This picture reminded me that Gina truly loved me. She really did, and she paid her dues by playing second fiddle to my mother for years.

The image changed to yet another photo of Gina and myself. This was getting freaky. Although we were together for five years, I only had twenty-seven pictures of us together. It was statistically impossible that four of them would play randomly back-to-back on the screensaver. Nor was it a good thing. The flood of memories they produced wasn't positive, especially this photo taken at her sister Kate's wedding.

The wedding was the closest Gina and I ever came to walking down the aisle together. Gina was the maid of honor. I was one of the groomsmen. We stood on the altar during the entire ceremony. Our eyes would periodically leave the happy couple and find each other. Her smile nearly melted my heart. To cement things, I even caught the bride's garter at the reception, which wasn't difficult since Kate had her new husband lob it directly at me.

Our marriage was a given to everyone but my mother. Neither of us doubted it. We often discussed where we would live and how many children we would have. The one thing we never discussed was *when*. Although, the answer was obvious—when my mother finally loosened her grip on me. Gina showed an extraordinary amount of patience during her long, emotional game of chess with dear old momma. She tried befriending her. She tried battling her. She tried indifference, but my mother remained resolute and unchanging through it all. Even cancer didn't weaken her. In the end, mom managed to keep her grip on me beyond the grave through those awful nightmares.

Gina thought it would be easier after my mother died. I know I did, but that was before the nightmares began. Still, even without the nightmares, I doubt the relationship would have ended in marriage. I just couldn't ask the question, and I couldn't bring myself to say yes when Gina did. Maybe if she waited until I was through the mourning process, but I suppose she felt she had waited long enough. She wanted a family, and it didn't look like I would ever provide it. Studying this photo with her arm looped around mine and that beautiful smile I took for granted, I wish I could have married her. Instead, I had to endure the guilt of having wasted five years of her life.

Then my cellphone rang. I turned to it. The Caller ID displayed Gina's number.

Impossible. This couldn't be a coincidence.

When Gina finally walked away, we resolved to remain friends, but our phone calls grew fewer and further in between. Most of her calls came when she needed a shoulder to cry on during her break-ups with her subsequent boyfriends. She also gave me a heads-up when she started dating a new guy. I got the latest call about two months earlier when she began dating Chuck. There could only be one reason for her call now: Chuck was out of the picture. I was fully prepared to console her as I reached for the phone because I was genuinely sympathetic. I knew what it was like to be alone, and I realized it suited me more than her.

"Hi, Gina," I said. My voice was cheerful. Despite the inherent awkwardness, I still enjoyed talking to her.

"Hi, Rick," she replied in a voice husky with excitement. "How are you doing?"

"Same as always," I replied. No lie there.

"I'm calling because I have some exciting news, and I don't want you to find out about it on Facebook first."

"I'm not on Facebook."

"I know, I know, but I'm still friends with Mike and Bob and your sister, and I don't want you to hear it from them first."

"What is it?" I asked, dreading the news.

"Chuck and I are getting married," she said, barely resisting the urge to squeal girlishly.

"Wow," I said quietly. Gina was getting married. To someone else. I knew it would happen eventually, but it still took me by surprise.

"I'm so happy."

"I'm happy for you," I said, before adding, "But isn't this a little sudden? You've only been going out with him for about two months, right?"

"Almost three," Gina corrected me, and then she added, "But, yeah, I know what you mean. The timing was a little unexpected. So was the way he did it. You know me, Rick. I'm a romantic. I expected a ring at the bottom of a glass of champagne at an expensive restaurant, but he just sprang it on me last night while we were driving back from his niece's wedding in Youngstown. God, it must have been three o'clock in the morning. I was sleeping. He just nudged me and asked me to marry him. I said yes. When I woke up this morning, I was afraid it might have been a dream, but it wasn't. We're off to buy a ring this afternoon."

"Well, congratulations," I said weakly as I turned to the computer where the screensaver shifted to yet another picture of Gina and myself, as if to mock me. "I'm really happy for you."

"Are you, Ricky?" she asked.

"Yeah," I said. "You deserve all the happiness in the world."

"Thanks. So do you," she said. "I'm sure there's a girl out there for you."

"You're more confident than me," I said.

"You just have to step out, Ricky," she said. "Sometimes, I think you're like *The Boy in the Plastic Bubble*. You've got to let someone in."

The Boy in the Plastic Bubble? Where had I heard that?

Lenny.

Last night.

That couldn't be a coincidence. What the hell was going on here?

"What made you bring up *The Boy in the Plastic Bubble*?" I asked, too quickly.

A cautious intake of breath came across the phone. There was a moment of silence before she replied, "I'm sorry, I shouldn't have said that. I don't want to make you mad."

"No, no, I'm not mad," I answered. "It's just that someone else said that to me last night."

"Who?"

Who? An honest answer to that question would send me to the loony bin. "It doesn't matter," I finally answered. "The only thing that matters is that you're getting married, and I couldn't be happier for you."

"Thanks, Ricky. That means a lot," she said. "You're always going to be one of my best friends."

"Same here, Gina," I said.

"I'll try to get you an invitation to the wedding," she added, "But the whole ex-boyfriend thing might be weird for Chuck."

"You don't have to invite me," I said. "I don't need to go to the wedding to know that you'll be a beautiful bride."

I heard her smile on the other side of the line.

"I'll tell you what, though," I added. "I promise I'll join Facebook to look at the wedding pictures if you post them."

"Will do, Ricky," she said.

Then she hung up.

I didn't know what to think. Our break up truly devastated me, but I also felt strangely relieved. I spent most of my life living under the pressure of my mother's expectations. Then, when she died, I had to contend with Gina's expectations. It wasn't until after we broke up that I felt I was truly charting my own course, as pathetic as it might seem to others. Still, part of me clung to the option of going back to her. She was my safety net. Now she was gone forever.

Man, I never wanted her as much as I did at that moment.

I chuckled at the irony. I didn't believe in God, but, if He did exist, this proved He was a cruel prankster. He fulfilled Gina's most heartfelt desire at the same time I nearly sleepwalked myself to death. Talk about freaky. I turned back to the screensaver expecting to see yet another photo of Gina and myself, but instead, I found the dark lady staring at me.

"No," I said aloud.

I refused to believe the unstated implications of that series of randomly selected photographs. The dark woman didn't have anything to do with this turn of events. It was just a coincidence. I grabbed the mouse and made her disappear.

Chapter Six: Tombstone Teri

Pushing thoughts of the dark lady aside, I decided to check my email. I was surprised to see a Resting Place email notification of a private message from Tombstone Teri. I opened the email and clicked on the link that took me directly to her instant message on the Resting Place website.

> You beat me. I took a picture of the Ritter grave, too,
> but you uploaded yours first.

I smiled.

But how to respond? Genealogy is a hobby dependent on the goodwill of others. I couldn't afford to gloat. I had to appear magnanimous, even though beating her was my primary goal. After a little thought, I typed my reply.

> I'm surprised I beat you to anything.
> You are putting up some impressive numbers.

Almost immediately after I pressed return, a response came back.

> Thanks, that means a lot. I really admire your work.

A first I thought she was mocking me. I viewed her as a rival, but, then again, there was no evidence she felt the same way about me. Maybe she *did* admire my work. I put a lot of effort into it. It meant more to me than my work at the hospital.

Suddenly Tombstone Teri looked a lot better in my eyes.

Thanks, Teri.

I typed, but what to say next? I didn't want to compliment her just because she complimented me. That would appear totally insincere. I decided to quit while I was ahead. So then I continued typing.

I look forward to running across you at a cemetery one day.

After pressing return, I prepared to close the browser, but Teri offered an immediate response.

I'll be at Holy Redeemer around 1pm.

I turned to her profile image. Instead of a photograph, she had chosen a cartoon illustration of a tombstone as her avatar on the website. My thoughts went back to how Rita at Eternal Faith described her: White, mid-thirties, kind of stiff like a high school math teacher. I mulled that description over in my mind briefly before I stopped myself. What did it matter what she looked like? She could weigh four hundred pounds, have a full beard, and still be a talented contributor. What did I have to lose by meeting someone who admired my work? This was just the boost I needed today.
I typed back.

I can be there.
Where do you want to meet?

She typed back.

You'll find me.

I had two hours to get ready, and I used every minute. After a long shower and both brushing and flossing my teeth, I agonized over what to wear. I normally wore slacks and white button down dress shirts at work, but the shirts made me look a tad overweight when I tucked them in. Outside of work, I generally wore Hawaiian-style shirts that didn't need to be tucked in. That's how I dressed on my cemetery expeditions, but I didn't want Tombstone Teri to think I wasn't sufficiently respectful of the dead. I eventually chose tan khakis and a short-sleeve, three-button, pullover Hopkins shirt. It never hurt to fly the Hopkins flag around Baltimore, or anywhere else for that matter. I was casual, but not too casual—and formal enough to take her to a nice restaurant, if things developed.

When I left the bedroom, I pointedly didn't look at the computer. I didn't want to see the dark woman's mocking smile. Keeping my eyes averted, I walked over to the computer and turned off the monitor. I would deal with her later. I had more important things at hand. I had a girl to meet. I only hoped that she wasn't already married with five children.

Holy Redeemer Cemetery was about twenty-five minutes from my apartment. I was very familiar with it. My father Stan was a mutt with mixed Bohemian, German, and Italian blood. His ancestors all immigrated directly to Baltimore between 1886 and 1919. They were all Catholic, and they were all buried on the grounds of Holy Redeemer Cemetery. All-in-all, counting spouses, about forty-five members of my extended family were resting under in its well-maintained thirty-three acres. I would happily buy a plot at Holy Redeemer if I didn't already have a space reserved for me at Eternal Faith.

I entered the cemetery through its ornate front gate. The front section was the oldest with graves dating back to the founding of the cemetery in 1888. Monuments ranging from simple marble tombstones to thirty-foot obelisks and angelic statues adorned the grounds around me. The further one drove back into the cemetery, the more recent and boring the monuments. Thankfully, most of my relatives rested in the more interesting front sections.

I stopped my car on the hilltop overlooking the green expanse. A typical post-church Sunday afternoon crowd was scattered about the premises. I spotted about fifteen cars, but where was Tombstone Teri? Using the telephoto lens on my trusty Nikon, I checked out the visitors one by one. Most of them were elderly couples, but I spotted a single woman parked near the grave of my great-grandparents, Jan and Kristina Bakos, with a camera hanging around her neck. That had to be her, or at least I hoped so. From a distance, she looked very nice. I set down the camera and started driving toward her. The closer I got, however, the more uneasy I felt.

Teri had nothing to do with my uneasiness. It was instead the grave of Kristina Bakos. When you live in a family decimated by suicide, it is only natural to search for the cause in the past. My search led directly to my great-grandmother. Kristina was the first member of the family to commit suicide.

Distraught over the death of her five-year-old son Vincent, Kristina killed herself by walking in front of a truck on Broadway, not far from her modest rowhouse on Chapel Street in East Baltimore. Sadly, Kristina passed her self-destructiveness to her progeny. Her son, my great-uncle Norbert, committed suicide after returning home from World War II. His military records showed that he saw heavy combat from D-Day plus six through the conquest of Germany. My father said he was quiet and moody after the war. Today, he probably would have been diagnosed with Post Traumatic Stress Syndrome, but back in his day, Uncle Norbert was on his own. He shot himself with a German Luger he had picked up on a European battlefield as a souvenir.

Norbert's older brother John also committed suicide. He drowned himself while fishing in the Chesapeake Bay a few years later. Initially everyone thought Uncle John slipped off the boat accidentally until they went to his house. Inside, they found that he had placed his will and all of his financial papers neatly on his desk along with detailed instructions concerning his burial. Despite his meticulous preparations, Uncle John left no explanation whatsoever for his actions. Neither of the brothers left any progeny. My grandfather Harold was Kristina's only child who lived to adulthood and died of natural causes. Our branch of the family was spared the pain of suicide until the death of my brother Lenny. I couldn't blame Kristina for my mother's death since she wasn't a blood descendant. Madness is not inherited by marriage.

As I parked my car, the photographer snapped photos of a classy, five-foot marble obelisk next to the grave of Jan and Kristina Bakos. She wore blue jeans and a sunny, flowered blouse. She obviously didn't see the need for solemnity. She turned to me as I got out of my car. I spoke first as I walked toward her.

"Tombstone Teri?"

She smiled. "Please, just Teri," she said as she walked over and extended her hand. "Teri Poskocil."

"I'm Rick Bakos," I said. Her handshake was firm and lingered just long enough to express some warmth.

"I know," she said.

"Well, here's something you don't know," I said, motioning to the monument beside us. "Those are my great-grandparents who came over from Bohemia."

"I know who they are," she replied. "That's how I discovered you."

Her words caught me off guard. I had already experienced too many coincidences since I took that picture. I wasn't in the mood for another one. Teri took a step back and motioned to the arched column monument beside my ancestors. I saw the name etched in stone and smiled: Poskocil.

"They're *my* great-grandparents."

"You're kidding," I said.

"Nope," she said. "Our families are neighbors, and that's how I discovered you in the first place. When I came here to photograph their grave, I photographed the entire row, too. When I started uploading them, I saw your memorial. I was really impressed with the photos and the biographical information you included about them. And I loved the way you linked your relatives together. I took a stroll through your whole family history."

"Thanks," I said.

"But what impressed me even more was the information you dug up on people who weren't even related to you: obituaries, death notices, census information, military records," she said, with genuine appreciation. "That's a lot of work, and it shows a true commitment."

"Or the total lack of a social life," I replied truthfully.

"Then I'm guilty as charged, too," Teri said with a laugh. "I don't know if you've been following me, but I've been adding quite a few graves, too."

"Oh, I know," I replied. "You're my biggest rival in the state."

"Rival?" she asked, amused. "Not colleague?"

"Maybe I'm just competitive," I answered before I confessed. "Yesterday I went out to Eternal Faith specifically to fill the Ritter request. When I went to the office, Rita told me that a woman was just in asking about her. I assumed it was you. I expected to find you in the mausoleum. When I didn't, I took the picture and hurried home to try to get it online before you did."

Teri laughed. "I have a confession to make, too," she replied. "When I said you uploaded your picture first, I was lying. I never got my picture. I went there, but something about the mausoleum scared me, and I left without it."

I felt strangely relieved that someone felt the same thing I did. It proved I wasn't insane. But I didn't say anything.

"I think it was the flowers," Teri added. "It was like every flower in the place was dead except down at that new burial."

"That wasn't a new burial," I said. "She's been dead since 2014."

"Must've been her birthday."

I shook my head no.

"Well, someone must really love her."

"I don't think so," I said quietly. Teri stopped and gave me a curious look. I think that was the first thing I said that surprised her. "There's something about that woman that scares me," I continued with unusual candor. "I can't imagine anyone loving her."

"Did you put up a memorial?"

I nodded.

"Do you have a picture of her?"

I nodded again.

"I gotta see it," Teri said, taking her cellphone out of her pocket.

"Don't," I said, touching her hand gently. "I've been a little freaked out since I saw it." Teri put the phone away. Suddenly embarrassed, I added, "I know how crazy it sounds. I mean it's only a photo."

"Native Americans used to believe photographs stole a person's soul," Teri added.

"To believe that, first you'd have to believe there *is* a soul."

"Mr. Bakos, are you an atheist?" Teri asked, as an eyebrow rose.

Damn. I recognized this as one of those moments that would decide what kind, if any, relationship we would have. I decided to answer honestly but circumspectly. "I wouldn't call myself an atheist," I replied. "But I'm definitely a skeptic."

Teri smiled. "That's okay," she replied. "We're all skeptical at times."

Not wishing to mislead her, I added, "I'm a skeptic most of the time."

"I'm only skeptical about five percent of the time," she replied. "The rest of the time I teach English at Mercy High School."

I laughed.

"What's so funny?"

"I asked Rita over at Eternal Faith to describe you. She said you looked like a high school math teacher."

"I am so insulted!" Teri laughed. "English teachers are so much cooler than math teachers."

I laughed, too. Then I added, "Do you like Mexican food?"

Chapter Seven: The Holy Redeemer Lonely Hearts Club

Teri indeed liked Mexican food so I invited her out to lunch at The Hacienda, a fabulous Tex-Mex restaurant about five blocks away from the cemetery.

Thank God this wasn't a date because I made the classic first date mistake: talking about your ex. As soon as we sat down, I just started talking about Gina, and I didn't stop for about twenty minutes. I described with surprising honesty my emotional ambiguities at every step of our relationship. To make matters even worse, I also revealed how I had chosen my mother over Gina. That's another big no-no. Geez. As I listened to myself, I was thinking, "Oh my God, you're going the full Norman Bates."

Teri took it all in stride. She let me tell my tale of woe, and then she told me about her ex with remarkable candor. Her ex was actually an ex-husband: Charles Allen Carson. They were mismatched from the beginning. She was a somewhat naïve Catholic high school teacher. He was a much worldlier plumber well versed in the art of love. (Her words, not mine.) She met him at a bar while she was at a going away party for a friend. He swept her off her feet with flowers, romantic dinners, and adventures. They went white water rafting, spent long weekends in the Bahamas, and even went skydiving. With Chuck, Teri experienced things she had only read about in books. It wasn't until after they married that she learned that their entire courtship was financed with credit cards.

Things went bad soon after the wedding. Her husband feigned a back injury at work and she had to support him while he battled endlessly for worker's compensation and disability. With only one salary, his credit card balances became a real burden. Chuck's strategy was to always shift the balances to new credit cards. She didn't know how to react. She always looked down on people who let material concerns like money ruin their marriages. She considered them shallow. To her, marriage was as spiritual as it was physical. Love always trumped money, except when she found herself in that situation.

Her resentment grew daily, but divorce was out of the question for a good Catholic. A divorce could endanger her job at the high school. She couldn't divorce Chuck unless he gave her a valid reason for an annulment. He unwittingly obliged when she discovered his affair with a former co-worker that began well before their marriage. Now she was free again in the eyes of Rome, her maiden name restored, and not interested in marrying again anytime soon.

"I've always been an excellent judge of character. I could always tell how my friends' husbands would turn out, who'd be great, who'd be a loser, but Chuck totally blindsided me. I didn't see it coming at all," she explained. Then, after taking a sip of her Corona, she added, "I'm never getting married again. I can't trust myself to make that kind of a decision."

"I think if Gina and I had gotten married, we would have stayed married," I replied. "But I don't think I would have made her happy. Not really."

"Then its good you didn't get married," she said. "If happiness looks out of reach, it's best to walk away before anyone gets hurt."

"Too late for that," I replied. "I definitely hurt her."

"And now you're hurt."

"Yes," I said honestly. "I guess."

"I hurt my husband, too," Teri replied, and she then smiled. "Or at least my lawyer did when he convinced the judge not to pile half of his credit card debt on me."

We both laughed.

"Maybe our expectations are the problem," I continued, more seriously. "I don't see any divorce in my family tree. None. Not my parents, grandparents, great-grandparents, and so on. They all stayed together. But you have to ask yourself how many of them were in love the way we expect it to be today? No one ever wrote any romance novels about my ancestors, but I hope that they at least found their niche with their spouses."

"Would that satisfy you?" she asked, meeting my eyes seriously. "Just finding your niche with someone?"

"Yesterday I would have said no," I replied. "But today I'm not so sure."

Teri gave me a weary smile before raising her bottle of Corona. "A toast to The Holy Redeemer Lonely Hearts Club."

I raised my bottle and tapped hers.

"To our first annual meeting," she said.

We both took a drink; then I added, "First annual? Does that mean you anticipate another meeting?"

"Well, Mr. Rick Bakos," she replied. "If you're looking for romance, you've come to the wrong place. But if you're looking for someone to help you document a cemetery or discuss genealogy, I hope there will be another one."

"Good," I replied, and I meant it. It felt nice to have a new female friend with similar interests to talk to without any romantic expectations. I always found it safer to talk about things of the heart with women rather than men, particularly safely married women who had no interest in me. I don't know why. I guess it was because I always felt competitive with guys, even my closest friends. I never wanted to seem weak around them. Whenever I had a problem with Gina, I turned to a couple of married women at work who would let me cry on their shoulders. They all thought I should have stayed with her. Then again, I never told them about the nightmares of waking up to find Gina dead. I didn't want them to think I was crazy.

I tried to pay the check, but Teri insisted on splitting it. She didn't want us to get off on the wrong foot. Then we took out our cellphones. She told me her phone number, and I dialed her, allowing her to capture my number. Our devices were now connected. When we left the restaurant, there was no friendly kiss on the cheek or even the shaking of hands before we walked off to our cars. That was a relief.

I was happy. I had a new friend, and, in all honesty, I didn't make them often.

Chapter Eight: A Mourner

I was on top of the world as I drove away from the restaurant. It was hard to process the wide range of emotions I had experienced over the last twenty-four hours. I went from haunted to heartbroken to happy. Amazing.

Despite my assurances to the contrary, I was already imagining what it would be like to date Teri, but I had no illusions. I would never violate our agreement by asking her out romantically unless she sent some very strong signals in my direction. I learned the hard way during my thirty-six-years that dating wasn't my strong suit. Friendship was a reassuringly open-ended thing. Dating wasn't. Every date was a pass/fail audition. I wouldn't risk a promising open-ended friendship with an attractive, like-minded woman for an uncertain romantic future. Still, I was already hoping that Teri would come to Gina's wedding with me. Going to her wedding alone, provided I was actually invited, was too pathetic for me to even consider.

My thoughts were so focused on Teri that I didn't put too much active thought to where I was driving. I planned to head straight home, so I was surprised when Eternal Faith came into sight as I crested a hill. I felt an instant pang of fear, as if some alien hand reached deep inside of me and twisted my intestines. I took a deep breath and closed my eyes for as long as my position in traffic allowed. When I opened my eyes, I took solace in the bright sunlight. It dispelled the evil. There were no ghosts or spirits. No undead. No haunting. No supernatural. Once again, my rational pride took over. I refused to become a victim of superstition. I decided to face my fear head on.

I turned into the cemetery. There were few cars in sight. Sunday was a big day for visiting the dead, but most people made their appearances after church services. It was three-thirty now. The rush was over. People had left their flowers and returned to the places of the living.

"What am I doing here?" I asked myself but quickly dismissed the thought. I had every right to be here. After all, one day, this place was going to be my permanent home.

The road took me past the rise where my immediate family was buried, but I tried to ignore them. My Catholic upbringing was to blame. I always remembered the lesson old Father Isidore gave us before our first confession. People who died with mortal sins on their souls, like suicide, were damned to hell. Although I turned my back on mother church decades ago, those words still haunted me, especially after the death of my brother. What cruelty! Lenny never had a chance in this world, and, if Father Isidore was right, he was damned to hell in the next one. The fate of my mother was even crueler. She lost a husband and a son and had to deal with cancer too. Now she was damned to hell because of one decision she made in a moment of weakness? A God who would do that was no God at all—even if He did exist.

Father Isidore's words got my blood boiling again, but I couldn't deal with those emotions now. I kept driving on the main road past the office. It was closed, but the mausoleum remained open until five o'clock. I often wondered about that. Did one of the employees actually drive into the cemetery and lock the large glass doors at five o'clock? I doubted it. I suspected that they only posted the warning signs to discourage curiosity seekers or possible vandals.

"What if they really locked it?" I asked myself aloud.

I shuddered at the possibility of getting locked inside the mausoleum overnight. I imagined hearing the click of the lock and racing toward the door to see Jose Garcia, the groundskeeper, driving away. That would be a true nightmare. With the mausoleum looming ahead of me, I quickly checked my watch again. Three-thirty-two. Still plenty of time for a quick visit.

But whom was I visiting? Why had I even driven there? This was definitely not something I planned to do. I drove those questions out of my head. Once again, my rational mind pushed back against my superstitious fears. There was no rational explanation for why I had driven to the cemetery, but I refused to turn away. Nothing in that mausoleum could hurt me. The dead were dead.

I should have invited Teri, I suddenly thought to myself. "No," I immediately answered myself aloud.

Why would I think that? That was crazy. I had no desire to involve her in this madness. I had even stopped her from looking at the Kostek memorial online.

I calmed considerably when a brown, four-door Mercedes sedan parked in front of the mausoleum. At least I wouldn't be alone inside. I didn't think I could face that prospect now, even in the bright light of day. I parked behind the Mercedes, grabbed my camera, and hurried over to the large, swinging glass doors of the mausoleum. I saw the other visitor, an elderly white man, walking slowly toward the Kostek vault.

I stepped inside as quietly as possible. I kept my distance, feigning interest in the other vaults as I slowly followed behind the old man. The same palatable sense of gloom that I felt the day before still filled the place, despite the fact that most of the dead flowers had been safely swept away. New flowers, recently placed by mourners in the decorative bronze vases alongside the vaults today, were already withering. They clearly wouldn't last the afternoon.

I discreetly returned my attention to the mourner. He was balding, but a few uncombed gray hairs made their presence known. He wore a bushy moustache and an old, navy blue suit. His overcoat might have seemed out of season, but it was quite appropriate in this marble-lined refrigerator. It made me wish I had worn a jacket. Goose pimples rose on my arms.

The man walked up to the Kostek vault and stood silently for a moment before he knelt briefly and placed a small bouquet of roses on the floor in front of it. Standing up, he quickly turned around before I had the chance to look away. We made eye contact. I'm not sure exactly what I saw in his eyes— indifference or disdain as he pointedly turned away and kept walking toward the door in a path that would bring him alongside me. It was unavoidable.

Over the course of the hundreds of hours I spent in cemeteries, I made it a point never to disturb a mourner. Often mourners asked me to help them find a grave, but I never approached someone on my own. I knew I had to break my rule this time. I needed to speak with someone who actually knew Elisabetta Kostek—and who could explain her strange hold over me.

As I started toward him, the old man pointedly turned his face further away from me. He veered toward the opposite wall, but there was no way for him to leave without passing me.

"Excuse me," I said. "May I ask you a question?"

No response. No eye contact. But he was passing me.

"Sir, may I talk to you for a second?"

Without even giving me a glance, the old man unexpectedly slapped my camera out of my hands. It hit the marble floor with an expensive-sounding crack. I raced after it as it skidded awkwardly across the floor in the direction of Kostek memorial. When I finally caught it, I noticed a large crack in my fifty-millimeter lens. There was no fixing that. The body of the camera seemed unscathed, and I still had my expensive telephoto lens in the case.

I looked up from my wounded camera to find Elisabetta staring at me from the photo on her vault. Her smile was smug, as if she had been expecting me.

"Who are you?" I asked aloud.

She didn't answer, of course. She just continued to smile.

I turned away. The mausoleum was now empty. The old man was gone. For a moment, I was tempted to check and see if he left any kind of note with his flowers, but I was afraid to go any closer to the vault. No, the door was the safer option. I started walking.

In a strange bout of paranoia, I thought I could hear movement in the vaults alongside me. It was a gentle rustling at first as the dead rose from their supposedly eternal sleep. Then they began struggling when they realized they were trapped. They banged the lids of their coffins against the roof of the vaults as their anger grew. As the glass doors loomed before me, I imagined the dead would soon break their coffins to pieces and then batter themselves against the vault doors until they were free. By then, their anger would be unquenchable.

My eyes remained glued to the door. I was afraid what I would see if I turned either right or left. Suddenly consumed by an additional fear that the old man had locked the door while I was inside, I began to run. I knew I needed to get the hell out of that mausoleum—or I would die.

Chapter Nine: War is Declared

Gasping for air and still shaking with fear, I became a man with a mission upon leaving the mausoleum. I refused to be manipulated like that again.

Elisabetta Kostek, whoever or whatever the hell she was, had already taken up too much of my time. I was going home to delete the photos of her from my camera and hard drive, and then I would delete her memorial from Resting Place. I didn't want to be responsible for anyone else looking into those dark eyes. Especially Teri. She had already expressed too much interest in Elisabetta after I mentioned her. I was tempted to call her and reiterate my warning, but I knew I couldn't. She would think I was crazy, and that would be the end of our budding friendship.

When I got to my car, I found a slip of paper under the windshield. I picked it up and read it.

Never come back.

The mourner obviously wrote it. There was no one else around. But what did he mean? Was it a threat or a warning? He left no signature or phone number. I wish I had written down his license plate number. Anything. He obviously knew something, but he was long gone.

I got into my car and headed out, passing our family plot along the way. As I did, I caught sight of a guy standing near the graves. From the familiar hunch of his back, I knew it was Lenny visiting mom's grave. I looked ahead again, thinking nothing of it, but then it struck me: Lenny was dead. He had never visited mom's grave because he died before she did. I hit the brakes and turned back to the grave. Just as I suspected, no one was standing there, but it was too real to just be my imagination. My eyes went to the nearby willow tree, which swayed in the light breeze.

"Probably just a shadow," I said, reason restored again.

I was tempted to back up to see if I could repeat the optical illusion again, but I decided against it. I feared the implications if I was unable to repeat it. It was one thing to have a bad dream. It was another thing entirely to see your dead brother in broad daylight. I was now willing to admit that something supernatural was taking place, but I didn't want to press the point. I just wanted to get my world back to normal.

While driving home, a great hunger overcame me, despite just having eaten a full meal with Teri. I ordered a super-sized Big Mac meal and a cheeseburger at the McDonald's drive-thru near my house. The previous afternoon, the pictures of their food made me nauseous. Not today. I took it as a sign that my new resolve had broken whatever spell the dark woman had placed on me. I was free.

I ate the cheeseburger on the way home, but my fries and Big Mac were untouched as I entered my apartment. I carried the food over to my desk and sat down. I turned the monitor on, fully expecting to find Elisabetta's image on the screensaver looking at me. In fact, I was hoping to see it, but instead, I found a random tombstone photo for one of the memorials I had created. I used the mouse to dispel the screensaver then turned my attention to my Big Mac. I took a bite. It tasted great. Putting the sandwich down, I went to my cemetery folder, where I kept my Resting Place photos. I knew the Kostek memorial was on the two most recent files: DSC_0591 and DSC_0592. I clicked on the second one to bring up the close-up of her face. She was still smiling in the face of digital death.

"Say, bye, bye, bitch," I said.

While I reached for the mouse again to do the deed, I took a big gulp from my Coke. As I did, I caught something out of the corner of my eye. I had just taken a bite out of the Big Mac, exposing those little onions they used—except they weren't onions. No. They were alive and wiggling. I turned to get a better look and realized that they were maggots. Tiny little maggots, and I had eaten them!

I immediately vomited everything out over my keyboard, mouse, and monitor. In the process, I spilled the rest of the Coke, too. I immediately jumped out of my chair and headed for the bathroom. This wasn't a paper towel spill. This was a bath towels spill—plural. By the time I raced back to the desk, there was already a large puddle of Coke and half-eaten food on the floor. I dealt with the desk first. The electronics in the keyboard were toast. No question about that. I unplugged it and tossed it directly into the trash. As I sopped up the sticky liquid and half-eaten food, I turned to the now drenched Big Mac. Just as I expected, there were no maggots. It was just another mind game, and I knew who was responsible.

Now I finally put aside my rational preconceptions and admitted to myself that I was involved in some sort of supernatural warfare. The hows and the whys and the parameters of the battlefield were still a mystery to me, but at least I knew the name of the enemy: Elisabetta Kostek. Everything started when I took that picture of her. No, I corrected myself. I think it started when I looked at her. That's what seemed to trigger it.

Whatever.

It didn't matter how it started anymore. I was going to end it.

I dropped the towel and turned my attention to the mouse. I didn't need the keyboard to delete those files. When I touched the mouse, the cursor moved. Good. I moved the cursor to the close-up file and clicked on it— or should I say I *tried* to click on it. Although the mouse still moved the cursor, the right and left buttons no longer worked.

"Damn it!" I shouted as I unplugged the mouse and tossed it in the trash.

The monitor turned black, and the screensaver started. Not surprisingly, I was greeted by the smiling image of Elisabetta Kostek. Actually, it *was* surprising. I set my screensaver to start five minutes after I last used the computer. This time the screensaver started only a few seconds after I unhooked the mouse. I took her appearance as a little show of force to prove that she had the power to manipulate more than just my mind. She could manipulate my electronics, too. Unless, I thought, I was only imagining seeing her on the monitor now.

Yikes. What was truly real? There was a lot to consider, but I didn't have time to wade into those weeds now. It was time to take offensive action.

"How you doing, Liz?" I asked with a smile as I turned back to the monitor.

I grabbed my camera and turned it on. I found her picture on it and turned the view screen around to the monitor.

"Recognize her?" I asked.

I pressed the little trash button on the camera. A dialogue box came up over Elisabetta's close-up. **Are you sure you want to delete this photo?**

"Yes, I do," I said aloud. Then I pressed the trash button again. The photograph was gone, and the wider one of the grave itself appeared in its place. Two quick presses on the trash button made that photograph disappear as well.

I half-expected to hear a faint ghostly wail of pain in response, but my actions were greeted by cold silence. Elisabetta herself even left the monitor. The screensaver replaced her with a photo of my mother, my father, Lenny, and me taken before my sister Janet was born. A superstitious person might have taken the photo as a warning that I would soon be joining them, but I wasn't spooked. Now that I knew what I was battling, I expected a quick victory.

Chapter Ten: The Motorcycle

I headed into my bedroom to throw the dirty towels into the hamper. Then I went into the bathroom to wash my hands. There was still plenty of cleanup to do, and I fully intended to go to the electronics store to get another keyboard and mouse, but when I sat down on the edge of my bed, I became deathly tired. I fell backwards, and I was asleep instantly.

The sound of a motorcycle woke me. Not *a* motorcycle—*the* motorcycle—*Lenny's* motorcycle.

Lenny rarely owned cars. He sold cars for a living and borrowed ones from the dealership for his personal use. On the weekends, he always rode his big Harley Davidson motorcycle for fun. It was also his primary form of transportation when he was out of his mind. The sound of that motorcycle during the middle of the week was a telltale sign that Lenny was off his meds. The roar of that engine at night always inspired dread in my mother, my sister Janet, and myself. I could pick out that specific engine out of a thousand others. It was ingrained into my mind. That roar meant we would soon be wrestling Lenny to the ground and dragging him off to the hospital to be forcibly committed.

I opened my eyes just as the motorcycle pulled into the driveway. I turned to my alarm clock. 3:00 am. But something was wrong. That wasn't my current alarm clock. It was the one from my bedroom in the old house. I looked around the room in the darkness. The contours of the furniture also told me that I was back in my second floor bedroom of our house on St, Helens Street, where I lived until I was thirty-one-years-old.

This isn't real, I told myself. *It's just another dream*. I shook my head back and forth quickly and opened my eyes again. My relief was palatable when I found myself back in my apartment bedroom. I fell back in bed and pulled the blanket over myself despite the fact I was still dressed from the afternoon.

Then I heard a key in the lock of my outer apartment door. I sat up. No one else had a key to my apartment except Gina, and I was sure that wasn't her. *Probably just a drunk neighbor at the wrong door*, I told myself, calming slightly.

Then I heard the door open. *WTF? Who could that be?* Like a scared child, I threw myself back in bed and covered myself with a blanket. A light went on in the living room. I could see it under the bottom of my bedroom door. I heard footsteps, but they didn't come all the way down to my bedroom. It sounded like they stopped near the kitchen. My guess was confirmed when I heard my cabinets open and close and the rattle of some pots and pans. Then came the voice.

"Mom, where's the hot dogs?"

It was Lenny, adult Lenny, with his stupid hot dogs.

When Lenny was crazy, he would disappear for days or weeks at a time only to show up in the middle of the night to cook some hot dogs. He'd boil them in a pot on the stove, but he invariably fell asleep before they were finished. The water would boil off, and the hot dogs would start burning. Before long, the smoke alarms would be ringing, and the house would smell like burnt hot dogs for a week.

"Mom, where's the hot dogs?" he shouted again, this time louder.

"She's dead," I shouted back, immediately regretting it. Note to self— you don't shout when you're trying to hide. It's counterproductive to say the least.

More footsteps. This time they came directly to my bedroom door. I could see movement underneath the bottom of the door. Someone was really standing there because this wasn't a dream. I had already woken up. Right?

There was a knock on the door. "You in there, man?" Lenny asked.

No way was I going to answer him. My thoughts went on the door itself. Did I lock it? No. Why would I? I immediately toyed with the idea of jumping up and locking the door, but instead, I just pulled the blanket the rest of the way over myself.

After another knock, the door creaked open. I heard footsteps as the person entered the room. I was shaking with fear as he stopped near my bed. "What are you doing under there, Ricky?" he asked. "Beating off?"

I stopped moving. Silence, then I heard a match being struck. I peeked out from under the blanket to see Lenny, looking more or less the way he did around the time of his death, leaning against my dresser drawers lighting up a cigarette. That was just like him. He was always so inconsiderate when he was off his meds.

"It's a smoke free building," I said, despite myself.

"Really? When did this stop being America?" Lenny asked, making eye contact with me as he took a puff. "I'm glad I'm dead."

"You're not Lenny," I said.

"Then who am I?"

"You're her," I replied. "Elisabetta Kostek."

"The lady from the picture?"

"Yeah."

"Ricky, you're supposed to be the smart one. Use your head," Lenny answered. "How would she know about The Kobayashi Maru?"

Good question, but my answer came quickly. "You can read my mind."

"And you were thinking about The Kobayashi Maru when?"

Good point. I hadn't thought about it since Charlie's funeral.

"I can prove I'm Lenny," he said.

"How?" I asked.

"Ask me something you don't know."

"What?"

"If you don't know the answer to the question, I can't be pulling it from your mind," he answered. "Right?"

"But how do I know you're not just going to make up an answer."

"Ask me the question. I'll give you the answer and someone who can back me up."

I didn't necessarily think this was a smart game to play with this person before me, but I couldn't resist. "What happened to your motorcycle?" I asked.

That was something I had wondered about. It disappeared a few weeks before his death, and its fate really worried our mother because the State of Maryland threatened to fine us over its missing license plates.

"At the bottom of the Gunpowder River about a mile east of Belair Road," Lenny replied; then he laughed. "I was really nuts then. Pete and me were doing some trails, and I saw a little hill that looked like a perfect ramp. I bet Pete twenty bucks I could jump over the river. He said I couldn't, and he was right. It's probably still there in about six feet of water. We tried to get it out, but it was wedged between some rocks. I'm lucky I didn't die that night. Ask Pete about it. He'll tell you."

Lenny took a contemplative drag from his cigarette.

"You know, I wish I would've died then. It would have been a much better way to go. More fun. People would still be talking about it," Lenny said.

"People still talk about you," I said quietly.

"That's cool," he said, and then he added, "I liked that memorial you put online for me. Very touching."

"You saw it?"

"Of course."

Silence.

"I have a question for you," I said.

"Shoot," he answered.

"If you really *are* Lenny, why did you try to trick me into jumping off my balcony?"

"Because you're my brother, man, and I love you," he said, before he turned and left the room. He called to me as he walked back toward the kitchen. "You sure you don't have any hot dogs?"

I got up and followed him. I didn't go into the kitchen with him. I stayed in the dining room and talked to him over the serving island. "If you love me, why do you want me to kill myself?"

Lenny stopped rummaging through my refrigerator and turned to me. "Cause I know where you're headed, Rick, and I'm trying to make it as painless as possible."

"Where am I headed?"

"Insanity and death."

"I'm not crazy," I responded angrily.

He really struck a nerve. Trust me, when you live in a family touched by multiple suicides, you constantly search yourself for any signs of madness. I had none, the last two days notwithstanding.

"Really?" Lenny asked with a smile. "Then go to work tomorrow and tell everyone you spent half the night talking to your dead brother. Trust me, you'll go from employee to patient lickety-split."

He had a point.

"Here's your options," Lenny explained. "One, you're actually talking to your dead brother. That's crazy. Two, a dead woman you took a picture of at a cemetery is masquerading as your dead brother. That's *really* crazy. Or three, you're sleepwalking yourself onto your balcony two nights in a row in order to jump off. That's lock 'em up and throw away the key crazy."

"I'm not going out on my balcony," I replied.

"Really?" Lenny replied. "Where do you think you are now?"

"My dining room."

"Think again," he replied, his expression sympathetic. "Open your eyes."

What did he mean? I was awake. I had been dreaming, but I pulled myself out of it already. Or did I? I squinted hard, and when I opened my eyes, I discovered Lenny was right. I was out on my balcony again. I was holding onto the railing and looking down ten stories toward certain death.

I backed away slowly until I reassuringly touched the outer wall of the building.

"Lenny?" I whispered, but there was no response.

Maybe he was never there, and maybe I *was* crazy.

Chapter Eleven: Suspended

Monday.

The alarm clock buzzed at seven o'clock as usual. I didn't hit the snooze. Instead, I slowly inched my head up and looked around my bedroom. Under the bright morning sunlight pouring in through my windows, the events of the previous night seemed utterly implausible.

Maybe I dreamt it all. A wave of relief swept through my mind and body with that thought, but I quickly pushed it aside. No. Lenny, or whoever he was, was right. Even if everything I had experienced was only a dream, it was a dangerous dream that hinted at mental illness. And I knew I wasn't mentally ill. I was completely sane; only my circumstances were insane. For some reason, a dead woman wanted to kill me—or more precisely, she wanted me to kill *myself*. I had to keep my guard up regardless of how implausible the situation seemed.

Work proved reassuringly ordinary. I found my job repetitive and boring, but today, I reveled in its normalcy. The smiles and nods from my co-workers as I walked toward my desk were so soothing, as was the constant ringing of the telephones. This was heaven compared to what I experienced over the weekend. My first goal that morning was to log onto Resting Place and delete the Kostek memorial, but instead, I allowed myself to be lulled into complacency by the warm camaraderie of the office.

I got a call from Bob Burgess, one of my oldest friends. He wanted to set up a lunch with Mike Phelan, another one of our old schoolmates, and me. Mike recommended the Cheesecake Factory in Harborplace, Baltimore's touristy waterfront Inner Harbor marketplace, which was near his office in the World Trade Center. Bob, a buyer for a supermarket chain, said he'd pick me up on his way downtown. That was great. I wouldn't even have to pay for parking. The call kept the battle out of my mind completely until I got a text message from Teri.

Your Kostek memorial is getting some hate.

I cringed. I never wanted her to see that memorial.

I didn't respond immediately. I needed to see what she was talking about. I went to the website, but the landing page looked different. I had been logged out. I quickly typed in my username and password and hit return. A pop up window appeared saying my account had been suspended for a Terms of Service violation.

WTF?

I couldn't believe it. I went to my personal email account and found a message from Resting Place. The form email said my account was suspended pending a Terms of Service investigation resulting from complaints concerning the Kostek memorial. I turned back to the Resting Place website. You didn't need an account to access the database. I typed Elisabetta Kostek's name in the search engine, and her memorial appeared. I was shocked by the response it was receiving.

Resting Place lets users leave digital "flowers" on memorials, usually accompanied by messages of condolence. Flowers flooded the memorials of famous individuals. The memorials of veterans, particularly those killed in action, were sought out and honored. The memorials for police officers and fire fighters were equally recognized. Generally, however, the vast majority of online memorials received no such recognition. That's why I was shocked by what I saw on the Kostek memorial. In less than two full days, she had received fourteen flowers, which was more than any of my other memorials.

Even more surprising than the number of flowers were the accompanying messages. They were all negative. People called the memorial "an abomination" and pleaded with me to "take her down" because "she's evil." I was dumbfounded. I had never seen negative comments about a deceased person on the website before. They were a violation of the Terms of Service. Resting Place didn't allow people to speak ill of the dead, but the messages soothed me on one level. They proved that I wasn't alone. The photograph of Elisabetta Kostek adversely affected everyone who saw it.

I picked up my phone. I decided to call rather than text Teri. She didn't pick up. I got her answering machine instead. I left a quick message: "Hey, this is Rick. Thanks for the heads-up, Teri. I think I'm just going to delete the memorial. Call me later. Bye."

Now, more than ever, I knew I had to delete the Kostek memorial. I went back and looked at the Resting Place email. It had been sent at 10:23pm EST. That meant if I had deleted her memorial as soon as I got to work, my account would have never been suspended. But I got distracted. She had beaten me again.

"I'm playing checkers, and you're playing chess," I said softly with disgust.

This was nuts. Over the course of a single weekend, I had gone from being a perfectly happy rationalist to not only believing in ghosts but even believing that a ghost could manipulate a website in order to stop me from deleting her memorial. Come on. Even if you acknowledged the possibility of her ghostly existence, why the hell would she even care about some stupid website? The flowers at her grave showed she was already getting more than her share of attention at the cemetery.

My cellphone rang. It was Teri. As I answered, I stepped away from the prying ears around my desk.

"Hi Teri, it's me," I said, wincing at both my informality and the functionality of my words. We weren't dating, but I still wished I could have come up with something wittier or more sophisticated.

"Sorry I couldn't answer when you called, but I was giving an exam," she replied.

"In June?" I asked.

"We're making up for some snow days. We have the girls imprisoned until Thursday," she answered before continuing. "Did you delete that memorial?"

"No, I couldn't. My account has been suspended."

"Why?"

"Because of complaints about the Kostek memorial."

"No offense, but I can see why." She paused for a long time. "There's something wrong with it. Really wrong with it."

"I know. I want to delete it, but I can't. It's like something always stops me." I hated hearing those words come out of my mouth. I was venturing a little too close to the border of Crazy Land.

Silence.

"I had the worst nightmare last night," she said finally.

"Did you dream about someone who died?" I asked. I had no idea why. I wasn't normally an intrusive person, but the words just tumbled out of my mouth on their own volition.

"Yeah, my uncle Hank," she replied quietly.

"Did he kill himself?" I asked again, cringing at my lack of discretion.

"Yes," she said after some hesitation. "Why did you ask?"

"I don't know," I replied. "But I've been having these really vivid dreams about my brother Lenny since I first saw that picture. He killed himself, too."

"I'm sorry," she said.

"I'm sorry about your uncle."

Silence. Then she added, "Hey, I've got to go, but we've got to talk again later. Okay?"

"Okay," I replied.

I hung up and looked at the clock. It was almost time to meet Bob on the street outside my building. Good. I needed some fresh air.

Chapter Twelve: The Harbor

When I stepped outside, I found Bob already waiting for me in his Chevrolet Malibu.

I think Bob enjoyed our lunches the best. His responsibilities as a father gave him little opportunity to socialize with his old friends in the evenings or on weekends. I rarely went to his home anymore. Not because his wife Barbara didn't like me, per se. She simply didn't know what to do with me. After my breakup with Gina, she tried to fix me up with single friends four times, to no avail. To her, an unmarried man approaching forty posed a threat to the natural order of things. As a result, I only found myself invited to their suburban house for large parties, but not the more intimate gatherings where my third wheel status would be more glaring.

We were only about fifteen minutes away from the Baltimore Inner Harbor, where, in theory, Mike was getting a table for us at the Cheesecake Factory in Harborplace. Bob was worried since Mike hadn't returned any calls or texts since ten in the morning. That didn't concern me. Mike was easily distracted—so distracted that I was surprised his fifteen-year marriage to Holly still survived. No woman escaped his notice: tall, short, fat, skinny, beautiful, or ordinary. It didn't matter. He lusted after them all. It was a situation made even more absurd because Mike was the head of human resources at his company. He knew the rules governing sexual harassment. Still, I never thought he would ever cheat on Holly. As ladies men went, Mike didn't rate much higher than me. He was lucky to get Holly, and he knew it.

When we arrived, we found Mike sitting at a table outside overlooking the water, just as I expected. He liked going to the Cheesecake Factory because it was close to work for him, but I knew the truth. He liked to sit outside during the summer months and watch the tourists walking along the waterfront promenade in their skimpy summer outfits. He was always the horn dog.

Usually our lunches were light affairs, dominated by recounting our nerdy glories spoken in our own coded language of *Mystery Science Theater 3000* and *Everquest* references, with occasional nods toward the Coen Brothers' classics *The Big Lebowski* and *Raising Arizona*. We could spend a whole afternoon riffing on Nicholas Cage films alone. Today, however, wasn't going to be our typical stress-free gathering. I caught a few worried glances between Bob and Mike. I knew what was up. They were building up the courage to tell me the bad news. I decided to let them off the hook.

"Hey, you're not going to believe this, but Gina's getting married," I said matter-of-factly.

They both seemed shocked that I knew. "How'd you find out?" Bob asked.

"She called me yesterday and told me."

"You guys still talk?" Mike asked.

"Sure, we're still friends," I replied, adding a little smile to sell it.

Mike and Bob exchanged a relieved glance. "Man, I thought we'd be breaking the news to you, Ricky," Bob said.

"She's all over Facebook showing off her new ring," Mike added.

"Can I see it?" I asked.

Mike and Bob shared a quick little glance before Mike took out his cellphone and produced the photograph. He handed it to me. The picture was taken in a jewelry store. It wasn't a selfie. From the angle, it looked like the jeweler took it. Gina and Chuck were standing happily with their arms around each other. Gina held up her hand with her big ring in front of herself.

Gina looked great, as usual. The warmth of her smile brought one to my lips. I remembered when I could elicit a similar response in her. Aware of Bob and Mike's eyes, I tried not to reveal any unhealthy emotion as I looked at Chuck. This was the first time I had seen a photograph of him. Good-looking guy. He seemed more athletic than me, but I had more hair. That was some consolation, I suppose. My eyes drifted down from the photo to the comments. They were all squeals of congratulations and delight. I recognized most of the names. I wasn't surprised to see that my sister Janet was among the chorus. They still talked, too.

I handed the phone back to Mike. "She looks good."

"Yeah," Mike said. "I'd do her."

"Holly might object," I warned.

"One question," Bob said.

We both turned to him. "When she called you," he continued, "did she ask you for one last quick one?"

"Don't you mean one last short one?" Mike asked as they both exploded into laughter. There was nothing like a small penis joke to break the ice. Guys are guys are guys.

My eyes drifted toward the water. They were drawn past the tourists to an older woman standing at the very edge of the concrete pier. She turned away from me just as I caught sight of her, but I saw enough of her face to notice her resemblance to my late mother. Even from behind, she looked like her. She was the same height, five-five, and she had the same mix of red and gray in her hair. Even her dress looked familiar. I was about to comment on her to Bob and Mike, when she suddenly stepped forward off the pier and dropped out of sight with a loud splash.

"No!" I shouted as I jumped up from my seat.

I started running. I jumped down from the raised patio of the restaurant and passed through the pedestrians walking along the brick promenade. They turned to me, startled and confused. I was appalled. Why were they looking at me? Why weren't they helping that poor woman? I plowed my way through them without hesitation, gaining speed with every step. As I neared the edge of the pier, I didn't see any disturbance in the water, but I took a deep gulp of air and dived in anyway.

My eyes were closed when I hit the water. I had my arms fully extended in front of me out of fear I'd hit the bottom since I had no idea how deep the water was. When I opened my eyes, I could detect some light trying to push through the greenish, brown murk, but I didn't see the old woman as I drifted lower. I wondered what happened to her, and I also began to wonder, fearfully, how deep was the water. It seemed to go on forever.

My lungs were aching when I finally saw the woman coming up toward me from the depths. I saw her hands first, reaching up toward me. Then her face slowly came into view. It was indeed my mother, but she looked younger than the time of her death. Her reddish brown hair swirling in the murky water hadn't turned gray yet. But she was still dead. Her freckles stood out like small pox against the deathly white pallor of her skin. Her eyes were wide open and angry. I had never seen her look at me with such undisguised rage while she was still alive.

She opened her mouth in a breathless scream. I screamed too, expelling the last of my oxygen, as I protectively put my hands ahead of me. She grabbed them, knitting her fingers together with mine. She dragged me downwards. I struggled for a moment, but I lost my strength when I lost my last breath. As I drifted out of consciousness, I wondered how far down she would take me.

Would it be all the way to hell?

Chapter Thirteen: Bad News Betty

When I regained consciousness, I vomited up what seemed like gallons of the worst imaginable filth into the mouth of a total stranger while Bob and Mike stood by helpless and confused.

Those first few minutes were a total blur. My chest ached, and my head throbbed. My mouth roiled under the taste of waste and pollutants from our large, dirty city's sewers. I kept gagging at the thought. I was sure I wouldn't survive an hour because of all the poisons. A large crowd of onlookers gathered around, despite the repeated pleas of the fireman to back away. One question was shouted to me time and time again— "Why'd you do it?"

"I was trying to rescue that lady," I replied; although, even in those first moments of consciousness, I knew there was no woman.

The mention of another potential victim led to a flurry of activity. People ran back to the water's edge to search for her, while other eyewitnesses shouted there was no woman. They said I had simply run and jumped into the water. Questions were thrown at me from all directions. The mood of the crowd quickly changed from exhilaration over my rescue to anger. The arrival of paramedics thankfully halted the Inquisition. I was happy to be loaded on the ambulance and taken away.

The paramedics wanted to take me to nearby Mercy Hospital, but I insisted on being taken to Johns Hopkins. They relented after I explained I was a hospital employee. Mike rode with me in the ambulance. Bob followed behind in his car. Amid the preliminary tests, I asked Mike, "Did you see the woman?"

He shook his head no.

I was admitted into the Emergency Room for tests. When Bob arrived, he told me that he called my sister Janet. She was on her way. I groaned audibly. That was the last thing I needed. I reached for my cellphone to tell her not to bother, but I couldn't find it. The phone was probably at the bottom of the Inner Harbor, if indeed there was a bottom. Just the memory of being pulled down into that abyss was enough to get me shaking again. I held my hands together to make it less obvious.

The police arrived during the examination to ask about the other victim. Under their firm questioning, I modified my initial claim that I saw a woman jump into the water. Instead, I said I *thought* I saw a woman jump into the water, which was the truth. That didn't placate them. They said if there were any possibility of another victim, they would have to drag the harbor for the body, which was a time-consuming and expensive process. I stood firm with the story that I had seen a woman. However, I conceded she probably stepped away while I was distracted, making me assume she had jumped when I looked back.

The police weren't satisfied, but I wouldn't budge any further. I certainly couldn't tell them that an evil ghost, disguised as my late mother, tricked me into jumping in the Inner Harbor with the intent of drowning me. That would have resulted in my exit from the Emergency Room and my entry into the Psych Ward upstairs, where my brother had spent a great deal of time.

When the police left, I called my supervisor Agnes Wilson on the hospital phone. I tried my best to make light of the situation. Bob and Mike listened to the exchange quietly, no doubt noting the subtle differences in my current story from the final version I just told the police. God only knows what they were thinking, and I wasn't about to ask. They were my best friends, but I still couldn't trust them with the truth. I could barely handle it myself.

After I finished my tale, Agnes applauded my misguided heroism and told me to take a few days off. I agreed. When I hung up the phone, I turned to Bob and Mike who looked at me curiously but seemed uncertain what to say. You could have cut the tension in the room with a knife, until I asked, "Who paid the check?"

They both started laughing. I raised my hand. Bob gave me the high five as he said, "Free eats."

I turned to Mike and said, "The next time, you jump in."

He gave me the high five, too.

We were still laughing when my sister Janet arrived. The last time I saw her was about five months earlier at our cousin Mara's wedding. Janet, a would-be sculptor who worked as a waitress to make ends meet, sported short, orange hair with red highlights and wore used, retro clothing that seemed more appropriate on an art student than a thirty-one-year-old, adult woman. Her look reinforced my opinion of her: she refused to become an adult and take responsibility within the family. Bob and Mike greeted Janet before taking off to return to their normal lives.

"I'm sorry Bob called you," I said to her after the guys left. "There was really no need."

She sat down beside me. Her expression was dour. "You don't think I need to know when you jump into the Harbor?"

"It was a stupid misunderstanding," I explained.

She studied me for a moment before she asked, "Did this have anything to do with Gina getting married?"

"No," I replied, insulted. "Do you think I was trying to kill myself?"

"Sorry for asking, but in this family..."

She didn't have to finish.

I hated confiding in Janet, but I knew I had to give her something, so I said, "I'm cool with Gina getting married. He seems like a nice guy. He makes her happy."

"Yeah," Janet said, nodding her head. "That's what she says."

Those words surprised me. I wanted to know how often they talked, but this was definitely not the time or place to pursue that subject. I had to deflect.

"Actually, I just started dating someone myself," I lied. "She's very nice."

"What's her name?"

"Teri."

"How long have you been dating?"

Saying yesterday would hardly bolster my point, so I said, "Just a little while, but it's good. She's really nice, and we have a lot in common."

"That's great," she said, smiling for the first time. "I'd like to meet her."

"You will, soon," I said. I forced a smile, too.

Awkward silence ensued, and then she leaned closer. "Rick, this isn't right. We're all we have left. We should be closer."

"Yeah," I said, and I meant it.

Granted, I harbored resentment toward her for escaping to college in California, but that was the past. Plus, if I was honest with myself, I was never there for her either. When I looked back, I always saw a sad, little girl desperate to tag along with her big brother after the death of our father. But I was too caught up in my own grief to give her much thought at all.

"I know we don't have a lot in common," Janet continued. "But I think we should make a commitment to get together at least once a month for dinner or something. You still go to the movies, right?"

"Yeah," I replied. I loved going to the movies, but I hadn't gone as much since I broke up with Gina. I found it depressing to go alone.

"Well, that might be a good place to start."

"I don't know," I answered. "I like real movies, not those stupid mumble core indies you watch."

"I can stand a Hollywood film every once in a while," she said, standing up. "You need a ride home?"

"No," I replied. "I lost my phone in the water, but I still have my keys and wallet."

Janet suddenly leaned over and gave me a quick kiss on the cheek. I couldn't remember the last time she did that. Even at our mother's funeral, the most we did was hug.

"You scared me, bro," she said. "Be careful, okay?"

"I will."

"Don't prove Betty right," she said under her breath as she left. She said it so quietly that I barely heard it, but I did, and the name definitely rang a bell.

Betty was a fortune-teller my mother visited at least monthly, more often when she was freaked out about something. Betty was supposedly the real deal. She was never wrong. My mother said Betty accurately predicted the death of both my father and brother—to the day. That's why my mother called her Bad News Betty because everything she predicted was tragic. She only made one happy prediction, as far as my mother was concerned: that Gina and I would never marry. I wasn't, however, aware of any other predictions about me.

Jumping down from the examining table, I sloshed over to the door. I called to Janet, who was halfway to the elevators. "Janet, what did you mean about proving Betty right?"

Janet turned to me. Her expression displayed her concern. "I shouldn't have said anything."

"Please," I said.

She weakened. She took a few steps back toward me. "Betty told mom that you were going to kill yourself, too."

I felt the blood drain from my face. "She never told me that."

"She was afraid to mention it," Janet said, stepping even closer and lowering her voice. "She didn't want you to feel predestined."

"Don't worry. I plan to make Betty a liar."

Then it hit me—Betty.

Betty was short for Elizabeth. Or Elisabetta.

Damn it! It was her—Bad News Betty. I knew it was true. It resonated through every pore of my body. Who else could it be?

"Do you remember Betty's last name?" I asked.

"No," Janet said. "But I think it began with a C or a K."

"Was it Kostek?" I asked.

"Yeah, I think so," she said. "Why do you ask?"

"I saw her grave over at Eternal Faith."

Janet spoke as she turned and headed back toward the elevators. "Good. I'm glad she's dead."

"Yeah, me too," I replied.

I just needed her to be a little deader, and I was going to make it happen.

Chapter Fourteen: Chapel Street

I refused to go home in my wet, diseased clothes. I went to a supply closet, snagged some medical scrubs, and left the hospital looking like a resident after a thirty-hour shift.

They released me at three o'clock. I had planned to head to Best Buy immediately after work to buy a new mouse and keyboard. However, my detour into the Inner Harbor necessitated a change of plans. Instead, I went directly home and took a long, hot shower followed by an even longer bath. I bet I nearly brushed the enamel off my teeth, and I gargled incessantly. Afterwards, I could still taste the lead, mercury, and feces contaminating that water. Maybe it was just my imagination, but it definitely took away my appetite.

I left to take care of business. Now, however, my main priority was getting a new cellphone. I didn't have a home phone anymore, so restoring cellular communication was essential, especially since Teri told me she would be calling. Fortunately, I got all three items at my local Best Buy store, but the phone purchase took more time than I anticipated.

While I waited, I tried to come to grips with the revelation that Elisabetta Kostek was Bad News Betty. It made complete sense. Although the photo appeared to have a negative effect on everyone who saw it, there always seemed to be something intensely personal about her attack on me. Now I knew why—pride. She wanted to fulfill her prophecy to my mother.

It wasn't going to happen.

I was hungry, but I knew better than to eat or drink anything while I headed home. I wasn't going to fall for that trick again. When I got to my apartment, I went immediately to my desk. I turned the monitor on to find the image of Betty waiting for me as the screen warmed up. She was smiling, but so was I. Knowing her identity and motivation gave me the confidence that I would beat her. Facts had a funny way of dispelling the terrors of the unknown.

"I know who you are, Betty." I laughed, wagging my finger at the screen. Her smile remained smug, but I knew this was the last time I'd have to see it in my own living room.

I quickly plugged in the keyboard and mouse. As soon as the mouse moved, the image of Betty disappeared with the screensaver. My cemetery photo folder was already open from the previous day. I highlighted the last two files, DSC_0591 and DSC_0592, and then pressed the delete button. The files disappeared. I opened the trash bin. There they were, right where they were supposed to be. Then I hit the empty trash button. Reopening the trash bin, I verified that the two files were indeed deleted. I felt a tremendous sigh of relief, but I had to admit I had an uneasy feelings. Things were going too easily.

I had won two thirds of the battle. The photos were gone from both my camera and my computer. Now all I had to do was delete the memorial on Resting Place, but I couldn't do that until the website restored my account.

I checked my watch: 5:32pm. I wondered when Teri would call. She had to be out of school by now.

I kept the data on my old phone backed up on my computer. I plugged in my new phone and began retrieving it. Sadly, I hadn't backed up my information since I met Teri. I had no record of her phone number.

I searched for Teri's number on the Internet, but it was unlisted. I had no choice but to wait for her to call. I was too on-edge to watch television or make something to eat, so I decided to do some research. I went to Resting Place and typed in the name Poskocil. Only a handful of memorials appeared. I recognized the names Antonin and Maria from their monument at Holy Redeemer. I clicked on Maria. The first thing I noticed was that she died in the same month and year as my great-grandmother Kristina Bakos. That was odd. I opened up my genealogy program to verify the information. I was correct. My great-grandmother Kristina Bakos died on May 8, 1932. Teri's great-grandmother Maria Poskocil died on May 12, 1932.

That was weird, but it explained how our families ended up as next-door neighbors in the cemetery. The two widowed husbands must have bought their plots within days of each other. The Poskocil plots were probably the next two available after my great-grandfather made his purchase. That made sense, but it wasn't the whole story. I remembered that Jan and Kristina Bakos weren't the first members of the family buried in the plot. Their five-year-old son Vincent died four days earlier, increasing the amount of time between the two purchases to around eight days. If the cemetery was simply selling the next available plots, they surely must have sold other plots during that period. I needed to investigate further.

I went to a genealogical website and looked up the Poskocil family in the 1930 Federal Census of Baltimore City, Maryland. I found them living at 2209 Chapel Street. Another coincidence. My family lived on Chapel Street, too. I checked their address. It was 2207 Chapel Street. I couldn't believe it. Our families were next-door neighbors in life as well as death. I checked Antonin's occupation. He was a tailor working in a factory. So was Jan. The records didn't indicate if they worked in the same factory, but at this point, I wouldn't have been surprised.

I decided to take a step back in time. I checked the immigration records and found that Antonin and Maria arrived in Baltimore from Bremen on February 10, 1919, five years after Jan and Kristina arrived. However, what caught my attention was Antonin and Maria's hometown: Bernartice, Czechoslovakia. That's where my Bakos family hailed from as well.

I was well acquainted with Bernartice. I never visited the town, but I had hired Czech researchers to study my family's roots there. They supplied me with reams of genealogical material and photographs of the houses associated with my family. The town was little more than a remote crossroads with a population of about a hundred people during the first decades of the twentieth century. It was highly improbable that our two families didn't know each other back in the old country.

A horrible thought suddenly crossed my mind—what if Teri and I were cousins?

I checked the surname index on my genealogy program for the name Poskocil. Nothing came up. That was a relief. My researchers traced back my Bernartice lines back to the late-sixteenth century. If Teri and I were related by blood, her surname would have shown up in the research.

Unless we were related through one of her maternal lines, I thought, sighing disgustedly.

There was no point speculating any further about it. I didn't have enough information about her family to prove it one way or another. Plus, what did it matter? It wasn't like we were dating anyway. But I *did* want to keep that option open—just in case.

"What a small world," I said softly to myself.

Then I had a chilling thought; maybe it wasn't a small world after all. Maybe meeting Teri wasn't a coincidence. Maybe I didn't even run across Betty's grave by accident. Maybe she drew me to it somehow to fulfill her prophecy. I couldn't imagine how Teri fit into the plan, but something told me she did. Why else would she suddenly be dreaming about a relative who had killed himself?

As if on cue, my cellphone rang. It was Teri. I answered immediately, with a voice that probably sounded more eager than I would have preferred. "Hi, Teri."

"Hi," she answered. "Did you manage to delete the memorial?"

"No, but I did learn something about Elisabetta today. She was a fortuneteller, and my late mother was one of her clients."

"You're kidding me," she said quietly.

"No, and that's not the worst part," I continued. "Bad News Betty— that's what everyone called her. She told my mother I would kill myself one day."

A long silence and then she spoke again. "If you're joking, it isn't funny."

"I'm not joking, Teri. I swear."

Silence.

"Rick, I don't know how to explain this, but I've been under a dark cloud since I first saw that face," she said. "I think this is something demonic."

Three short days ago, I would have openly scoffed at such a statement, but not today. Not anymore. "We've got to talk," I replied.

Teri suggested meeting at the Bel-Loc Diner, an authentic fifties-style joint not too far from my apartment on Joppa Road. Of course, I said yes. She arrived before me. I joined her at an isolated corner booth where we could speak without being overheard by the normal people scattered about the establishment.

She was dressed casually wearing jeans and a white, button down shirt. Her short auburn hair brushed against her collar every time she turned her head. She smelled great, too, but I couldn't tell if it was perfume or shampoo. Teri possessed a wonderful, unforced beauty, and normally, my thoughts would have drifted toward possible romance, but not tonight. I saw the fear in her blue eyes. I felt it, too. The confidence I felt earlier after discovering Betty's identity vanished once I found the link between our families. I now feared we were part of a plan a very long time in the making, which wouldn't be easily undone.

"I did some research on your family," I continued. "They weren't just neighbors in the cemetery; they were next door neighbors in real life, too, on Chapel Street."

I gave her printouts of the census records. She quickly examined them before softly saying, "Wow."

"If you think that's something, look at this," I said as I handed her a printout of the immigration records. "They were also from the same small village in Bohemia."

"They probably knew each other there."

I nodded in agreement.

"Do you think we're cousins?" she asked.

"I don't see a direct link," I replied. "But all I know about your family is what was posted on Resting Place."

She nodded.

"I know you've been to both graves," I continued. "But did you notice the dates of death of our great-grandmothers?"

She shook her head no.

"Mine died on May 8, 1932," I said. "Yours died on May 12, 1932."

She thought about that for a moment, then asked, "How did yours die?"

"The death certificate said accident. She was struck and killed by a truck while crossing Broadway," I replied. "But my family thought it was suicide. Someone said she shouted out the name of her son Vincent, who had died five days earlier, right before she ran out in front of the truck."

"My great-grandmother drowned in her own bathtub," Teri said quietly. "The official story is that she slipped and hit her head and drowned, but I heard they found pills beside the tub. My great-grandfather hid them from the police because he was afraid the church wouldn't bury her on sacred ground if they thought it was suicide."

"Was she depressed?" I asked.

"I have no idea. I'm lucky to know as much as I do," she replied. "I heard my father and my great-aunt Maggie talk about it once when I was a kid, and half of that conversation was in Bohemian."

"I never heard anything about my great-grandmother committing suicide until my brother died," I explained. "Afterwards, my mother was quick to point out that suicide ran down my father's side of the family, not hers. She gave my sister and me all the gory details to back up her point. Trust me; they were not what we needed to hear at the time."

"If you don't mind me asking," Teri said. "How many people committed suicide in your family?"

"My great-grandmother. Two of her sons. My brother and my mother, although I don't think my mother is relevant because she's not from Chapel Street," I answered. "And, according to Betty, I will, too."

"Never ever say that!" Teri replied sharply. Then she took a sip of her coffee before she continued. "My family's similar. My great-grandmother and two of her sons, Martin and Hank."

"I think we're outside the statistical norm."

"Agreed."

"What I don't understand is what any of this has to do with the picture. Or Betty," I said. "Is it possible your mother went to see her, too?"

"Oh, heavens no," Teri answered. "My mother is the original Miss Super Catholic. She views any kind of divination as being on the same level as devil worship. She'd never even let a newspaper in the house because of the horoscopes."

"Is she still alive?"

"Yes, both of my parents are," Teri replied. "They retired to Fort Myers, Florida, last year."

Our conversation stopped as the waitress brought our food. With all of the photos of Betty deleted from my personal computer, I felt safe eating again. Once the waitress disappeared, I continued. "Teri, you said your Uncle Hank came to you in a dream. Did he ask you to do anything?"

"Whatever I saw in that dream wasn't my uncle," she replied. "I was only about six when he died, but I remember him clearly. Whenever he saw me, he'd always smile and pick me up and spin me around. I know he loved me. He'd never..."

"Ask you to kill yourself," I interrupted.

"No," she said. "He didn't put it like that. He said I should join him. Is that what your brother asked you to do?"

"He told me he doesn't want me to go through what he went through," I answered. "He said it's peaceful where he is." I considered telling her about my experiences on the balcony and at the Inner Harbor, but I was afraid they'd be too much for her. I couldn't afford to lose my only ally now.

"Would your brother ask you to do that when he was alive?" Teri asked.

"Possibly," I answered. That was an answer she didn't expect. "My brother was genuinely insane at times, bipolar, and the illness was a definite burden on him. That's why he did what he did. I could see him recommending that same choice to me if he felt I was suffering like him."

Teri shook her head no. "It's not my uncle. It's not your brother. The Bible says there is a gulf between the living and dead that no man can cross. Luke 16:23, the parable of the rich man and Lazarus."

"Then who is it?" I asked. "Betty?"

"It can't be her either," Teri replied. "She was a human being, just like us. It has to be a demon."

"Then why does it all seem to hinge around these pictures I took of her?"

"I don't know, Rick," she said. Then she reached over and touched my hand. "But I believe we are both in a great deal of danger."

That was an opinion we both shared.

Chapter Fifteen: The Herd

Teri managed to scare me more than I already had been. I nearly jumped out of my skin when my phone rang while I was driving home. I picked it up to see that the call was from Portland, Oregon. That was surprising. I didn't know anyone in Portland. I assumed it was a sales call, but it was ten p.m. What salesperson calls a cellphone at that hour? I answered.

"Hello, is this Richard Bakos?" the voice asked.

"Yes," I said.

"Hi, this is Herb Norton from Resting Place."

I couldn't believe it. Herb was the founder of Resting Place. I always imagined that one day he could recognize my efforts on behalf the website. I often fantasized about getting a full-time job with the company, but I suspected this call wasn't going to be the pat on the back I envisioned.

"I hope I'm not calling too late," he continued.

"No, no, no," I stammered. "It's fine."

"Good," he said. "First, I want to apologize about the suspension. That was an automatic function triggered by the complaints about your Kostek memorial. We found no terms of service violations."

"How many complaints did it get?" I asked.

"Fifty-seven, as of now."

"Fifty-seven," I said, astonished. "I can't imagine fifty-seven people even saw it."

"It is out of the ordinary," Herb replied. "The average memorial in Eternal Faith cemetery is viewed three point four times a year. Your

Kostek memorial has received over nine hundred unique visits in the last four days."

I couldn't believe that. "Why?"

"We have no explanation. It's an anomaly," Herb replied. "No outside sources are linking to the memorial. It is all internal traffic from unrelated ISPs all around the world. People aren't even searching specifically for her. They seem to surf to the memorial randomly. We've never seen anything like it before."

I didn't know how to respond, but it was clear to me that Betty was drawing the users to herself the same way she had drawn me.

"Considering the unsettling effect the memorial has been having on our users, and, quite frankly, ourselves, we plan to delete it," Herb said.

"Good," I replied.

"Before we do, I was wondering if you knew anything more about her? We haven't been able to find anything about her on the Internet. It's like she never existed."

"No, she existed," I answered. Normally I wouldn't confide in someone I barely knew, but his tone of voice told me he was now a brother in arms. "My mother knew her. She was a fortuneteller. People called her Bad News Betty because she only predicted bad things."

A long silence followed. "May I talk with your mother?"

"No, I'm sorry," I replied. "She died."

More silence. Then, "Thank you, Mr. Bakos, Rick. We will be restoring your account soon."

"Do you want me to delete it?"

"No, that's not necessary. We'll do it here," Herb replied. "We have better tools. We can eliminate all traces of it from cache and any mirrored sites."

"Good," I said. "The sooner she's gone, the better."

"Yes," Herb replied.

What a relief!

As soon as I got home, I called Teri and told her the good news. She was relieved, but asked if I thought that would end the nightmares. I told her I hoped so, but at the very least, it would limit the number of people she could affect. Still, I wasn't anxious to go to bed after I hung up with

Teri. Since I didn't have work the next day, I planned to stay awake until the memorial was safely deleted. The Orioles were on a West Coast road trip playing the Seattle Mariners. That would be a good start. Hopefully, the game would run into extra innings.

Despite my best intentions, I dozed off some time during the eighth inning. I awoke somewhere around three a.m., as usual, to find an infomercial for a workout device playing on the television. As I picked up the remote to turn off the television, I heard a voice say, "I know what you're thinking. Boy, I thought Mom was clingy when she was alive!"

I turned to find Lenny sitting in an armchair catty-corner to the sofa. He was wearing a Washington Nationals T-shirt strictly to annoy me. He never followed the National League when he was alive. I doubt he suddenly became a fan in the afterlife, despite the great year the team was having.

"You're not Lenny," I said.

I was going to stand up and go to my bedroom, but I stopped myself. Anytime I moved in one of these dreams, I ended up on the balcony. It was safest just to stay put.

"We're back on that again?" Lenny asked, disappointed. "Did you call Pete and ask him about the motorcycle?"

"No, I didn't," I said. "I was a little busy today."

"Yeah, I know," Lenny replied. He got up and headed for the kitchen. "Can I get you a beer?"

"No, thanks."

"I can't believe you jumped into the harbor, Ricky-boy," Lenny said as he bent over to rifle through the refrigerator. "People are going to start thinking you're crazy."

"Was that you?" I asked.

"Hell, no," Lenny replied. I heard him pop open a beer before he stood up. "That was Mommy Dearest."

"No it wasn't."

"That's right, we're all demons," Lenny said as he walked back into the room. "I'll tell you what, Ricky. You go into work tomorrow and tell somebody that a demon tricked you into jumping in the harbor and almost drowned you. I betcha you'll be strapped down in the psych ward in about fifteen minutes."

He was right about that. A grieving son could be forgiven for mistaking someone for his late mother, but as soon as you started talking about demons, it was game over.

Lenny sat down at the desk. "I noticed you didn't tell your new girlfriend about the harbor. Or the balcony. Why?"

I didn't answer.

"I'll tell you why," Lenny continued, waxing philosophically. "You don't ever really see human beings for what they are until you find yourself on the outside looking in. The human race is like a huge herd of Wildebeest moving slowly across the African plains. All they do is walk and eat. Walk and eat. For them, happiness is an endless sea of grass that they never have to lift their snouts up from. But sometimes you're so busy walking and eating that you accidently step into a gopher hole and injure your leg. Next thing you know, you're limping. That worries the rest of the herd because they know your limp will attract the lions. Think about it, Ricky; the lions would never spot a limping Wildebeest if the others kept it in the middle of the herd, but they don't. Nope. They push the wounded member as far away as they can because they don't want to see the approaching lions. They just want to keep munching on the grass, without ever acknowledging that one day the lions will come for them, too."

Lenny took a drink from the beer then made eye contact with me. That was him alright. I'd seen that look a thousand times as he laid down some mostly insane big brother wisdom. I turned away. This was getting too real.

"Yesterday, you disturbed the herd. You took a real fall, but you're not limping yet. Your friends and co-workers will cut you some slack about the harbor thing, provided you don't pull another stunt like that. If you do, they'll push you out to the edge of the herd for the lions. And she is ready to devour you, the way she devoured me."

"Who?"

"You know who—Bad News Betty," he answered and then saluted me with the beer can. "Kudos for figuring that out, but you have to admit you got a valuable assist from Janet. God, I love her. I think she might actually make it."

"I'm going to make it, too."

Lenny gave me a dismissive smirk. "Not a chance, Ricky. Once Betty focuses her attention on you, it's time to cash in your chips," he said. "Man, I wonder how different our lives would have been if Mom had never gone to her in the first place. I think I was doomed one way or another, but she might still be alive."

I offered no response. He continued.

"You give mom a lot of crap, but she really loved you."

"Yeah," I replied. "Too much."

"Damn right, " he said. "She died for you."

I gave him a skeptical look. Lenny continued.

"That old witch gave Mom a prophecy about our family. She said, 'Two will die by their own hand and wipe their name from upon the land.' Mom knew that the prediction meant you and I would kill ourselves before we passed on the family name. Mom thought she could spare you if she became the second one to die by her own hand. She was wrong, but her heart was in the right place."

What nerve, I thought furiously. That was it. "No, no, no," I said standing up. "You're not going to pin her death on me. You're the one who killed her when you killed yourself. You took away her will to live."

"I know I hurt her," Lenny conceded. "But I was a burden on her, too. How many more times do you think she could have endured the cycle of me returning to sanity only to drift back into madness? It took as much out of her as it took out of me. And what about you? How much longer was it going to be before you gave up on me?"

Those words silenced me because I had already given up on him prior to his death. I was always online trying to find a place that would take him indefinitely and get him out of our lives. My mother was more patient. She fought the idea. She wanted us to stay together as a family.

"Right up until the minute I died, Mom believed she could stop Betty's prophecy without bloodshed," Lenny said quietly. "When she realized she couldn't, she tried to save you. So don't give her too much crap."

Sitting down, I tried to absorb Lenny's words. Was there any truth in them, or was this all some kind of mind game? My mother held onto Lenny and me in a selfish, psychotic way, but she was also fiercely protective. I had no problem believing she would sacrifice herself for us. But why did she have to do it? I turned back to Lenny.

"What does Betty want?" I asked.

Lenny said nothing.

"You know."

He nodded yes.

"If you really are Lenny, you'd tell me so I can protect myself."

Lenny stood up. "You can't protect yourself," he said wearily. "You have no idea what she's capable of. Right now, she's toying with you like a cat with a ball of yarn. She'll pull you and stretch you to see how much you can take, but, trust me, the reckoning will come. The only way to stop the game is to stop playing."

He went to the door and left my apartment. The slamming of the door woke me up. When I opened my eyes, I found myself not in my living room but instead on the balcony seated on a deck chair. I was genuinely surprised. Every other time, I had walked in my dreams, but I made a conscious decision to stay put this time. So how did I physically end up on the balcony? Did something move me? Or did I simply not remember?

My thoughts were interrupted by the sound of Lenny's motorcycle. That was unsettling. How could I hear that while I was awake? I went to the railing of the balcony to see Lenny pull out of the garage onto Joppa Road. The engine roared as he accelerated toward an intersection. The light was red, but Lenny barreled through it, forcing a car coming from the other direction to slam on its brakes to avoid him.

"Oh my God," I said softly.

The other driver saw him, too. He was real.

Unless this was all a dream, too.

Discerning what was real and what was a dream was becoming increasingly difficult.

Chapter Sixteen: Research

Tuesday.

I woke up early. Like the last couple of mornings, the purifying rays of the sun seemed to wash away what I had experienced at night, but I refused to be lulled into complacency. I was in the midst of a life or death battle. I had to figure out a way to take the offensive. My boss gave me a few days off. I had to make the most of them.

Teri texted me while I was showering.

Go to Resting Place.

I went into the living room and sat down behind my desk. I opened my browser and went to the website. The landing page was now a tribute to founder Herb Norton. I couldn't believe it. A drunk driver killed Herb while he was crossing the street to get to his car the night before.

The so-called accident brought to mind my own father's death. He was killed when a drunk driver went through a red light and slammed into his car at sixty miles an hour. My mother said Betty had accurately predicted his death. That's why she took Betty's words as gospel. But what if Betty hadn't just predicted his death? What if she made it happen somehow?

The thought chilled me, but I tried to put it out of my mind. I had more than enough reasons to fear Betty without inventing more through speculation. However, I couldn't believe that Herb's death was an accident. His words and tone of voice hinted that he and his staff were already under heavy supernatural attack. I was sure Betty killed him to protect her memorial. That meant I was ultimately responsible. I had unleashed her.

My heart sank as I read about Herb's wife and four young children, one of whom had special needs. I knew what they were going through. My father's death had thrown our family into a psychological tailspin from which we never recovered. None of us, not even Janet. You didn't have to be Sigmund Freud to see that. I was reasonably happy, but I knew I was screwed up. Gina and Lenny were right. I was the Boy in the Plastic Bubble. I knew I would never really let anyone all the way into my heart out of fear of losing them.

Would Herb's kids face the same fate? I hoped not.

I knew I would live forever with my guilt about Herb, but I couldn't fall into that rabbit hole now. I had to stop Betty's killing spree first. I hoped that Herb or someone on the staff had managed to delete her memorial. That would certainly contain her influence.

I typed Betty's name in the search engine. Her page came up. They didn't delete it. Not wanting to see her face again, I didn't click on the memorial itself, even though I was curious how many more negative flowers she had received. Then I wondered what would I find if I checked the names of the people attacking her memorial against the death notices in their hometowns? For all I knew, Betty could be killing people all over the world.

I picked up the phone and dialed Teri. She answered on the first ring.

"Can you believe that?" she asked.

"Yeah, I can."

After a pause, she spoke quietly. "I woke up this morning in my bathtub with the water running. That's how my great-grandmother died."

I closed my eyes and winced. I couldn't allow that to happen. Nor could I let her suffer alone by letting her think she was the only crazy one. I had to lay all my cards on the table. After all, she was probably the only person who would understand.

"My brother Lenny jumped off a six-story balcony in Ocean City," I told her. "I wake up on my balcony after every one of my brother's visits. I have no idea how I get there."

"We have to stop this," she said.

"I know," I replied. "Unfortunately they didn't delete the memorial, and I don't think they've restored my account."

"It's going to take more than deleting the memorial," she said. "One way or another, I think she'll still come for us."

"Yeah, this feels personal," I replied.

We needed to do something more but what?

"I'm going to talk to our Chaplain, Father Kubera, today at school," she said.

"Are you sure that's a good idea?"

"We need somebody who understands spiritual warfare."

True enough, but I thought Teri was being naïve. "What if he doesn't believe you?" I asked. "It could cost you your job. Or worse."

Teri laughed. "Come on, Rick. You were raised Catholic. You know about the confidentiality of the confessional," she said. "I could tell him I was stealing the girls' lunch money, and there isn't anything he could do about it."

I had to smile, but that wasn't the case with me. Lenny was right about the herd. I considered everyone in my office a friend, but they wouldn't be supportive if I started talking about ghosts and demons. They would have me locked up for my own good and theirs! The only person I could trust now was Teri. And Lenny, provided, of course, Lenny wasn't Betty in disguise.

"I'm not going to work today," I told her. "I'm going to do a little research."

"Be careful."

"I will."

"Text me if you learn anything," she said. "I'll call you back when I can."

I hung up and thought about what to do next. First, I decided I had to figure out who or what Lenny was. I decided to call Pete and ask him about Lenny's motorcycle. I turned to my address book program on my computer, but I didn't have a listing for him. I found dozens of Peter Thompsons in the area in an online directory, but none of the addresses looked familiar. I decided to call Janet. She wrote all the thank you cards to the people who attended our mother's funeral. She answered on the third ring.

"How you feeling today, Rick?" she asked.

"Pretty good," I replied. "But I think I'm going to take a few days off."

"That's good."

"Hey, I was wondering if you had Pete Thompson's phone number."

"Why?" she asked. "You looking to buy some meth?"

That was a surprising response. "Why'd you say that?"

"He's obviously on something," she responded. "You saw him at Mom's funeral. He definitely had that homeless guy puts a tie on for Thanksgiving dinner at the shelter look."

"He wasn't that bad."

"He was missing teeth."

"I don't think his family stressed oral hygiene," I replied.

"Or impulse control."

"He's not a bad guy," I answered defensively. "He'd never hurt anyone. Except himself."

"Those are the ones who hurt you most."

I couldn't argue with that. Our mother and brother's self-destructiveness shredded both Janet and me emotionally, but this wasn't a discussion I could afford to have now. I had too much work to do. "Do you have the number?" I asked.

"Yeah, I'll get it to you."

"Thanks," I said.

"Bye."

I hung up. So far so good. My next goal was to head over to Eternal Faith and see what I could learn about Betty. They undoubtedly had the address of her next of kin. My phone rang again. Thinking it was Janet, I answered without looking.

"Got it?"

"You lied," the voice said softly, edged with pain, both physical and psychological.

My heart stopped. I began to shake, a little at my torso but more wildly at my extremities.

"You promised to stay with me forever."

It was my mother's voice—but devoid of any of her warmth. She was reminding me of the promise she had elicited from me as a nine-year-old boy immediately after the death of my father. It was a promise I made willingly, as did Lenny and Janet. And it was more than just words. Our only desire at that moment was to hold ourselves together in love as a bulwark against cruel, unblinking death. Of course, I didn't realize the implications of the oral contract or how seriously my mother would take it.

"Richard!" she screeched.

That was a tone she rarely used except when she thought I had snuck off to call Gina when I should have been tending to her instead. She wouldn't tolerate that. No, no, no. There was absolutely no room for Gina in "our" life, especially then. Guilt still plagued me on occasion concerning those last days. The night my mother died, I had gone out for a late dinner with Gina. I often wondered if she was screeching for me before she swallowed the pills that ended her life and, in theory, reunited her with her husband and her older son.

"Richard! I'm talking to you!"

I dropped the phone. I was afraid to look down at it until I heard the faint sound of the dial tone. Then I bent over to look at the phone. The Caller ID indicated that the call had come from my own mobile number.

"Of course," I told myself. She had my phone. The one I lost in the harbor.

That was insane, of course. My dead mother wasn't calling me on my phone I lost in the harbor. She wasn't in the harbor. She was rotting in a box beneath the soil at Eternal Faith. She didn't have my phone or any other phone. No, this was just another one of Betty's mind games. And I wasn't going to take it anymore.

I nearly dropped my phone again when I stood up and turned to the computer. The screensaver was back on and with it, came Elisabetta Kostek. Her smile appeared more bemused than ever.

"What the..."

I moved the mouse to eliminate the screensaver. Then I sat down and opened up the photo directory. I clicked on the cemetery folder. The two most recent files were DSC_0591 and DSC_0592. I didn't have to click on them. I knew what they were, and I knew I had deleted them the day before. Why weren't they gone? I looked down the list. The next file was DSC_0589. Two other files were missing. I had obviously deleted the wrong ones.

I knew it wasn't a mistake. It was more mental manipulation, and I wasn't going to let it happen again. Now, instead of just deleting her two files, I decided to delete all of my cemetery photos. It wasn't an easy decision. I had spent years taking them, but I didn't want to see that face on my screensaver again.

"Take that, Betty," I said boldly as I deleted the folder, but I was afraid. I didn't think Betty would take that lying down.

Chapter Seventeen: Flowers

I left my apartment and headed over to Eternal Faith. I was relieved to see that there were not any customer cars parked in front of the office. I needed Rita's undivided attention—and her good will.

"Don't you ever work?" she asked, hardly looking up as I walked in.

"Taking a vacation day."

"Oh, joy," she replied. "Who are you looking for today?"

"Elisabetta Kostek," I replied.

Now she looked up. Her eyes were wide, and the blood quickly drained from her face. I could tell there was no need for her to check the files. She knew exactly whom I was talking about.

"Why are you asking about her?" she asked. Her voice was deadly serious.

I didn't expect to be grilled in the office about this request, so I didn't have a story ready. Obviously, the truth wouldn't be helpful, but I came up with a great answer that was actually somewhat truthful.

"She was an old friend of my mother," I said. "I saw her in the mausoleum and wanted to pay my respects to her next of kin."

That answer caught Rita off guard. Her expression indicated that she believed me. Jose Garcia, the head groundskeeper, appeared in a nearby doorway. I always respected Jose. Most of the cemeteries I visited were in some degree of decline, but Jose maintained Eternal Faith meticulously like it was his personal mission in life. He was also normally a chatty, happy-go-lucky guy, who always had time to give me the ins-and-outs of the cemetery business. Now he was as deadly serious as Rita. They exchanged a glance before she turned back to me.

"We don't have any next of kin information," she said.

"Nothing?" I replied incredulously. "You must have something."

"We tried contacting her family about a month ago, but the information wasn't any good anymore," she replied. "I guess her husband, or next of kin, or whoever, died or moved without a forwarding address."

I had a strong feeling she was lying to me, but how could I push her? I was lying to her, too. "Can I have what information you do have?" I asked.

"No."

"Please?"

"No, Rick, I can't," she said in a voice imploring me to stop. "I couldn't even if we had it. It's private. I could lose my job." She turned to Jose for confirmation. "Right?"

Jose nodded in agreement and then turned to me. "Let the dark lady be," he said. "Walk away, my friend."

I knew I wasn't going to get any further, so I turned to leave the office. When I reached the door, Rita called out to me. "And whatever you do, don't put her up on that stupid website."

Now you tell me, I thought.

I left the building frustrated. I expected to wheedle all of the information I needed from Rita, but that obviously wasn't going to happen. I had seen her happy, and I had seen her angry, but I had never seen her afraid. In fact, she seemed almost as frightened as I did. And the normally affable Jose…he called her The Dark Lady. Did he see her in his dreams, too?

My phone chirped as I got back into my car. Afraid it might be my mother, I looked at it cautiously. It was a text from Janet with Pete's phone number. I called it immediately.

Pete sounded hung over when he answered, but he became downright chipper when he recognized my voice. I tried to ask about Lenny's motorcycle, but Pete had other ideas. He thought we should get together that evening for drinks at Brendan's, an old school Hamilton bar on Harford Road. When I tried begging off, he became evasive. He obviously wanted to sell his memories to me for a drink or two. I resented that. However, when he began waxing poetically about how good the burgers were at the bar, I decided to say yes before I ended up on the line for a seven-course meal. I agreed to meet him at six o'clock.

I hung up, but I didn't want to go home empty handed. I drove over to the mausoleum and parked nearby. I thought about going inside and checking the vaults around Betty. Families often bought more than one. I hoped one of the nearby vaults belonged to a more-easily traced family member. There was only one problem. I couldn't bring myself to enter the building again. I could sense Betty inside waiting for me. Her presence had grown stronger. The sense of gloom I felt inside now radiated outside, too. It hung over the building like the scent of rotting meat. There was no way I was going inside.

As I considered my next move, an old Chevy drove past me and parked closer to the mausoleum. An elderly woman carrying a single rose got out and walked toward the glass doors. Grabbing my camera off the seat beside me, I got out of my car just as she disappeared inside the heavy glass doors.

I walked across the road onto the grass. I wasn't going to make the same mistake I made with the old man again. I checked the position of the sun and smiled. If my guess was right, the sun wouldn't leave any glare on the glass doors, and I would be able to see inside from the field of graves. I walked quickly, pretending to be looking at the ground-level monuments as I moved in front of the door.

I was right. When I got into position about fifty yards away from the mausoleum, I had a glare-free, unobstructed view inside through the glass doors. I raised the camera up from the ground and looked through the door with my zoom lens. The old woman had her back toward me. As I expected, she walked straight up to Betty's vault. When she reached it, she knelt down and placed the roses on the floor before her. The mourner seemed to linger a moment in some silent contemplation or supplication before she slowly stood up again.

I turned the camera away toward the ground before the old woman could see I had been spying on her. I never even turned my eyes in her direction as she left the mausoleum and started up her car. I just walked from grave to grave, photographing the monuments as I had done many times in this cemetery. As the sound of the Chevy retreated, I heard the sound of another vehicle. I turned to see Jose approaching in his golf cart.

Jose was headed straight for me. I considered fleeing toward my car, but that seemed entirely too undignified for an adult man my age. Plus, I wanted to hear what he had to say. We had an agreeable relationship. He often chatted amiably while I photographed graves, but he didn't seem happy now as he neared me in the golf cart.

"You had to put her up on that website, Mr. Rick," Jose said, unnerved, as he stopped alongside me.

"I'm sorry."

"You have to take it down. Now."

"I can't," I answered. "They suspended my account."

"Madre de Dios," Jose replied. "You have no idea what you did."

"I think I do," I said. "What do you know about her?"

Jose got off the golf cart and turned his back to the mausoleum, as if he was afraid she could read his lips. He spoke softly. "She's evil."

Thanks for the news flash, dude. I barely contained the urge to roll my eyes. "Do you have her next of kin information?"

"I don't know for sure. I don't do the paperwork," he replied, "but I think they tried to call her family before we moved her."

"You moved her?"

"Yeah. She was in the ground. The Beatitudes section."

"Why'd you move her?"

"It was the strangest thing," he said, lowering his voice further. "She was killing the grass. We re-sodded it three times, but the grass always died, radiating out from her grass." He pointed to a rolling hill nearby. "I don't know if you noticed it, but that was all brown for a while."

"Yeah," I said. I actually did notice that.

"We knew it was her. Anyone who looked at her picture knew. Mr. Farber, the old manager, told us to move her into the mausoleum where she could do less damage," Jose explained. "But it was a big mistake. The grass grew back, but now more people saw her picture in there. Just look at how many flowers she gets now."

Silence.

He leaned in close. "I'll tell you, Mr. Rick," he said very quietly. "When we pulled her coffin up, Manny and I were so tempted to take that old bruja out back into the woods and burn her body. But I was afraid."

"Of what?"

"That she was alive in there," he answered, shivering suddenly and then crossing himself. "The whole time we had her coffin out, I could feel her eyes peering at me through the lid. She sees us now, you know."

I nodded and said, "She's trying to get me to kill myself."

Jose nodded. The news didn't surprise him. "Yeah," he said. "That's the way she does it." He pointed to a section near the office. "Mr. Farber's buried over there. He wouldn't leave a flower."

"What do the flowers do?" I asked.

"If you pay her respect, she shows mercy," Jose explained.

Jose spotted some fresh flowers on a nearby grave. He went over, removed one from the vase, and handed it to me. "Just go in, kneel, and place the flower before her," Jose said. "Then she'll leave you alone."

"It's that easy?" I answered, amazed.

Jose shrugged. "Well, it's a little different for everyone. Some people leave one flower, and that's it. Other people come once a week. Other people, like me, leave a flower every day," he said, and then lowered his voice again. "I think it's because I disturbed her grave."

Silence. I looked at the flower in my hand. The solution couldn't be that simple. Sure, placing the flower at her grave would be giving her the victory, but what did I care? I just wanted to go back to my normal life.

"Just do it," Jose said, as if he knew what I was thinking.

Why not? I didn't have to beat her. That was probably impossible anyway. How can flesh and bone beat an entity from another plane of existence, whether it was spiritual or dimensional? Why not call it a draw? She could go her way, and I could go mine. I took a step toward the mausoleum before I suddenly stopped. Why? Because I heard that little voice again that warned me not to put the photo on the website. The voice was now telling me that putting the flower on the grave would be a terrible mistake.

Once again, the irony of the situation struck me. I spent almost thirty years rejecting the supernatural, and now I was being tossed back and forth by voices and dead people. The absurdity angered me. Damn it, I was the master of my soul. If it suited me, I would put a flower on her grave and end this madness. Why should I obey some voice that never did me any good anyway?

As I looked up from the flower to the mausoleum, it struck me. My pride got me into this whole mess in the first place. Had I listened to that warning voice the first time, I wouldn't even be in this predicament.

"Was she in a family plot over on the hill?" I suddenly asked Jose, distracting myself from the decision at hand.

"Yes, I think she was buried with her parents."

"Can you take me over?"

Jose sighed. He climbed back onto the golf cart and drove me over to the former resting place of Elisabetta Kostek. Despite my emotional state, I still found time to admire the way Jose drove his golf cart, carefully avoiding riding directly over coffins. He was a great caretaker who took pride in his work. Most cemeteries I visited were not fortunate enough to have someone like him on staff. Even Holy Redeemer, despite their large staff, suffered from weeds and the occasional overturned monument. Jose would never allow that.

Jose stopped near the grave and pointed. "There it is."

I got out of the cart. I left the flower on the seat, but I took my camera with me. I followed Jose's finger over to the monuments belonging to Frank Popek, 1923-1980, and Helen Popek, 1922-1994. I turned to Jose.

"Popek?" I asked.

"That's them," he answered.

Popek sounded Bohemian to me. I wondered if they went back to Chapel Street, too. Perhaps they were the link between our families. I took pictures of their markers for reference, and then I turned to the empty space beside Helen. The grass was perfect. You couldn't tell where the new grass blended with the old.

"Is that where she was?"

"Yes, sir," Jose answered.

"Does anyone leave flowers here?"

"Nope," Jose replied. "That's the funny thing. The people seemed to know where she went without even asking at the office."

I walked back to the golf cart. "Does Rita know about her?"

"Yes, she puts down her roses, too."

Jose reached over and took the rose. He held it up to me. "Are you going to pay your respects?"

Oh, God.

I felt like hapless Larry Groger character in the film *Animal House* with an angel on one shoulder and the devil on the other one whispering into my ears. For a recent agnostic like me, the situation would be as comic as it was in the movie if the stakes were not so deadly high. One voice offered me peace if I submitted and laid down a flower. The other voice didn't offer me anything if I resisted the urge. No guarantee of eventual victory. It simply said things would be worse if I laid down a flower.

In the end, my decision wasn't about whom I trusted. It was about whom I didn't trust. Betty came at me with such fierce malevolence that I knew she wouldn't be satisfied with such a small sacrifice. I realized the most I would be doing was prolonging the agony, or as Lenny called it, the game. More importantly, how could I reward Betty for driving my mother and my brother, and possibly even other members of my family, to their deaths? What the other voice whispered was irrelevant. If it was God, great. If He had a plan, even better! I would like to hear it. However, if that voice was just my pride coming at me from another direction, that was cool, too. It didn't matter. I wasn't going to bend a knee to Betty. Ever.

"No," I said to Jose. "I'm going to beat the bitch."

Jose gave me a sad look as if he knew he was going to be burying me soon.

Chapter Eighteen: Pete

I went straight home and researched the Popek family.

I found the death notice for Frank Popek in the archives of the Baltimore Sunpapers. The death notice identified his wife as Helen Popek, nee Jindra. It also listed one child—a daughter named Elizabeth Kostek, the wife of Emile Kostek. I had the right people.

I shifted to a genealogical website. I looked Frank Popek up in the 1940 Federal Census of Baltimore, Maryland. I found him living with his parents, Vincent and Marie Popek, on Duncan Alley, not too far from my family's Chapel Street home. Frank was born in the United States. His parents had emigrated from Czechoslovakia. No immediate connections.

I turned my attention to his wife Helen Jindra. In addition to identifying her husband and daughter, her death notice listed her parents as Matthew Jindra and Anna Jindra, nee Novak. I looked them up in the 1940 Federal Census. I found Matthew, a widower born in Czechoslovakia, and his American-born daughter Helen living on 25th Street in Baltimore. That was nowhere near Chapel Street. But what happened to Anna? I turned my attention to the 1930 Federal Census. I found Matthew and Anna—and their only daughter Helen living at 2218 Chapel Street. That was the same block where our families lived, just across the street and a few houses up.

Now I finally found a connection, but it proved to be a dead-end online. I couldn't find the immigration records for Matthew Jindra. It was pointless pursuing Anna Novak without further information. The surname Novak was the equivalent of Smith in Bohemia. I knew I could find more information about them at the Maryland State Archives in Annapolis, Maryland and perhaps. in the newspaper archives at the main office of the Enoch Pratt Library in Baltimore, but I couldn't do it now. I had to meet with Pete Thompson.

Teri called as soon as she left work. She said I was right. Her chaplain, Father Kubera, wasn't sympathetic. He suggested that she seek immediate psychiatric help. He even printed up a list of recommended doctors and put it in her mailbox at work. She wanted to get together that evening. I told her I was meeting with Pete to talk about my brother. She asked if she could go. I said yes. It would save me the trouble of recapping the conversation later. We were in this together.

Pete wanted to meet at Brandon's at five o'clock. Now that Teri was coming, I wished we had picked anywhere else. Harford Road, the main artery through my old neighborhood, was now known as Restaurant Row after a number of trendy restaurants, brew pubs, and coffee houses sprang up to take advantage of the relatively safe streets and low rents. Many of those places were perfect for a nice, educated girl like Teri. Brandon's, however, wasn't one of them. The shadowy, drinking hole called to mind the blue-collar, working class origins of the area. Its clientele was strictly local—people who grew up in the neighborhood and never left. I wouldn't take Teri by choice, but Pete was calling the shots this time.

I made sure I got to Brandon's early. I didn't want Teri beating me there and catching some sort of disease without me. The dimly-lit bar was nearly empty when I arrived, only about six customers. I was never a regular here, but Lenny was when he was off his meds. For him, Brandon's was a place where he could hang out without being judged. Trouble wasn't uncommon here. He was only one of many characters in residence. I only came around when they needed someone to help restrain Lenny. Brandon's was often Lenny's last stop before the hospital.

"How you doing, Ricky?" George Brandon, the owner, shouted from behind the bar.

"Pretty good," I lied.

"What can I get you?"

"A cranberry juice," I replied, wanting to keep my head clear.

George didn't mock my request, but it brought some stares in my direction from the rest of the clientele. George slid the glass to me as I reached the bar. "Damn, I miss your brother," he said. "He could be a handful, but deep down, he was always a good guy."

"That he was," I replied.

"How long has it been?" he asked.

"Six years."

"Seems like only yesterday," George said.

"You ain't kidding, George. I feel like I was talking to him just last night," I replied, truthfully. "Has Pete been in?"

"No, but he will."

It wasn't long before I heard the door creak and a shout, "Ricky-boy!"

I turned to see Pete step inside the bar. He seemed genuinely happy to see me, but his appearance saddened me. Everything from his clothes to his grooming told me he was on a downward spiral. *Well*, I thought, *that's two of us.*

Pete ambled over to the bar. "You got a tab running?" he asked me with a smile, which wasn't toothless but getting there.

I turned to George. "It's on me."

George nodded. "Jack and a chaser," Pete told him, before turning to me. "Have you eaten?"

"No."

Pete grabbed two menus and headed to a relatively isolated table. I followed him and sat down. Pete studied the menu intently, despite the fact that it only offered about ten items—and he ate here often. "The burgers are really good," he said. "You should get one."

George brought Pete's drinks over. Pete ordered a burger and fries. I ordered two appetizers, mozzarella sticks and boneless chicken wings, with the intention of sharing them with Teri when she arrived.

"Man, I'm so glad you called," Pete said. "I was just thinking about Lenny last night. He was one of a kind, man."

"Yes, he was."

Pete leaned forward with a smile. "Last night, I saw Barbara Darrah. She was talking about how Lenny and I took her and her sister Bonnie to Atlantic City when she turned twenty-one. Man, we lost at the tables but won upstairs if you know what I mean." Pete laughed.

I heard footsteps behind me, and I turned to see Teri walking toward us. I stood up. "Hey, Teri," I said, as I motioned to an empty seat at the table.

"Hi," Teri said, as she sat down. She turned to Pete.

"Teri, this is my old friend Pete," I said, and then added. "Pete, this is my new friend Teri. I hope you don't mind that I invited her to join us."

"No, no problem," Pete said. "I always enjoy the company of a pretty lady."

"Thank you," she said, smiling back.

I checked if Teri wanted any food or drink. She declined both, saying she was having a problem with her stomach. I understood. Betty was obviously playing the same games with her that she had played with me. I decided to use Teri's problem as an excuse to force my meeting with Pete to a head. What Pete had to say about my brother seemed less important than what I had learned from Jose.

"Hey, Pete," I said. "There's one thing I've always been wondering about. What ever happened to Lenny's motorcycle?"

Pete started laughing. "You're not going to believe this, but it's at the bottom of the Gunpowder River," he said.

That proved Ghost Lenny knew things I didn't know. He got the facts right, but how about the motivation?

"How'd that happen?" I asked.

"It was kind of narrow there. He thought he could jump it," Pete said. "I tried to stop him, but I couldn't. You know how he was."

"He was probably under orders from the Illuminati," I replied.

The Illuminati?" Teri asked.

I turned to her and explained, "When he was crazy, Lenny said he got orders from a member of The Illuminati who kind of looked like Chancellor Palpatine from the *Star Wars* prequels."

"Yeah, that was messed up," Pete said.

"Yeah," I answered. "If you're going to take orders from someone in *Star Wars*, make it from the original trilogy."

Teri didn't laugh. Pete did. I guess you had to be there.

"You know, in the end it wasn't The Illuminati anymore," Pete added. "It was some dark woman."

Teri and I both turned to him.

"What dark woman?" I asked.

"I don't know," Pete answered. "He didn't say much about her, except that she was rising and that she was out to get him."

"What year did your brother die?" Teri asked.

"2010," I answered.

"Betty didn't die until 2014," Teri replied. "How could she be rising?"

"Beats me," I said to her, before I turned back to Pete. "Did Lenny ever mention someone named Betty?"

"Betty Forester from Northern High?"

"No, another Betty," I said. "Not someone from the neighborhood."

Pete shook his head no.

"Did he ever mention going to a fortune teller?"

"No. Not that I remember," Pete answered. His voice trailed off as he spotted someone behind me at the bar. I looked over my shoulder, half-expecting it to be Lenny, but it wasn't. It was just a shady looking guy I had never seen before. Pete leaned toward me and whispered, "Hey, buddy, could you lend me twenty? I'll get it back to you."

"Sure, man," I said.

I took out my wallet and handed him a twenty. Pete got up and walked over to the man. "Who's he?" Teri asked in a whisper.

I was about to answer when Pete pulled some additional bills out of his pocket to join my twenty and handed it to the man with zero discussion. I didn't see the stranger hand Pete the drugs, but the nature of the transaction was obvious. I leaned over to Teri. "He's a drug dealer."

Pete left the dealer and walked back past the table toward the restroom. "I'll be right back, okay?" he said.

"Okay," I said.

Pete disappeared in the restroom. I called to George at the bar. "Check when you can, George," he said.

"Will do, Ricky," he answered back.

I turned back to Teri. "We can leave when he comes back," I said. "I think we got all we're going to get."

"Thanks," Teri replied, resting her head in her hands. "This was a rough day. I've got some things to tell you."

I heard the creak of the restroom door. Pete, smiling blissfully, left the restroom and half-walked, half-staggered back to the table. I wasn't surprised, but I was saddened. Pete was Lenny's friend, not mine, but he certainly loomed large in my childhood as one of the older kids I always wanted to emulate. Seeing him in this sorry state served as yet another reminder that the safe, little world I grew up in prior to the death of my father was gone forever.

Pete's chair squeaked uneasily as he sat down. I reached out instinctively to prevent him from falling, but he successfully anchored himself against the wall. I should not have worried. Pete was certainly capable of navigating through the world in this state. I, however, didn't have to watch.

"Pete," I said. "Teri's not feeling very well. We have to take off."

Pete smiled. He turned slightly to look at both of us and then said, "We're a long way from Chapel Street, children."

My jaw dropped. I couldn't believe it. It was her! Teri found my hand and squeezed it hard under the table.

I was terrified but also strangely exhilarated. I often wondered whether there was life after death and a realm beyond what we could see and feel. Now I had proof, real, honest-to-God proof that such a realm existed. An unseen spiritual entity was communicating with us through Pete. He wasn't faking. How could he? He had no idea what we were dealing with. He certainly knew nothing of Chapel Street. I felt like Roald Amundsen standing on the South Pole. The only difference is that I would probably be in less danger on the South Pole.

Pete turned to Teri. "I gave your boyfriend a way out, but he didn't take it. He wanted to keep playing instead."

Teri turned to me briefly, but I kept my eyes on Pete.

"Why are you doing this to us?" I asked.

"Because I can," Pete replied. "Your name will die with you, but the game will continue. Your sister will meet a man soon. They will marry, and, in due time, they will have children, and then the game will go on."

I felt my blood turn cold.

He turned and met Teri's eyes with utter malevolence. "Make the sacrifice, and I may spare you," Pete said, but it was no longer his voice anymore. He now spoke with the voice of an old woman.

That was it. I released Teri's hand. Leaning forward, I angrily grabbed Pete by his shirt. "Damn you, you monster," I shouted.

The expression on Pete's face instantly changed to one of utter befuddlement. "What the hell?" he said fearfully.

Pete obviously had no memory of what he said or why I was yelling at him. My anger left me instantly, leaving me mortified. I wasn't a man given to public anger—or any other extreme emotion. I released Pete and looked around the bar. I was embarrassed to see every eye in the place on me. I turned back to Pete.

"I'm sorry, man. It's not you; it's me," I said, my mind stretching to think of a suitable excuse. "Teri and I, we've been fighting, and you just got in the middle of that."

"You should treat your woman right," he replied, turning away from me.

"I'm sorry, Pete," I reiterated. I took sixty dollars out of my wallet and put it down on the table. "I'll take care of everything, okay?"

Pete didn't answer or meet my eyes, but he pocketed the money.

I hustled Teri to the door. As I did, I made eye contact with George behind the bar. "Sorry for the disturbance," I said.

"You call that a disturbance?" George laughed. "Come back anytime, Ricky."

As the door was closing behind us, I heard the patrons erupt into laughter. They all had their share of crazy stories about Lenny Bakos. Now they had one about his brother.

For all they knew, the whole family was crazy.

Chapter Nineteen: Idolatry

I took Teri right across the street to one of the yuppie bars. It was small and crowded, but we found a corner private enough, provided we kept our voices down. Being a firm believer in the spiritual world, Teri was less impressed with the fact that Betty spoke to us than I was. Her concerns were not philosophical or theoretical. They were more immediate. She was only interested in defeating the entity.

"What was the way out that she was talking about?" Teri asked quickly.

I told her what Jose had told me about the flowers left at her grave. The thought chilled Teri. "That's idolatry," she said quietly. "Like during the persecution of the Christians in the Roman times, they would let you go free if you made a sacrifice to an idol of the Emperor."

I made a dismissive gesture. "She just wants to see us grovel."

"Why would that be important to her if she's just the ghost of a fortune teller trying to fulfill her last prophecy?" Teri asked.

No brainer. "Because she's evil," I answered.

"That's a given," she replied. "What we have to do is figure out her motivation, and I think there's a spiritual aspect you're missing."

"I can't argue with you there," I said with all honesty. "Last week I was an agnostic. I didn't even believe in spirits of any sort."

"Then hear me out," she continued. "Why did Satan fall?"

"I don't know."

"Satan was cast out of heaven because he wanted to be like the Most High," she explained. "He wanted to be worshipped by the other angels."

At this point, I was willing to believe what I had personally experienced, but I was still hesitant to buy into the whole Bible thing. I'm sorry, but I wasn't about to risk my life and sanity on some Bronze Age mythology. "Trust me," I glibly replied. "If Satan exists, he has more important things to do than possess Pete Thompson."

"I'm not saying she's Satan," she answered. "I'm just saying that we're dealing with a demonic entity."

"Ghost. Demon. It's just semantics to me," I said. "Let's look at the facts. We are dealing with an intelligent entity. Call it what you like, but it's outside of the normal plane of existence with the power to manipulate what we see and hear—and obviously physical reality."

"Here's something I need to tell you," Teri said quickly, cutting me off. "I saw my Uncle Hank today in broad daylight. It was right after I spoke with Father Kubera. I went back to the classroom, which faces Northern Parkway, and I saw him sitting on the bus stop across the street looking at me. He was there the whole afternoon."

"Did anyone else see him?"

"No, the girls couldn't because of the angle. Their desks are too low."

"What about the people on the bus stop? Did anyone interact with him?"

"I'm not sure," Teri replied. She thought before she continued. "Other people stood around him at times, and a woman sat down next to him for a while, but I don't remember him talking to anyone. Between classes, I was tempted to grab Father Kubera and show him, but I knew he wouldn't have been able to see him."

"I'm not so sure about that," I replied.

I told her how the other motorist saw Lenny on the motorcycle. "So he was real," she said in response.

"Who knows?" I replied. "For all I know, the other driver was a ghost, too. Once you throw objective reality out of the window, anything is possible."

She was silent for a moment, and then she continued. "I could handle this when it was just a night-time thing, but this is too much." I could see her hand shaking as she continued. "Every time I heard someone walking down the corridor, I thought it was him. What could I do if he came into my classroom? How could I protect my girls? Or myself?"

I took her hand. "I don't think she's after anyone but us."

"What about Herb at Resting Place?"

Teri had a point. "He wanted to delete her," I replied. "He would probably still be alive if he left her alone."

Silence. She lowered her eyes. "How much longer can this go on?"

That question made me think about Lenny again. What if he was never crazy after all? What if Betty had just been toying with him the whole time? For ten long years. That was a sobering thought and one that tore at my heart. None of us ever believed any of his claims, but what if they were true? Maybe my mom and I might have saved him, if we had only taken him seriously.

At least I had Teri and she had me. As long as we had each other's back, we would never be isolated like Lenny. We were the key to each other's survival.

"Okay, let's say you're right," I replied. "What's the downside of paying our respects to her?"

She looked up at me horrified. "We'd lose our eternal souls."

I had a funny feeling that was what she was going to say. I didn't need to be a theologian to figure that out. I'd seen enough horror movies.

"But wouldn't God forgive us if we just laid down a few flowers until we figured out a way to beat her?" I asked.

"Maybe. Maybe not," she said. "I don't know, but I'm not going to take that chance. Here, Betty can only kill us. In hell, she could torture us for eternity."

That little voice told me it would be worse.

I was out of my depth. We needed help. "It's a definite no from your priest friend?"

She nodded.

"Maybe if we showed him the picture," I mused. That would certainly bring him into the fight.

"Richard Bakos, that's a horrible thought," she said, pulling her hand away from me. "I can't believe you said that."

"I'm sorry," I said.

"I didn't even tell him her name so he wouldn't look her up out of curiosity."

"What *did* you tell him?" I asked. "Maybe you didn't give him enough information."

"I was very detailed. I told him everything but her name," she replied. "And he was completely dismissive of me."

"Do you know any other priests?"

"I don't think my parish priest would be any good," she said. "He's nice, but he's old and frail. I can ask around."

"Please do."

I couldn't believe those words came out of my mouth. Me asking for a priest? My mother had a priest come to the funeral home and say a few words over Lenny. That got my blood boiling. I knew the good father believed my brother was burning in hell for taking his own life, even if he did offer the crowd some platitudes. I didn't request a priest for my mother's funeral. The people at the funeral home said they could arrange it, but I said no. My mother had not been to church in years. To me, having a priest there would be the height of hypocrisy and pointlessness. What good would it do her anyway? Back then, I thought dead was dead was dead.

But it looks like I was wrong.

What other options did we have than the Roman Catholic Church? I didn't have any faith in secular authorities. Ghost hunter and paranormal investigator shows filled cable TV every night. They all seemed like fakes to me. Even if they were real, none of them could handle Betty. In the shows, the investigators always jumped at loud noises or picture frames falling over. An entity like Betty would eat them alive.

I didn't have any faith in the Protestants either. Switching through the channels a couple weeks earlier, I ended up on a televangelist casting out demons at a revival service. It was ridiculous. He would cast the Demon of Lust out of one person. He cast the Demon of Envy out of another one. These so-called demons he was casting out were just the deadly sins personified, but it even got more ridiculous. The funniest part was when he cast the Demon of Smoking out of someone. I wondered what that poor demon did for the thousands of years before people invented cigarettes. I imagined how difficult it would be for him to introduce himself at parties ten thousand years ago.

"Hi, I'm the Demon of Smoking," he would say, offering his hand, only to be greeted by a confused look in response.

"What's Smoking?" the other Demon would say.

"I don't know yet," Smoking would say, "But I bet it'll be badass."

Geez. If I were at that revival service, I wonder if the preacher could have cast the Demon of Walking With Your Shoes Untied out of me. I always had a problem with that when I was a kid.

No, I didn't anticipate getting any help from the Protestant side of the aisle. They trivialized the concept of demons too much to be useful. If that preacher met Betty, I'm sure she'd be playing basketball with his head in about five minutes flat.

I didn't have much faith in the Catholic Church in general, but if the film *The Exorcist* was any sort of guide, they seemed to know how to deal with these things.

Chapter Twenty: Hell

Teri and I stayed at the yuppie bar for a couple of hours discussing my research concerning Betty's family. Our conclusions, however, were all simply guesswork without more facts.

We couldn't see how Chapel Street fit into the demon scenario. If our antagonist was a demon, why did Chapel Street matter? Chapel Street didn't fit into the ghost scenario either. How could Betty have been responsible for the suicides of our great-great-grandmothers? They died a decade before she was born. But Chapel Street seemed to be the unifying touchstone in the whole affair. The first thing she said was, "We're a long way from Chapel Street, children."

Were we, Betty? I thought.

No one in my family lived on Chapel Street during my entire lifetime. Neither Teri nor I had anything to do with Chapel Street.

After a while, we both realized we were talking simply to avoid going home and facing whatever terrors laid in store for us. Had Teri been a guy, I would have invited her to my place for the night. Since she was a woman, I had to worry about the appearance of sexual overtones. I hoped she would take the initiative and invite me to spend the night at her house. She told me she lived in a small, two-story suburban townhouse. I would be hard-pressed to fall to my death from that height, but the invitation never came.

We left the bar with plans to see each other the following afternoon. Teri was scheduled for half days through Thursday, and then she was off for the summer. I told Agnes, my supervisor, I would take the rest of the week off. Considering that I had nearly four months of sick leave saved up, I could essentially stay out of work indefinitely. The only problem was that I needed a doctor's approval to go on long-term leave. It would be easier to take the following week off as vacation, but that wouldn't win me any friends at work. Agnes always liked a few weeks' notice.

I walked Teri to her car. She gave me a quick hug after she opened the door. That caught me by surprise, and I was grateful for the gesture. I needed a little human warmth. I guess she did, too.

"Thanks for doing all the research, Rick. We'd be flying blind without it," she said, and then she paused before she added, "You're a problem solver."

Me, a problem solver? I was tempted to laugh. I couldn't remember the last time I actually solved a problem. I was pretty good at tests back in college, but I never solved any problems at work. I was just a bean counter. Whether the beans added up or not was somebody else's problem. I certainly wasn't a problem-solver in my personal life, either. I had five years to figure out a way to reconcile Gina and my mother, but I failed.

"If I was a problem-solver, I would have been able to work things out between my mother and Gina," I answered.

"I don't think your mother was the problem with Gina. I think she was just your excuse," Teri replied. "I think deep down in your heart you knew Gina wasn't the one for you, and she wasn't."

"What makes you say that?"

"She gave up on you," she answered. "If Gina truly loved you, she would have waited."

Teri's analysis infuriated me. Who was she to judge Gina? She never even met her. I was the one who failed her, not vice-versa. Long-suffering Saint Gina was my last remaining idol. I still found time to worship at her altar, even if I couldn't bring myself to embrace the flesh and blood woman herself.

"How can you say that about her? I could say the same thing about you. If you really loved your husband, you wouldn't have given up on him," I replied defensively, immediately regretting my words.

"You're right," she answered, lowering her eyes. "I didn't love him. I was just lonely. My parents had just moved, and my friends were all getting married. I needed someone, and suddenly, there he was. Mr. Charming. I wanted to believe him, so I closed my eyes, ignored my better judgment, and let myself be swept away." Teri looked up and met my eyes. "It take a lot of discipline to wait for the one God has in store for you. I couldn't wait. You could."

I didn't know what to say. I certainly didn't keep Gina on the line for five years because I was waiting for the one God had in mind for me. The thought never entered my mind.

Teri must have seen the wheels turning in my head. She smiled and gave me a pat on the arm. "Don't doubt me, Rick. Remember, I'm always right about other people's relationships," she said. "I'm only ever wrong about mine." She sat down in her car. "Text me when you wake up so I know you're okay, okay?"

"Okay," I said.

"See you tomorrow," she said as she started her engine.

"See you tomorrow," I answered.

She closed her door and she was gone.

Instead of thinking of ways to defeat Betty, I spent my ride home contemplating Teri's analysis of my relationship with Gina. Had I used my mother to hide my unwillingness to make a commitment? Definitely not, I thought, but I had to admit my mother was a useful shield against Gina's anger. The longer we stayed together, the more frustrated Gina grew over our lack of progress, as she put it. We fought about it, directly or indirectly, practically every month near the end. The fights usually started when I had to cancel one of our plans to help my mother. Gina generally reacted by angrily denigrating my manhood and withholding her affection, but only briefly. She was quick to forgive because she viewed me as a fellow victim. But her anger against my mother would simmer for weeks. I shivered at the way Gina's eyes narrowed and the venom that crept into her voice when she talked about my mother. I was grateful that I never saw that anger directed at me.

Perhaps it should have been.

I was a grown, adult man. I didn't have to obey all of my mother's whims. I willingly chose to do so. Gina should have directed her anger at me. If she did, our relationship probably would have ended years earlier. My mother gave Gina an excuse to view me in a better light than I deserved and allowed me to evade responsibility for our stalemated relationship. Did that mean that I felt Gina wasn't the one for me? Well, I guess the proof was in the pudding. I didn't marry her even after I was free to do so.

Damn. Maybe Teri *was* right.

It was nearly midnight when I got home. Thoughts of Gina left my mind as I took the elevator to my floor. When I stepped inside my apartment, I went to the computer and checked my email. There was nothing from Resting Place. I went to their webpage, and I typed Betty's name into their search engine. Her memorial showed up on the list. I knew it would. Herb's death probably spooked everyone at the company. No one there was going to touch it. It would ultimately come down to me, and that was only fair.

I went back to my email and found the terms of service complaint. I quickly typed a response.

To Whom It May Concern.

I apologize for putting up the memorial for Elisabetta A. Kostek. Please restore my account so I may delete it.

Thanks, Rick Bakos.

It took me about an hour to write that short email. I kept adding more details and then subtracting them. I eventually felt additional words were unnecessary. If they were experiencing what I thought they were experiencing, they would reach for my little email like a life preserver. I was more confident they would restore my account then I was that I would be able to delete Betty's memorial.

I went to bed after pressing the send button. I was determined not to wake up on the balcony again. I locked the bedroom door, but that was pointless. The doorknob lock prevented people from opening the door from the outside, but it unlocked automatically when you turned the knob from the inside. That did me no good. Instead, I pushed a large cabinet in front of the door. It made an ugly scrapping sound as I did. I smiled. Pushing it aside again would definitely wake me up. Still, as a precaution, I went to bed wearing shorts and a T-shirt. If I did end up splattered in the fountain in front of the building, I didn't want to be wearing the Star Wars footie pajamas Gina bought me as a joke.

Sleep came easily, but it didn't last.

"Are you freaking crazy?"

I opened my eyes and turned to see Lenny standing beside my bed. The clock near him read 3 a.m.

"She gives you a way out and you spit in her face?" he asked. "You're crazier than I am."

"It's idolatry," I said yawning.

"Who the hell cares?"

"Teri says I could lose my immortal soul."

"So? Since when have you and God become buddy-buddy? Seems to me that He never cared much for you," Lenny replied. "Where was He when you needed Him? Or when Mom needed Him?" Lenny sat down beside me. "She was a real believer once. She trusted God. She deserved better than she got."

That was true. Despite my periodic bouts of self-pity, I realized my mother suffered more than the rest of us. Janet and I lost more people than either Lenny or my mother, but I knew there was more to the equation than numbers. My mother lost a husband and a son. That had to be worse than losing your parents and a brother. After all, you expect to lose parents. That's a given, whether you acknowledge it or not. As for siblings, you do not expect to lose them, but their loss cannot be as painful as that of a child. There was no question my mother had suffered the most.

"Is she in heaven?" I asked.

"Nah, she's down at St. Helens Street," Lenny replied. "Why do you think the house has sold two more times since you and Janet unloaded it?"

"She's haunting it?"

"Don't say haunting, Ricky; that's a pejorative term, like calling a short person a midget," Lenny answered. "Just say she's living there."

I got up and sat at the edge of the bed beside Lenny. He was wearing jeans and a Rolling Stones T-shirt and boots. His hair was messy, like it usually was when he was off his meds, but his eyes were calm. It was strange. Although I strongly doubted the entity sitting beside me was truly my brother Lenny, I found it very comforting to talk to him.

We talked endlessly when we were little kids and shared a bedroom, but we drifted apart when he became a teenager. It wasn't cool having your little brother tag along, especially when your main goals were meeting girls and getting high. As adults, I think we only had serious, sane conversations once or twice a year at most. I guess I was more to blame for the distance than he was. I couldn't bring myself to continue making an emotional investment in him once he became mentally unstable. Now we had a chance to talk again. It was like a heaven-sent opportunity, even if Betty was the one behind it.

"Think she'll make it to heaven?" I asked.

Lenny shrugged. "She's not ready, Ricky," Lenny answered. "She wants the three of us to go together."

"The three of us?" I asked. "What about Janet?"

"You know Mom," Lenny answered. "It's always been a boy's club with her. Janet can come along later."

That was true, too. Mom always favored us. In retrospect, I could see how Janet was always acting out to get her attention, but she rarely received it. That was why I tried not to hold Janet's resentments against her. She was entitled to them. And she certainly didn't deserve her mother's fate, as Betty had threatened.

"You saw what happened with Pete?"

Lenny nodded yes.

"Was that Betty?"

Lenny nodded again.

"She said she was going to let Janet live and then come after her children."

"Did she?" Lenny asked.

"You just said you were there."

"When she showed up, I skedaddled," Lenny replied.

"Can she hurt you?"

"Uh, yeah," Lenny replied, as if I were an idiot for even asking. Then he explained. "She really doesn't give a damn about people once they're dead, but if you provoke her, watch out. She's got quite a few tricks up her sleeve."

"So there's nothing you can do to help me?"

"I've been trying," he said, and then he stood up. "Damn it, why didn't you just take the flower and lay it down? How hard is that? If I were given that chance, I would have done it in a heartbeat."

"Even if it meant going to hell?"

"Do you want to know what hell really is?" Lenny asked, getting agitated for the first time in our post-death conversations. "Hell is being institutionalized seventeen times in ten years. Hell is having everybody looking at you all the time like you have a third eye in the middle of your forehead." He calmed slightly as he looked out of my bedroom window. "You have no idea what it's like walking out some hospital so full of drugs that you're practically a zombie. Then you have to go and rebuild your life, but you can't because each time, the people you need trust you less and less."

Lenny turned to me. I averted my eyes.

He continued. "But it really didn't matter what other people think about you because you're doomed anyway. The drugs they give you leave you with so little energy that it's hard to do anything but sleep. So you cut back on the dosage. Just a little bit, and you feel better. Then a little more, and a little more, and the next thing you know you're back in the hospital."

"I'm sorry I wasn't there for you, Len," I said softly.

"It's okay, bro," he said, giving me a pat on the shoulder. "I know I didn't make it easy for you. Or Mom. Or Janet. I just don't want you going through the same damn thing."

"I won't," I answered. "We're different. You had a chemical imbalance."

Lenny smiled wearily. "When was the last time you had your blood tested?"

"I don't have to," I said defensively. "I'm sane."

"Here we go again," Lenny said, sitting down beside me. "You know how many doctors I've seen? They all had a different theory about bipolar disorder. Some thought brain chemistry affected behavior. Others said behavior affected brain chemistry. Mom thought it was all the pot I smoked, but let me tell you something that I didn't know until right up to the end. It was her. Betty played me like a yo-yo, taking away my mind one piece at a time."

"How could she do that to you while she was still alive?" I asked.

"How the hell am I supposed to know?" Lenny answered. "I'm no expert. All I know is that she's coming for you now."

"I'm going to beat her."

Lenny smiled and shook his head as he stood up. "The only way to beat her is to stop playing the game on her terms," he said as he walked toward the bedroom door. He turned back to me as he opened it up. "I don't know what you think you're holding onto. It's not so bad here, and you'd certainly make Mom happy."

He didn't wait for an answer. He left and closed the door behind himself. I didn't see the cabinet blocking the door anymore. I was tempted to get up and see whether it was really there or not, but I was afraid if I moved, I would end up on the balcony again.

Instead, I just laid back and fell asleep.

Chapter Twenty-One: Father Kubera

Wednesday.

I woke up late, around ten o'clock. Much to my surprise, I found myself safely ensconced in my bed. I turned to the bedroom door. Despite Lenny's easy access, the cabinet still safely blocked it from my own nocturnal movements. I smiled. It looked like I had solved my balcony problem. Now it was time to go on the offensive.

The first thing I did was text Teri.

Alive and well. Had a visitor but didn't end on the balcony.

Her text came back almost immediately.

In class. Call you soon.

Good. She was alive, too. That was a promising start to the day.

After my morning grooming rituals, I went to the computer. I was hoping for an email from Resting Place concerning my suspension but no such luck. Then it hit me. I forgot to look Betty's grandparents up on Resting Place. I opened the browser and typed in Matthew Jindra. His name came up. He was born in 1892 and died in 1950. He was buried in Holy Redeemer Cemetery. That information didn't surprise me. Matthew was a Bohemian from the old neighborhood. Most of them ended up in Holy Redeemer eventually. His wife Anna was probably buried there, too.

I clicked on a button that showed you other people with the same surname buried in the same cemetery. Only two other Jindras showed up: Vincent and Maria. They were buried in the same section as Matthew, and their dates made me think they were his parents. Where was his wife Anna? I typed her name directly into the search engine, and I found her buried in Baltimore Cemetery: Anna Jindra, 1896-1932.

1932. I wasn't surprised. That was the same year my great-grandmother Kristina and Teri's great-grandmother Maria died. What was the connection? I clicked on the memorial. Fearful she would have the same effect on me as her daughter, I was relieved to see that there was no photograph of Anna, or the grave itself, on the memorial. The memorial only listed her years of birth and death. I was hoping that her monument would give the actual date of her death. I suspected it would be early May, just like our great-grandmothers.

My cellphone rang. It was Teri. I picked it up.

"How was your night?"

"Not good," she replied with a disconcerting weariness in her voice. "I ended up in the bathtub again."

"I think there are some precautions you can take to stop that," I replied. "We should get together when you get off work."

"Actually, I was hoping you could come here," she replied. "Father Kubera pulled me aside this morning. He believes us now. He wants to talk to us this afternoon. Can you come by when we let out around 12:15?"

"What a change of heart. I definitely need to hear how that happened," I replied. "See you then."

"Thanks," she said, and she added before she hung up, "I have to get back to class. See you in a bit."

This was a tremendous relief. We definitely needed some spiritual help. I just hoped he didn't want me to start going to church or something in return.

I checked the time: 11:10 am. I was hoping to drive down to Baltimore Cemetery and check Anna Jindra's tombstone for her date of death. Once I had that information, I could go to the Enoch Pratt Library and check their microfilm library for a death notice or news story about her. The fieldwork was necessary because none of the old Baltimore newspapers were available online, but there wasn't enough time now. Teri and I could do it later.

I pulled into the Mercy High School parking lot around noon against the tide of vehicles heading out. I texted Teri when I arrived while I waited in the car. I didn't think it was appropriate for me to enter the building and wander the halls without an escort. Before long, Teri appeared at the back door and waved me in. I could see how popular she was with the students as she led me toward Father Kubera's office. She had a smile for everyone, and there was a lot of good-natured bantering, but her eyes told me she had had a hard night. I kept my mouth shut and tried to remain as inconspicuous as possible.

I hoped Father Kubera wasn't one of those non-judgmental, hippie, "let's all love each other" priests who dressed in civilian clothes and always had an acoustic guitar handy for a rousing chorus of *Kumbaya*. I wanted a stern, fire-and-brimstone priest with all the trappings, full vestments, and totally fluent in Latin, Greek, and Hebrew. I wanted a classic, old school priest from the 'fifties. Not the nineteen-fifties mind you: The thirteen-fifties.

Father Lawrence Kubera was waiting for us in his small office. He was thin and parted his trim blonde hair on the side. He wore black pants, a black shirt, and a clerical collar, but a civilian jacket. He was younger than I was. He couldn't have been thirty. I wasn't entirely impressed. He extended his hand to me as Teri closed the door behind us.

"You must be Rick," he said with a fake smile hiding some fear.

"Yes," I said.

Kubera motioned to some seats crammed in front of his desk. Teri and I sat down in them as he took his position behind the desk. "I don't know if Theresa told you, but I was quite skeptical of her story when she first told me," he said.

"What changed your mind?" I asked.

"The conversation was very disturbing, especially coming from someone as stable as Theresa," he replied. "Something told me I should do some investigating so I drove over to Eternal Faith. I knew the place well; I did quite a few funerals over there when I was assigned to the Church of the Annunciation. I drove right up to the mausoleum and got out of my car, but I literally couldn't go any further. It was like there was a wall, a wall of evil, around the building."

I nodded. I knew how he felt.

"It was a profound spiritual experience," Kubera continued after a pause. "When I gave myself to the Lord, I experienced a profound, transcendental sense of love and peace that has truly sustained me through my calling. What I felt yesterday was the mirror opposite, and, frankly, it scared the hell out of me. I tried convincing myself that I was just falling victim to Theresa's psychosis, but I knew what I felt was real. There is evil at work here. True, demonic evil."

A feeling of relief washed across me like a wave. An authority figure with the power to help us actually believed us! "Thank you, Father," I said. I turned to Teri. She was smiling, too. I turned back to Father Kubera. "What do we do?"

"Frankly, I don't know," he answered. "My training was in psychology and sociology before I became a priest. I have zero experience in anything like this, but I know someone who does—Father Thomas Mubita, who works at the Helping Hands Mission downtown. I called him, and he offered to help us."

"Does he have experience in these things?" I asked.

"Yes," Father Kubera answered. "He's African–Zambian–and the people there engage in more spiritual warfare than we do in this country. Father Mubita has participated in a number of exorcisms, though this situation is somewhat different inasmuch as no one here seems to be possessed."

"Betty," Teri volunteered.

"She's dead," Father Kubera said authoritatively. "She can't be possessed anymore."

My phone rang. I pulled it out of my pocket and gave it a glance. The blood drained out of my face as I saw my own number on the Caller ID.

"Who is it?" Teri asked, concerned.

"My mother," I said in a voice that was much more matter-of-fact than I imagined it could be. I guess I was getting used to this madness.

"Hang up," Teri said.

"No, no, no," Father Kubera said, turning from Teri to me. "Teri told me your mother was dead, is that correct?"

I nodded yes as the phone rang again.

Father Kubera pointed toward the top of his desk. "Answer it, and put it in speaker mode. I want to take her measure."

I didn't like the look in his eyes. A detached curiosity replaced the genuine fear he expressed earlier while telling his story, as if this were some sort of college science project. I suppose I couldn't blame him. I felt the same way when I heard Betty speak through Pete. I turned to Teri. She closed her eyes.

The phone rang again. Father Kubera leaned forward expectantly. I placed the phone face up on the desk and answered it, pressing the speakerphone button.

"Hello," I said weakly.

"You promised, Ricky," said my mother. Her voice was quiet and pained.

I hated hearing her like that. Ghost Lenny was right about one thing. I was too hard on my mother. She was mostly cheerful, upbeat, and supportive. She certainly did everything in her power to help Lenny. She would have done the same for me, too. She only became unreasonable when something or someone tried to come between her and her family.

Father Kubera reached forward and pressed the mute button. "Is that her voice?" he asked.

I nodded my head yes.

"Ricky, are you still there?" my mother asked.

Father Kubera unmuted the phone and nodded for me to answer.

"I'm still here, Mom," I said softly.

"You left me," she answered, wheezing slightly in her death voice. "I woke up, and you weren't there. You were with that bitch."

I didn't want to hear this. I looked up at Father Kubera, but he didn't even meet my eyes. He was too fascinated by the voice.

"What did it get you, Ricky? She left you just like I always said she would," my mother continued. "So will this one. She couldn't make it work with her first husband. What makes you think she'll stick with you?"

Teri gasped. That was it as far as I was concerned. It was bad enough for her to berate me. I wouldn't let her attack Teri. I reached to turn off the phone, but Kubera raised a hand to stop me. He leaned forward.

"Mrs. Bakos, my name is Lawrence Kubera and I..."

"I know who you are, priest," my mother spat, cutting him off. "If you think that collar gives you the right to step between me and my family, you've got another thing coming."

"And I know who you are," Father Kubera said, cool and collected. "You are not Mrs. Bakos."

"You don't know crap."

"Tell me your name, demon."

"Tell me how long you think you're going to live," she hissed back.

"What is your name?" he asked again.

"You're going to die."

"Not before I send you back to hell," Father Kubera said confidently. I was amazed. I exchanged a glance with Teri. She was equally impressed. It looked like we came to the right person.

"I will see your life drain out of you this weekend," my mother, or should I say the thing pretending to be my mother, said.

"Our father, who art in heaven," Father Kubera said, as he began to slowly recite the Lord's Prayer.

Almost immediately, my mother let out a low, guttural moan.

"Hallowed be thy name. Thy kingdom come."

The moan increased in pitch intensity.

"Thy will be done on earth as it is in heaven."

The moan intensified into a high-pitched scream.

Father Kubera's voice wavered as he continued. "Give us this day, our daily bread."

The volume of the scream increased dramatically. The phone started vibrating on the table. I was afraid the sound would break the glass. Teri put her hands over her ears.

"And forgive us our trespasses," Father Kubera continued, his fear becoming evident in his voice.

Unbelievably, the volume of the scream continued to rise. As I began to shake, I realized something. The scream wasn't one of pain. It was meant to cause pain in the listener. Father Kubera felt it, too. His prayer stopped. He looked at the phone, breathing hard for a moment before he swept it off his desk. The scream stopped as the cellphone bounced off his door.

"Hey, that's a new phone," I said as I jumped up to retrieve it.

Kubera hurried over to the door and looked out at the corridor. No one gave him any notice. It was as if no one outside the room had heard anything. Closing the door, he walked back to the desk. "Is that the way these conversations usually turn out?" he asked, still reeling from the call.

"My mother always seems angry," I replied. "But my brother is okay, when he's not trying to get me to kill myself."

"You can't talk to them anymore," he replied. He turned to Teri— "Either of you."

"That's easier said than done," Teri replied quietly. "He just keeps pleading with me until I talk to him."

"Did you try praying?" Kubera asked.

"Yes," she answered.

"Aloud?"

"No."

"Try it next time," he answered. "It seems to work."

I wasn't so sure it worked. It only seemed to make her angry. She was only silenced because the phone turned off when it hit the door. Still, I didn't say anything, but I lost a little confidence in the good Father.

"When can we talk to Father Mubita?" I asked.

"I'm going to meet him tonight down at the mission," Kubera answered. "I'll try to set up a meeting with all of us tomorrow."

"Thank you, Father," Teri said, reaching out and touching his hand.

She seemed very relieved. That relieved me because she seemed under greater strain than I did. Therefore, despite my skepticism, I wasn't going to voice any opinion concerning Father Kubera that would detract from what she was feeling now. I just hoped Father Mubita knew what the hell he was talking about.

Chapter Twenty-Two: Anna

Teri immediately agreed to accompany me on my field trip to Baltimore Cemetery. She didn't want to be alone and, frankly, neither did I. After dropping her car off at her townhouse, we headed downtown in my Toyota Corolla.

Teri was on edge. She told me she had woken up in the bathtub again, but there was a twist. This time she found an empty bottle of Percocet beside her. Her doctor prescribed her five pills after taking a hard fall on the ice last winter. Being skittish about using a narcotic, she only took two of them before switching over to industrial-strength Ibuprofen for her pain. Last night, she took the final three in her sleep while she got into the bathtub.

"If that had been a full bottle, I'd be dead now," she said softly, realizing now how high the stakes had become. "When I got up, I flushed every pill and dangerous substance in my house down the toilet."

I told her about the success I had building a barrier to prevent myself from walking to the balcony. She said she would try it tonight. However, she wasn't very optimistic.

"Betty could just as well strangle me in my bed as drown me in my bathroom," she said.

"I don't think she would," I replied. "It would ruin her fun. I think she has already decided how we're going to die: me in a fall and you drowning. If we don't die that way, she loses." After I spoke, I realized I was echoing Lenny's sentiments. That couldn't be a good thing. He was having a greater impact on my thought processes than I had imagined.

"If my uncle comes again tonight, I'm going to try praying," she said.

"I don't know," I replied cautiously. "I don't think it worked with my mother. I think it only made her mad."

"God is stronger than the devil," she answered.

"Then why doesn't He stop him?" I asked.

Teri didn't have an answer—or perhaps she wasn't in the mood to debate theology.

We decided to go to Holy Redeemer first to check out the grave of Betty's grandfather Matthew Jindra since it was on our way to Baltimore Cemetery. I pulled up to the office. Teri went in with me. Louise Preller, the receptionist, seemed nearly as old as the cemetery itself. I liked Louise a lot. She loved the cemetery and its visitors. She had a million stories and would talk for hours if you let her, and she had a story for us.

"Vincent and Maria Jindra purchased six plots in 1895," Louise reported after finding the file. "They are buried there with their son Matthew, and their daughter Veronica Reese and her husband Andrew."

"So there's an empty space?"

"Yes, the space next to Matthew was reserved for his wife, but she was denied burial," Louise said, pulling a yellowing handwritten note from the file. "This is a note from the pastor of St. Wenceslaus Church denying Anna Jindra funeral rites and burial on consecrated ground."

"May I see it?" I asked.

Louise handed me the slip of paper, which stated little more than what she had already told us. "He doesn't give a reason why," I said, disappointed.

"Why would they deny her burial?" Teri asked Louise.

"Back then, they were much stricter about who could be buried in a Catholic cemetery," Louise explained. "It's possible she that might not have been a Catholic, although most Catholic cemeteries would bury non-Catholic spouses. It's more likely that the parish priest felt she died in a state of mortal sin."

"Like committing suicide?" I asked. I had no reason to suspect Anna committed suicide. I just wanted to see how my family would have fared at the time.

"Yes, at that time Holy Redeemer wouldn't bury suicides without special dispensation from the parish priest," Louise answered. "But it could have been something else, too. Like if the deceased died while openly involved in an adulterous affair, or committing a crime, or involved in witchcraft or occult practices."

Bingo, I thought. Betty was a fortuneteller. It wasn't too much of a reach to imagine her grandmother doing it as well.

"Do you know any way we can find out the reason?" I asked.

"No, I don't think so," Louise answered. "You might find something in the records of St. Wenceslaus Church, but I doubt he would be more specific there than he was in this note."

Louise gave us the section and plot number, and Teri and I ventured out onto the grounds to find the Jindra graves. They were located nearby. Teri suggested we walk. It was a good idea. The weather was great. It would have been a perfect day to hit the beach if we were not fighting a demonic entity.

"Thanks for inviting me," Teri said as we walked. "I was really dreading going home. If it wasn't for you, I'd probably be curled up in bed now, crying, and waiting for the night."

"I don't believe that," I answered. "You're a strong, confident woman."

"That's how my students see me, too," she answered forlornly. "And I guess I was, in my twenties and early-thirties, but now I just look at myself and ask, 'Is this all there is? A house? A car? A job? Happy hour with my friends?'"

I gave her a look.

"Don't get me wrong," she added quickly. "I'm not one of those women waiting for a man to complete them. After Chuck, I know a man is just as likely to tear you apart. I just need to find a why for myself."

"Doesn't the church give you that?"

"The church gives me a where. I know where I'm going to go when I die. But it doesn't give me a why I am what I am now. I guess that's why I turned to genealogy. Hoping to find the key to the present in the past."

"What's past is prologue," I said quickly, hoping to impress the English teacher by trotting out every genealogist's favorite Shakespeare quote.

"The past is never dead. It's not even past," Teri retorted. "William Faulkner, *Requiem for a Nun*."

One-upped. What was I thinking challenging an English teacher to a quote battle? I decided to go back to The Master again. "Now is the winter of our discontent," I said.

"Made glorious summer by this sun of York," Teri said, continuing the quote from *Richard III*, before adding with a smile, "Is that all you got for me?"

It was great seeing her smile. She was quite beautiful, exuding a warmth to rival the sun. She didn't deserve this madness. And she could certainly do better than me. I wondered if she would ever consider me suitable boyfriend material.

"Hey," she said suddenly. "I think we found it."

She pointed to a large granite tombstone with the word Jindra carved across it. We hurried over, but it was a wasted trip. There was nothing suspicious written on any of the monuments, just the conspicuous absence of a spouse.

"Do you think she was a suicide, too?" Teri asked softly.

"No," I said. "She's not a victim. She's the *cause*."

We went back to the car and left Holy Redeemer. We continued down Belair Road to Baltimore Cemetery, which was located only a couple of miles south at the intersection of North Avenue. At eighty-five acres, it was over twice the size of Holy Redeemer. It was a municipal cemetery open to people of all religions, and the owners apparently had no problem burying people who died in a state of mortal sin. Although I suspect the color of a person's skin might have been a deterrent, at least until the mid-nineteen-sixties.

I was familiar with the cemetery, but I rarely spent much time there. One of the worst neighborhoods in the city surrounded the grounds. I was genuinely afraid one of the locals would end up with my camera if I spent too much time documenting the graves there. However, I did contribute to an online campaign to buy a headstone for former Little Rascal Norman "Chubby" Chaney. The former child actor died in 1936 at the age of twenty-two, but no one ever put a monument on his grave. That was a shame. I was only too happy to contribute to the fund.

When we got to the cemetery, Teri and I went to the office. Neither of us were regulars so the receptionist treated us with the respect due potential customers rather than the annoyance frequently assigned to genealogists. I asked for the location of Anna Jindra's grave, alluding that she was a family member. I must admit I was a little disappointed when the mention of Anna's name didn't inspire any noticeable fear. Instead, the receptionist simply disappeared for a moment before returning with the burial record. I photographed the burial card with my iPhone, which documented her dates of birth and death, address, next of kin, and burial plot. Anna died on May 2, 1932—six days before my great-grandmother—ten days before Teri's great-grandmother. No cause of death was given.

The burial card gave us everything we needed to go downtown to the Enoch Pratt Free Library and search their microfilm collection for further information, but we couldn't resist going to her grave. I didn't expect any satanic symbolism carved into the monument, but I hoped something there might offer some clue to the mystery of Chapel Street.

The receptionist provided us with a detailed map to the grave from the office. It entailed a few twists and turns along the way, but that was no problem. Teri acted as navigator as I drove off into the vast field of white marble and limestone monuments.

"I think you were right about me and Gina," I confessed sheepishly as we drove.

"Well, it didn't take any great insight, Rick," Teri answered as she followed our route on the map. "You said it yourself a couple of different ways at the restaurant on Sunday."

"That was so embarrassing," I said. "I can't believe I did that."

"It was kind of scary," she answered.

"Yeah, you must've thought I was Norman Bates or something."

"No, that's not what I mean," she said, adding quickly. "Left up ahead."

I made the turn.

"It was scary to me because I tend to be very empathetic. When someone really opens up their heart to me, I tend to care about them, and, no offense, I didn't want to care about you—aside from genealogy. Make a right."

I made the turn.

"If you felt that way, why'd you tell me all that stuff about yourself?" I asked.

"See? That's just it. You opened up so completely that I didn't feel I could leave you hanging," she replied, looking up at me. "I wanted to let you know that you weren't the only one who failed at love." Her eyes went back to the map. "We're almost there," she said. She looked back up and added, "It should be right over there on that rise. Near that woman."

Teri pointed toward a woman. I turned to her as I drove. At first, I thought she was standing up, but I quickly realized she was sitting perched on top of a tombstone with her feet dangling down. My blood began to boil. That was both disrespectful and dangerous. Many of the stones here were over a hundred years old, and it wouldn't take much to topple them over. Kids like her ruined cemeteries.

Then I noticed something. She wasn't a kid. No. She appeared to be in her early-to-mid-thirties with attractive features—long dark hair, a seductive smile, and penetrating eyes. I could tell they were an emerald green, even from the distance. They were mesmerizing. They grabbed a hold of me completely.

"Stop," Teri said in a cold, frightened voice.

I didn't. The woman drew me forward with her eyes and her smile, which exuded a raw sexuality. At that second, I wanted her—badly.

"Richard, stop!" Teri said again, this time louder as she grabbed my shoulder. "It's her."

I hit the brake and turned to Teri. Her breath was heavy with fear. "It's her, Rick," she said. "Anna."

I turned back to the woman. Now I noticed her hair was styled in some bygone manner and that her dress was something I would expect to see Myrna Loy wear in a *Thin Man* movie. The woman was indeed from a different time. I looked up at her face again. Her smile broadened. She knew we figured out the truth, and she wanted to play.

Anna jumped down from her perch on the tombstone. No. Jumped is the wrong word. She drifted down in a manner that defied gravity.

"Let's get out of here," Teri said as her fingernails dug deeper into my shoulder.

I shifted the Corolla into reverse as Anna started walking toward us. I put my foot on the gas and gently started backing up. My eyes never went to the rearview mirror. I couldn't take them away from the spectral Anna. She started about eighty yards away from us, but moved steadily toward us in an abnormal manner. Although her steps seemed natural and human, the distance between us closed disproportionately. Every step she took brought her five steps closer to us.

"Hurry, Rick," Teri pleaded.

Trust me; I didn't need any prompting along those lines. I sped up, but the distance between us continued to shrink. The nearer she got, the more Anna changed. The formerly alluring specter transitioned into something hideous. The hair on her head fizzled away as if consumed by fire. Her skin blackened, and her eyeballs collapsed inward leaving empty lifeless sockets. She was all hate now. And anger. And every evil thing.

Teri screamed. Almost immediately afterwards, the Corolla shuddered to a stop with a loud thud. I looked over my shoulder to see that I had left the road after passing through an intersection, knocking a massive granite tombstone from its pedestal.

"Rick!" Teri screamed.

I looked forward. Anna was now only about thirty yards away and gaining on us steadily. I had no idea what she intended to do when she reached us, but I wasn't going to wait and find out. I put my foot to the floor. The tires spun wildly on the grass, churning up the dirt. Gritting my teeth, I grew terrified that the tires would sink into the earth and trap us. Fortunately, after what seemed an eternity, the vehicle lurched forward toward the pavement. By the time the rubber hit the road again, the vehicle accelerated wildly.

I turned left at the intersection and drove away from our pursuer. I glanced through the mirror as we raced away at nearly sixty miles an hour. Anna, with her skeletal smiles, slowed before she dissolved into a strange mist, but I still didn't feel safe. She wasn't human. For all I knew, she could reappear in front of us or pop up in the backseat. I had only one goal—get the hell out of that cemetery, and quick!

I barreled through the narrow cobblestone lanes of the cemetery at about eighty miles an hour, sliding through turns as I headed for the exit.

I doubt any other car had raced out of the imposing front gate of the cemetery, designed to recall the Battle Abbey in England, as fast as we did. The busy intersection of Belair Road and North Avenue lay at the bottom of the hill right outside the cemetery. Fortunately, we had a green light because we were going too fast to stop. Better to die on the street than in that evil place.

Chapter Twenty-Three: Murder

Teri and I were still shaking as we joined the westbound traffic on North Avenue. We needed to stop and catch our breaths, but the open-air drug markets lining the thoroughfare didn't appear much safer than the cemetery.

"Do you want to go home?" I asked Teri.

She shook her head no. Then, after a moment, she said, "Thanks."

"For what?"

"Getting us out of there alive," she answered. "I never saw driving like that before. Chuck was Mr. Macho, but he couldn't have done that."

I took being favorably compared to her ex-husband as a compliment, but after hearing about their relationship, besting him didn't sound like much of an accomplishment. Still, I couldn't help but smile as I confessed, "Well, I did knock over a tombstone."

"We'll send them a check," she replied.

I laughed. So did she. The further we got from the cemetery, the more relaxed we became, and analysis became possible. "So what are we dealing with here?" I asked. "Do you think that was Betty's grandmother or just her in disguise?"

"I don't think it was her *or* her grandmother," she answered. "I agree with Father Kubera. We're dealing with a demon—or demons."

"That's what I'm really asking," I replied. "Do you think we're dealing with one or *more* entities?"

"I wish I knew, Rick," she said softly.

"Somehow it relates to Chapel Street," I said. "You still up for heading over to the Pratt?"

"Boy, nothing stops you, does it?" she asked with some admiration.

"What choice do we have?" I asked.

"Some men would just pop open another beer and turn up the volume of the television."

"Do you mean some men?" I asked. "Or one man?"

Teri smiled forlornly. "One thing I can say about Chuck is that he had boundless courage when it came to things that didn't matter, like skiing or whitewater rafting or skydiving. But he had no fortitude whatsoever when it came to real, everyday challenges like holding onto a job, living within his means, or trying to figure out why his wife was sad. He wasn't steadfast like you."

"I don't think my mother, Gina, or even Lenny would say I was steadfast," I answered. "I let them all down."

"I bet you gave them everything you had."

"Maybe," I said. "But it wasn't enough."

We drove the rest of the way in silence. I found a parking place right outside the mammoth main branch of the Enoch Pratt Free Library on Cathedral Street. I found it unusually reassuring that the Basilica, the first Catholic cathedral built in the United States, sat right across the street. Previously, I never thought much of the squat building. When I thought of cathedrals, I always pictured the European gothic masterpieces like Paris' Notre Dame. The neoclassical style of this building always left me a little cold. It more resembled a museum than a place of worship. Of course, a few days ago, I would have preferred a museum to a place of worship. Now I considered the building a possible place of refuge. I wondered if Betty could pursue us in there?

We hurried inside to the microfilm collection on the first floor. I had frequently visited the collection during my early days as a genealogist before the Federal census records slowly came online. Now I mainly visited the library for its extensive microfilm collection of old, local newspapers. Those records weren't online yet. I went to one of the black filing cabinets and pulled out a microfilm of the Baltimore Morning Sun for the first week of May in 1932. The story was easy to find. It was front-page news on May 3rd. Teri gasped when she saw the headline.

"Noted East Baltimore Spiritualist Dies in House Fire."

We poured over the story.

Ann Jindra, 36, a noted spiritualist and fortune-teller, died last evening around 8:15 in a suspicious fire at her home at 2218 Chapel Street. The three-fire alarm blaze burned for more than an hour. Mrs. Jindra's charred remains were found in her bedroom on the second floor. She was the only person at home at the time of the conflagration.

Baltimore City Fire Department Investigators suspect arson was the cause of the fatal fire. Captain Martin Ernst believes two buckets of kerosene or gasoline were thrown through the first floor front windows and lit with a torch of some sort.

"This wasn't an accident," Captain Ernst said. "This was murder."

Mr. Matthew Jindra, husband of the deceased, claims his wife had received death threats after predicting the death of a neighborhood child. Fire Department and Police investigators canvassed the neighborhood but found no witnesses to the crime. The investigation will continue.

Mrs. Jindra was known throughout East Baltimore for her well-attended séances and her ability to predict the future. In addition to her husband, a daughter Helen survives her.

No funeral plans have been announced.

"Charred remains," I said softly, turning to Teri. "You saw her changing, right?"

Teri nodded weakly.

"I thought she was just decaying, but she was showing us how she died," I said.

Teri nodded.

"I bet I know who that neighborhood child was," I said as I quickly rewound the microfilm and found the death notices on May 2nd. Sure enough, I found the one for my great-uncle Vincent Bakos, who died at the age of eight. I had obtained a copy of his death certificate from the

Maryland State Archives, which reported he had died of a cerebral hemorrhage.

"They killed her the night of my great-uncle Vincent's funeral."

Teri said nothing. I quickly scanned through the rest of the week and the rest of the month of May, but there were no further stories about the house fire. Considering the lurid, exploitative coverage of crime during that period, I was certain the newspaper would have followed up on the case if the police pursued it. However, they didn't. Either the police didn't have any evidence or they simply chose not to pursue it. Why?

I wanted to switch over to the microfilm of Baltimore's other daily, now defunct, newspaper, The Baltimore American, but then Teri broke her silence. "Can we just go?" she asked quietly.

I would have preferred to stay, but I could tell she was troubled. I quickly paid for a printout of the story, and we left the library. After closing her eyes for a moment and taking a deep breath, she turned to me and asked, "Do you really think they killed her?"

"Yeah, I do," I said. "That would explain everything."

"No, it doesn't explain anything," she replied. "They didn't talk a lot about my great-grandmother, but everything they said about her was good. How sweet she was. How kind."

Teri pulled out her cellphone. She clicked on the Resting Place app and brought up the memorial to her great-grandmother Maria Poskocil. Teri clicked on a picture of Maria with three of her children. Her smile was warm, and her eyes were bright. Teri handed me the phone.

"Does she look like someone who would burn a woman alive?" she asked.

"No," I answered.

Nor did my great-grandmother Kristina Bakos. I only found three photographs of her. They were all portraits taken on formal occasions, and, as was the custom of the day, she didn't smile in any of them. Still, despite the seriousness of her expression, nothing in her face hinted she could commit murder either. These two women were not criminals. They were both good Catholic wives and mothers.

"Teri, if they killed her, I'm sure they thought they had a good reason."

"There's no good reason for murder," Teri said.

I was surprised by how much this news upset her. It seemed to threaten her bedrock assumptions about her family, and, by extension, herself. Me? I wasn't troubled by the news. No, not at all. I was proud my family took action, but there was no point saying that to Teri. I knew she wouldn't be responsive to that viewpoint.

"We're the bad guys," Teri said after a moment of reflection.

"We are definitely *not* the bad guys," I said firmly. I reached out, took her chin, and turned her face toward me. "Even if our families did this thing, *we* didn't. It happened fifty years before we were born. It has nothing to do with us."

Teri turned away and spoke quietly. "The Lord is slow to anger and abounding in steadfast love, forgiving iniquity and transgression, but He will by no means clear the guilty, visiting the iniquity of the fathers on the children, to the third and the fourth generation. Book of Numbers."

I cringed. Did I really have to be partnered in this disaster with a Catholic schoolteacher with a working knowledge of Old Testament?

"Teri, can you please do me a favor," I replied. "From now on, when you quote the Bible, quote something nice, like 'Jesus loves puppies and daisies.'"

"This is no time for joking, Rick."

"I know, I'm sorry," I replied. I reached out and touched her hand. "You know what? We could be jumping entirely to conclusions. I wish my grandfather were still alive. He would know what happened."

"My aunt Maggie," Teri said. "She's still alive. She was born in 1925. She would have been around seven at the time. She should remember. We can talk to her."

"Are you sure?" I asked. "Everyone we discuss Betty with becomes a target. Do you really want to do this?"

"If it's true," Teri answered, "She's already a target."

I couldn't argue with that.

Chapter Twenty-Four: Aunt Maggie

Teri's great-grandaunt Maggie Poskocil was ninety-one-years old and lived at Stella Maris, a Catholic nursing home in Baltimore County. She was the last surviving child of the Bohemian immigrants Antonin and Maria Poskocil. Two of Maggie's three brothers died by their own hand; only Teri's grandfather lived long enough to reproduce before eventually dying of natural causes.

Teri said Aunt Maggie never married or had a serious boyfriend either. She worked as a clerk at the Woodlawn offices of the Social Security Administration. She spent her retirement taking bus trips to various casinos with her dwindling number of girlfriends until she eventually became infirm and moved into the nursing home. Mentally, she was still sharp as a tack.

Teri called her aunt while I drove and asked if she could visit. I could hear Maggie's response. Her voice was frail but alert, and she was delighted to see Teri. I was concerned when Teri didn't mention me or the reason for our visit. That wasn't something I would want to spring on a ninety-year-old woman without warning. Then again, springing it on her on the phone didn't sound like a kindness either. But I didn't say anything. I trusted Teri's judgment. She was a teacher. She knew how to handle people. I had no appreciable talent for that myself.

We pulled into Stella Maris about a half an hour after the call. The facility was bright and clean, and the residents in the common area seemed happy enough. Teri went straight to Aunt Maggie's private room. She knocked on the door before she stuck her head inside.

"Aunt Maggie?" she said.

"Come in, dear," Maggie replied.

"Are you dressed?" she asked, opening the door a crack. "I've brought a friend."

"Oooo," Maggie exclaimed curiously. "A boy?"

"Yes."

"Bring him in," she said.

Teri and I entered the room to find Maggie sitting in a wooden rocking chair between her bed and a dresser lined with dozens of framed photos. She wore green sweat pants, tennis shoes, and a floral print blouse. She was thin. Her skin stretched across her bones like paper, but her eyes were bright, and her smile was broad. Ignoring Teri, she rose up slightly from her chair and extended her hand. "I'm pleased to meet you, Mister…"

"Bakos," I said as I gently took her hand. It seemed so frail that I felt I could break it with half a squeeze. "Rick Bakos."

"Bakos," Maggie said as she released her hand. She put on a smile, but I could tell her mind was clicking. "I knew a Bakos family once."

"He's one of them," Teri said as she pulled out a seat for me across from her aunt. "His family is from Chapel Street, too."

I sat down. Teri took a seat on the bed closer to her aunt.

"What was your father's name?" Maggie asked.

"Stan," I answered. The name brought no look of recognition from her, so I added, "His father was Harold Bakos."

Her eyes lit up. "You're Harold Bakos' son?" she said.

"Grandson," I corrected.

"Oh, my goodness. He was so handsome and athletic," she said, and then she turned to Teri. "I had a huge crush on him when I was little girl." Teri smiled. Maggie turned back to me. "Did he ever marry that Italian girl, Sadie? I forget her last name…"

"Mastracci," I said. "Yes, he married her."

"She was a beauty," Maggie said. "Are they still with you?"

"No," I said, "But they both died of natural causes."

Maggie met my eyes warily. She knew what I meant. There was an awkward moment of silence before Teri spoke up. "Aunt Maggie, I love you, and I don't want to hurt you, but we have to know what happened on Chapel Street. It's a matter of life or death."

Maggie closed her eyes. "Is she talking to you?" she said quietly, little above a whisper.

"She comes as Uncle Hank," Teri replied, and then she motioned to me. "She comes to Rick as his brother Leonard, who killed himself."

"What does she say?" Maggie asked.

"She wants us to kill ourselves," Teri answered.

Maggie's face cracked. She lost all composure and was barely able to hold back her tears as she reached out and took Teri's hand. "I thought it ended with our generation," she replied. "How much longer do we have to pay?"

"What happened?" Teri asked.

Maggie hesitated. Her expression indicated she was stepping back into a long nightmare. It was painful for me to watch. I doubt I could have pressed her, but Teri continued. "We were just at the library. We saw a story about the fire. Was it arson?"

Maggie nodded yes.

"Why?" Teri asked.

"The Jindra woman was a čarodějka," Maggie said softly, quickly crossing herself. "A witch. Our families did what they had to do, but she didn't die. Not really."

Teri took Maggie's hand in both of her own. "Please," she pleaded. "We need to know everything,"

"Her name was Anna Jindra," Maggie said. "She was from the old country, and she had powers. Great powers. She told fortunes and put spells on people. The priest told us to shun her, and most did, during the day. But many went to see her at night when they were in trouble. No good ever came of it. She only gave people bad news."

Teri and I exchanged a glance. That was Betty's M. O.

"I remember her very clearly even now," Maggie said. "She was very beautiful and wanton. They said she had the appetite of a prostitute but never asked for money. She did it for pleasure only. She slept with whoever she wanted, even though she was married herself. That's how it all started."

Maggie raised a finger toward us before she continued.

"There's one thing you must remember. We were a close-knit neighborhood. Half the people on Chapel Street were from the same town in the old country. That's how it was. One came here, then another, and another. Most of us were cousins or related some way," Aunt Maggie said, turning to me. "Like our families."

She turned to her dresser and picked up a framed photo of two smiling women standing behind a row house. She handed it to me. I recognized them immediately. They were my great-grandmother Kristina Bakos and Teri's great-grandmother Maria Poskocil. The genealogist in me leapt with joy to see a new photograph of one of my ancestors. Normally, my priority would now switch to making sure I left with a copy of that photograph, but not today. Today I needed information, not mementos.

Aunt Maggie continued. "Your grandmother Kristina and my mother Maria were like sisters, here and back in the old country. In a way, they *were* sisters. Your grandmother's parents took my mother in when her parents died. They grew up together and dreamed of coming to America together—and they did."

Wow. Although she confused her generations, Aunt Maggie was a genealogist's dream come true. She knew more about the Bakos family history than any of my living relatives.

"There was another girl from our village, Emma Kostohryz, who lived on Chapel Street, too," Maggie continued. "She and her husband ran a fruit stand on Collington Street. She was seven months pregnant when the witch took an interest in her husband. They had an affair, but, unlike the other women who kept their mouths shut out of fear, Emma made a scene. One day, she cursed at the witch and threw fruit at her. The witch said nothing. She just pointed at her, and Mrs. Kostohryz had a miscarriage right there on the street. The baby didn't survive."

Teri and I shuddered.

"That was the final straw for the women in the neighborhood," Maggie continued. "Back then, everyone sat out on their front stoops in the evenings and talked. The mood that night was terrible. When the witch came home, the women taunted her. But she just smiled, and that made them even madder."

Maggie turned to me. She reached out and touched my hand.

"Your grandmother was the bravest," she said. "Just as the witch was stepping into her house, she threw a rock through her front window."

"What did she do?" I asked.

"She just turned to her and said, 'You should look after your son.' That very moment, your uncle Norbert came running out of the house. He said little Vincent was having a seizure. They took him to the hospital, but he died."

"His death certificate said he died of a cerebral hemorrhage."

"He was murdered," Maggie said firmly, as if she thought my statement had contradicted her story.

"I know. I believe you," I answered, and I *did* believe her. Being chased out of a cemetery by a burning ghost would make even the most fervent skeptic open to practically anything. But it was more than that. I knew in my heart of hearts that Maggie was telling the truth. She was exposing the cancer at the heart of our families, which had claimed one life after another for decades.

"Now the witch went too far. She forgot that most of the people on the street were from the old country. They knew how to handle witches," Maggie continued. "The anger grew until little Vincent's funeral. Then Father Stegskal, the old priest down at Saint Wenceslaus, lit the fuse. He said we faced an evil that could only be cleansed by the fire. Everyone knew what he meant. I don't know if there was any planning or anything. I was too young, and no one ever talked about it later, but the street was quiet that night until Mr. Jindra left with his daughter. Then it all happened at once. People ran up to the house and threw bricks through the windows while others tossed in buckets of gasoline and torches. The house went up in an instant."

"Did she try to get out?" Teri asked.

"Right after it started, she appeared in one of the upstairs windows," Maggie answered. "She shouted something. I think it was Bohemian, but a dialect I didn't know. Then she disappeared back inside. No one saw her again until the fire department dragged out her body. Considering how long the fire burned, I was surprised there was anything left. They carried her out on a stretcher covered by a blanket. My brothers and I watched from our upstairs windows. When her blackened arm fell out from under the blanket, I fainted."

"The newspaper said the police knew it was arson," I said.

"Of course," Maggie replied. "It was obvious. Some people even blocked the street with their cars to slow down the fire trucks."

"Why didn't they prosecute anyone?"

"Who could they prosecute?" Maggie asked. "The deaths started almost immediately. First, it was Mrs. Kostohryz, the one who had the miscarriage, then your grandmother, then my mother, then Mrs. Cunat and Mrs. Klima and Mrs. Rynes and her sister. All suicides. The street was cursed. They called it Suicide Street. Everyone scattered. If they couldn't sell their house, they just abandoned it, but it didn't matter. She was so strong in the beginning."

"What do you mean?" Teri asked.

"She could get into your mind and make you see things," Maggie answered, and then she met Teri's eyes. "Did you ever wonder why I never married?"

Teri nodded yes.

"It was her," Aunt Maggie answered. "Almost from the beginning, when I was still a little girl, I had these horrible nightmares. The details would change, but it always took place in a maternity ward. I had just given birth to a baby, and doctor or nurse would bring it to me wrapped in a blanket. However, when I opened the blanket, the baby was always terribly deformed. I woke up screaming every night for twenty years. Her powers eventually faded, but after all of those visions, I couldn't take a chance on marriage and getting pregnant."

Teri got down off the bed and gently hugged her aunt. "Oh, sweetie, that's horrible," she said. "She stole away your family."

"She stole away a lot of families," Maggie continued as Teri released her. "Pretty much all of the families from Chapel Street are gone now. Extinct. It was one suicide or quote unquote accident after another for twenty long years. I'd see their names in the newspaper, but we stopped going to each other's funerals. We couldn't face each other because we knew what we did." Then, lowering her eyes, she added in Bohemian, "Každý ptáček svým nosem se živí."

I turned to Teri for a translation. Teri turned to her aunt. "What does that mean?"

Aunt Maggie looked up and said, "It's something my father used to say—'We all gnaw on the bone we are given.'"

Geez, I thought, *does anyone in this family know an upbeat quote?*

Teri and I sat in silence trying to absorb the implications of the story. It was stunning. Betty, or Anna, or whoever she was, had essentially wiped out entire families. The situation was worse than I ever imagined, and I imagined it being pretty damned bad. I only had one question. "Why did she stop?"

Maggie shrugged. "Lord only knows. Her voice just became fainter and fainter, until about thirty-years-ago or so. Then she grew louder again, but I learned how to deal with her."

"How?" Teri and I asked almost simultaneously.

"I don't talk to her, no matter what form she takes," Maggie answered. "The more you talk to her, the more power she has."

"Who does she come as?" Teri asked.

"She comes as my mother," Maggie replied. "She's so much like her, a carbon copy, but it's not her."

Teri gave Aunt Maggie another hug. As she did, I put the photo of Kristina and Maria back on the dresser, but I couldn't resist getting a copy. I took my cellphone out and turned to Aunt Maggie. "Miss Poskocil, may I take a picture of this photo? I have so few of my great-grandmother." I asked.

Aunt Maggie turned to me and smiled. "You can have it."

"No, I can't take it," I replied.

"I insist," Aunt Maggie answered.

She reached over and took the picture. As she removed it from the dresser, Teri suddenly said, "No, no, no." Teri quickly reached over and turned another photograph face down.

"What's wrong?" Aunt Maggie asked, suddenly concerned.

"I told you this picture was strictly verboten," Teri said.

"Which one?" Aunt Maggie asked.

Teri carefully showed the picture to her at an angle, which prevented me from seeing it. "But you're so beautiful," Aunt Maggie exclaimed.

"I'll find you another one of equal or greater beauty," Teri replied.

Teri tried to pull the photograph back, but Aunt Maggie grabbed it. Teri reluctantly released it. "Maybe you should let your young man see what a beautiful bride you make," Aunt Maggie said as she turned the picture toward me.

It was a formal wedding photograph of Teri and her ex-husband Chuck. Teri did indeed make a very beautiful bride in her flowing wedding dress. It was hard to take my eyes off her, but I had to see what kind of man could win her heart, albeit briefly. Chuck was a good-looking guy with a toothy grin. He definitely looked more athletic than me, but he was already balding. At least I still had my hair.

Then it struck me. There was something familiar about him. I had seen him before, but where? When I finally figured it out, I was too stunned to say anything until we got out into the car.

Chapter Twenty-Five: Candlelight

"No way!" Teri exclaimed.

"It's him," I said. "I swear."

Teri took out her cellphone as I drove. She clicked on her Facebook app. "What's your ex's name, Gina..."

"Holt. H-O-L-T."

Teri typed the name into the search engine. "Great, there's a million of them."

"She's the one standing with your ex-husband in her profile picture."

Teri silently scanned down the list of Gina Holts. Then she clicked on one of them. I glanced over to see she had successfully located the photo of Gina and Chuck posing with their engagement ring.

"Oh my God," she said softly.

"My thoughts exactly."

Teri clicked off her phone and sank back into the seat. "This isn't a coincidence," she said softly.

"I know. It's Betty."

Teri nodded.

"I don't know what the hell she's up to, but I'm not going to let it happen," I said. "I have to call Gina and tell her."

"No, don't," Teri said.

"Why not?"

"It won't help."

"What do you mean?" I asked. "I can't let her marry that jerk."

"What are you going to tell her? That a demon got my jerk ex-husband to propose to her? Do you think she's going to believe that? Especially since we're seeing each other?"

Under normal circumstances, I would have been thrown off-balance trying to figure out exactly what Teri meant when she said we were seeing each other, but I was too worried about Gina now. "What do you expect me to do?" I asked.

"Nothing."

"Nothing?"

"Look, Rick, I don't mean to be rude or insulting, but you don't know anything about women," she said. "If you say anything to Gina, she's just going to think that it's all a sick, manipulative ploy to get her back. She'll think that you tracked me down just to get the dirt on Chuck."

Damn. She was right, but I didn't like it.

"Did she say when they were getting married?" Teri asked.

"No," I answered. "She was still dealing with the surprise of getting engaged."

"Okay, here's the way I see it, Rick," Teri said. "Obviously, Betty is behind this. My guess is that she arranged this relationship to distract us. Do you agree?"

I nodded.

"We've got to put this aside and concentrate on sending her back to hell. If we do, my guess is that their relationship will fall apart on its own. Okay?"

"Okay," I answered reluctantly.

We drove in awkward silence for a moment. I don't know what Teri was thinking, but I was wrestling with the enormity of my mistake. "How many innocent people have to be hurt just because I took that stupid picture," I asked rhetorically.

"Don't beat yourself up. Remember I went to the mausoleum before you," Teri replied. "She was drawing me, too."

"Yeah, but you were smart enough not to take a picture."

"It was only a matter of time," she replied. "I was already intrigued by all the flowers. I would have been back. Probably Tuesday after exams. Then you would have found the memorial and contacted me."

"I don't know about that," I answered. "I'm not very good at contacting women."

"You would have contacted me," she answered. "I honestly believe with all of my heart that we were fated to face this together."

"Fated or doomed?"

"I suppose that depends on how it works out," she said, smiling weakly. "Here's the funny thing. I'm afraid of Betty, but, in a strange way, I have more faith than I ever had."

"Why?"

"This thing we call Betty proves what I believe is true—that there is something beyond this world," she said. "Even Catholic high school teachers have doubts sometimes."

"I felt the same way when she spoke through Pete," I answered. "At that moment, I knew we were actually dealing with an intelligent entity from beyond the realm of our senses, but that didn't suddenly make me believe in the Bible or some loving, all-powerful God. If anything, God seems as absent from that realm as He does from this one. Otherwise, why would Betty have such free reign?"

I was spared a theological rebuttal from Teri when her phone chirped. It was a text. She quickly checked it. "Father Kubera wants to know if we can meet with Father Mubita and him tonight after six at the Helping Hands Mission on Read Street."

"Definitely," I said.

She sent back the message and then turned to me. "What do you want to do until then?"

The clock on the dashboard read 3:52pm. What I desperately needed was a little sleep. Lenny's visits had left me exhausted, but I didn't want to sleep alone. I wanted to sleep with Teri so we could watch over each other, but that was something I couldn't suggest. So I did the next best thing. "Do you want to get something to eat?"

From her expression, I knew the prospect of eating didn't necessarily appeal to her. "Yeah, okay," she finally said. "But can we drop by my place first so I can freshen up?"

"Yeah, sure."

I drove directly over to Teri's townhouse. She invited me inside. It was a small place, very narrow. Despite its two floors, I doubted it had more square feet of living space than my apartment. Unlike my place, however, her house reflected excellent taste. Her furnishings and knick-knacks were all chosen with care. I picked out all of my furniture in less than an hour at IKEA. Fascinating artwork hung on her walls. My only decorations were a few movie posters and some sports memorabilia. In other words, she was living as an adult woman. I was a nerdy teenager in comparison.

Teri immediately ran upstairs to freshen up. I used the half bath downstairs. When I finished, I checked out her living room. It had a large, comfortable sofa. By the time Teri came back down, I had a solution to her problem.

"Have you tried sleeping down here?"

"Why?" she asked.

"You only have a half bath down here," I answered. I stepped out of the living room and into the entrance hall and motioned toward the kitchen. "All you need to do is stack a couple of those dining room chairs here on your stairs. It doesn't have to be an impenetrable wall. It just has to be difficult enough that you can't move them while you're asleep. That way you can't get upstairs to the tub."

"I hope that won't be necessary," she replied. "As soon as my uncle shows up, I'm going to start praying. I hope that drives him away."

I still wasn't sold on that tactic, but I didn't want to discourage her. If it worked for her tonight, fine. To me, the problem was less about tactics than desire. The truth of the matter was that I liked talking to Lenny. I knew he was probably a counterfeit, but he was so close to the real thing that the good it was doing me emotionally was worth the risk. Plus, I didn't feel threatened by him anymore now that I was able to control my environment.

"Hey, instead of going out, how about me fixing something here?" Teri asked.

"Sure," I said.

"I have a great recipe for chicken fajitas," she said as she walked into the kitchen. "How does that sound?"

"Great."

I followed Teri into the kitchen and sat down at the table while she prepared the food on the counter near the table. She explained each step of the process and how she grew many of the herbs herself in her small garden. I enjoyed the lecture, but once the cooking began in earnest, I took out my phone to check my mail, but there was no cellular signal.

"Zero bars?" I asked, looking up at her.

"Who's your provider?" she asked.

"Verizon."

"I have Verizon, too." She picked up her phone. She didn't have any bars either. "Maybe the tower's down."

I saw a computer on a small desk in the dining room. "Can I use your computer to check my email?"

"Go right ahead, Rick."

I went into the next room and sat down at the desk and accessed my email account. It was mostly junk mail, but my eyes went right to the message from Resting Place.

"Resting Place," I said aloud. Teri put down her spatula and joined me. She watched over my shoulder as I opened the email. The message was short.

We have restored your account.
Please delete the Kostek memorial immediately.

Underneath the message was a link to the memorial. I looked up at Teri.

"Do it," she said.

I clicked on the link. The Kostek memorial appeared on the computer screen. It was the first time I had seen Betty in days. Now, knowing her death toll, I must admit I shuddered. Her eyes met mine, unafraid, and, if anything, her taunting smile seemed even smugger. Teri averted her eyes from Betty's gaze.

"If you can't do it, I will," she said softly.

No, I had to do it. I brought the cursor up to the delete button on the right corner of the memorial but, before I could click, the computer screen went blank.

"What the..." I said.

Teri turned from the monitor to the lights. "Everything's off."

"Where's your fuse box?" I asked.

Teri got up and headed through the kitchen to the basement door. I followed. As I did, I noticed that the chicken was still cooking. "The stove's still on."

"It's gas," she replied.

Teri grabbed a flashlight from a drawer, and we descended into the basement. I was actually a little frightened as we walked down the steps. I expected Betty to jump out at us from the shadows, but Teri kept her basement very neat and organized, leaving no real shadows for Betty to hide in. Teri went right to the fuse box and opened it up. The fuses were all switched in the same direction.

"Did she switch them all off?" Teri asked.

"No, they're all in the on position," I replied.

We headed upstairs again and stepped out of the front door. One of Teri's neighbors was also standing outside. She turned to Teri. "Did you lose your power, too?"

"Yeah," Teri answered.

"This is ridiculous. It's not like there's a storm or something." The neighbor then added, "Maybe a car hit a pole or something."

Maybe that was how Betty did it, I thought to myself.

She already manipulated drunk drivers to kill my father and Herb Norton. She could have made some unwary driver ram his car into an electric pole in order to save her online memorial. That was a frightening thought. It meant she could be in more than one place at the same time. The timing was too perfect. She had to be in the room watching us— waiting until I was about to click the button, but also elsewhere guiding the driver. Then again, perhaps entities outside our realm were not bound by our rules concerning time and space. Or maybe she had other minions doing her bidding as well. The possibilities were endless and dizzying.

I didn't to share my thoughts with Teri as we went back into the house. Things were already bad enough without adding further speculation. I followed Teri back into the kitchen where she flipped over the chicken breasts. Afterwards, she left the room and quickly returned with a candle and placed it on the table.

"I hope you don't mind eating by candlelight, Mr. Bakos?" she said with a smile.

"Not at all," I said.

Betty might have been an evil, demonic bitch, but her counter measures certainly made our dinner more romantic, in a strictly friendly manner, of course.

Chapter Twenty-Six: Father Mubita

Teri and I arrived at the Helping Hand Mission early, while the staff was still feeding the guests their dinner along a buffet line.

I hate to seem mean or callous, but the place repulsed me. It was filled with homeless people who obviously hadn't bathed in weeks. The pungent smell of grimy sweat and urine completely overwhelmed the aroma of the food. Something else also permeated the place that I couldn't articulate: a palatable sense of gloom and hopelessness. Sort of like what I smelled at the mausoleum. I was tempted to turn around and leave, but I knew I couldn't. We needed the priests.

I spotted Father Kubera standing behind the buffet counter with the volunteers serving the clients. Another priest, a large, imposing black man around forty-something-years-old with a warm smile and wearing a black shirt and the telltale collar, also served the guests. When the priest spotted us, he came out from around the counter and walked over to us, displaying a rather pronounced limp.

"You must be Rick and Teri," he said with a gentle Zambian accent.

"Yes, Father," Teri answered.

"Good, I'm glad you could make it," he said as he quickly shook our hands. "I am Father Thomas Mubita. We are still serving our guests, but if you'd like, you can wait in my office." He motioned to a half-open door right off the main room.

"Thanks," I said, as I guided Teri toward the room. As she walked, Teri looked back and watched Mubita take his place on the serving line again.

"We should help," she said.

"Nah," I replied. "It looks like they've got things under control."

"Come on; it'll be fun," she said, breaking free of me.

Teri was a natural do-gooder. I wasn't anymore. I felt I paid my dues caring for my mother and my brother for years. A less generous analysis would be that I became very self-centered since the death of my mother. That was probably the truth. Still, I knew I had to join Teri in the serving line. If I didn't, I would look like a total jerk, and I wanted Teri to think I was a nice guy.

Teri and I were quickly outfitted with aprons by one of the regular volunteers, and before long, the last homeless person was served. Father Mubita had mercy on us. He left the cleanup to his regulars and invited Father Kubera and us back to his private office. When he closed the door, the stench of the guests receded, and I relaxed a bit.

"Thank you for your help," Father Mubita said as he sat down behind his desk.

"It's the least we could do, Father," I said.

He turned his attention to me. "I understand you were baptized and raised Catholic, but you no longer practice?"

"Correct," I answered.

"Do you believe in Jesus Christ?" he asked.

"I'm starting to believe in the Devil," I answered. "Is that enough?"

"Not if you hope to survive," Mubita answered in deadly seriousness. "Only the blood of Christ can protect you now."

I didn't like being under his glare—or being told what I had to believe. So, I shot back. "A lot of good the blood of Christ has done our families," I replied. "She's killed dozens of people from Chapel Street."

"Chapel Street?" Mubita asked, turning to Kubera for clarification.

Teri jumped in and gave Father Mubita the Cliff Notes version of our research that evolved into a full-throated confession for the sins of both of our families. She was in tears by the time she finished with that same gloomy quote from the book of Numbers she laid on me earlier about God punishing the children and grandchildren of sinners.

"No, no, you misunderstand the scriptures. Ezekiel 18:20, is very clear: 'The son shall not bear the punishment for the father's iniquity,'"

Father Mubita said. "You and Rick are not being punished for the sins of your ancestors. However, their sins have opened the door to the Beast."

"What do you mean?" Teri asked.

"God has erected a wall between us and the demons," Mubita explained. "They cannot, by their own will, enter the human realm. If they could, the human race would be extinct. But God has given us free will, and we have the power to invite them into our world. That is what happened here. The witch, or one of her ancestors, invited the Beast inside of her and left her descendants susceptible to possession. Later, by their unrepentant act of murder, your families left you vulnerable to retaliation. It is a terrible chain of events, but it *can* be broken."

"How?" Teri asked.

"Genuine repentance," Mubita answered.

Here it comes, I thought. Mubita would help us, but he was going to exact a price. We were going to have to become good Catholics and buy into the whole religion thing. That was fine for Teri. She already believed, and I had no problem with that. For her. Me, I had my own problems with God, and I wouldn't be blackmailed into believing. A God worth following wouldn't have put me in this mess in the first place.

"Well, I didn't do anything to her," I replied defiantly. "It was eighty-years ago. I don't see why *I* have to repent."

He turned to me. "When the Beast comes to you, does it play on the guilt of your ancestors?" Mubita asked. "Or your own?"

I turned away. That was indeed an excellent question. Lenny never directly pointed the finger at me, but our nightly conversations always churned up my own feelings of guilt about our relationship. How I had emotionally, if not physically, abandoned him in his time of need. That guilt grew the more I came to understand how he had been battling Betty all alone. He never had a chance. Had I taken him and the voices he heard seriously, I might have been able to save him.

Yeah, maybe Mubita was right. Perhaps Lenny was a Trojan horse designed to enter my heart and weaken me by manipulating my guilty conscience. I recognized that fact. Still, I had no desire to drive him away. These were the most honest and straightforward conversations I had with him since childhood. There were still things I wanted to say to Lenny. If there were the slightest possibility that he really *was* my nightly visitor, I would take the chance.

I turned back. Father Mubita's eyes were still on me. There was nothing accusatory in them. No judgment. But I decided not to answer the question. My guilt about my brother wasn't relevant. It was just a distraction. We had to maintain focus.

"Look, Father, what I did or what my family did is irrelevant," I finally said. "What I need to know is what we have to do to stop this thing."

"I am not sure yet," Mubita answered.

Teri closed her eyes. This wasn't what either of us was expecting.

"I have been praying and fasting, but no answer has come yet." Mubita continued. "This is an odd situation. Normally, I deal with people who are possessed. In those cases, we cast out the demon, and the victim is healed. Sometimes, a demon is attached to a specific place. In those cases, we cast the demon from the place, and the problem is solved. This is different. Neither of you are possessed, and although the presence of the demon is very strong at the cemetery, it does not seem to be tied to that specific place since the Beast visits you at your homes and elsewhere."

Great. The expert had no idea what to do. That seemed par for the course, but at least he seemed more cognizant of the danger than Father Kubera.

"What do you recommend?" I asked.

"We must wait upon the Lord," he replied.

"Father," I said. "I can't emphasize enough that there is a certain degree of hurry-up needed here."

"I understand your fears, but you must have faith—both of you. The Lord is our only protection. If we step beyond His will, we will be placing ourselves at the mercy of the Beast, and it *is* formidable," Mubita explained. "I went to the cemetery with Father Kubera. The presence of the Beast was so powerful that we dared not enter the mausoleum. That's when I realized we're not dealing with a normal demon, but rather a devil."

"What's the difference?" I asked.

"Demons are hell's foot soldiers. They can be very fierce, but they yield quickly to the word of the Lord," he explained. "Devils are their commanders. They are infinitely wiser and more powerful. The Apostle

Paul described them in the book of Ephesians as the powers and principalities of the air. They are our true enemy, and even the twelve had trouble casting them out while our Lord still walked the Earth."

"Have you ever cast out a devil before?" I asked.

"A Devil? No," Mubita answered.

"But you have cast out demons?" I asked.

"Yes, many," he answered.

"Did any of the people you tried to help die?" Teri asked cautiously.

Mubita turned to her. "Yes," he answered. Both Teri and Father Kubera shuddered. This was obviously news to him as well.

"How'd they die?" I asked.

"Mostly drug overdoses," he answered.

"Drug overdoses?" I replied incredulously.

"Yes, it is almost impossible to separate drugs and demonic possession," he explained. "From the pagan oracles of ancient Greece, to the village shaman of my homeland, to California's hippies, human beings have always used drugs to cross into the spiritual realm, opening the door to the demonic in the process. In fact, the Greek word that Apostle Paul uses for sorcery, pharmakeia, is also the basis for the English word pharmacy. They are interchangeable. And America is the world's greatest drugstore. Every time I walk out among our guests, I can detect the presence of the Evil One like a scent in the air."

Wow. That explained what I was feeling out in the dining room. Perhaps this drug connection wasn't as far-fetched as it sounded. My mother and I both initially credited Lenny's madness to his drug use. And my mother's suicide only occurred after she became dependent on painkillers during her battle with cancer. Then there was Pete. Betty spoke through him right after he shot up.

"What do you want us to do?" Teri asked.

"I want all of you," Mubita began, taking both Father Kubera and myself under his gaze as well. "To pray and fast and listen for the Lord, and, whatever you do, do not communicate with the Beast anymore. Every time you speak to it, you open the door wider."

After those words of wisdom, Father Mubita ended our meeting in prayer. He had us all hold hands. I was never big on holding hands with guys. I was glad I had Teri on one side of me. That was nice. Father Kubera was on my other side. He seemed as awkward as I was with the whole holding hands thing. I think it was a little too Protestant for him.

The prayer was long and sprinkled liberally with quotations from the Bible. He called upon God to protect us from the evil one. A week ago, Mubita's words would have inspired laughter from me, but today, I soaked up every word hungrily. It still amazed me to think this whole thing had started only six days ago. The world was now an entirely different place – a much more dangerous one.

I liked Father Mubita, and I believed he could beat Betty.

If we lived long enough, that is.

Chapter Twenty-Seven: The Ledge

Teri seemed relatively upbeat when we left the Helping Hand Mission, but her mood darkened along with the sky as the sun slowly set. I knew exactly how she felt. It was easy being optimistic about our prospects in the light of day, but the night belonged to Betty.

I pulled into a parking place near her front door and turned off the engine. "Are you going to be okay?" I asked.

"Yeah," she replied, but the flatness of her voice belied her answer. "How about you?"

"I don't think I'm in any danger if I block my bedroom door again," I replied. "Are you going to try sleeping in your living room and blocking your stairs?"

She shook her head no. "If he comes again tonight, I'm not going to talk to him and just start praying."

I said nothing. She turned to me.

"I want you to do the same thing, Rick," she said. "You've got to stop talking to him."

I said nothing.

"For me," she said.

"What if it really is him?" I asked after a moment. "Even if it's one chance in a hundred that it's him, I gotta take it. When he was alive, the sicker he got, the more I pushed him away. I won't do that again."

Her eyes narrowed. "Is that what he's telling you?"

"He didn't have to," I replied. "I know what I did."

"Rick, it's not your brother."

I wanted to object, but she raised a finger to silence me.

"One day I'm sure you're going to see your brother again, and, when you do, you're going to find out that he knew you loved him."

"I'm not so sure I loved him," I answered softly. "Not in the end."

"Don't believe that," she said firmly. "That's the enemy talking, trying to weaken and destroy you the way she's trying to destroy me."

"What does she say to you?" I asked.

Teri paused. She had never discussed the actual content of her conversations with her would-be deceased great-uncle. I could tell it wasn't going to be easy for her despite her more outgoing nature.

"Everything he says is always couched in love," she replied. "He always calls me his little angel, just like he did in life. He says I'm too good for this world and goes through the litany of ways people betrayed or hurt me. Then, invariably, he brings up things I did to hurt other people. It's scary. It's like he knows all my private hurts and sins. When he's done, I don't think I'm too good for the world at all; I think I'm too bad for it."

"That's crap" I said.

"I've done many things I'm ashamed of, Rick," she said, lowering her eyes. "There was this one time, near the end of my marriage, I was commiserating with a guy friend, Todd Evans, whose wife just left him. We went out to happy hour together, and the next thing you know, we were making out in his car in the parking lot. I mean really making out. If he had a bigger car, there's no doubt in my mind we would have gone all the way. No doubt at all."

"But you didn't."

"I know what was in my heart, Rick," she said. "I had a million ways to justify it, but that didn't make it right. And here I am, teaching moral values to high school students. What hypocrisy. I can see why part of me wants to end up in that tub."

"That's Betty talking, not you," I said, genuinely alarmed.

"I know, I know," she replied, and then she turned to me. "Have you wondered how long she's been in our heads? I know I've changed. I was a different person. I was confident, happy. I knew who I was and what I wanted. When I was twenty-five or twenty-six, I would have seen right through Chuck and all his crap. I always attributed the change to getting older, but what if it wasn't? What if it was just Betty whispering in my ear, tearing me down bit-by-bit, setting me up for the kill?"

That was a terrifying thought. Because I knew it was true. I could see now how my entire personality, my fears and insecurities, were a result of Betty's intervention in my life. She stole my sense of security by murdering my father. Then she began pouring poison directly into my mother's ear, twisting her and our family into something sick. My adulthood was defined by my embarrassment and guilt about Lenny and his illness. Since then, I pushed everyone away, especially Gina. People were too painful to deal with. I felt I was better off alone, sinking into isolation. I was easy pickings now.

"Yeah," I said quietly. "She's been setting us up the whole time."

Teri nodded. "Think about her patience," she said. "She waited until we were ready, and then she called us over to the cemetery."

"She didn't count on the priests," I added. "They'll see us through."

"I hope so," she answered, in a voice tinged with doubt.

"Do you need me to stay here with you?" I asked.

She considered the proposal before gently shaking her head. "No," she said. "I think the best thing I can do is devote myself to prayer and fasting tonight, and you would be too much of a distraction. But I do need you to do one thing for me."

"What?"

"Don't talk to him," she said, imploring me. "Pray instead."

I didn't answer immediately. She continued.

"Rick, I need you to break free of her," she said. "I'm glad we have Father Kubera and Father Mubita on our side now, but neither of them really understands what we're going through. How could they? We're all we have. I'd be lost without you."

How could I refuse her? Even if the apparition was truly Lenny, nothing I could do or say could change the past or bring him back to life. Teri, on the other hand, obviously needed me now, in the present, to help her survive. What I did now for her mattered. She had to be my priority from now on.

"Okay, I will," I said.

She smiled and gave me the gentlest but sweetest kiss on the cheek before she left the car. I smiled as I waved goodbye, but I wasn't sure whether I just lied to her. It was going to be hard giving up Lenny.

When I got home, I headed for the refrigerator. Then I remembered the prayer and fasting thing. What did that even mean? I went to the computer and googled fasting. Zero help. There were a million ways to fast. Some people abstained from food entirely, others only abstained from food during the day, others abstained from a single meal, and others just gave up a favorite food. Father Mubita gave me his phone number, but I wouldn't waste his time with a question like this. I decided to make my own rules. I would abstain from everything except water until the morning. Then I would do what Teri was doing, unless she was doing something extreme.

I closed my browser and sat back. When the creak of the chair receded, I was suddenly struck by the silence. When I first moved into the apartment, the noise coming from my neighbors or the street below constantly annoyed me. Over time, I tuned out most of it, but now, it seemed I went too far. My apartment was as quiet as a tomb–an analogy I found very uncomfortable. Closing my eyes, I silently prayed that the Gehrets, the couple next door, would have another one of their periodic, wall-shaking fights.

God didn't answer my prayer. When I opened my eyes, the unnatural silence remained. I turned to the clock on the wall. It read: 8:46pm.

But was it?

What if it was already three am? What if I had come home hours ago and fallen asleep? What if I was only dreaming it was 8:46? Anything was possible with Betty.

I got up and went over to the balcony. I cracked open the door, and I was relieved to hear the traffic from the street below. Of course, that didn't mean I was actually awake. I closed the door and considered my options. I usually spent the evening watching television before going to bed around eleven or twelve. However, since Betty had the ability to make me drowsy, I didn't want to take the chance of falling asleep before my preparations.

I retreated into my bedroom. I pushed not one but two dressers in front of the door. I smiled as the furniture scraped loudly across the floor. I could never sleep through that sound. Once again, I opted against pajamas. I changed into shorts and an Orioles T-Shirt in case I woke up in an embarrassing position. I wasn't tired, but I drifted off into sleep almost immediately.

"You're screwing up, Ricky."

I opened my eyes. The alarm clock read 3am. I rolled over to see Lenny standing at the other side of my bed in his car salesman best, wearing dress pants, a white shirt, and a skinny tie. His hair was trim and combed. He looked about twenty-four or twenty-five. His eyes were a little dull, as if he were faithfully taking a heavy regimen of pills.

"Those priests, man, you're just going to get them killed," he continued. "Haven't you figured it out yet? She targets anyone you involve."

"When you say *she*, who do you mean?" I asked. "Betty or Anna?"

"They're both the same person," he answered.

"How about you?" I asked. "Are you the same person, too?"

"What do you think, Ricky?" he answered. "You spent thirty years of your life with me. Am I Lenny?"

I didn't offer him an immediate answer. But I knew one thing—I lied to Teri. I was doing exactly what she begged me not to do.

"Come on, Ricky, I'm your brother doing what I always do—looking out for you."

"You looked out for me?" I asked.

"Yeah," he answered. "Who took the heat for you when Mom found that Penthouse magazine in your drawer?"

"It was *your* magazine. I stole it from you."

"And Mom found it in your drawer," Lenny replied. "I didn't have to say it was mine, but I was the oldest, and I took responsibility."

"Okay, that was one time," I answered angrily. "How many times did I have to take you kicking and screaming to the hospital? How about that for taking responsibility?"

Lenny leaned in toward me, meeting my angry eyes. "Maybe I wouldn't have gone to the hospital so many times if you just believed me."

There. He said it, sticking the knife into my heart without even blinking. And yes, I was guilty as charged. Lenny earned the right to judge me, but did this apparition? There was only one way to find out.

"Our Father, who art in heaven," I began, the words leaving my mouth slowly.

"You're really doing this?" Lenny asked incredulously.

"Hallowed be Thy name..."

"You're going to choose your girlfriend over me…"

"Thy kingdom come, Thy will be done."

"…the way you chose Gina over Mom…"

"…on Earth as it is in heaven…"

"She died calling out your name."

My voice faltered. The thought of my mother calling for me in those last moments haunted me. That, perhaps even more than the nightmares, shattered my relationship with Gina. Every time I saw her, part of me blamed her for my mother's death. Of course, it wasn't her fault. It was mine. I was responsible.

"Remember the look on her face when you found her?" Lenny asked.

Yes, I remembered only too well. I closed my eyes and found myself transported back in time. The light was on in her bedroom when I got home. Her door was open. I could see my mother lying in her bed in her pajamas half covered by her blanket. I knocked on the doorframe and called her name, but she didn't answer. I ventured inside slowly, thinking she was only asleep. However, as I neared her bed, I could see that her eyes were open and unblinking. Her mouth was misshapen as if she died emitting a final scream. I froze. I couldn't bring myself to check her pulse or close her eyes.

"Mom died calling your name while you were with Gina," Lenny quietly hissed. "I hope you at least got laid."

I turned to Lenny. He was smiling smugly.

Just like Betty in the picture.

"Give us today our daily bread," I said defiantly.

Lenny straightened up. "Don't," he said.

"And forgive us our trespasses…"

Lenny backed up a little. "Stop it, Ricky," he said.

"As we forgive those who trespass against us."

"I can't protect you anymore."

"And deliver us from evil…"

In a broad gesture, Lenny waved his arms in front of himself and disappeared. I fell back into bed and closed my eyes. "Amen," I said.

I was overwhelmed by a profound sense of relief but not victory. The relief came from learning that prayer was indeed an effective weapon. Still, I didn't label it a victory because I still wasn't certain Lenny was Betty in disguise. Sure, the prayer sent him packing, but maybe because he was damned due to his death by suicide. I was afraid I might have simply inflicted more punishment on my brother who, in my opinion—if not God's, had suffered enough.

I didn't have long to contemplate the situation before I heard a voice say, "Please, don't do it, Rick."

It wasn't Lenny.

It wasn't Betty.

It took me a second to place it—Patty Gehret, my next-door neighbor.

"Just calm down, man," David, her husband, added.

What the hell?

I opened my eyes I found myself on the balcony again. But, worse than before, I was now standing on the wrong side of the metal railing. Only the heels of my bare feet rested on the three inches of concrete that extended out on the death side of the railing. When I instinctively turned toward the Gehrets, who were standing on the adjacent balcony, my left foot slipped from the narrow edge of concrete. Losing my balance, I fell forward, and my other foot also left the concrete.

Patty Gehret screamed. She might have even fainted.

Thank God my arms were wrapped behind me around the railing. The metal creaked ominously while my hand grabbed at the supports as I dangled partially off the ledge. The view below was too frightening to contemplate, so I closed my eyes. Arching my back, I managed to get my right foot back on the concrete. I sighed in relief. The worst was over. Now, using my right leg to lift myself up, I managed to get my left foot back up to the concrete.

Only then did I open my eyes to gauge the proportions of my predicament. Aside from the Gehrets, I saw other neighbors watching me in horror from their balconies. What the hell were they doing up? I guess it was all the sirens, which I only heard now. Looking down at the street, I saw a veritable roadblock of police and fire vehicles parked in front of the building with their emergency lights flashing. To make matters worse, there was even a news truck down there, too. Great. Maybe I was on CNN live.

There was no way for me to walk away from this situation clean. This was a life-changing event. Everybody I knew, everybody I worked with, everybody I'd ever met, was going to know about this incident. I was now officially crazy like Lenny.

"Shit!" I shouted.

"Calm down," David said. "You don't have to do this."

I tried calming down. I closed my eyes and took a deep breath. As I did, I could hear the concerned voices of others all around me on their balconies. Yes, they were all concerned now, but I knew that the next time I got on the elevator with them, they would subtly shift away from me. Lenny was right about the herd. They would never accept me again. They would push me to the edge for the lions to devour.

My life was over.

I was tempted to just release my arms and fall forward. There wouldn't be any pain. If I landed head first, my brain would be destroyed by the impact before the nerves could relay the sensation. Then I wouldn't have to answer the questions or face the stares from everyone I knew.

Damn it, this wasn't fair. I had spent my adult life being the anti-Lenny. Stable and ultra-reliable. Now I was just another Lenny. A suicidal lunatic.

To be or not to be.

This would have been an easier choice in my agnostic days. I didn't believe in an afterlife, so there would be no regret if I let go. Just a nonjudgmental nothingness. Now that I acknowledged the possibility of the afterlife, I also had to consider the possibility that I might leave this life for a worse one. What if Lenny really was Lenny? Did I want to condemn myself to wandering the Earth as a spirit like him? Worse yet, what if there really was a hell? If I let go now, would I wake up in hell after hitting the pavement?

Ultimately, I didn't make my decision in accordance with my own needs but the needs of others. As I contemplated death, I wondered if Teri's prayers had backfired as well. Where was she now? Was she drowning in the tub? If not, would she have the strength to hold on if I died? She needed me. So did my sister Janet. Her father died when she was just a little more than a baby. Then her brother and mother killed themselves. She deserved better than that from me.

I had to live.

Chapter Twenty-Eight: Rescue

"Just hold on, Rick," David said from his balcony.

"I'm not jumping," I said. "I'm just going to turn around."

There was no way to get off the ledge without turning around toward my apartment. But I couldn't move. I was paralyzed with fear. Finally, I took a deep breath and moved my left hand across my body and grabbed the rail. As I did so, my left foot followed, and I found myself facing my balcony door. Now I just had to climb over the railing itself. But how? Lifting myself up slightly, I felt the metal shudder under me. I doubted it would sustain my weight. I stopped immediately.

"How did I get over here?" I asked aloud. I couldn't imagine climbing over the railing in my sleep and surviving. Did Betty transport me here somehow? Was it a dark miracle?

Just then, I saw movement in my apartment through the glass balcony door. The front door swung open, and a tide of firemen, policemen, and EMTs flooded inside. It looked like the stateroom scene from the Marx Brothers' *A Night at the Opera*. They slowed as they neared the balcony door. The bulk of the men remained in the living room. Two burly firemen and a police sergeant moved toward the door. They exchanged a glance before the Sergeant began sliding the door open.

"Mind if we talk?" he asked.

"I was hoping you could come out and help me," I replied.

"Okay, we're coming out," the Sergeant said.

The Sergeant and the two firemen cautiously stepped out onto the balcony. "We're going to grab you by your arms and pull you over, okay?" one of the firemen said in an extremely calm voice, as if he were speaking to a child.

"Okay," I said.

Each of the firemen grabbed me by the upper arm and shoulder. "Are you ready?" one of them asked.

"Yes," I answered.

The two firemen easily lifted me up and set me down on the balcony to cheers of my watching neighbors. They didn't, however, release me. If anything, their grip on my arms tightened.

"Thank you very much," I said without making any attempt to break free. I had seen Lenny in this position many times, and, the more he struggled, the more force the authorities would use. My freedom depended on remaining calm and unthreatening.

"Our pleasure, Mister..." the Sergeant began.

"Bakos," I said. "Rick Bakos."

"Mr. Bakos, I'm Sergeant Gary Klado, Baltimore County Police Department, Towson Barracks," he said, smiling, although without extending his hand. "I think we should continue our conversation inside."

"Yeah, sure," I said.

"Good," Klado said, nodding to the firemen.

The firemen started moving, practically carrying me inside. Once we were inside, the other emergency personnel stepped aside to reveal a waiting stretcher. I knew what that meant, and I didn't like it. I shuddered inwardly but tried to remain outwardly calm.

"I want to thank you all for your help," I said, "but this isn't what you think."

"It isn't?" Klado asked. The fireman continued half-carrying, half-guiding me toward the stretcher.

"I wasn't trying to kill myself," I said, my voice rising fearfully despite my efforts to remain calm. "I've been sleepwalking the last couple of nights, and I just woke up out there."

"On the other side of the railing?" Klado asked dubiously.

"I don't know how I ended up there," I said truthfully.

"Well, I think that's something you may want to discuss with a doctor."

The two firemen turned me so that they could lay me back onto the stretcher. As they did, I saw my cellphone charging near the computer. I knew I needed to call Teri. She could help.

I decided to break free and grab the cellphone. That was a big mistake. I got free of the unsuspecting firemen, but Klado and two other police officers were on me before I could cover the five steps to the desk. I was thrown to the floor. My chin hit the wood hard. I felt a sharp knee dig into the small of my back as the officers grabbed my hands.

"No, please," I said.

Then I heard a telltale metal jingling.

"Don't, I'm alright, I swear," I said.

I felt the handcuffs snap around my wrists.

"I was just trying to get my cellphone," I said as the officers yanked me to my feet.

"You won't need it where you're going," Klado said.

With the help of the firemen, the police officers laid me down face up on the stretcher. They held me in place while the EMTs tied me down. I knew I was supposed to stay calm, but I couldn't. I was sane. I didn't deserve to be treated in such a humiliating manner.

"There's nothing wrong with me," I shouted, as I struggled. "I'm not crazy."

"Then you have nothing to worry about," Klado replied.

"Just untie me. I'll go with you peacefully."

"Not going to happen," Klado said, smiling.

I felt a prick in my arm. I turned to see an EMT pulling a needle out. I wanted to object, but everything collapsed, both my mind and my body. Suddenly, it seemed like I was watching and hearing everything through five feet of water.

The stretcher began moving.

"Where you taking him?" Klado asked the EMT, his voice slowed to blurry drawl.

"Hopkins," the EMT said.

"Not Hopkins," I said, though I don't know if they actually heard me. No one responded.

My mind was misfiring, but I remembered some details from my experiences with Lenny. The State could only commit you against your will for three days, provided you weren't a threat to yourself or others. That meant, in theory, I could still show up for work on Monday, or at least call in sick, without anyone knowing about my committal, provided they didn't take me to Hopkins. If they took me to Hopkins, my co-workers would find out. My work took me around the entire facility. Everybody knew me. Someone would recognize me. They would talk. My life would be over.

"Not Hopkins," I said again as they rolled me down the corridor toward the elevators.

The apartment doors opened on both sides of the corridor. My neighbors stared at me with concern. They seemed genuinely sympathetic but also strangely detached. None of them offered to help. None of them said anything to me. They just watched, like I was a TV show or something.

This was the end of my life here. They would never see me as a peer again. I was no longer one of them. From now on, I would be a freak. A curiosity.

Lenny was right. You don't really understand human beings until you're on the outside looking in.

Chapter Twenty-Nine: Committed

They brought me to Johns Hopkins Hospital despite my pleas.

I don't remember when I feel asleep, but the lights of the emergency room woke me up. They seemed to blur and follow me as I rolled past them on the stretcher. I was hallucinating. Stripes on the shirts of the people we passed glowed like neon lights. I wondered if this was what it felt like to get high on a hallucinogenic drug like LSD. I was never much of a drug user. I only smoked pot twice as a teenager, and I didn't like it. I never tried anything harder, and if this was what it was like, I'm glad I didn't bother. Who'd pay money for this? Geez.

They wheeled me into a private room. Well, perhaps room was too strong a word. It was a small, equipment-filled area cordoned off by thick curtains. It wasn't until the EMTs removed me from the stretcher and placed me in the hospital bed that I realized my handcuffs had been removed while I slept. Still, they applied restraints to hold me in bed. I tried to struggle, but all my strength was gone. Whatever they gave me really did a number on me.

After the EMTs left, a nurse came and hooked me up to the machinery of modern medicine. I didn't recognize her. I really didn't know the staff on the night shift. If I were lucky, I would be out of the ER before the day shift started. If I were really lucky, I would be released by then.

The rules slowly came back to me. I learned quite a bit about involuntary committal in the state of Maryland during my years with Lenny. You could only be held against your will in the Emergency Room for six hours. After that, they had to release you if they couldn't find a bed for you in a psychiatric unit. Man, I hated that law. Once it took us weeks to get Lenny into the hospital, only to have them release him after the six hours because all the beds were filled. Lenny ended up rampaging around for another three weeks before we got him the help he needed.

"Nurse, what time was I admitted?" I asked, hating the weakness I heard in my voice.

"It's four-thirty-two," she replied, smiling.

Four-thirty-two? I probably woke up at three like usual. Where was I for the last ninety minutes? Were they driving me around the city? Was I sitting in the waiting room? I found it extremely unsettling to lose time like that. It made you feel helpless.

"No, I need to know when I was officially admitted," I replied.

"I don't know if you are officially admitted yet, sir," she replied.

Great.

"I want to be released," I said.

"We can talk about that after the doctor examines you."

"Can you at least untie me?"

"No, I'm sorry," the nurse replied as she prepared to leave. "Can I get you something to drink?"

"No," I said defiantly, but after she left, I wished I hadn't. The offer itself made me thirsty, but I wasn't about to shout for her. Shouting would only make me appear like a lunatic. I had to maintain a calm demeanor.

"You're thinking about the six-hour rule, right?" a voice asked.

I turned. It was Lenny, of course. He wasn't wearing the suit anymore. He looked sloppy, like he normally did when we got him to the emergency room. His eyes, however, were clear.

"It's not going to work," he continued. "I heard them talking down at the nurses' station. They found a bed for you at Bayview."

"They wouldn't get me a bed before they do an exam," I replied.

I knew I should not have been talking to him, but I felt it would prove less damaging to my prospects for release than confronting him. Praying the "Our Father" aloud would only make me look like a religious fanatic.

Lenny laughed. "Dude, they pulled you off a ten story balcony at three o'clock in the morning with half the city watching. That's all the examination they need," he said, before adding, "It was different with me. Most of the time I had been drinking, too. So they had to figure out whether my behavior was a result of mental illness or just alcohol."

He was right. He was always right.

"You see, you'd have been better off spending the night out drinking with your new girlfriend than hanging with those stupid priests," Lenny said. "Who knows? You might've gotten laid, too. I think she likes you."

I was tempted to ask why he felt that way. I certainly liked her, but I thought I was still locked in the friend-zone. Had he seen something I hadn't seen? I opened my mouth to speak, but I stopped myself. This was crazy. I couldn't hope to win Teri over by doing the one thing she asked me not to do.

"Don't sulk, Ricky," Lenny continued, moving closer. "Bayview has a pretty good unit, as nuthouses go. It's nicer and cleaner than here, and a hundred percent better than Shepherd Pratt. They house some real homicidal maniacs. Stay away from there."

"I will," I answered, despite myself.

"Take some advice from someone who knows," he continued. "Don't argue with the staff. You'll want to, but don't. They're not going to believe you anyway. And take the pills. If you don't, they'll think you don't want to get better, and you can end up in the deep freeze. You can always stop taking them later."

Lenny stopped suddenly. He had his ear cocked as if he were listening to something. After a moment, he turned back to me. "I better go. Janet's coming."

I cringed. Great. The last thing in the world I needed was Janet seeing me like this now.

"Just reassure the docs you're no threat to yourself or others, and you'll be out in three days," he said. "And whatever you do, don't tell Janet you saw me. She won't believe you."

"I don't even believe it," I replied, but he was gone before I finished.

Lenny was replaced by the sound of hurried footsteps. My eyes followed the sound to an opening between the curtains. Janet stepped inside. She looked a mess. Her clothes were a thrown together, and her eyes were red. I hated to see her like that. It kind of made me wish I had died, but I had to look on the bright side. They obviously called Janet because she was my legal next of kin. Her voice would weigh heavily with the authorities. I had to convince her that I was calm and reliable, but, in my drugged state, emotions overwhelmed reason. "Janet, you've got to get me out of here now," I bluntly pleaded, my voice cracking.

"Damn you, Rick," she said as the sorrow in her eyes switched to anger instantly. "I hope they lock you away."

"Janet, it's not what you think."

"What the hell was it then?" she replied. "The police said they pulled you off your balcony."

"I was sleepwalking," I answered.

"Were you sleepwalking at the Harbor, too?" she asked.

"No, I was trying to rescue Mom."

Mom? I couldn't believe I actually said that. Damn! Whatever they gave me certainly loosened my tongue. I had to watch myself.

"Mom?" Janet asked, confused.

"The woman I saw jump in the water kind of looked like Mom from behind," I stuttered, compounding my problem.

"I thought you said no one really jumped in," Janet added.

"No one did," I said, correcting myself to remain consistent with my police report. "I thought I saw someone, but she must've just stepped away or something."

An awkward silence followed, broken only by the beeps and chirps of the machines attached to me. I could tell Janet was trying to calm herself. After a moment, she took a seat beside me "What's going on, Rick?"

"I'm not trying to kill myself," I said as firmly as my drugged-out voice would permit. "I swear."

"If you did, it would be a really crappy thing to do to me," she said. "You know that, right?"

"I wouldn't be doing myself any favors, either."

Janet just stared at me. Unconvinced. I had to try another tactic.

"Have you been following the Orioles?" I asked. "They're leading the league. Do you think I would kill myself and miss the opportunity to see them in the World Series?"

Janet smiled despite herself. "Only you would come up with something like that."

"Janet, seriously, you remember what Lenny was like when he was crazy?"

She nodded yes.

"Now, forgetting about this week, have I been behaving like him?"

"Not that I'm aware of," she answered. "But before Monday, I haven't seen you in three months. For all I know you've been crazy the whole time."

"But I'm not."

"Then what's going on?"

I wish I could tell her. She was my sister. If anyone had a right to know what was going on, it was her. But I knew I couldn't. One, it would make her a target. Two, it would make me sound like Lenny. I couldn't risk either.

"Was it Gina?" Janet volunteered helpfully.

No, it wasn't Gina, but clearly that was an explanation Janet could accept, so I went with it. "That's when the sleepwalking began," I answered. That was almost true.

From her expression, I could tell Janet was relieved. She just needed something understandable to get a grip on the situation. She reached out and touched my hand.

"I know it's hard," she said.

"I am happy for her," I said. "But it kind of took me by surprise."

"I understand," Janet said. "But don't you have someone now, too?"

"Yeah," I answered. "Can you call her the first thing tomorrow morning and tell her where I am?"

"You sure?" Janet asked.

"Yeah."

"Must be love," Janet said as she reached into her purse for a piece of paper and a pen. "What's her number?"

Damn it. Even after losing Teri's number on my phone in the Harbor, I didn't take the time to actually memorize the number. And I was a numbers guy.

"I don't remember. It's on my phone, and they wouldn't let me bring it," I said. "But she's on Facebook. Her name is Teri Poskocil. Teri, T-E-R-I, Poskocil, P-O-S-K-O-C-I-L."

"Got it," she said as she finished writing it down. "What do you want to tell her?"

"Anything she asks. I have no secrets from her."

"How about Gina? Do you want me to talk to her?"

"Definitely not," I replied. "This is a happy time for her. I'm not going to ruin it."

Janet was satisfied with that response.

"Could you do me another favor?" I asked.

"What?"

"Could you talk to the doctors and try to get me out of here?"

"Rick, I think it'd be best if you stayed and talked to someone," she said firmly.

"I'll get my own doctor," I responded. "I promise."

"Look, even if I wanted to get you out of here, I couldn't," she replied. "They didn't call me to ask my permission. They were calling me just to inform the next of kin."

That was that. I was headed to Bayview, and, if Lenny's experiences were any guide, the doctors would knock me out completely the first day to calm me down and then gradually bring me back to what they considered an acceptable level of coherence. I dreaded it. Drugged up like that, I would be a sitting duck. Worse still, Teri would be left alone. I just hoped the priests could protect her.

Janet stayed with me until transport arrived. It was the longest amount of time the two of us had spent alone together in years, visits from nurses and doctors notwithstanding. We didn't talk much, but I felt strangely comfortable. It also reminded me of the stakes. If Teri and I didn't succeed, Betty would eventually come for Janet's yet unborn children. I couldn't allow that to happen.

We had to end this curse now.

Chapter Thirty: The Idol

Bayview was part of the Johns Hopkins Medical System, but it was an acquisition that didn't share our reputation before we acquired it. I never visited the facility on official business. My duties kept me on the main campus on Broadway. However, I visited the hospital many times. Lenny spent most of the time he was institutionalized on its third floor.

I was reasonably rested and alert when I finally arrived at Bayview around sunrise Thursday morning. They took off my restraints when they removed me from the stretcher. New ones were not applied. Nor were they necessary. The psychiatric unit was essentially a minimum-security prison. Escape was possible, but not easy. The doors were always locked, and the orderlies were large and well trained. Lenny never even raised his voice while an orderly stood nearby. Punishment awaited those who misbehaved.

Troublemakers were sent into isolation. Everyone else was encouraged to stay in the common areas to watch television or play board games. Once, Lenny asked my mom and me to bring him our old Monopoly game to play at the facility. When he was released, he came home without it. He told our mother not to worry—he left it with some friends, and they would bring it to her when they got released. My mother wasn't pleased. One lunatic around the house was enough for her.

A nurse took blood and urine samples before sitting me down to answer some psychiatric questionnaires. Do you suffer from extreme mood changes? Are you more talkative or louder than usual? Have you lost interest in sex? Can you concentrate properly? Geez. It was one test after another. I answered them as honestly as possible, though I suspected the doctors would assume I was lying. The outward circumstances of my committal indicated I was crazy, but I wasn't insane. I was normal. Completely normal.

After the tests, I was taken to my room. It wasn't a padded cell, but it would be safe to call it a cell. The room was small, about eight feet wide and ten feet long, with one bed and no window, unless you counted the small one on the door. A nurse and two orderlies escorted me inside. You wouldn't have thought that many people could fit in the room. It was as intimidating as they no doubt intended. The nurse handed me a paper cup with three pills and a glass of water.

I had been pliant and agreeable ever since I made the mistake of trying to grab my cellphone back at my apartment. My resolve to be a good little soldier weakened as I looked at the pills in the cup. Lenny's word rang out in my ears. "You can always stop taking them later." He was right. Things would certainly go better for me if I did as I was told. It didn't take a rocket scientist to figure that out. Still, Father Mubita's words about the link between drugs and the demonic chilled me. Would I be walking right into Betty's parlor if I took the pills?

"What are these pills?" I asked.

"They'll calm you down and help you sleep," the nurse said, smiling. "You'll feel much better in the morning when you wake up."

"It's already morning," I said.

The edges of the nurse's smile dipped a little. She gave the orderlies a quick glance. The two men lazily shifted to attention as the nurse turned back to me.

"Mr. Bakos," she said. "Are you going to let us help you?"

The bigger of the two orderlies rolled his head to crack his neck. His neck, I must report, seemed twice as thick as my thigh. The internal debate came to a quick end. One way or another, I was going to be medicated. The question was whether I would do so restrained or unrestrained. I chose to be unrestrained. I took the pills and drank a sip of water. I didn't even think of trying to fake swallow them until it was too late.

The nurse smiled. She took back the glass and paper cup and said, "Say, aaahhh."

I opened my mouth to show her that I swallowed the pills. She smiled and said something. I don't remember what because my head was already swimming, and I was overcome by a profound drowsiness. I don't even know whether I fell back in bed or forward on the floor. I was just out.

After I took those pills, I became unmoored from reality and time. What was real and what was imagined was almost impossible to discern. My mind was like a deck of cards shuffled into a completely random order. Vivid dreams, or should I say dream fragments, raced through my mind without discernible order or meaning. One second I'd be fishing with my father and brother at Loch Raven Reservoir. The next second, I was in bed with Gina. Then I'd be trying to wrestle Lenny into the car to get him to the hospital. The next image would be something as simple as watching a baseball game at Camden Yards. It was weird. They say before you die your life flashes before your eyes. I suppose that was what this was like. But I didn't glean anything from it. Nothing stayed in my mind long enough for me to be happy or sad about. I felt no pride or regret.

Then I started seeing things that weren't part of my life. Little flashes of people and places I didn't recognize. It wasn't like a movie or photographs. I saw real people in real life, just not my life, at least not at first. The vignettes got longer and longer, but none of them seemed connected to me. At first the images were innocent. For example, I saw a woman in a wig putting on makeup in candlelight, two kids playing on a rope swing, and a man in a suit from the twenties shoveling snow. Then images of death and mayhem became interspersed with the more innocent ones. I saw a man strangle a woman with a wool scarf, and then I saw a soldier kill an enemy with a bayonet on some long, forgotten battlefield. When I saw a man hang himself on a construction site, even in my drugged state, I knew where this was headed, and I didn't like it.

The images finally slowed to real time in my mother's large, second-floor bedroom in our home on St. Helens Street. The lights were on. So was the television. Some Randolph Scott film I didn't recognize played on Turner Classic Movies. My mother was sleeping uneasily until a coughing fit aroused her. Her face was thin and skeletal. I hated remembering her that way. I wanted to close my eyes, but I couldn't. They were already closed, or were they? Was this a dream, a vision, or had I been transported back in time? I really had no way of knowing.

My mother's eyes opened after the coughing stopped. She looked around the room as if she didn't recognize it.

"Ricky," she croaked.

Of course, there was no response. I was out with Gina, but she knew that. Well, not that I was with Gina. She said she was feeling fine and even suggested that I should go out with my friends.

"Ricky," she croaked again, this time louder.

I didn't deceive my mother on the last night of her life. I didn't specifically say whom I was seeing that evening. She may have assumed on her own that it was Bob and Mike, since they had come over and visited her the previous weekend, and we had talked about getting together in her presence. I didn't dissuade her. She would have been angry if she knew I was seeing Gina, but she didn't ask, and I didn't tell her.

"God, where are you?" she muttered under her breath.

From her tone of voice, I assumed she was talking about me and not the Almighty.

My mother's hand reached out from under the blanket toward her nightstand. She got a hold of her cellphone, but it slipped free and fell to the floor.

"Damn it," she said.

My mother threw back her covers a bit and leaned over the side of the bed. She reached down, but because the height of her antique bed frame, she was barely able to touch it with her fingertips. When she did, she inadvertently pushed it under the bed.

"Damn it," she said softly.

She leaned further over the bed. She remained motionless for a long moment as if she was deciding whether or not it was worth getting up to retrieve the cellphone. With a long sigh, my mother eventually collapsed back into her bed. She turned her glassy eyes to the television and watched the movie.

After a moment, my mother turned to her nightstand. She reached for the yellow, plastic prescription bottle that held her oxytocin. The lid was already off. Then, without any further ado, she poured all of the pills into her mouth. Then, slowly, she worked her way through all of her medicines. Putting the last bottle back on the nightstand, she grabbed a glass of water. She brought it over to her mouth, but it was empty. She put the glass back on the nightstand as she began loudly crunching on the pills, trying to summon up enough saliva to swallow them.

Death came mercifully quicker than I expected. Another coughing fit began as soon as she stopped chewing. When it stopped, her head tilted to her side. Drooling slightly, she gave a few final wheezing breaths, and then she softly said, "Ricky."

Silence followed. She was gone to wherever the supposedly-merciful God sent people who died committing a mortal sin.

I wish I could have cried, but it was like I had no tears in this nether realm. My anguish was greater now than it had been when I found her dead or even at her funeral because I knew now how easily her death could have been averted.

Had I been home, she wouldn't have taken her life. Had she not dropped her phone, she probably wouldn't have taken her life. Had she found the movie on television more engaging, she probably wouldn't have taken her life. It would have been so easy to prevent her death. It shouldn't have happened.

Suddenly, I found myself being pulled backwards at an impossible speed into the blackness until the light of my mother's bedroom was little more than a tiny dot in the distance. Before I had the opportunity to consider where I was, I found myself being pushed forward again in another room.

I had never been in this room before, but I knew where I was immediately—the sixth floor of the Sand Castle Motel in Ocean City, Maryland. Beer cans littered the floor, along with plastic bags filled with clothes. Early Van Morrison blared from a boom box while my brother Lenny paced around the room with long, determined strides like a caged animal. He wore blue jeans, boots, and a Jack Daniels T-Shirt. His eyes were wild, and his hair was disheveled. His lips muttered some phrase repeatedly that I couldn't make out over the music.

The sound of someone banging on the door could be heard. A voice followed. "Mr. Bakos, you have to turn down the music! We're getting complaints."

Lenny gave the door a quick glance.

"Mr. Bakos, the police are on the way!" the voice shouted.

That was it. Lenny stopped. He glanced at the door as the banging continued. Then he turned to the open sliding door to the balcony. He suddenly charged toward it, running through the open door. When he reached the railing of the balcony, he grabbed the top with both hands, lifted himself up, and swung his legs over in a single move, the way we used to hop chain-link fences when we were kids. Once Lenny was free of the building, he extended his arms as if he intending to fly and dropped out of sight.

As heart wrenching as the scene was, I was relieved that I didn't actually see him die—or see his corpse. Neither my mother nor myself saw his dead body. The police identified him through his fingerprints. When the body was brought to the funeral home in Baltimore, my mother asked to see it, but the funeral director advised against it. He said the damage was too severe. I requested his autopsy and toxicology reports for genealogical purposes, but I couldn't bear to read more than a few sentences before I threw them away. It was too horrible.

Once again, I was suddenly yanked back into the darkness. When I was pushed forward again, I found myself poolside at the Sand Castle Motel. Lenny laid face down on the concrete a few feet from the lip of the large swimming pool. He had hit concrete with his forehead. His head had exploded like a ripe watermelon, splattering brain and gore across a wide area. Thank God the funeral director wouldn't let my mother see the body. She would have died then and there. I didn't know how I would ever be able to unsee this.

Poor Lenny.

God, he didn't deserve this fate.

Mercifully, the unseen hand yanked me out of this grisly vision. As I was pushed forward again, I hoped to find myself asleep in my hospital bed, but no such luck. Instead, I found myself on the stern of a large, rented fishing boat. The sun hung just above the horizon as the ship headed north, back up the Chesapeake Bay towards Annapolis. The coolers were filled with Rockfish and emptied of beer.

Most of the men, in their long slacks and button-down short-sleeve shirts stood around the wheel laughing and drinking with the captain. One man sat on the edge of the stern with his back toward the Bay. I never met him, but I recognized him from our family photos. It was my great-uncle

John Franklin Bakos, pipefitter, fisherman, confirmed bachelor—who committed suicide.

He sat watching the others. Nothing in his expression indicated a desire to join them in their laughter. Nor did I see any regret. Whatever he was thinking in those last moments was hidden away deep in his heart. He uttered no words and surrendered no clues to his decision as he gently pushed up with his feet and fell backwards into the water. You wouldn't have heard the splash above the sound of the engine unless you had been specifically listening for it. The others weren't. I heard they didn't realize he was gone until they were practically back to the dock.

I wish I had had the chance to meet him.

Before I had a chance to contemplate Uncle John's fate any further, I was yanked back and forth again in space and time. This time I found myself somewhere I had been—inside the family home on Evergreen Avenue. It was at the top of a hill in Hamilton, the neighborhood I grew up in. My great-grandfather moved the family into the modest Cape Cod home after they fled Chapel Street around 1934. At the time, the surrounding area was still dotted with small farms and pastures. The real housing boom didn't begin until after World War II. That's when this vision took place.

I found myself in the middle bedroom on the second floor. My great-uncle Norbert was putting on his old uniform. He served in the 79th Infantry Division, the Cross of Lorraine, during the Second World War. He saw some very heavy action and had won the Bronze Star and two Purple Hearts. Now I watched him put on his old uniform one last time, in 1948. He had a hard time getting all the buttons buttoned over his belly, but he silently persevered until he finished. Then he went to the top drawer of his dresser and took out his medals. He stood in front of the mirror and pinned his medals on his chest. He gave them a pat when he was finished and walked over to the closet. He pulled down a cardboard box filled with battlefield souvenirs from Germany.

Removing a German Lugar from the box, he checked the clip before he sat down at the edge of the bed. I knew what was going to happen next.

"Don't," I shouted.

Uncle Norbert couldn't hear me. In a precise military fashion, he put the barrel of the Lugar in his mouth. He wrapped his lips around it and pulled the trigger. The back of his head disappeared in a red mist. His lifeless body hunched forward slightly as his hand lost its grip on the pistol. Then he fell over on his side on the bed.

Another life snuffed out, but it wasn't the end of the show. I was yanked back into the darkness again. When I pushed back into the light, I found myself on a busy street in Baltimore, sometime in the past. I wasn't a car nut, so I couldn't discern the year from the vehicles around me, but I had my suspicions. All my visions shared the common theme of suicide, and there was one more to go in my family.

I recognized the intersection since it was only a few blocks from Johns Hopkins Hospital at Broadway and Lombard Street. The date had to be May 8, 1932, the day of my great-grandmother Kristina Bakos' death. There was no other reason to transport me to this location. I expected to see her, but I didn't. I instinctively turned to look for her, and I was surprised that I could move this time. In the other visions, I had been locked into a stationary position. After a moment, I spotted her about a half a block away, down the busy street. I trotted quickly toward her.

Her hair was wrapped up in a babushka, and she was wearing an ankle length dress more suited to Bohemia than Baltimore. She was only forty-seven at the time, but she easily looked twenty years older. Her gait was unsteady, zombie-like, but no one seemed to notice or care. Where was her family? Why did they leave her alone in the midst of her grief?

Moving through the Baltimore streets of 1932 was surreal. The air was hotter than I expected for that day in early May. No clouds. I didn't see a lot of smog, but the smell of smoke and exhaust emissions was much more omnipresent. Everything, the buildings, the vehicles and the people, looked like they were from an old newsreel, but in vivid color. In other circumstances, I would have reveled in the opportunity to explore this world, but my great-grandmother had my entire attention. She was walking south toward her home on Chapel Street. I was gaining on her. I was only about fifteen yards away when I heard a child's voice say, "Matka!"

That was one Bohemian word I knew. It meant mother.

Kristina's head shot in the direction of the voice. So did mine.

Across the street, I saw the recently-deceased eight-year-old Vincent Bakos, dressed in his little burial suit, waving to his mother.

"Vincent," Kristina exclaimed in her thick Bohemian accent.

Vincent opened up his arms to her. She started toward him. I turned from her to the oncoming traffic. A large truck rattled along its way in the second northbound lane from the sidewalk. I knew what was going to happen, and I knew I had to stop it—or die trying.

The unsteadiness of Kristina's recent gait belied how quickly she was capable of moving when she wanted to do so. She charged into the street in the direction of her dead son. I sprinted into the street, too, hoping to intercept her before she reached the path of the truck. It was a losing battle from the start. I was just too far away. I heard the brakes on the rumbling truck begin to screech. Kristina turned to the threat as I made a desperate leap. Throwing myself forward toward my doomed great-grandmother, my right hand managed to reach the bottom of her dress. I might have actually been able to yank her back out of the path of the truck if I made true physical contact, but my hand went right through the material.

I fell to the street as the truck horn blared. I watched the truck knock her off her feet. I don't know how far she flew into the air before she fell back to the ground, but from my vantage point, I could see her bounce up and down between the asphalt and the bottom of the truck. She was a tangled, bloody pulp by the time the truck finally skidded to a final stop. To make matters worse, if that were possible, an automobile crushed her head before it slid sideways and slammed into the truck.

Of all the visions, this one was the worst and most brutal. I don't know why. I never met her. Even had she lived to a ripe old age, I would have never known her. Still, in a very real sense, I came from her. She was the matriarch of our whole family. She didn't deserve this death. And it wasn't suicide. It was a trick.

She was murdered.

I turned back to Vincent, but he wasn't there anymore. Instead, I found Betty enjoying her handiwork—not Anna Jindra, her contemporaneous grandmother. Betty herself. They were one and the same, different skins on the same monstrous snake. Betty turned to me. She, alone in this dream world, could see me, and she gave that small smug smile from the photo on her grave. These visions were her way of displaying her power, and she wasn't done yet.

Betty raised and crooked her finger for me to come. I tried to resist, but this was her world, not mine. I felt myself propelled toward her and through her into the dark void again. When I fell back into the light, I had no idea where or *when* I was.

I found myself in the main room of a stone, torch-lit temple crowded with people. The ceiling seemed to be about forty feet high supported by rows of pillars lining both sides of the room. Worshippers dressed in tunics and robes filled the large hall and swayed in a strangely sensual religious fervor. The people appeared Middle Eastern in appearance, but I had no idea what country. Some of them sang while others moaned to the low, rhythmic sound of horns and drums. A dense smoke, smelling of both incense and marijuana, permeated the entire building. I began coughing at first before a feeling of euphoria began to overwhelm me. I turned to the altar, which sat on a raised dais at the end of the room. A team of priests, garbed in white robes coated with blood, sacrificed a cow.

Beyond them stood a twelve-foot statue of a woman on a pedestal. The idol was made of stone, but it wasn't as finely finished as the classical Greek statuary I remembered from my history classes. However, the level of detail on this statue seemed greater than the statues I remembered from Ancient Egypt. Where was I? How long ago was this? Three thousand years? Five thousand years?

The intoxicating smoke billowed out of large bronze censers on either side of the idol. I watched the dark plumes rise into the air. As I did, I saw what appeared to be dark, hideous shapes hiding within the smoke. Looking around I saw them everywhere, hovering above the eager supplicants. Every so often, one of the swarming shapes would dive down through the smoke into the open mouth of a person. Once it entered, the worshipper would shake convulsively and start emitting high-pitched utterances.

I turned back to the idol to find that its head had moved. Its crudely carved eyeholes now faced me. Slowly, the stone became flesh. The face morphed quickly from one person to another: some male, some female, some black, some white, and some Asian. Hundreds, no, thousands, of faces were revealed before it came to rest upon Anna, and then it slowly morphed to Betty.

Then, to my horror, the idol took on my own face.

She was inside *me* now.

Chapter Thirty-One: Humiliation

I don't know how many hours of drug-induced nightmares and revelations passed before I first stirred in my sleep.

With no outdoor windows, my room didn't allow for the natural passage of time, much like the floor of a casino. I felt trapped in an unyielding, perpetual now. Dim overhead fluorescent lights illuminated the room along with the constant light from the corridor. All I remembered was being pulled out of the dark void by the sound of a wordless lullaby that took me back almost as far as the womb. I opened my eyes to find myself in bed with my head resting in my mother's lap. I turned and looked up at her. She looked like she was about twenty-five or twenty-six-years-old, before the horrors of life stole the joy from her eyes. She smiled as she hummed and stroked my hair.

"Mom," I said weakly.

"What about her?" Janet asked.

I turned to her voice to find myself sitting at a table in the cafeteria. Janet sat beside me feeding me some soup. Before I could answer, I noticed Lenny standing behind her. He brought his finger to his lips.

"Nothing," I answered. "What day is it?"

"The tenth," Janet replied.

"What day is that?"

"Friday."

Oh, no. I had to make sure I got out of here by Monday morning, or the people at work would find out for sure what happened to me. I had to do something; I just couldn't quite remember where I worked. Many of the details of my life seemed just out of reach.

"Where do I work?" I asked.

"Don't worry," Janet answered. "I talked to your boss and told her you would be out for a while."

Closing my eyes, I thought, *Oh, no.*

"Don't worry. Everything will be alright," Lenny said.

I opened my eyes to find myself in a shower. I think I was sitting in a chair, but I wasn't sure. Someone was scrubbing me–too hard.

"Ouch," I said.

I closed my eyes again. When I opened them again, I found myself sitting up in my bed in my room. The nurse was handing me a paper cup filled with more pills. Lenny stood over her shoulder.

"Just keep taking the pills, and you'll be okay."

I took the pills.

I shook myself free of that vision to find myself sitting across from a doctor. I didn't remember his name or whether we were even formally introduced, but his words came as a shock.

"Mr. Bakos, the results of our tests indicate that you have a chemical imbalance in your brain," he said. "We're going to prescribe you medication to increase your level of serotonin."

Lenny was right. He knew I would fail the tests just like he did. But I wasn't like him. I wasn't bipolar. I was a normal, happy guy until I took that picture.

"I'm not crazy," I said.

"Mr. Bakos, that term is an ugly throwback to a time before we understood mental illness," the doctor explained. "People attach a stigma to bipolar disorder when they shouldn't. It's no different than having a broken leg or the measles. They are all conditions that simply need to be treated in order to allow a person to return to their fullest potential."

"No, you don't understand," I said, as I stood up wobbly. "There's nothing wrong with me."

Two large, strong hands firmly grabbed my shoulders from behind and forced me back down into my seat, which I discovered was a wheelchair. The doctor's eyes rose to the person behind me.

"Take Mr. Bakos back to his room."

I don't know how many times Janet visited me, but it seemed like she was there every time I woke up and found myself in the cafeteria or common area. My first question always seemed to be what day was it. I was pretty loopy. I also constantly asked about Teri. I was worried to death about her. I knew she still had Father Kubera and Father Mubita to look after her, but I needed to know she was okay. Janet said she found her on Facebook. She sent her a friend request and an instant message.

When I was alone in my room, I always had Lenny and my mother for company. My mother hardly ever said a word. She seemed content just to be spending time with me. Lenny, on the other hand, was a complete chatterbox. He knew most of the older staff from his many visits and gave me the rundown on practically everyone we saw. Most it of the time it was easy not to respond. He gave most of his running commentaries while I was being wheeled around the facility. I couldn't answer without appearing insane. Back in my room, the drug-induced sleep spared me much conversation. But sleep offered no relief. I found myself at Betty's mercy in my dreams as she took me on her magic carpet rides.

If the first night was devoted to death, the second night was devoted to my humiliation on a more intimate and personal level at the hands of one Charles Allen Carson. Every time I fell asleep, I found myself in the bedroom with Chuck and Gina. Sometimes it was her apartment. Sometimes it was his place. Sometimes it was somewhere else completely. It was unbelievable. The more I saw, the more I realized I never knew Gina at all.

The Gina I dated and loved would never have sex with me standing up in a stall in the ladies' room while people washed their hands at the sink. This Gina did. Stunned, I watched her with her skirt hiked up, her legs wrapped around him, and biting his shoulder as he pounded away at her like an animal. I don't think I could have made that work even if she asked me. I don't think I was tall enough to get the right angle—or strong enough to hold her in place.

The only time Gina and I attempted to have sex in a public place was during the late-night third feature on Saturday at the Bengies Drive-In during one of those stupid *Twilight* movies that the girls loved. We were in the backseat of my Corolla. We tried to do it sitting up, but the cramped quarters made it too awkward. We resorted to the good, old reliable missionary position, but she hurt her back against the receiving end of one of the seatbelts right after we started. That was that.

When I first saw a picture of Chuck, I consoled myself that I had more hair than him. Well, let me tell you; he made up for the hair in other places. Chuck was extremely well endowed, and the angles from which Betty forced me to watch their frequent couplings only emphasized my inadequacies in comparison. But it was more than size. It was technique, too. As Teri had said, he was well versed in the art of love, but it was in their post-coital intimacy where I felt most betrayed.

After sex, Gina often took on this sweet, girlish, persona. It was all about snuggling and little nicknames and rhymes. Those moments, rather than the sex itself, were the ones I treasured most after our relationship ended. I knew she had sex with other men before me and that she had sex with other men after me, but I thought those playful, post-coital intimacies were something belonging to the two of us alone. Not so. She did the same thing with Chuck, and she even used some of the same nicknames. If watching Gina have sex with Chuck was painful, hearing her talk to him like that tore my heart apart.

Since our break-up, memories of Gina fueled my solitary sex life. In my mind, she was the pinnacle of human sexuality. Now that she had Chuck, I'm sure she never gave me a second thought. Compared to Chuck, I wasn't minor league; I was strictly sandlot. From now on, in her mind, I knew I was only going to be that funny little loser who couldn't break free of his mother.

I awoke in my cot utterly helpless and humiliated. Betty had set the table for our final showdown. The previous evening, she revealed that she was an ancient, god-like entity who killed more people than smallpox. The next night she totally emasculated me. I was nothing in comparison to Chuck, let alone her.

More importantly, what would be the point?

Even if I beat Betty, my life was over, and I knew it. I was officially diagnosed as bipolar, and everybody I knew would know it before long. I couldn't imagine going back to work. Sure, they were my friends. They would be sympathetic, but they would never really trust me again. I would be a pariah.

I was totally screwed.

At least I still had my mother.

She still had my head cradled in her lap when I woke up. I could feel her fingers gently running through my hair as she hummed that old wordless lullaby. I turned to see Lenny sitting on the floor by my bed reading a tattered paperback of Hunter S. Thompson's *Fear and Loathing in Las Vegas*. It was his favorite book, although it probably wasn't the best choice for someone in his mental state. Lenny looked up at me and smiled. I smiled back. This little family reunion was strangely reassuring. I only wished my father were here, too.

That thought made me ask, *Why wasn't he?* And what about my grandparents? Why didn't Betty ever appear as them?

For me, it was always Mom and Lenny. For Teri, it was her Uncle Hank. For Aunt Maggie, it was always her mother. Betty only seemed to appear as victims of suicide.

Why? Did their manner of death give Betty special access to them? Were they under her demonic authority now? Was this finally proof of what Father Isidore told me as a child? That people who died committing a mortal sin, like suicide, were consigned to eternal torment?

What did that mean for me?

Father Mubita said we must rely on God to beat Betty. What if I did? What if I made peace with Him? Did that mean I would join my father and grandparents in heaven but remain eternally separated from my mother and brother? Was God really some sort of sadistic Divine Divorce Court Judge who'd make a child choose between his parents? That was cruel, but I didn't have to contemplate it for long. Betty wasn't done. She had one more thing to show me. After an evening of sexual visions, she gave me a final one of violence.

In this final vision, I found myself walking down the buffet line at the Helping Hand Mission. I wasn't dishing out the food like a volunteer this time. I was on the receiving side of their generosity. Father Kubera was the next server, spooning out mashed potatoes. He didn't recognize me when our eyes met. Then, much to my surprise, I literally jumped over the buffet and attacked him. I saw a knife in my hands. There was blood everywhere and screams.

I looked up from Father Kubera. People fled in every direction, except Father Mubita. He stood looking at me. I got up and started toward him. Thankfully, the vision faded before I saw what happened next.

Chapter Thirty-Two: The News

Sunday.

"Feeling better, right?" Lenny asked.

I opened my eyes. I was still in my little room slash cell. Mom was gone, but Lenny was sitting on the floor near my bed.

"They're pulling you back now," he said. "They zonk you out first to get you out of the manic state, and then they stabilize you."

"I wasn't in a manic state," I answered.

"True," he answered. "But they weren't taking any chances that you'd hurt yourself. The cops did pull you off your balcony."

Thanks to you, I thought, but I let it go. I sat up. That's when I first noticed I was wearing a hospital gown. "What happened to my clothes?"

"They're long gone, bro." Lenny laughed. "They've been leading you around here bare-ass for two days."

"Even around Janet?"

"Sorry."

Great. That was just what I needed. I was sure Janet was going to find it increasingly difficult to differentiate between Lenny and myself. There was a knock at the door. I turned to the door as it opened. A smiling nurse stepped inside. "I'm glad to see you're up, Mr. Bakos," she said. "Are you ready for breakfast?"

"Yeah," I said. I was suddenly desperately hungry. I remembered eating, but it couldn't have been much.

The nurse led me in my opened-back hospital gown to the cafeteria where I was treated to scrambled eggs, sausage, toast, and orange juice, plus another paper cup of pills. The food was surprisingly good, and I had a second helping of everything. The pills weren't bad either. They didn't knock me completely on my ass this time. They just left me, as Pink Floyd would say, comfortably numb.

Janet arrived for a visit before I was finished. She brought me a bag of clothes. They were all new. She didn't know my size so she bought me some sweatpants, some T-shirts, and a pair of sandals. Thankfully, she didn't buy me any underwear. I preferred going commando to having my sister decide whether to go with boxers or briefs. I went to the nearest restroom immediately and changed, leaving my hospital gown on the floor. In those new clothes, I felt myself for the first time in days.

"You look a lot better, Rick," she said when I rejoined her.

"Thanks."

"Did you talk to the doctor?" she asked.

"Yeah, I guess."

"Did he give you a diagnosis?"

Ugh. I didn't want to go there. Not now. "I don't know," I answered. "I was pretty much out of it when we talked. I guess I'll see him again soon. Did you talk to him?"

"Yeah, but he didn't tell me anything," she answered.

I nodded. I felt sorry for her. I remember how frustrated I felt when the doctors refused to tell my mother or me anything about Lenny's condition. Now, however, I saw the situation from Lenny's point of view. I didn't want my family knowing about my bipolar diagnosis, especially since it wasn't true. Thank God for doctor patient confidentiality.

"Did you talk to Teri?" I asked, changing the subject.

"Yes," she replied. "I talked to her last night. She said she was going to come by and see you this morning."

"How'd she sound?"

"Worried."

I nodded. She was probably going out of her mind.

"I talked to Gina, too," Janet continued. "She wants to see you."

Normally, I would have jumped at the opportunity to see Gina. Even after our breakup, I always found her presence emotionally soothing, but

I couldn't take that chance now. Teri was right. I was bound to say the wrong thing if I saw her, especially after the recent visions. Just the thought of her and Chuck together had me simmering with a combustible mix of anger, jealousy, and inadequacy.

"No," I said softly. "Not now, not here."

Janet seemed surprised by my decision.

"Do you have Teri's number on you?" I asked.

"I got it on my cellphone."

"Let me call her."

"Uh…"

She looked around the room for a staff member.

"It's okay. Patients aren't allowed to have cellphones, but they are allowed to make phone calls," I said. "Lenny called us all the time when he was in here. He used to have me get cheesesteaks for him from Zorba's."

Janet reluctantly took her cellphone out of her purse. She handed it to me. "I want it back when you're done," she said.

"Sure."

I took her phone. I found Teri's number on her list of recent phone calls. I stood up and walked away to a more private area as I pushed the button. I turned back and gave Janet a reassuring smile as the phone rang. She smiled back as her fingers tapped nervously on the tabletop.

"Hello," Teri said.

"Hi, it's me," I said.

"Thank God!" she said. "How are you, Rick?"

"They had me drugged out 'til this morning, but I'm feeling better now," I answered. "Did my sister tell you what happened?"

"No, but I assume someone saw you on the balcony."

"Not someone, everyone," I answered. "There were police, the fire department, even the news."

Her tone of voice changed. "Have you been watching the news?"

"No, I've barely been awake."

"Well, don't watch the news," she warned. "Not until I talk to you."

"Why?"

"Just trust me, okay?"

"Okay," I answered.

"Now, I hope you don't mind, but I called a friend of mine whose husband is a lawyer," Teri continued. "He says you're in what they call a seventy-two hour evaluation period. After that, if the doctors decide you meet the standards for involuntary admission, you have to be given a hearing within ten days."

Ten days? That sounded like a death sentence to me. "They always released my brother after three days, and he was nuts."

"Thanks!" Lenny said, sarcastically.

I turned to see Lenny standing nearby. I raised my forefinger to my lips to silence him.

"Craig, the lawyer, can't do anything today," Teri continued. "But if they don't release you by tomorrow, he'll file a writ of *habeas corpus* with the courts. He said that almost always results in an immediate release in non-criminal cases because the facilities don't have the time or money to fight the motion."

"Thank you, thank you," I said. "But I hope that won't be necessary. I've been a good, cooperative patient. I've been taking the pills, and I'll agree to anything they say to get out."

"Good," Teri said. "Do you mind if I come down and see you?"

"Anytime," I said, and then I added, "How are you doing?"

"I've been better."

"What happened?"

"I'll tell you when I get there, okay?"

"Okay."

"Bye."

"Bye."

I took a moment to memorize Teri's phone number as I walked the cellphone back to Janet. "She sounds very nice," she said as she put the phone away.

"She's great," I said.

"The funny thing is that she seemed more relieved than surprised that you were in here," Janet said.

"Did she tell you why?"

"No," Janet answered. "She did more listening than talking."

I didn't want to go where Janet was going, so I changed the subject: "There were TV trucks out front," I said. "Was I on TV?"

"No, not you." Janet answered. Her expression immediately indicated that she felt she said too much.

"Then who?"

I could see Janet debating internally whether to tell me or not. "Come on," I said.

"Pete."

"Pete?" I asked. I didn't expect that answer.

"Yeah, you're not going to believe this, but he stabbed two priests downtown at a homeless shelter."

Oh, no. My heart sank. That was the final vision. Betty showed me the attack through Pete's eyes. "Did they die?" I asked.

"One of them did; the other one is in the hospital," Janet answered.

Teri and I were the ones who got Kubera and Mubita involved in this mess. We were responsible. Pete was just a pawn, and now his life was ruined, too.

"I knew Pete had fallen on hard times," Janet continued, "But I never imagined he'd do anything like that."

"He didn't," I answered. It was Betty.

Janet gave me a curious look. I know my words required an explanation, but obviously, I couldn't tell her. Maybe later, in the unlikely event we defeated Betty.

"Mr. Bakos?"

I turned to the voice. It was a nurse holding a clipboard. "The doctor would like to talk to you," she said with that cheery hospital voice.

I turned back to Janet. "I've got to go."

As I stood up, Janet said, "I was talking to Gina. She really wants to come down and talk to you."

"Today is not good," I said. "Tell her I'll call her later in the week."

Janet left as the nurse led me back to the same doctor who gave me the bipolar diagnosis. Now, however, I remembered him: Dr. Christopher Levin. My mother and I had spoken with him many times about Lenny. He seemed reasonably compassionate, but his adherence to the rules of confidentiality always pissed me off.

"How are you doing today?" Dr. Levin asked without getting up from his desk.

"A thousand times better," I replied honestly. "I feel like a new man."

"Good," he said.

"Doctor, do you remember me?" I asked as I sat down. "My mother and I talked to you a few times about my late brother Leonard Bakos."

"I remember your brother," Levin replied, finally looking up. "Your sister said he passed away. I was sorry to hear that."

"Yeah."

"Your sister also said that your mother took her own life as well."

"Yes, that's true," I answered. "But the circumstances were different. I don't think she was mentally ill like Lenny. I think it just came down to not having enough strength to battle the cancer anymore."

"Illness is often a triggering event in such decisions," Levin said. He studied me for a moment before he continued. "Do you remember our last conversation?"

"No, not really. I was kind of out of it."

"Well, I told you that our tests indicate that you are suffering from a bipolar disorder and that I felt you needed medication to restore your serotonin levels."

I realized this conversation wasn't a simple sharing of information. It was a test. The doctor was evaluating my response to see whether I could be trusted to take my medicine on the outside. I had to thread this needle carefully. If I was defiant, he might fight to keep me locked up. If I gave in too quickly, he might suspect I was just saying what he wanted to hear.

"Would I have to take this medicine forever?"

"Possibly."

"And if I don't, I'll end up like my brother?"

He nodded yes. I had to resist a bit.

"I don't see how this could have happened. I was normal a week ago. I swear."

"Your sister mentioned that a woman you loved recently became engaged to another man."

"That couldn't change the chemistry of my brain, could it?"

"In and of itself, no," he replied. "However, traumatic life events of that sort could trigger an episode in someone with a genetic predisposition toward bipolar disorder, like yourself." Levin opened up another file. "In addition to your mother and your brother, it seems there were other instances of bipolar depression in your father's family."

"There were instances of suicide," I replied quietly. "It wasn't necessarily bipolar depression."

I pushed back too hard. Levin lowered the file and gave me a look over the top of his glasses that seemed to say, 'Boy, are you questioning my judgment?' Behind him, Lenny stood with his head lowered and his arms crossed in front of himself indicating that I was about to crash and burn.

I lowered my eyes. "What kind of medication are we talking about?"

"I'd like to start you off with lithium carbonate to reduce any mania."

"My brother said that used to knock him out."

"Yes, it can do that," Levin said. "That's why I am also prescribing Latuda which, in addition to limiting any depression and lightening your mood, should increase your appetite and energy level."

"Are there any other treatments?" I asked, after a sufficient pause.

Levin smiled. "Let's see how you respond to these medications, and we'll go from there."

It was that easy. I left his office with a starter pack of drugs, two prescriptions, and permission to leave the facility. I used the phone at the nurses' station to call Teri. She said she would be there in about thirty minutes.

I sat down on a sofa in the common area to watch television while I waited. The local news at noon was playing. The lead story was about Pete. They reported he had hung himself during the night in central booking. Interviews with Pete's mother Darlene and an aunt followed the announcement. I had to bite my lower lip to resist the urge to cry. A sudden outburst of tears could cost me my "get out of jail free" card, but it was almost impossible not to cry. By most people's standards, Pete was just a loser and an addict, but he had a good heart. He didn't have to die like that in a prison cell, another innocent victim of Bad News Betty.

Lenny sat down beside me. "The poor bastard." he said.

And here she was to rub it in.

I loved my brother, and I wanted to say I was sorry and that I could have done more. But this thing next to me wasn't Lenny. Teri and Mubita were right. It was Betty.

"I'm not talking to you anymore," I said very quietly, barely moving my lips in case anyone was watching.

"I've heard that before."

"Our Father, who art in heaven," I began quietly. "Hallowed be Thy name."

"Don't," he said as he stood up.

"Thy kingdom come, Thy will be done. On Earth as it is in heaven."

He raised his hands in a gesture of surrender. "You can cut the crap," he said. "If you want me to go, I'll go."

I stopped and turned to him.

"Do you want me to go?" Lenny asked.

"Yeah."

"Okay, but screw you, Rick," he said. "Turning your back on me again. I thought you changed, but even here, you're still the same."

Lenny turned and walked away, giving me one final glance over his shoulder. I had seen that mix of anger and disappointment in his eyes before. I normally received it from him as I was leaving the hospital after getting him successfully locked up. I tried to never to let it show, but it always left me wracked with guilt. I felt the same way now, even though I was the one being locked up, and he was the one walking away.

I should have been a better brother.

Chapter Thirty-Three: Couples

My heart leapt when Teri finally arrived, but I have to admit she looked terrible. Her hair was disheveled, and her eyes were sunken. Her complexion was gray. She looked like she had a worse time on the outside than I had on the inside. I was concerned enough about her to delay my escape in order to sit her down for a moment.

"Are you okay?" I asked.

"I've got terrible news," she answered without meeting my eyes.

"My sister told me about Pete," I answered, not wanting go into the actual specifics now. "I know Father Kubera's dead. How is Father Mubita?"

"I saw him at the hospital last night," she answered. "He has defensive cuts on his arms–some pretty deep–but he'll be out tomorrow in time for Father Kubera's funeral."

There was a long silence before she looked up at me. "He wouldn't be dead now if we didn't talk to him. Neither would poor Pete."

I knew exactly how she felt because I felt the same way. No one was better at wallowing in guilt and self-pity than me, but we didn't have time for it now. The only way to survive was to keep moving. Father Mubita said to wait upon God. I couldn't. If I didn't keep moving, the hopelessness of the situation would overcome me.

"We didn't kill them," I said with more conviction than I felt. "Betty did, and she will continue to kill until we send her back to hell."

"But how?"

"I don't know," I answered. "But we're not going to do it from in here."

I led Teri out. The sunlight felt great on my face, despite what I was hearing. While we walked, Teri told me about her last two nights. Her prayers worked. Every time she prayed, her uncle left, but he returned every time she fell asleep. She doubted she got more than an hour or two of sleep a night since I went into the hospital.

We were nearly at Teri's car in the parking lot when I heard a familiar voice happily call my name. "Rick!"

I turned to see Gina waving to me as she leaned out of the passenger side window of a black Dodge Charger. The glare of the sun on the windshield prevented me from seeing who was driving, but I assumed it was Mr. Sex Machine himself. I closed my eyes and shook my head for a moment. This was the last thing in the world I needed. Of course Betty would arrange for Teri and Gina to arrive at the same time. She was working overtime to torment us.

"Gina?" Teri asked softly.

I nodded yes as I opened my eyes.

The car stopped about fifteen feet away from us in the middle of the lane. Gina opened her door to get out, but she suddenly leaned back into the car to talk to her companion. When she finally got out, her smile wasn't quite as natural, and she definitely eyed Teri up and down as she walked over. The magic man remained in the car.

"How are you feeling?" she asked as she gave me a genuinely warm hug.

"Much, much better," I said.

"I'm so glad," she replied sincerely. However, her expression changed as she broke off the hug and turned to Teri.

"Gina, this is my friend Teri," I said quickly.

Teri extended her hand. Gina touched it briefly. "A pleasure," Gina said in a voice oozing with condescension. "I've heard so much about you."

Teri's eyes widened, but she didn't have an immediate response.

Gina turned to me. "Can we talk for a second? Privately?"

"Sure."

I gave Teri a helpless glance as Gina, and I walked away. When we were out of earshot of Teri, Gina spoke quietly but firmly. "What are you doing with her?"

"Gina, I swear I didn't know she was Chuck's ex until Thursday when her aunt showed me one of her old wedding photos."

"Then how'd you meet?"

"On a genealogical website. Our great-grandparents are from the same village in Bohemia."

"How convenient. Who contacted who?" Gina asked.

"She contacted me first," I answered.

Gina smiled and shook her head knowingly. "Thought so."

"It's not like that. She was as surprised as I was."

"Rick, you are so naïve," she said, anger entering her voice. "You know nothing about women. Well, let me tell you something. You gotta steer clear of her."

Gina turned and motioned toward Teri who, while we had been talking, had gone over to the driver's side window of the Charger to talk with Chuck. That didn't please Gina. She turned back to me even angrier.

"I've heard nothing but horror stories about her. She used Chuck. She ran up all of his credit cards, then dumped him, and left him with all the debt."

"That's not what she said."

"I'll tell you another thing about her. She's stuck up and frigid."

That was it. Something inside of me, perhaps my good judgment, snapped. The images I saw the night before certainly didn't help either. "Just because she doesn't have sex in ladies rooms' stalls doesn't mean she's frigid," I replied, immediately regretting my words. What the hell was I thinking?

If I had any doubts about whether the images were true, Gina's expression dispelled them. Her jaw dropped. Her face turned red, first in embarrassment, and then even redder in anger. "Have you been following…"

She stopped in mid-sentence. She answered her own question as she glanced over her shoulder at Teri. "That bitch."

Talk about the Koybiashi Maru. I couldn't defend Teri without indicating that I was stalking Gina myself. How else could I possibly know about the stall? One of us had to be there. I certainly couldn't tell her about Betty. If I did, I would immediately end up back in the loony bin.

Gina turned back to me. "If you ever cared about me at all, you better break up with that stalker."

She turned and marched back toward the car. She called to Chuck as Teri backed away from the window. "Let's get out of here, Chuck."

Chuck was revving the engine before Gina got to the door. Gina turned to Teri as she got inside. "Nice meeting you," she said, pouring on the sarcasm.

Teri just lowered her eyes in response. Once Gina closed her door, the car peeled away at an inappropriate speed. I walked over to Teri. "Well, that could have gone better," I said.

"You didn't tell her about Betty?"

"No, but for some stupid reason, I mentioned something Betty showed me."

"What did she show you?"

God, why couldn't I just keep my damned mouth shut? This wasn't a subject I wanted to discuss with Teri or anyone else. Still, I suppose it was best for us to be as honest as possible with each other. We both faced the same enemy.

"I had a lot of dreams, or visions, or whatever, while I was drugged out," I said. "Last night they were all about Gina and Chuck. In bed, next to the bed, in the car, in the woods, on that stupid sofa that she'd never even let me hold a glass of water around out of fear of stains. You get the picture."

Teri nodded.

"Well, when she told me that Chuck said you were frigid…"

Teri cut me off. "Chuck said I was frigid?"

I nodded and continued while she seethed. "I'd had enough by then. So I said just because you wouldn't do something I saw her and Chuck do in a public place, that didn't mean you were frigid. Well, that really pissed her off because she assumed one of us was spying on her."

"Me," Teri said disgustedly.

"Yeah."

She simmered for a moment and then she just shrugged defiantly. "Who cares what they think, right?"

I nodded. She started walking toward her car again. I followed. "So what did you and Chuck talk about?" I asked.

"He was his typical smartass self," Teri replied. "He said, 'So you left me for a mental case.' I said, 'Yeah, he's an improvement.'" We got into the car. While we put on our seatbelts, she turned to me and said, "Don't worry about Gina. Once we deal with Betty, her relationship with Chuck will fall apart. I guarantee it. He can't hold onto a decent girl for long."

"I don't know about that," I answered quietly. "She seems to be enjoying her time with him a great deal. Much more than she did with me. He's quite a man."

Teri reached over and lifted my face until our eyes met. "If he's such a wonder, why am I here with you instead of driving off with him?" she asked with a smile.

The smile she gave me practically undid the damage Betty spent all night inflicting upon my masculinity, but the moment came to a premature end when her cellphone rang. She retrieved it from her purse and checked the Caller ID. "It's your sister," she said, handing it to me. I answered it.

"Hi, Janet," I said.

"So you're out of the hospital?" she asked. Her tone of voice told me she was both peeved and concerned.

"Yup, the doc gave me some prescriptions and sent me on my way."

"And you didn't think to call me?"

"I was going to call you when I got home."

"Well, we've got to talk," Janet said, and then she lowered her voice. "About your new friend."

"Don't worry; it's not what Gina thinks."

"Then what is it?"

"Look, it's complicated. I'll call you later," I said.

"This isn't healthy."

"I'll talk to you later, bye."

I hung up and handed the phone back to Teri. "Gina called her."

"I gather." She turned the key and started the car. "Where do you want to go?"

"I don't know," I answered. I took the prescriptions out of my pocket. "Do you think I should get these filled?"

"What do you think?"

"I don't think I need them," I answered. "But any time Lenny told me he didn't need his meds, I knew we were in trouble."

"You want to ask Father Mubita?"

"I don't want to bother him about this."

"No, we should go over and see him. He was very worried about you."

A lunatic killed his friend and stabbed him yet he was worried about me? A guy like that was definitely worth talking to.

"Okay," I answered. "Where is he?"

"Hopkins."

Great. I was spending more time at Hopkins now than when I was working.

"Okay," I said, "But can we drop by my place first so I can take a shower and change?"

"Sure."

I got another taste of Lenny's life when I stopped at the rental office to get a copy of my apartment key. Clara, the receptionist whom I amiably chatted with dozens of times, didn't know how to react to me. Her voice betrayed a slight stammer, and her hand even shook a little bit. I wasn't boring old Rick Bakos anymore. Now I was the crazy guy who tried to jump off the tenth floor balcony.

When she went to the inner office to get the key, I could hear the concerned whispers of other members of the staff. Rob, the superintendent, and Carol, the rental supervisor, even took furtive glances at me through the open door. Yes, I had disturbed the herd. I knew I had to move sooner rather than later. If I survived, that is.

I was relieved when Teri and I got to my apartment. The circus hadn't left too much of a mess. Just some furniture pushed out of place.

"This is nice," Teri said as she walked into the living room.

"Thanks. Can I get you something to drink?"

"No, thanks."

"Well, let me change," I said as I walked to the bedroom door.

I turned the handle and stepped into the door with a thud. It only moved about a quarter of an inch. I pushed against it using my shoulder this time. The door only moved about an inch this time with a screech.

"What's wrong?" Teri asked.

"The door's blocked," I said.

I slammed against the door again. Harder. This time it opened about a half a foot. I stuck my head and shoulders inside. I couldn't believe what I was seeing.

"No," I said.

"What?" Teri asked as she moved behind me.

"The furniture is still where I left it when I went to bed," I answered.

"How can that be?"

I backed up a bit and slammed against the door hard. It moved about two feet, enough for me to get inside and push past the two dressers. Teri followed me inside.

"I can't believe this," I said.

"This is how you blocked yourself in?"

I nodded.

"How you'd get out to the balcony?"

There was only one way. I turned to my bedroom window. It was wide open. A breeze was pushing the curtains. I hurried over, almost slipping on the wet floor, and looked out the window. The balcony was about five feet away.

"No, I couldn't have."

Teri joined me. She gasped audibly as she examined the distance between the window and the balcony—and the ground below. "You couldn't get there from here," she said softly.

"I'd have to hang from the window frame and swing myself over to the railing of the balcony," I said as I sank down and sat on the slick floor. "She's just playing with us. If she wanted me dead, she could have had me fall when I made the leap."

Teri closed the window with a definitive slam. Then she sat down beside me. "I don't think you're safe here," she said.

"I don't think either of us is safe anywhere anymore."

"I know, but I don't want you staying here anymore," she said firmly.

I nodded as I got to my feet. "I see a first floor hotel room in my future."

After the shower, I decided to pack enough stuff for three days, but I chuckled at the thought. Thinking I was going to live another three days was awfully optimistic. I didn't check my email, but I took my phone and charger. There were a few messages from friends, but I couldn't bring myself to listen to them as Teri drove us back downtown to Hopkins. Our trip turned out to be a bust. When we arrived at Father Mubita's room, he was gone for tests. The nurses had no idea when he would be back.

"Do you want to wait?" Teri asked as we stood in Mubita's empty room.

No. I didn't want to wait. Not anymore. I waited three days in the hospital while Betty buffeted and abused me. I was through being her pinball. Now, more than ever, I knew Betty would kill us. However, I wasn't going to take it lying down. I needed to take action somehow.

What did we need to know?

I initially felt I had done a pretty good job of genealogical detective work. Now I suspected I was just following crumbs Betty left for me. She wanted us to know about Chapel Street. She wanted us to know why she was punishing us. That was the first thing she mentioned when she spoke to us directly. I also suspected Aunt Maggie was kept alive, despite Betty's renewed strength, to tell us the story. Betty was spoon-feeding us what she wanted us to know—both in the real world and in the visions.

Then I heard that little voice again—the same one that warned me not to take the picture and upload it. The voice asked me, *What doesn't she want you to know?*

Good question. I thought back. The only information I wanted but I couldn't get was Betty's next of kin information. That information was inexplicably wiped from the internet, and the cemetery pointedly refused to supply it. "Let me check something," I said to Teri.

I sat down and googled Elisabetta Kostek. Nothing came up. Nothing.

"What are you doing?" Teri asked.

"Trying to find her next of kin, but there's nothing," I answered. "You have to wonder why. She's all about glory and exposure, yet she erases her immediate past. I think she's hiding something. Some weakness."

"There's got to be some online forum where they rate fortune tellers or something. We can post something there and see if anyone remembers her," Teri said.

"Good idea," I said, but then I retracted my words. "No, we can't do that. We can't post anything about her. I don't want to be responsible for anyone else seeking her out and looking in those eyes."

"Right, right," Teri said, nodding quickly.

"We have to head back to Eternal Faith and convince Rita to give us the information. I know she's lying. They have to have something."

"What if they don't?"

"Then we'll stake out the mausoleum. People are dropping off flowers all the time. One of them must know her."

Chapter Thirty-Four: Emile

It was about three-thirty in the afternoon, bright and sunny, when Teri and I arrived at the cemetery, but it felt like midnight on a chilly Halloween. Teri instinctively switched from air conditioning to heat in the car as soon as we entered.

The presence of the thing we called Betty had expanded beyond the mausoleum. She was everywhere now. The place smelled of death. Not that I ever smelled a decaying body, but I had smelled rancid meat, and that's what I detected here. So did Teri, but I think we were the only ones. A number of mourners were parked around the cemetery. They didn't seem to notice. They still lived in the safe, normal world.

As we wound around the narrow lanes, I suddenly remembered something. "Oh, no, it's Sunday, right?"

"Yeah," Teri replied.

"The office is closed."

"Damn it," Teri said, and then added quickly. "Let's get out of here."

"No wait," I replied, but as the office came in sight, I saw a pick-up truck parked out front. "Look, there's someone here."

We pulled in next to the truck and went to the door. We knocked. No response. We knocked again. Finally, Jose appeared and opened the door slightly. His eyes indicated he wasn't happy to see us.

"We're closed," he said.

He started to close the door, but I pushed back. "You've got to help us, or we're going to die."

Jose stared at me for a moment before he looked beyond me to Teri. He let the door open and spoke as we entered. "I don't know how I can help you when I can't even help myself," he said. "I'm next."

"What do you mean?" Teri asked.

"Four of us moved her. Mr. Farber, the boss, and me and two of my men, Manny and Nick. Mr. Farber was the first to go. He shot himself. Then Nick hung himself. Manny tried to escape. He went to live with relatives in Florida, but he died Saturday night. Drove into a bridge embankment at ninety-miles-an-hour."

Jose sat down behind Rita's desk. "The flowers don't work anymore," he continued. "She comes to me every night."

"You have to fight her," I said.

"You fight her," he replied. "I'm going to do the smart thing—buy a big, fat insurance policy while I can."

"We have a priest," Teri said.

"Nick went to a priest," Jose replied. "Lot of good it did him."

Silence. I could understand his hopelessness. I was only a few steps away from it myself and wasn't working in her shadow. Still, even if death was inevitable, we still had a choice as to how. Motioning to Teri and myself, I continued. "We might die, but we're going to die fighting. Will you help us?"

"What do you want?" he asked, looking up at me.

"Her next of kin information, and anything else you have on her," I answered.

"Okay," he said, standing up. "But I'm not responsible for what happens."

Jose headed out of the lobby. Teri and I followed him past the large room filled with the black filing cabinets. He led us instead into the manager's office. He removed a manila folder from the front drawer of the boss' desk. Obviously, Betty was receiving a lot of attention from the staff.

I opened the folder. It had everything I wanted: her death certificate, burial information, and documentation from the funeral home. Most importantly, it also listed her next of kin: Emile Kostek, her husband, and it provided his contact information.

"Can I get a copy of this?" I asked, nodding to a copier in the corner.

"Go ahead," Jose answered.

"Is her husband still alive?" I asked as I copied the documents.

"Yes," Jose answered. "He leaves flowers about three or four times a week."

"Do you ever talk to him?"

"Only once, about the reburial. He said we should burn her," Jose replied, and then added, "I wish we did."

"I wish you did, too."

I thanked Jose for the information, and Teri and I took off. The information included Emile's phone number. Teri suggested that we call him first. I said, no. I wanted to see him in person. Plus, I had to keep moving. Tasks gave me at least the illusion of control.

Betty lived in the waterfront Canton neighborhood on South Kenwood Avenue in downtown Baltimore. The once working-class area became increasing gentrified since my mother began visiting Betty. I had even considered buying a rowhouse in that area before I got my apartment in Towson, but I balked at the price tag.

Betty lived one block north of O'Donnell Street, which was a frequent destination for Gina and myself when we were dating. A number of cool restaurants and bars lined the street. I had nothing but great memories of O'Donnell Street. Now I shivered to think how Betty might have physically watched us walking the streets like a spider in the middle of her intricate web. I imagined that smug smile on her face as she patiently put all the pieces of her plan together. Now it was finally bearing fruit.

Betty's modest two-story rowhouse sat at the end of a block on South Kenwood. The adjacent house was vacant. A dusty For Sale sign sat in a window. The two houses across the street were also for sale. It was unusual to see that many vacant homes in such a trendy neighborhood, but I knew why. Teri and I both felt Betty's presence while we searched for a parking space. It wasn't as strong as it was at the cemetery, but we knew she was here, too.

"Do you want to wait here?" I asked as she squeezed her car into one of the rare parking spaces.

"No, I'm going with you," she answered quickly.

I didn't argue the point. She was entitled to go. We walked slowly to the house, side by side. Our hands brushed against each other accidently. Instinctively, our fingers wrapped around each other. We were in this together, spiritually, mentally and physically.

A sense of dread touched me when I recognized the old brown Mercedes parked in front of the corner unit. I realized I had already met Mr. Betty. He had to be the mourner who knocked the camera out of my hands. But I couldn't stop now. I had to face him again if I wanted to live.

Releasing Teri's hand, I stepped up the three marble steps to the front door. I knocked, but there was no immediate answer, at least not from the Kostek house. In the silence following my knocks, Teri and I both became aware of other eyes. We looked around to see curtains moving in nearby windows. I doubted we would have garnered as much interest if we had knocked on any other door.

I knocked again. This time I heard movement inside the Kostek house. Before long, Emile Kostek opened the front door a crack. It was him all right, but nothing in his eyes indicated that he remembered our previous encounter. He looked at the two of us with an expression betraying no emotion whatsoever. "Mr. Kostek?" I asked, already knowing the answer.

"Yes," he answered.

"We need to talk to you about your wife," I said.

He didn't answer, but he tried to slam the door instead. I instinctively stuck a foot between it and the doorjamb like some cliché door-to-door salesmen. It hurt like hell. Emile looked down at my foot, and then he met my eyes. Still, I couldn't read him.

"Please," Teri pleaded from the lower step. "She's trying to kill us."

Emile turned to her. "Then you will die," he said quietly, and then he turned back to me. "Please remove your foot."

I removed my foot, and he closed the door without further comment. I couldn't believe it. I really hoped we would find something here. It seemed like that little voice I heard was full of crap after all.

"What do we do now?" Teri asked.

I was lost. I had nothing. "Do you want to eat?" I asked.

"You can eat now?" she asked, incredulous.

"I haven't had real food, in what, three days," I answered. "I'm famished."

"Okay," she answered, stepping down from the stoop. "If you want, but I'm not eating. I'm still fasting."

"No, you're not," I replied. "You need to build up your strength."

"I'd rather be strong spiritually," she answered.

"God will understand."

I took her by the arm and guided her across the street and south toward O'Donnell Street. Almost immediately, we heard a door behind us. We turned to see Emile leave his house. He stepped down from his stoop and stopped on the sidewalk. He looked up into the sky and took a deep breath. After a moment, he turned and gave us the slightest possible nod before he started walking south on his side of the street. The nod was so imperceptible that I wasn't completely sure I really saw it.

"Did he just nod to us?" I asked Teri.

"I'm not sure," Teri whispered back.

"Well, let's follow him," I answered.

Teri and I followed a few yards behind him on our side of the street. When Emile reached O'Donnell Street, he crossed the eastbound lane and entered St. Casimir Church, which sat in the island between the east and westbound lanes of the road. Teri and I hurried across the street and went to the church. The large glass doors revealed the dark interior. Only a few lights illuminated the large sanctuary. It seemed empty.

"Wait here," I said to Teri.

I opened the door and stepped inside. My footsteps echoed as I walked through the vestibule into the dimly lit sanctuary. It took me a second to spot Emile sitting at the far end of the third pew from the back. He motioned for me to come over. I raised a hand in a gesture to wait before I hurried back to the door. I opened it for Teri, who stepped inside cautiously. As we entered the sanctuary, she blessed herself with the holy water and crossed herself. We walked over to Emile. He spoke before we sat down.

"I am sorry about your camera, but we couldn't speak there."

"But we can here?" I asked.

He nodded. "This is consecrated ground. She can neither see nor hear what we do in God's house," Emile explained, and then he added. "She'll know I talked to you. She will be angry, but I don't think she'll kill me. If she does, may God have mercy on my soul."

We sat down in the pew behind him.

"Thanks for talking to us," Teri said.

"Talk is all I have to offer," he replied. "Do you know about the flowers?"

"Yes, but I can't do it," Teri said. "It's idolatry."

"True," he answered. "She hungers for worship—worship and blood. That's what she wants, and I have given it. I tell myself that I only placate her so I will have time to destroy her, but that's not true. I offer the flowers out of fear. I hope the Lord will forgive me my weakness."

"Can she be destroyed?" I asked.

Emile smiled wearily. "You don't know what you're dealing with, do you?"

"Your wife was possessed by a devil," Teri volunteered.

"Yes," Emile said, and then he turned to me. "How can you destroy a Devil? It is an immortal being. He was alive before the first man took breath."

"He?"

"He? She? It doesn't matter," Emile answered. "It can take whatever form it chooses. Now it is my Betty."

"How'd it happen?" Teri asked.

"Was it because of her grandmother?" I interjected before he could answer.

Now Emile offered me an appreciative smile. "You've done your homework, young man," he said, nodding. "Yes, it was because of her grandmother. She brought this curse into our house. I met my Betty back in 1964. She was twenty-two, still living at home with her parents, and working as a waitress at The Palmist. She was such a beauty, long black hair, vibrant eyes. Friendly. Everybody loved her."

Friendly? Everybody loved her? Those were things I had a hard time believing.

"Are you familiar with The Palmist?" he asked.

We both shook our heads no.

"After the meal, the waitresses would read your palm. Betty loved it. She always fancied herself a fortuneteller. She said the gift ran through her family. She'd make a little money on the side reading palms and Tarot cards. But she was a fake. She just knew how to read people. I would listen sometimes and have a hard time not laughing. The people couldn't see how they were unconsciously guiding her every step of the way, but I could see it. She couldn't tell the future or talk to the dead. No one can, but God Almighty."

Teri nodded in agreement.

"It frustrated her," Emile continued. "She was good enough to leave her job as a waitress, but she sought real power, like her grandmother. She became obsessed with her. She made a shrine to an old picture of her. She lit candles and said prayers, and then she changed. Not all at once. It was gradual. I remember when I first noticed. I was in the dining room reading the sports page while she sat in the parlor with a client. She went into one of her trances, like she often did, but this time, she spoke in a different voice. Normally, she used this lower, almost male voice, but this voice was much more subtle, much less theatrical, and I couldn't believe what she said. She told the woman her husband was sleeping with his secretary. She never did anything like that. My Betty always said the key to repeat business was giving people reassuring news, but the Beast only gave her bad news. Always bad."

"Bad News Betty," I said.

He nodded.

"My Betty didn't care at first. She found it exhilarating, but she slowly began to lose control to the spirit, and as she did, she came to realize that it wasn't her grandmother after all, but a Devil."

"Do you know its name?"

"Yes," Emile answered, "But I will not say it here. It would desecrate this holy place."

"Did your wife try to get it out of her?" Teri asked.

"Not at first. She enjoyed the power too much, but it slowly began taking control of her normal life, too. My poor Betty didn't become frightened until she realized the Beast couldn't predict the future. It made the things happen. If it predicted you or your relative would die on a certain day, it or one of its minions would kill them. That's why she was never wrong. I still have all of her notebooks. She'd write down her predictions, thousands of them, and then tape the death notices next to it later."

Teri and I exchanged a glance. I saw despair in her eyes, and I wasn't far behind. I knew Betty specifically targeted the families on Chapel Street, but the degree of her general carnage astounded me.

"Once my Betty realized this was murder, not fortunetelling, she tried to break free, but it was too late. The Beast had her. I only saw occasional glimpses of her after that. The last time I saw her, for sure, was about two years before her death. We were in bed together, and I woke up in the middle of night to find her looking at me. She said, "Help me, Emile." And that was it. I don't know if I ever saw her again."

"Is that why you stayed with her? To help her?" Teri asked.

"I wish I could claim such altruism, but it would be a lie," he answered. "Yes, I wanted to save my Betty, but I obeyed the other Betty out of fear. I could deny her nothing. Still, I hoped to end her reign of terror."

"How?" I asked.

"In her lucid moments, when the Beast was elsewhere, my Betty shared its secrets with me," Emile continued. "She told me it needed a physical form to maintain power in our world. It joined with her grandmother but slowly lost its power as her grandmother's body turned to dust, leaving only a shadow of itself in images taken of her. As my wife was dying of cancer, I had an idea. I would expel it by cremating her body and destroying every image of her."

"Why didn't you?" I asked.

"The Beast made its own funeral plans. I hoped to override them, but it gave me a stroke three days before my wife died, leaving me unable to communicate or even attend the funeral."

"You can still have her cremated. You have the authority. You're the next of kin."

"Impossible. It is perfectly capable of defending itself. It would reach into my chest and stop my heart before I could finish the paperwork," Emile said, and then he leaned closer. "But I have gathered up all of the pictures of her. I went from friend to friend and relative to relative asking for them. It took years, but I have every photo of Betty ever taken in my house now, except the one on her grave. All it would take is one match to accomplish half of my plan."

Emile stood up.

"You should see them, all those pictures and books of predictions," he said. "It could prove fatal for me to invite you into my home, but I often forget to lock the back door, especially nights like tonight, when I go bowling at around six."

He started walking away. I stood up and called to him.

"Will burning her body really work?" I asked.

He turned to me. "I believe so."

"We need more than that," I said. "We'll be risking our lives."

"If what you said is true, your lives are already over," he said. "Live your remaining time as you see fit. Good day."

Then he left.

"It makes sense," I said to Teri. "It fits right in with what your aunt said about Anna's power slowly fading. That must've been while her body decayed. Then she suddenly came back as strong as ever. I bet if we knew the dates, it would correspond with the spirit entering Betty."

"What do you want to do?" Teri asked.

I checked my watch. It read: 4:45. "It's almost five," I said, "I say we stay here until six and then pay a visit to the Kostek house."

Teri sighed forlornly. "What if it's a trap?"

I believed him, but I had to take into account the fact that I *wanted* to believe him, and that may have colored my judgment. Betty was the queen of the mind game. This could all be another layer. "We have to test him," I said.

"How?"

How indeed? Then it came to me. "He said she can't see or hear what we do in here, right?"

Teri nodded.

"Let's test it."

I pulled out my cellphone and clicked on the Resting Place app. Teri moved closer, and watched as I found the Kostek memorial. With my account finally restored, a little delete button appeared again on the corner of the memorial. I gave Teri a glance; then I pressed the button. The memorial, photos and all, disappeared.

"Oh. My. God," she said.

"Double check it on your phone."

Teri quickly pulled out her phone and searched for the Kostek memorial. No trace of it remained. It was gone. "It's gone; it's really gone," she said.

"Wait a minute," I said. I went to Google and typed in her name. Pages of information showed up, including her home address. "The information was there the whole time. She was just blocking it somehow."

"Now we've proven there are limits to her power," Teri said. "She can be beaten." Teri sank down into the pew looking totally relaxed for the first time since we met. "I wish I had known about this church thing. I have keys to school. I could have spent the last couple nights sleeping in the chapel."

What a great idea. Finally we could both have a real night's sleep. "We can go there tonight," I said, before adding with a smile, "If boys are allowed."

"I'll make an exception for you," Teri replied, giving my hand a quick squeeze.

She closed her eyes and fell asleep almost instantly. I understood the peace she felt. We were both actually free of Betty for the first time since I took the picture, but I knew the sensation would be short-lived. Soon we would have to leave the church and face her fury. She, no doubt, already knew her memorial had been deleted. She killed Herb Norton to protect the memorial. I had every reason to suspect we would be punished as well.

But there was no point talking about it now. What would happen would happen, regardless of what we said. Yawning, I felt the need to sleep, too. I set the alarm on my phone for six, and then I fell asleep, too. It was my first sleep without any nightmares or visitors in what seemed like an eternity.

Chapter Thirty-Five: Predictions

The alarm sounded at six p.m.

Teri and I had slept for little more than an hour, but we both felt incredibly refreshed when we awoke. I gave Teri the opportunity to remain safely in the church while I checked out the Kostek house, but she insisted on going along with me. I wish she hadn't. I knew it would be dangerous.

I could detect the presence of Betty as soon as we stepped outside. Her scent permeated the whole square, although none of the innocent bystanders seemed to detect it. My greatest fear involved crossing O'Donnell Street. Betty seemed to enjoy destroying her enemies in automobile accidents. I didn't want us to suffer the same fate. I waited until there wasn't a single moving car in sight before I finally led Teri across the street.

We proceeded up South Kenwood Street along the same side as the Kostek house. As we passed the house, I discreetly checked through the front window. The lights were out. Emile had obviously gone bowling to establish his alibi. The house was an end unit. Teri and I turned down the side street and entered the backyard through the alley. I felt eyes on us from the neighboring houses as we stepped up onto the creaking wooden back porch. I reached for the door handle and turned it. The door was unlocked.

Teri and I stepped from the porch right into the kitchen. The room was large, but the bulky, white appliances looked like they hadn't been upgraded since the nineteen-fifties. The gas stove looked like it might have been original to the house. We closed the back door only to be overwhelmed by the smell of gasoline. A five-gallon plastic gas container sat on the table on top of a pile of old newspapers. The smell of gasoline, mixed with the rancid scent of Betty's presence, was almost unbearable.

"I can't see how he can live here," Teri said, stifling a cough.

Teri and I proceeded from the kitchen past a small half-bath into the dining room. The table and chairs were too large for the room. They seemed to be antique but weren't maintained with any particular care. A bookcase against the outer wall was filled with occult and New Age volumes, mixed with a few books about sports. None of them looked particularly old or rare. The other walls contained framed pictures of Betty and Emile. It was weird seeing her as a wife rather than a monster. It was hard to believe she was once beloved. At that moment, despite everything, I honestly felt sorry for the human part of her.

Teri and I left the dining room and entered the narrow foyer. The staircase against one wall led to the second floor. A door in the wall beneath them concealed stairs to the basement. We walked past the photos on the wall toward the front door and the inner doorway near it. In the narrow confines of the foyer, I felt like we were walking down the throat of a sleeping dragon. A sense of gloom and impending death grew with each step. Teri grabbed my upper arm, and her nails dug into my skin. I wasn't alarmed. I was grateful for the human contact.

We turned and looked into the front room when we reached the doorway. A large antique, mahogany desk sat near the curtained front windows. Back, further in the room, four seats circled a round table. That table, no doubt, was where my mother once sat to receive Betty's predictions. And now here I stood, too, and I had to wonder why. Was it my own decision? Or had she drawn me here? Either way I couldn't stop now.

"The belly of the Beast," I said quietly.

Teri nodded. She reached into her shirt and pulled out her little silver cross. She kissed it before she let it hang outside of her shirt.

I stepped into the front room first. Teri followed. I walked over to the desk. A couple of photo albums and cardboard shoeboxes of loose photographs sat on top of it. This was obviously the collection of photos Emile had painstakingly collected over the years. What did he say? He was only one match away from completely half of his plan.

Yeah, right, I thought. He wasn't one match away because he would never light it himself. He was too afraid. He wanted someone like me to do it. He even bought the gasoline to make it easier. In his own way, he was just as manipulative as his evil wife. Screw him.

I turned from the photos on the desk to a small table alongside it. A framed photograph sat in the middle surrounded by burnt candles and the petals of long-dead flowers. I recognized the woman in the photo from our visit to the Baltimore Cemetery. It was Anna Jindra. This was obviously the little altar Betty used to summon the Beast back into our world. What sympathy I felt for Betty earlier evaporated. If it weren't for her lust for supernatural power, my family would still be alive now.

"Rick, come here," Teri said softly.

I turned to see her standing in front of the bookcase lining the inner wall further back in the room. I walked over to her. Unlike the books in the other room, these books looked old and musty. The bindings were often broken, but, where they could be seen, they were often in other languages. But Teri wasn't looking at the old books. She was looking at a group of marble-covered notebooks like the ones we used in school.

I grabbed one of them at random. A large, ornate R was written by hand on the cover. I opened it up. The notebook consisted of page after page of handwritten notes with death notices and newspaper stories taped to them. I didn't bother reading any specific entry. I just flipped through the pages trying to comprehend the scale of her carnage. It was immense. Betty seemed to steal a loved one from everybody foolish enough to step into her lair.

I threw that notebook down and searched for the B one. All of the entries in the book involved surnames that began with the letter B. The names weren't listed in alphabetical order. They seemed to be listed in the chronological order in which her customers came to visit her. It took me a minute to find the name Bakos.

According to the notebook, my mother first visited Betty on March 25, 1988. She wanted to speak with her mother who had died the previous month. During the session, my "grandmother" told my mother that my father would die in July. The newspaper article about the accident that killed my father and his obituary was taped in an empty space under the prediction. My mother returned to Betty in August and became a regular, monthly customer. I couldn't bear to read the summaries of the following sessions. They were too private. It was like reading my mother's diary.

I skipped ahead to the page where I found Lenny's obituary taped. Betty accurately predicted on April 17, 1999 that Lenny would take his own life on September 14, 2010. Damn. She predicted it eleven years early. Eleven years! Talk about long-term planning. She was one patient bitch. I skipped ahead until I found an empty space. Above it, on December 12, 2010, Betty predicted I would die on June 13, 2016. I looked up from the book to Teri. "What's today's date?"

"The Twelfth," she answered.

I saw she had the P volume in her hands. Her eyes were dead. "Don't read that," I said as I reached for the book.

She backed up and turned a page out toward me. "June thirteenth."

I grabbed the book out of her hand. "Screw that, and screw…"

My voice failed me as I turned back to the bookcase and noticed the picture hanging above it. It was the eight-by-ten portrait of Betty that was used on her grave. Her eyes seemed to dance in amusement as they looked down at me, and, yes, her smile was smugger than ever. I couldn't help but think she wanted us to see the predictions so that we would know that we were still playing the game according to her rules.

"Well, if you're not going to kill us until tomorrow, that means we can do whatever we want today," I said defiantly to the picture.

I threw down the book and stepped out of the room. Teri followed me into the entranceway. "What are you doing?"

"You know what I'm doing."

We walked back to the kitchen, and I grabbed the plastic gas can. "Do you have a match?" I asked Teri.

"No, I never smoked."

I looked around. Emile conveniently left us a stack of newspapers and gas stove. "Use the stove to make a torch out of these newspapers, but wait until I'm out of the room. I don't want these fumes setting it off now."

"Okay," Teri said.

As I carried the gas can through the dining room, I couldn't help but think how shocked the people at work would be to see me burning down a house. That would probably surprise them even more than me ending up on the balcony. I'm sure Teri's students would be equally shocked to see her committing arson in Canton, too. I couldn't help but smile. We were finally taking charge of the situation.

When I got to Betty's office, I poured the gasoline liberally over the photos on her desk. Then I went over to the bookcase and knocked the well-maintained notebooks to the floor and poured gasoline on them. They would make good fuel, too. Then I heard Teri shout from the entranceway, "I got the fire!"

"Wait out there by the dining room," I shouted back.

I started pouring the gasoline on the floor, leaving a flammable trail as I retreated from the office back into the foyer. I saw Teri standing at the end of the long narrow room. The fire was burning through the newspaper quickly. Hurrying, I continued making my trail of fuel about halfway down the corridor. Then I threw the half-filled gas can back toward the front door.

"Now!" I said as I started back towards Teri.

She tossed the burning newspapers toward the end of my gasoline trail. Neither of us were experienced arsonists, so the ensuing explosion, which occurred when the fire reached the gas can by the door, caught us both by complete surprise. I was blown face first into the wall at the end of the corridor. Teri was blown back into the dining room.

I don't know if I was truly knocked unconscious, but when I became aware again, I was coughing. The air was thick with acrid smoke as flames consumed the floor and walls just feet from me. Fire was everywhere. Before I even began struggling to my feet, I heard a deafening roar, not of pain—but of anger. I watched in horror as the flames down by the broken front door joined together and took on a human-like form. Much to my horror, this creature started walking toward me.

Oh my God, I thought. Was this the actual form of the Beast itself?

As it walked toward me, shaking the floor with each fiery step, its form became more and more detailed. A narrow face took shape. It had thin lips and a long chin. I saw no eyes, just fiery, deep hollows where they belonged. More frightening was its sinewy musculature. I could tell it had the strength to tear me limb from limb, and that seemed to be its intention as it slowly raised its fiery hands toward me.

This is it, I thought. *I'm going to die.*

I couldn't imagine a worse way to do it than being dismembered by those fiery hands. Lenny was right the whole time. I should have taken the leap when I had the chance. It would have been less painful. I closed my eyes as the Beast neared me. My only prayer was that Teri would have the chance to escape as the creature devoured me.

"Run, Teri!" I shouted.

The heat of the Beast was upon me. I could feel its scalding breath. Then I suddenly heard another roar, but this time it wasn't anger but pain. I opened my eyes to see the Beast flying back against the front door where it lost its form in an explosion, becoming indistinguishable from the other flames. I looked up over my shoulder to see Teri standing in the dining room doorway holding her small cross out in front of her. She had saved me.

"Let's get out of here," she said.

I didn't need to be asked twice. She helped me to my feet, and we stumbled through the thick smoke to the back door. We tumbled out of the back door to find neighbors approaching from all directions.

A woman and a man ran up to us. "Are you okay?" the woman asked.

"Yeah," I answered.

"Then you better get out of here," she replied.

The couple steadied us and helped out of the backyard into the alley. The neighbors gathered to watch the fire in a weird silence. No one made any effort to stop us, despite the fact we were clearly leaving the burning building. Everything was so calm. The only disturbance came from a millennial couple running up the street toward the fire. They were shouting directions to 9-1-1 on a cellphone. Then the strangest thing happened. One of the neighbors grabbed the phone out of the guy's hand and threw it.

Teri and I staggered to the adjacent street where her car was parked. As she pulled away, I watched in amazement as people blocked the street behind us with their vehicles. It was just like Chapel Street. They weren't going to let the Fire Department in. They wanted the house to burn. They instinctively knew that it took fire to cleanse the world of evil.

"Thanks for saving my life," I said to Teri, as we left the carnage behind us.

She just smiled in response.

Chapter Thirty-Six: The Leopard

We needed to see Father Mubita now more than ever, so we were off to Johns Hopkins Hospital again. Still smelling of gasoline and fire and covered by grimy smudges, Teri and I stepped into Father Mubita's room to find him, arms bandaged, reading the Bible in his bed.

"We burned down Betty's house," Teri said proudly.

"I see," he responded with remarkable calm.

Teri opened her mouth to continue, but I stopped her by putting a hand on her shoulder. "We shouldn't talk here," I said, and then I turned to Mubita. "Do you think the chapel here is sufficiently blessed and consecrated?"

"If it isn't, I can make it so," he answered.

We went to the chapel. Father Mubita was perfectly capable of walking, but the nurse on duty insisted we push him in a wheelchair. While we walked, I explained how Betty was unable to hear what was said on consecrated ground, without mentioning Emile. I didn't want Betty to hear us talking about him.

"I should have thought of that myself," Father Mubita replied, shaking his head.

The hospital chapel was empty when we arrived. Mubita hopped out of the wheelchair immediately. I was relieved to find him so vigorous, aside from his normal limp. I knew we were going to need him at full capacity to survive the coming ordeal.

"Will you bow your heads?" he said to us.

Teri and I bowed our heads. Teri crossed herself. I was tempted to do so, too, but I felt it would be hypocritical.

Mubita raised his hands and prayed. "Bless, O Lord, this place built in Thy name, for Thy people who shall come into this place. Hear their prayers on high for Thy sole glory. Preserve this Thy house, O Lord, that Thy name may be invoked in it: that it may be a house of prayer and supplication for Thy people. We beg of Thy immense mercy, to visit whatever we shall visit, and bless whatever we shall bless, so that it be to the increase of our humility, the merit of Thy Saints, the flight of demons, and the entrance of angelic peace. Through Christ our Lord. Amen."

"Amen," Teri replied.

Yes. I said it, too. Mubita lowered his hands.

"Is that it?" I asked.

Mubita turned to me with a smile. "The ritual of consecration is normally performed by a bishop and takes quite a bit of time, but I think I hit the necessary points."

"Are you sure it was enough?" I asked.

He put a hand on my shoulder. "Put your faith in the mercy of the Lord, not ritual, Rick. 'For I delight in loyalty rather than sacrifice, and in the knowledge of God rather than burnt offerings,'" he said, and then pointed at Teri.

She thought for a moment. "Ezekiel?"

"No, Hosea 6:6," he answered, as he motioned to the pews. "Please."

We sat down, and I gave him a recap of the events since I saw him last. He listened intently, asking the occasional question to focus my tale. I told him about Emile's theory about how the demon was attached to Betty's body and image and how his own plan to cremate her failed. I also explained how perfectly Emile's words dovetailed with Aunt Maggie's story. Teri mentioned our predicted deaths. Mubita nodded.

"Yes, I am supposed to die tomorrow as well," he added.

"She came to you?" Teri asked.

"Yes. She came last night as the leopard."

"The leopard?" I asked.

Mubita seemed surprised. "Father Kubera didn't tell you about the leopard? That's usually the first thing he tells people about me."

Mubita lifted up his hospital gown to reveal horrible scarring on his left leg.

"A leopard did that?" I asked.

"Yes, when I was eleven," he answered. "I was raised in the capital of Zambia, Lusaka, a modern city, but we used to visit my grandfather's rural village in the East. Once, I was playing football, your soccer, with some boys there, and the ball went into the brush. When I retrieved it, the leopard sprung out on me."

"What'd you do?" I asked.

"I grabbed a stick and started hitting it. Then the other children came, shouting and waving their arms, and it released me and fled," he said. "I don't think it wanted to kill me. I had just startled it. I spent two months in the hospital learning to walk again. The men in the village killed the leopard, but it was back last night telling me that I would die tomorrow after the funeral of Father Kubera."

"What time is the funeral?" I asked.

"Twelve noon at the Church of the Annunciation, where he once served, which is located near Eternal Faith."

"He's not being buried there, is he?" Teri asked with a shiver in her voice.

"No, he is being buried at St. Joseph Cemetery," Mubita replied. "Then, sometime later in the evening, we three, the condemned, will go to Eternal Faith and burn the body of Mrs. Elizabeth Kostek and send the Beast back to hell."

He said it so calmly, with his pleasant, lilting accent, that it didn't sound insane at all. But it was. There was no other word for it. We were going to go to a cemetery and break into the mausoleum, break into a vault, open a coffin, and then burn a body. If we got caught, we'd make the national news, and not a single person would believe us. I would be sent back to the loony bin. God only knows what they would do to Teri and Father Mubita.

"Are you sure this is the right thing to do?" Teri asked.

"I have been praying for guidance, and this morning the Lord told me that you," Mubita said, turning to me, "would show us the way."

Teri, surprised, turned to me. I was surprised, too. I was the only heretic in the group, yet God left it to me to show them the way. Then again, I couldn't take any credit. That little voice got me wondering what Betty was hiding. I only wished I listened to it more often, although part of me believed these events had to play out one way or another. Had I listened, however, perhaps there would have been fewer fatalities.

"We will gather supplies tomorrow," Mubita continued, and then he turned to me. "Do you know if there is an alarm system at the mausoleum?"

"No," I answered. "I'm not even sure they lock it at night. This could be much easier or much harder than we anticipate."

"I anticipate that it will be hard," Mubita answered. "Is there anyone at the cemetery who might help us?"

"The guy today," Teri interjected.

I shook my head no as I turned from Teri back to Mubita. "The groundskeeper gave us Betty's file today, and he told me before he was tempted to burn her body when they moved it, but he's too scared to help now."

"I will pray tonight that the Lord will strengthen his heart and that, at the very least, he will turn off any alarms and unlock the door."

"I'll try to talk to him tomorrow while you're at the funeral."

"No, you will attend the funeral," Mubita replied firmly. "We must not forsake the company of believers and their prayers before we battle this creature. Remember, the battle is not against flesh and blood, but the powers and principalities of the air. We wage spiritual war, so we must strengthen our spirits first. There will be sufficient time afterwards for preparations. My major concern is your safety tonight."

"We have that taken care of," Teri answered. "I have keys to the school. We're going to spend the night in the chapel."

"Excellent!" Mubita said. Then his face soured a bit. "No offense, but I do not know your chapel. I think you would be safer in the sanctuary of an active church tonight."

"Which one?"

"The Church of the Annunciation, where we will be having the funeral tomorrow," he replied. "Father Justin Sobczak, the pastor, is a friend. I will arrange it for you."

"What about you?" Teri asked.

"I will spend my night here, in my room, and they will release me in the morning."

"Will you be safe?"

"I trust the Lord to protect me."

"What about Father Kubera?" I asked. "The Lord didn't protect him."

"I cannot tell you why Father Kubera died," Mubita answered. "He was my friend and my brother. To us, his death is a tragedy, but I know he stands in awe before the throne of God Almighty now beyond any fear or pain. I pray he pleads our case before the Lord that we might find the courage and strength to do His will."

Mubita smiled. Despite his imposing size, he had the smile of a carefree child. He had true faith. I knew he would battle Betty even if he believed he would die in the process. Anybody with the guts to beat a leopard with a stick that was gnawing on his leg certainly earned his position in the badass category. Having him in our corner gave me a lot of confidence.

I probably had more faith in him than God.

Chapter Thirty-Seven: First Choice

Teri and I finally hit the road around eight o'clock after many prayers on our behalf, courtesy of Father Mubita. I felt surrounded by a wall of supernatural protection as I left the hospital, but the feeling quickly faded. The sun had already set. The sky was a rich, deep blue above the lights of the city, but I took no pleasure in the sight. The night belonged to Betty.

Although Betty predicted Teri and I would die the next day, I couldn't discount the possibility that she might act tonight. I still believed she wanted us to see her predictions. She knew it would unnerve us to know she had planned our demise for over a decade, and she was now within a few hours of making it happen. However, her rage in the hallway seemed genuine. I think the fire surprised her, and I don't think she liked it. She had to know what our next step would be. I can't believe she would just let it happen.

Teri drove. I wish I had volunteered instead. Weakened by a lack of sleep, she wasn't very steady behind the wheel. She over-reacted wildly every time a nearby vehicle changed lanes. I couldn't blame her. Knowing how Betty used cars like bullets, I winced and twisted in my seat every time, too. I knew we wouldn't be safe until we reached the church.

We stopped by Teri's house first. It was on the way. She needed to pack for our unwanted vacation. She, at least, knew where we were going and packed something appropriate for a funeral. I had packed some slacks and a decent shirt, but I normally wore a suit to a funeral. Oh, well. I wasn't going home to get one. We were in danger every second we spent away from the church. Thankfully, Teri packed quickly. In less than five minutes, we were on our way with two sleeping bags and a couple pillows and blankets in tow.

As Father Mubita instructed, we pulled around to the back door of the large, modern church building. A very confused Father Justin met us at the door. It was clear Mubita had told him nothing about the situation, except for our need to sleep in the sanctuary. The priest offered us rooms in the attached rectory. We politely declined, and I'm glad we did. The closer I got to the sanctuary, the better I felt. Outside, I felt weighed down. Here, the pressure was gone. I could breathe easily again.

Teri crossed herself with the holy water as we entered the sanctuary. I did the same to reassure Father Justin that I held the place in sufficient esteem.

"Can we sleep on the altar?" Teri asked.

Father Justin was aghast. "I don't think that would be appropriate," he replied.

Teri quickly nodded in agreement.

Father Justin watched silently as we spread out our sleeping bags and blankets on the hardwood floor near the altar. We laid them out head-to-head, with a good amount of room between us, so Father Justin wouldn't worried that we were up to some shenanigans. I knew he wanted to ask what was going on, but he resisted the urge. The only thing he asked was "Can I get you anything to eat or drink?"

"Sure, that'd be great," I answered.

"We have a lot of food for the funeral," Father Justin replied. "But you'll have to come to the kitchen. We don't allow food in the sanctuary."

I was ready to go, but when I turned to Teri, she shook her head no and said, "Fasting."

Drat. I turned back to Father Justin. "No thanks, we're fine," I said.

"Okay," he replied, obviously more confused. "Well, we're going to need you out by around seven. That's when we'll be doing our final preparations for the funeral. It's going to be very crowded."

"I hope so," Teri said. "Father Kubera was a good man."

"You knew him?" Father Justin asked.

"Yes," she answered. "I teach at Mercy High School, where he was the chaplain."

"He loved it there," Justin said.

"We loved him, too," Teri replied quietly.

Father Justin seemed visibly relieved now that Teri had successfully established her Catholic bona fides. He could now trust his sanctuary to us. "Well, I'll be in the rectory if you need me," he said as he walked away.

"Thanks, Father," I said.

After he left, Teri sat down on her sleeping bag. I sat down on mine. It wasn't comfortable. I knocked on the floor. The sound echoed lightly around the room. I turned to Teri as I nodded to the red carpet around the pews. "Maybe we'd be more comfortable over there," I said.

"I don't think so," she said.

"I don't think so either," I said with a smile.

She reached over and gave my hand a squeeze. We shared a weary smile. It was amazing. In little over a week, Teri had gone from a competitor to the most essential and trusted person in my life. I knew she felt the same way about me. I only hoped those feelings would survive this ordeal. Our quiet little moment ended when my phone rang. I pulled it out of my pocket and looked at the Caller ID. "It's Gina," I said.

I went to answer it, but Teri grabbed my hand. "Don't answer it," she said. "It could be Betty."

"Nah, she always calls from my number," I replied.

"It could be a trick," Teri said. "Think about it. If you let her in here, even through the phone, you might desecrate the place, and we'll lose our protection."

"I'll go out to the lobby and call her back," I said. "That should be safe."

I got up and left the sanctuary. I saw a sad look on Teri's face as I pushed through the thick, wooden doors and stepped out into the lobby. Dim light from parking lot illuminated the room through the large glass doors. Fearing Betty might have corrupted my speed dial, I hand dialed Gina's number. She answered on the first ring.

"Hey, Rick," she said.

"Hey."

"How are you doing?"

"Pretty good, or should I say, much better."

"That's good," she said. "I'm just calling to apologize. I'm sorry for going off on you like that. That was wrong. Whatever psychodrama is going on between Chuck and Teri is their problem. It shouldn't come between our friendship."

"Thanks," I said. "I agree."

There was a long silence before she continued. "I wish I knew what was going on in your heart, Rick. If I knew how strongly you really felt about us, things could have been so different."

I didn't know how to reply. I hated perpetrating the fiction that her engagement sent me out on the ledge, but what good would the truth do now? If I tried to explain, she'd call Janet the second I hung up. Then Janet would be on the phone with the doctor trying to get me locked up again. No. I had to remain free, not only for my sake, but also for Teri and Father Mubita. Something told me they couldn't beat Betty alone.

I also had to consider the other side of the coin. There were other possible repercussions of the lie. How would it affect Gina if I ended up dying the next day in a manner that could be misconstrued as suicide? That was a distinct possibility. I didn't want to burden her with any unnecessary feelings of guilt. I was in a bind.

"There's one thing I want you to know, Gina, and that's that I'd never do anything to hurt you," I replied. "If something were to happen, it would have nothing to do with you."

"Don't talk like that, Ricky," she said, interrupting. "Nothing is going to happen to you."

"I know, I know," I said. "I just want you to know that when I look back on my life, you were responsible for most of the happiness I felt."

"Rick…"

"Let's be honest; you put up with a lot of crap. I know what a whiny, selfish little bastard I've been. You were always the giver."

"No, that's not true, Rick. You were always sweet to me," she replied. "Why do you think I stayed with you for so long? It wasn't for the Orioles season tickets. God, sometimes I wish Chuck was more like you."

Not when you're in bed, I couldn't help thinking.

"Like tonight, we had this huge fight…"

"Did he hit you?" I asked, interrupting.

"No, but he might as well have for all the screaming," Gina continued. "I mean, everybody fights, but I couldn't believe the words coming out of his mouth. The vicious things he was saying. After a while, I just stood there thinking that you'd never treat me like that. Never, ever, ever."

It was so good to hear Gina say that. I mostly assumed Gina's opinion of me mirrored my own sense of self-esteem, or lack thereof. When I looked back on our relationship, my biggest fear was that the years we spent together were wasted. I dreaded that I would be forgotten once Gina finally found the man of her dreams. It was unbelievably reassuring to my ego to hear that she actually weighed another man against me and found him wanting.

"You know, Rick, I would've never left if I thought we could make it work someday," she continued

"Yeah, I know that."

"Do you ever imagine us getting back together?"

"Yes, I have," I answered honestly.

"I have, too," Gina answered.

I practically sighed. Although we often talked during her rebound periods, she never confessed to wanting to get back with me.

"I've just never felt as comfortable with anyone else," she continued. "I trusted you completely. I never felt I had to hold anything back."

I closed my eyes. I could easily picture Gina on the other end of the line. Lying in bed on her stomach in a T-shirt and panties with her legs up and crossed at the ankles. I could see the sadness in her eyes and her hunger for genuine intimacy–the kind Chuck could never give her.

"I'll always remember the way you held me after we made love. It's like you never wanted to let go. I always felt so safe then, like I could say or do anything. I was at peace."

I knew exactly how she felt. Those were the memories I cherished, even more than the sex itself. That's what I missed.

"I want to feel that again, Rick," she continued, her voice softening. "With you."

I wanted to feel it, too. More than anything in the world.

Why did I let Teri drive? If I had driven, I could make up some excuse and head straight over to Gina's apartment. But now I couldn't. There was no way I could get Teri's keys without an extensive third degree. *That bitch*, I thought. I didn't owe her an explanation. Or anything for that matter. We weren't even dating.

Whoa. What the hell was I thinking?

My sudden anger toward Teri stunned me and yanked me from my reunion fantasy. Teri was no bitch. She was my partner. My lifeline. She had just saved my freaking life. And she was also right.

Teri thought the call was a trick, but it wasn't the kind she expected. She thought Betty herself would be on the other end of the line. She wasn't. This really *was* Gina. I knew that, but I also knew now that Betty was the one behind this call. She was the puppet master. She caused the fight between Gina and Chuck, and then she played on Gina's emotions to draw me away from safety.

No, I thought. There was more to it than that. This call wasn't about drawing me out into the open. As the scales fell away from my eyes, I could see Betty's goal was to crack the bond between Teri and myself. Together, we were more of a threat to her. She had to separate us, and having me run off, panting, to sleep with Gina would do the trick nicely.

No, I wouldn't do it. Nor would I even toy with the thought. I quickly backed out of the situation as gracefully as possible. I might not have met her sexual needs by the time I hung up the phone, but she certainly knew she still had a friend she could count on. And I knew that's all we would ever be.

"You're nuts, bro."

I turned to see Lenny standing outside the glass front doors of the church. "That was a total freebie," he said with a smile. "And, trust me; she is much improved since you were with her last. It would have blown your mind."

I didn't answer him. I just turned and walked back toward the wooden doors of the sanctuary.

"You think you're going to get something from her? Not a chance!"

I opened the door and stepped inside the sanctuary.

"You'll never sleep with her, and even if you do, you'd never satisfy her. Not after Chuckie-boy," Lenny said, laughing.

When the door closed behind me, Lenny's laughter faded away. I was safe and free again. I walked up toward the altar to find Teri already asleep in her sleeping bag. Her breath was soft and gentle. Her face was relaxed. This was the most relaxed I had seen her since the day we met at Holy Redeemer Cemetery. She was so confident then. How long ago was that exactly? Nine days? Ten? It seemed like a whole lifetime ago.

I went over and sat down on my sleeping bag. I took off my shoes and slipped inside.

"Was it Gina?"

I turned to Teri. She was looking at me through sleepy eyes.

"Yeah."

"What did she want?"

"She wanted to apologize for this afternoon."

"That's nice," Teri said.

"Yeah," I replied. "She had a big fight with Chuck. She's beginning to doubt their relationship."

"See? I told you."

"Yeah," I answered.

Teri got up on her elbow and studied me in the dim light of the church. "Do you think you'll get back with her after this is over?"

I turned away. "This whole thing has changed me. It really has. I can honestly say now that I don't want to go through my life alone anymore," I answered before turning back to her. "But Gina wouldn't be my first choice, and if she's not my first choice, it wouldn't be fair to go back to her at all."

Teri reached out and took my hand. I held it until I fell asleep.

Chapter Thirty-Eight: Azardon

Monday.

Father Justin woke us up promptly at seven o'clock in the morning. You would think I would still be tired, but I was refreshed. More importantly, away from the drugs and Betty's pernicious influence, I felt completely sane for the first time in days. That thought, however, had some troubling implications. Anytime Lenny had told me he felt completely sane, I knew he was entering the manic state. I would have to watch myself for any signs of madness, but I wasn't going to fill my prescription until after we dealt with Betty.

I could tell Teri felt better, too. She was all smiles as we quickly packed up our sleeping gear and retired to separate bathrooms in the rectory to prepare for what Betty planned to be our last day of life. You would have thought that both of us would have been paralyzed with fear under that looming deadline, but the purifying light of day, as always, took the edge off Betty's predictions. I was sure the fear would return at full-force the closer the sun got to the horizon.

When Teri and I returned to the church proper, we found preparations for the noon funeral in full swing. Lay people and members of various religious orders decorated the church with flowers and banners and prepared food in the Fellowship Hall. I could tell it was going to be an enormous event attended by hundreds of people. This was news. Real news. A drug dealer getting shot on a street corner wasn't news. An innocent priest getting stabbed to death while serving the poor was definitely news. I saw four news trucks parked outside. The crews were getting ready for the show.

Teri, true to form, volunteered. She helped lay out the food in the Fellowship Hall. I helped set up folding chairs in the sanctuary and the adjacent Fellowship Hall. There was a buzz of excitement as the Archbishop of Baltimore, Daniel Grzymski, arrived. He seemed like a nice guy. Father Justin told me the Archbishop would be officiating the funeral mass. There was no sign of Father Mubita yet. I was tempted to call him, but I resisted the urge. I was sure he was okay. If he were dead, someone would have mentioned it by now.

Around eleven-twenty, Teri joined me in the sanctuary. We took seats in the last pew, as far as possible away from the door. We didn't speak. The initial euphoria of being alive and Betty-free was gone. We were both finally coming to terms with what had happened. Until now, Father Kubera's death had remained an abstract thing. Now, we were hit by the reality of what had happened. He was dead, forever, because we had gone to him for help. Teri and I both felt the guilt, but I carried an extra burden. I felt terrible for being dismissive of him as an amateur demon fighter, especially in comparison to Father Mubita. He might have had more curiosity than sense, but he laid down his life for us. I don't think I would have willingly done that for him, at least not when this started.

Teri and I didn't have much time to consider these matters privately. Practically the entire staff of Mercy High School, and many of the students, filed into the church and sought out Teri when they saw her. Their grief compounded Teri's guilt exponentially. She woke up secure and confident, but the emotional cracks began showing, and the fissures widened the more she talked with her friends. Now, not only did she have to bear the burden of Father Kubera's death, but she also felt responsible for the grief of her friends. That was one burden I didn't think I would have to endure myself until I spotted Pete's mother, Darlene and his sister, Sharon, entering the church.

I was the only one who recognized them. They walked right past the press, who were setting up their cameras in the back, without a second glance. If the reporters recognized them, they would have descended on them like vultures. Now I had to wonder what to do myself. They were right in my direct line of view. Only a slight turn of either of their heads and they would spot me. If they saw me, they would no doubt come over, and I couldn't allow that. Meeting Pete's family would be too much for Teri now. I was sure she would crack.

"Excuse me," I whispered into Teri's ear before I left to intercept Darlene and Sharon and guide them away.

I was halfway across the church when Sharon spotted me. "Rick!" she said with a smile. She moved ahead of her mother and hugged me. "What are you doing here? Do you know Father Kubera?"

"My girlfriend works over at Mercy," I answered. "She knew him." Okay, that was an evasion; I admit it, but it was better than a lie.

Darlene gave me a hug.

"I'm so sorry about Pete," I said softly. "Have you made any arrangements yet?"

"No," she answered as she finished hugging me. "They haven't released him to us yet."

"I heard you saw Pete last week," Sharon continued. "And you got in a fight."

"No, we didn't get in a fight." I answered. "I hope that wasn't his last memory of me." They waited for more. I continued. "I was thinking about Lenny, so I called Pete to talk about him. We met at Brendan's, and everything was cool at first. We were eating and a having a few beers, and then he asked for twenty bucks. I gave it to him. He went to the bar and bought something from a guy; then he went to the bathroom, and when he came back, he was…"

They both started nodding their heads.

"…a different person."

"It's the drugs," Darlene said.

"Did they make him violent?" Sharon asked.

"No, I was the angry one," I answered. "I hated seeing him like that. I mean, when I was a kid, I used to look up to Lenny and him and Charlie Woods."

"And now they're all gone," Darlene added, barely able to hold back her tears.

I put my hand on her shoulder. "I want to tell you something. That wasn't Pete who did what he did," I said. "It was his body, but it certainly wasn't his mind or his heart. You know that, right?"

Darlene burst into tears as she nodded her head.

"That's what the other priest said," Sharon added.

"What other priest?" I asked.

"I can never pronounce his name. It's Mu…."

"Mubita?"

"Yeah, that's him. The other priest from the shelter."

"He offered to officiate Pete's funeral," Darlene added.

"Wow, that's nice." I replied.

Boy, Mubita continued to rise in my estimation. Severely wounded and battling a demon, but he still has time to reach out to his attacker's family. He truly was the man.

"Will you come to his funeral?" Sharon asked.

"Definitely," I answered.

Just that moment, Father Justin walked by with another priest. Justin told him, "They're two minutes out."

I turned back to Darlene and Sharon. "We better find you some seats fast," I said.

Darlene and Sharon turned to the main sanctuary. "I don't think there's any seats left there except reserved ones," I said as I motioned toward the adjacent Fellowship Hall, "But they set up some more seats in there."

I guided them to seats. I gave them both a kiss on the cheek as I said goodbye. They were smiling. They were so happy to see me. I, of course, felt terrible knowing that Pete would still be alive now if I had not gone to talk to him about Lenny. But that was a problem for another day. If there was indeed another day for Teri, Father Mubita, and myself.

When I stepped back into the sanctuary, I noticed a little commotion near the front door as the news crews jockeyed discreetly for position. I went over and saw that the hearse had arrived. The pallbearers were positioning themselves at the back. I smiled when I saw that Father Mubita, despite his injuries, was serving as one of them. My smile left my lips, however, when I saw my brother Lenny standing in the crowd behind him. Wearing a dark blue suit, a white dress shirt and a narrow tie, Lenny was better dressed than me. He had his eyes lowered reverently and his hands crossed in front of himself. As if he knew I was looking at him, Lenny raised his eyes up a little and gave me a wink.

I retreated into the sanctuary. I made my way through the crowd and found my seat next to Teri, who seemed very tense. She leaned over and whispered in my ear. "Who were they?"

"Who?"

"The two women."

"Friends from the old neighborhood," I answered, not quite lying.

She gave me a disappointed look. She knew I was hiding something.

"It was Pete's mother and sister."

Teri nodded, then said, "I thought I recognized her from television."

"Did Father Mubita tell you he's doing Pete's funeral?'

"He's doing his funeral?" Teri asked, surprised. "I bet that'll be a comfort to them."

"It is," I replied.

Our conversation stopped when the organ music suddenly began. The large crowd hushed as the remaining mourners quickly took their seats. From the doors leading to the rectory, a long line of priests, probably fifty of them, followed Archbishop Daniel Grzymski into the sanctuary. Their varied vestments and robes bespoke the number of orders represented in the service. Some of the priests swung incense thuribles on chains. The rising smoke brought to mind the ancient pagan temple Betty showed me in her vision, but the incense here was sweeter and didn't have the same narcotic effect of the smoke in the temple.

After the priests took their places on and around the altar, the music changed, and the pallbearers brought the coffin into the sanctuary. I could tell that Teri's sorrow at seeing Father Kubera's coffin was mitigated by the sight of Father Mubita. Despite the crowd, Father Mubita's eyes found us. He gave us a quick but reassuring nod. Teri sighed with relief. I was also relieved when I was sure Lenny didn't follow them inside.

Father Mubita joined the other priests on the altar, and the service began. I often called myself The Funeral King, but I didn't deserve that crown. Back at the height of my genealogical research, I attended two or three funerals a month, but I rarely attended funeral masses. I mainly went to viewings at the funeral homes. Personally, I hated viewings. I found the open coffins creepy, an unnecessary vestige of our superstitious past. Still, I found viewings preferable to funeral masses, which forced me to view my own mortality through the eyes of the church, rather than my formerly rationalistic viewpoint. I left every funeral mass feeling I was doomed to hell, and it sometimes took me weeks to successfully reassure myself that there was no hell.

Today, however, I found the ritual quite haunting in a beautiful way. Previously, I experienced the rite from the perspective of an outsider looking in rather than an insider looking up toward God. Now I saw the purpose and meaning behind each word and gesture. If you believed in God, and if you believed in an afterlife, the funeral mass served as a profound reminder that death wasn't an end but a beginning.

Archbishop Daniel Grzymski officiated the funeral, but Father Mubita gave the heartfelt eulogy. He explained how they met in Zambia, when Father Kubera took a group of schoolgirls to his parish on a mission trip. They became close friends when Mubita was transferred to the United States. Father Mubita offered a word of comfort to every member of Father Kubera's family in attendance, most of whom he already knew. It was very moving.

Then Father Mubita moved to his more general theme. He called Father Kubera a martyr who died battling evil. He never laid the blame for his death at Pete's feet. He specifically called Pete another victim. His message worked on two levels. If you were a good social-justice Catholic, the evil that killed Father Kubera was poverty and inequality, and the powers and principalities we battled were unfettered capitalism and governmental indifference. That was the safest interpretation. Teri and I, however, knew Father Mubita wasn't speaking in metaphors. His words could be taken literally. Father Kubera actually died battling the devil. I wondered how many other people realized that.

The most awkward moment of the service came when they called the people forward for communion. When I was an unbeliever, I never considered taking communion, even for the sake of social conformity. Now I wasn't quite an unbeliever anymore. I wasn't necessarily a believer either, but I was definitely an acknowledger, which meant there were things I had to acknowledge about myself as well.

Teri started moving with the rest of our pew when our turn came, but I stood still. She gave me a disappointed look. I leaned toward her and whispered into her ear. "I haven't been to confession," I said.

Teri's eyes widened a bit. That wasn't what she expected to hear, but she gave me an understanding nod.

As Teri followed the others down to the altar, I acknowledged that if I drew strength from the church, I should honor its rules. My mind went back to old Father Isidore, who warned us against going to communion with sins on our souls. You had to go to confession first, and I hadn't been to confession since I was eight or nine years old. Back then, I didn't have much to confess. Now I suppose I had fewer sins than most people, but I definitely had some. I wasn't going to add to them by going to communion inappropriately.

After the service, Teri and I left the church to join the procession to the cemetery. The temperature was in the low nineties. Cheerful, puffy white clouds drifted across the sky, oblivious to our fate. The scent of the freshly mowed grass of the church reminded me of the carefree summers of my youth. But I was more concerned about another reminder of youth: Lenny. I knew he was there, but I didn't see him. As a result, I almost had a heart attack when Father Justin put a hand on my shoulder.

"Father Mubita asked me to give you a ride," he said.

"That's okay," I responded after catching my breath. "We have a car."

"He knows," Father Justin answered. "He wants me to drive you so that you can drive back with him."

"Okay," Teri said quickly, before I had the chance to do the same. We walked with Father Justin to his Ford Taurus.

I don't know how long the funeral procession was, but it had to be well over a mile. The only time I had personally seen one that long was for a police officer who died in the line of duty. I was pleased that Father Kubera was getting the same consideration. He had died in the line of duty as well.

The driver of the hearse had to wind us around the narrow lanes of St. Joseph Cemetery in order to get the entire procession inside. Our car was about twenty back from the hearse. By the time we reached the grave, Father Mubita and the other pallbearers already had the coffin in place over the open grave. Father Kubera's immediate family sat weeping in the front row of chairs near the grave.

Archbishop Grzymski officiated the committal ceremony. Although the funeral mass lifted my spirits, I found the committal ceremony depressing. In the church, I found it easy to imagine Father Kubera standing in heaven before

God. Out here, in the cemetery, he was just another dead body in a box, like the thousands I had memorialized on Resting Place. What little faith I possessed seemed to waver wildly. That was worrisome. I had no idea if I could count on it during the coming battle.

After the ceremony, Teri and I worked our way toward Father Mubita, who motioned toward one of the black limousines behind the hearse and said, "Come with me, please."

We followed him without any small talk. There were too many people milling about. Father Mubita opened the back door of the limousine for us. Teri entered first. As I followed her, I was shocked to find us sitting across from Archbishop Grzymski. Father Mubita got inside and closed the door behind himself. He took the seat across from us beside the Archbishop.

The Archbishop turned to the driver sitting in front of the vehicle. "Randy, could you give us a little privacy?"

"Yes, your eminence," the driver replied.

The glass partition between the driving and passenger compartment rose up. Almost immediately afterwards, the vehicle began to move. The Archbishop turned to us and said, "Father Mubita told me about your situation."

Teri sighed in relief. I must admit I was overjoyed too. Having the full weight of the Catholic Church on our side certainly evened the scales a bit.

"I want to tell you that the Archdiocese is very familiar with the late Elizabeth Kostek and her demon familiar Azardon."

I couldn't believe it. They were already on the case. They even knew the name Emile refused to speak. What shocked me was the Archbishop's willingness to say it. I let the syllables roll over my lips, but I wouldn't dare say the name.

"Under my predecessor, Father Charles Karwacki, the pastor of St. Casimir Church, began an official investigation at the request of the woman's husband and other members of the parish. He researched the case back a number of generations. He gathered a lot of information on her grandmother, Anna Jindra, from the journal of Father Josef Stegskal, the former pastor of Saint Wenceslaus Church. He also uncovered information about Anna Jindra's grandmother, Petronilla Valesova, in the Czech Republic. This demon has a long affiliation with this family."

The Archbishop paused long enough for me to ask a question. "Your honor, can we talk with Father Karwacki?"

Teri nudged me and whispered, "It's Your Excellency."

The Archbishop turned to her with a smile. "Let's make it Dan," he said, but his expression became more serious as he turned back to me. "That's not possible. Father Karwacki died before he was able to complete the investigation."

"Suicide?" I asked.

"The circumstances indicated suicide, but we know he was murdered by the evil one."

"What did you do?" Teri asked, suddenly disheartened.

"I hate to say it, but no one was willing to continue the investigation," he replied. "Then, with the subsequent death of Mrs. Kostek, it seemed unnecessary. Obviously, they, we, were wrong."

"Can you help us?" Teri asked.

"I do not have the authority to officially assist you without Vatican approval, and that could take two to three months upon the completion of the investigation."

"We don't have that long, Dan," I said.

"Yes, I am aware of that, so I have been trying to assist from behind the scenes, as it were," he replied.

Father Mubita injected himself into the conversation. "The Archbishop has been extremely helpful, particularly with the cemetery."

"Yes," The Archbishop continued. "Eternal Faith is one of five properties owned by the Stillmeadow Corporation, which specializes in non-denominational Christian cemeteries. They have always strived to maintain good relations with the Archdiocese since forty-five percent of their burials are Catholic. I called the owner, George Bonner, an acquaintance, and told him, unofficially, there was a problem at Eternal Faith. He acknowledged the problem and offered us a free hand to deal with the situation as we saw fit."

The Archbishop reached into his pocket and pulled out a scrap of paper.

"He offered us the assistance of the groundskeeper, a Mr. Jose Garcia."

"He'll be happy to hear that," I said sarcastically under my breath.

"You know him?"

I nodded.

"Excellent," the Archbishop said.

"More importantly," Father Mubita added. "The Archbishop was kind enough to arrange a prayer vigil tonight at the Basilica while we do our work. Prayer, more than anything else, will be the key to our success."

Teri nodded quickly in agreement. I no longer doubted the need for prayer. That said, however, I would have preferred if the Archbishop had somehow managed to find a flamethrower for us, unofficially, of course.

Chapter Thirty-Nine: The Recruit

When we arrived back at the Church of the Annunciation, the post-funeral repast was already underway. The limousine took us up to the front entrance of the church. We got out and followed the Archbishop into the sanctuary. When we got to the altar, the Archbishop took out a small vial of oil. One by one, starting with Father Mubita, and then Teri and myself, he anointed our foreheads with a cross and pronounced a blessing upon us.

I didn't know whether this was a formal blessing or whether it was something the Archbishop ad-libbed on the spot. He spoke about battling the evil one, but in a non-specific manner. The little ceremony managed to attract an audience in the crowded church. Both priests and civilians stood and watched from a discreet distance. When the Archbishop finished with us, one of the spectators asked if he could be blessed, too. The Archbishop agreed, but I suspected he regretted his decision when other people began lining up behind the first one. He was going to be there until he ran out of oil.

While we were walking toward the adjacent Fellowship Hall, Father Mubita took his car keys out of his pocket and tossed them to me. "Why don't you go over to the cemetery and get our new recruit," he said.

Teri gave me a worried look. She obviously didn't want us to separate. Father Mubita smiled at her. "Don't worry, he'll be safe."

"How can you be sure?" Teri asked.

"I'm not, but I have faith," he said. "Not only in God, but also in the arrogance of the Beast. She set the date for this showdown and worked toward it for over a decade. I doubt she will pick us off one by one now when she can display her full powers to us all at once."

"That doesn't necessarily reassure me," Teri replied.

"Fear not, for what can separate us from the love of God?" Father Mubita asked.

"Neither life or death, nor angels nor rulers, nor things present nor things to come, nor height nor depth, nor anything else in creation," Teri answered.

"Yes, yes!" Father Mubita replied. "When this night ends, we will be praising God; the only question is whether we will be doing it in the mausoleum or heaven itself." Then he turned back to me. "I'm afraid I am giving you an unpleasant task. I fear our recruit is more a draftee than a volunteer."

"I just hope he didn't quit his job," I answered.

"If he did, I'm sure the Lord will provide someone else," Father Mubita answered.

"I'm sure he will," I answered, actually meaning it. The more I hung around with religious people, the more I bought into their faith. I saw its value.

"Be careful," Teri said as I turned to leave.

"You, too," I replied.

I touched her hand reassuringly before I turned and left. When I got to the parking lot, I realized I didn't even ask Father Mubita what kind of car he drove. I looked at the keychain. A Buick. I just clicked repeatedly on the unlock button as I walked and waited for some blinking headlights. I spotted them on a blue, dented mid-aughts LeSabre. Father Mubita seemed to be taking his vow of poverty seriously.

Eternal Faith was only about five minutes away from the church. After the mass and blessing, I felt relatively confident about my survival until the cemetery came into sight. Betty's overpowering scent of death and decay had now expanded beyond the physical borders of the cemetery itself. I instinctively rolled up my windows and shut the vents, but it did nothing to block the stench. I found it disheartening that her power was expanding rather than receding. I hoped the destruction of her photos and her removal from Resting Place would have weakened her, but it seemed like I was wrong.

I deliberately tried not to look at the willow tree on the hill as I entered the cemetery. However, out of the corner of my eye, I saw Lenny and my mother standing over their graves. My mother wore the dress she was buried in. Lenny was wearing the suit he wore earlier to the funeral. Still, the family reunion remained incomplete. Once again, my father was absent. Why? Was he watching us all, both the damned and the condemned, from a safe perch in heaven?

The question spoke to my change of heart. The last shades of my agnosticism were gone. I no longer doubted the existence of heaven and hell. My only problem now involved the qualifications for entry. I felt heaven might be too exclusive a club for me, even if I were allowed admittance. If tortured souls like my mother and brother were denied, I didn't want to go there either.

"No," I said suddenly aloud.

I had to stop those thoughts. Even if they came naturally to me, I knew they only served Betty's purposes now.

But I now wondered whether they really were my natural thoughts. Prior to my father's death, I accepted the basic tenets of Christianity, as I understood them, despite the fear caused by Father Isidore's periodic fire and brimstone pronouncements. I said my prayers every night like a good little boy. I didn't even mind going to church with my family on Sundays. I had to wonder if I would have been a Christian if Betty hadn't twisted my personality through her predations. I had to concede that possibility. Had I given God a fair chance?

I drove straight to the office. I saw Jose's pickup parked alongside it. I smiled. That meant he had not quit his job upon receiving his assignment. Then again, perhaps he hadn't received the good news yet. I parked and stepped inside. Rita looked up from her desk as if she were expecting me.

"Is Jose in?" I asked.

"He's preparing for a burial down in the Parables section," she replied. "You can find him there."

"Thanks, " I said.

As I headed back to the door, she called to me. "Rick."

I stopped and turned to her.

"Be careful," she said.

"I will."

I left and got in my car. I rode over the Parables section of the cemetery where Jose and his team prepared a grave. They weren't very far off the road. Jose paid no attention as I drove up in Father Mubita's car. He didn't recognize me until I stopped and got out. After giving his guys some instructions, he started walking toward me. "I should kill you, but what's the point?" he said as he neared me. "We're both dead already now."

"We shouldn't talk here," I said.

"Why?" Jose asked. "She's everywhere."

"She can't hear things said in church," I replied. "Have you checked Resting Place lately?"

Jose stopped. He put out his cellphone and clicked on the Resting Place app. "Damn, you actually did it," he said, looking up at me with new respect.

"Do you have time to come with me and talk?"

"Whatever you want, Mr. Rick," Jose replied. "I got no choice. The boss told me I was supposed to work with someone today about a problem in the mausoleum. I had a feeling it was going to be you."

I turned and headed back to my car. He followed. "I'm surprised you didn't quit."

"So am I."

We got into my car. We both buckled up. "I was watching the news on TV," Jose said. "Seems like someone burned down a house in Canton."

"Heard about that," I said.

I looked over at him. He seemed disappointed I didn't say more. Turning away, he added, "She's pissed. She came to me in a dream last night and said I was going to die tonight."

"You won't be alone," I answered as I started the car.

The crowd at the repast for Father Kubera had diminished by the time we got back. Jose crossed himself with holy water as he entered the sanctuary. I was glad to see he was Catholic. That made it more likely he would follow Father Mubita.

The Archbishop was gone, but people still milled around the sanctuary. I'm sure Father Mubita would have preferred to meet in the privacy of the rectory, but safety dictated we huddle near the altar instead. Father Mubita, speaking in hushed tones, explained the situation and the plan quickly to Jose, with little comment from Teri or myself.

"We would greatly appreciate whatever assistance you could grant us, Mr. Garcia," Father Mubita said in conclusion. "However, considering the danger, we would understand if you preferred not to participate. In the end, all we ask is that you leave the gate to the cemetery and the door to mausoleum open tonight. We will take care of the rest."

Jose considered the proposal, and us, for a long moment before he replied. "I gotta go with you," he said in resignation. "No offense, Father, but none of you look like you know your asses from your elbows when it comes to cemeteries. If you blow it, she's going kill me anyway, just for opening the door. I might as well go with you and make sure it gets done right."

"Thank you, sir," Father Mubita said with a smile.

Teri gave me a smile and squeezed my hand. I was happy, too. Jose always impressed me with his devotion to duty at the cemetery. We needed someone like him.

"We must remember, as always, that our battle tonight is spiritual," Father Mubita continued. "To prepare myself, I have made my confession, and I strongly suggest that each of you do the same."

Yikes. When Teri first suggested contacting Father Kubera, I feared it would come down to this: accepting Catholicism again. A week ago, I would have never submitted. Now I recognized the value. We couldn't win without God. However, needing God and loving God were entirely two different things. I needed God, and I was prepared to accept Him. I wasn't, however, prepared to love Him, despite my suspicions that Betty had insidiously colored my perceptions.

Oh well. One way or another I knew I had to make my confession. I started to raise my hand to volunteer, but Teri beat me to the punch.

"Will you hear my confession?" she asked.

"Of course," Father Mubita answered.

He stood and motioned to one of the old school confessionals along the side of the sanctuary. They walked over to it and disappeared out of sight. Jose glanced at his watch and then turned to me. "We should get our supplies now," he said. "There's a hardware store down the street that should have everything we need."

Taking Father Mubita's car, we drove over to the nearby mom and pop hardware store. Once inside, Jose grabbed a shopping cart and took the lead. First, he grabbed two five-gallon plastic gasoline containers. Ten gallons. That seemed excessive to me. "Don't you think we're overdoing it?" I asked.

He gave me an annoyed look. "Have you ever burned a body before?" he asked.

"No." I replied.

"Well I have," he explained. "The last place I worked had a crematorium onsite. It takes a lot of heat for a long time to burn a body to ash."

"Okay," I said, nodding. Next he grabbed two metal buckets. "What are they for?" I asked.

"You think she's just going to let us pour gasoline on her?" he asked. "She's alive in there. I know it. I could feel her eyes on me. We're going to have to fill these up with gas and toss it on her before we light her up."

Speaking of fire, I grabbed one of those butane grill lighters from a nearby shelf and put it in the cart. Jose looked at it with bemusement as he lifted it up. "What? We having a cookout?" Jose said as he put the lighter back on the shelf. He pulled a cigarette lighter out of his pocket and lit it. "You think she's going to let you walk up to her with something like this?" Jose blew out the flame. "Now you're dead. And so am I and the priest and your pretty girl." He walked down the aisle and pulled a road flare down from a shelf. "There's no way she's going to blow out this bad boy," he said.

I smiled. He grabbed four more and threw them into the cart. We quickly finished shopping without further comment from myself. Jose picked up two screwdrivers, two hammers, and a crowbar. I have to admit he knew more about how to accomplish the mission than I did. I would have been satisfied with a couple containers of gasoline and a few matches. I hadn't even thought about how we were going to open the vault itself.

Jose was definitely proving his worth.

Chapter Forty: Deliberate Consent

Jose and I filled up the gasoline containers on the way back to the church. The parking lot had emptied out considerably by the time we returned. However, I did see one unwelcome visitor standing near the front door of the church. It was Lenny, dressed in a suit and smiling. Jose fearfully stiffened in his seat when his eyes drifted over to the door.

"Manny," he said softly.

"Manny?" I asked.

Jose shook his head. "Yes," he answered as his tough composure melted. "My friend. He killed himself in Florida."

"No, that's my brother Lenny," I replied.

Jose looked at me like I was crazy. "No, it's Manny."

"No, it's Betty," I said firmly.

We were both looking at the same entity and seeing different people. That proved to me, once and for all, that I wasn't seeing Lenny. It was never him. It was Betty. Always Betty.

Man, what kind of fool was I? How many times had Teri and Father Mubita told me not to talk to him, but, no, I never listened. Idiot.

I gave Betty a wide berth. I pulled around to the rear of the church. We left the supplies in the car. When we got inside, Jose went to the front door. His cocky composure returned once Betty was nowhere to be seen. I was glad to find Teri and Father Mubita still in the confessional when we returned to the sanctuary. I knew Teri would be worried if she got out and we were gone. Still, I had to wonder why her confession was taking so long. How many sins did she have to confess?

Jose seemed surprised, too. "Is she your girlfriend?" he asked me.

I nodded.

"She's busting you in there, man," he said. "The priest is gonna be on your ass."

I smiled. Just then, Teri emerged from behind the curtain. Her eyes were red with tears. She barely gave us a glance before she headed to the front pew and knelt in prayer. That didn't look good. Father Mubita must have put her through the wringer.

Father Mubita stepped out of the confessional and turned to us.

"Heads or tails?" Jose whispered.

I turned to him. He had a quarter in his hand.

"Heads," I said.

He flipped the coin. It came up tails. "I guess you're next," he said with a smile.

"I guess so," I said as I started walking toward the confessional. "You may want to go and get something to eat. I might be in there a long while."

I stepped behind the curtain and sat down. I could see Father Mubita's profile on the other side of the screen. "Bless me, father, for I have sinned," I said, after I crossed myself. "It's been thirty, thirty-one, years since my last confession."

"That's a long time, Rick," Father Mubita replied.

"Yeah," I answered. "I don't know where to start. I mean, how do you want to do it? Do you want to hear my sins chronologically? Or the worst first?"

"Let us start with the worst," he replied.

Theologically, I didn't know what my worst sin was, but I knew what I felt most guilty about. "I left my mother alone the night she killed herself," I said quietly.

"Were you afraid your mother might kill herself?"

"No," I answered. "She just had a couple of good days. That why I thought it was okay to go out."

"So your worst sin is a sin of omission, not commission?"

I couldn't believe Mubita was downplaying my worst sin. "No, I wouldn't say that," I answered defensively. "I honestly believe she wouldn't have died that night if I chose to stay at home. In the vision Betty showed me…"

"Do not believe the Beast," Father Mubita said firmly, interrupting me. "It will always mix lies with the truth to feed your guilt and insecurity."

"Well, I have reason to feel guilty," I answered. "I wasn't a good son. I was there for her, most of the time, but I resented it, just like I resented having to care for my brother. I gave up on him years before he died, and now I see, if I had listened, I might have saved him. Him and my mother."

"Every caregiver experiences doubts and moments of weakness."

"These weren't moments," I said, the emotion welling within me. "It was day-after-day, for months and years. Are you telling me that wasn't sin?"

"Sin means to miss the mark, to fail to behave as Christ Jesus would in a situation," Father Mubita explained. "The Lord wouldn't have grown weary of doing good in your circumstances. Nor would he have failed to see the hand of the Evil One on your mother and brother. So yes, you missed the mark. You have sinned."

I felt strangely relieved to have my sin confirmed. I had lived so long in a world where nothing mattered, good or evil. I believe that your actions died with you. And when the last man finally went extinct, the universe would be no different than before the first one arose. It was good to know that my actions mattered, even if they were wrong.

"Can you forgive me?" I asked.

"It is not I who forgives, but Christ. He paid the price for your sins with His blood on the cross," Father Mubita answered. "Are you willing to accept his sacrifice?"

Now it was time to sign on the dotted line. And what choice did I have? In about five hours, I would face Betty head on. She spent decades arranging this showdown, preparing for any eventuality. She probably had tricks up her sleeve we had not even imagined. I knew we couldn't beat her on our own. I needed God to survive, which meant I had to join His team, even if it meant eternal separation from my mother and brother.

"Yes," I answered. "I accept His sacrifice. I will do whatever He asks, but I will never love him."

Silence. Then he asked, "Rick, why would you withhold your love from someone who died for you?"

"Because He's asking me to choose between Him and my family."

"How?"

"If I obey God, I'll end up in heaven and never see my mother or brother again."

"Why? Because of the way they died?" Mubita asked.

"That's what good old Father Isidore taught me—that people who die with mortal sins on their souls go straight to hell."

"Did this Father Isidore also teach you what a mortal sin is?"

"A sin that damns you, like murder."

"Rick, I see why this weighs heavily on you, but you are making some false assumptions," he replied. "A mortal sin must meet three conditions. First, the act must be a grave matter. Obviously, suicide is one. Secondly, the person must have full knowledge that what they are doing is wrong. Both your mother and your brother received at least some religious training so that would be a safe assumption. Finally, the act must be done with deliberate consent. Do you think either your mother or your brother were in a condition to make an unfettered choice?"

"What do you mean?" I asked.

"The church realizes that mental illness, extreme hardship, and fear or anguish make it impossible for a person to give deliberate consent. Therefore, they are not fully culpable for their actions morally," Father Mubita explained.

I couldn't believe what I was hearing. "Are you telling me that my mother and brother are in heaven?" I asked.

"Rick, I wish I could tell you that they were both in heaven, but I do not know. Only God knows what was in their hearts at the time of their deaths," he answered.

My heart sank. "So they could be in hell?" I asked.

"Rick, you must also take in account the love of God," Father Mubita added. "God loved your mother and brother—even more than you do. He created them expressly for His pleasure. Do you think after that God would surrender them willingly to the Devil? No, no, no. The Lord vied for their souls until the very end, of that I am sure. His arms were always open to them, and we can only pray that, as they left this troubled life, they fell softly into them."

"Do you really believe that?" I asked. I could feel the tears filling my eyes.

"Rick, I have staked my entire life, all that I am and all that I ever will be, on the love of God," he answered. "Do you think I could walk into the battle tonight if I didn't trust him entirely?"

Mubita's commitment to both God and us made a compelling argument about faith. Betty attacked Teri and me. We had to fight her. Father Mubita didn't, but he chose to help us despite the death of his friend. He was the kind of person who would have faced the lions in the Roman coliseum with a smile on his face and a hymn on his lips. He was a man of true faith. I envied him, but then I realized something. I had no reason to envy him. *I* could have the same faith.

In a moment of true clarity, the last vestiges of my spiritual resistance collapsed. I proudly believed my agnosticism was a product of my rigid rationalism, but now, I saw it as an emotional reaction to God's silence at the loss of my father. But God was never really silent. In that moment, words and images flooded my mind. I could clearly see Him reaching out to me through my family and teachers and even the church, but I had petulantly stopped listening. I rejected the peace He offered. My anger at God hardened even further after the death of my brother as Betty continually projected Father Isidore's hurtful words into my mind. My mother's death was the final blow. That locked and bolted the door of my heart forever. Or so it seemed.

I left the confessional a changed man. Teri could tell. She looked up from her prayers when she heard me. A giant smile crossed her face. I walked over to her as Jose sheepishly took my place in the box. Emotionally drained, I practically collapsed onto the wooden pew.

"How are you feeling?" she asked.

"Good," I answered. "How are you doing?"

"I feel clean, Rick," she said. "It's as if all the hurt and doubt that's plagued me for the last ten years is gone."

"I can't remember the last time I felt this kind of peace," I replied. "I've always gone through life waiting for the other shoe to drop. Now I'm not afraid anymore, even if we don't make it."

"Neither am I," said Teri.

I put an arm around her shoulder. She nuzzled closer.

I pulled out my cellphone. It was five-thirty. Three hours to nightfall—and our potential deaths. I wondered about my mother and my brother. Did they know three hours earlier that they would die? I doubted it. My mother seemed perfectly fine before my little tryst with Gina. I detected no gloom or resignation in her voice. I think the same was true of Lenny. He spent the last week of his life working a construction job in Ocean City. Why would he spend the week working if he just planned to kill himself? It didn't make sense.

I think Father Mubita was right. Their deaths were not premeditated. They had not made deliberate consent. The irony, of course, was that I had. I was going to the cemetery tonight with the full knowledge that I might die. It wasn't quite suicide, but the end result could be the same.

And I was ready.

Chapter Forty-One: Sunset

I don't know how long Jose spent in the confessional. Maybe an hour. Maybe a little longer. When he finally emerged, he seemed a little shaken. However, when he spotted me looking at him, he forced a cocky smile.

Father Mubita emerged from the booth soon after him and declared the fast over. Now it was time to replenish our physical strength. We retired to the fellowship hall to pick through the plentiful leftovers as some old ladies from the parish cleaned up. The food tasted good, and none of us had any trouble eating it or holding it down. I didn't know whether it was because we were still outside of Betty's reach in the church Fellowship Hall or whether she was too busy setting up her defenses at the cemetery to play her little food games.

Sitting at a table in a corner by ourselves, we talked about everything but Betty and the showdown ahead of us. Teri asked Jose about his background, and we were treated to his story. He was born in Los Angeles. When his parents saw him hanging out with gang members in high school, they sent him to live in Baltimore with an uncle who owned a landscaping business. Jose felt the lure of the streets in Baltimore, too, but this time, he saved himself by joining the United States Marines at seventeen. He served two tours in Iraq and one tour in Afghanistan. That was enough for him. He came home to work with his uncle again. When they got a contract to clean up a cemetery, he discovered he had an affinity for the work. After all of the killing he had seen, he found peace honoring the dead. He soon quit his uncle's business and started working directly for cemeteries.

When Jose finished, I prodded Father Mubita to tell him about the leopard. He retold the story in greater detail, but with a more comic tone. There was much laughter, but it ended abruptly with the beeping of Father Mubita's cellphone. We all turned to him as he pulled it out. "Sunset. They're starting the prayer vigil now," he said as he turned off the alarm. Turning to Jose, he asked, "Do you think it's dark enough now?"

Jose walked over to the window. "Well, provided we don't catch the whole damned place on fire, I don't think anyone will be able to see us from the road," he answered after a moment of consideration.

Father Mubita turned to Teri and me. "Ready?"

Ah, the moment of truth. It was finally here. Teri turned to me. Her eyes told me what I already knew. We were in this together. I nodded to her before turning back to Father Mubita. "Let's do it," I said.

"I'm ready," Teri said, nodding.

Father Mubita turned to Jose.

"Who wants to live forever anyway?" he replied with a smile.

"Let me get a few things; then we can leave," Father Mubita said before he disappeared back into the sanctuary.

"I'm sorry I got you involved in this, Jose," I said.

"Don't worry. I've been wanting to do this for months, but I didn't have the guts to do it alone, and I couldn't ask my guys," he said as he walked over and put a hand on my shoulder. "We end this thing tonight. We burn this witch or die trying."

I nodded my head firmly in agreement.

"You and me will handle the coffin," he continued. "It'll be around four hundred pounds. You good with that?"

"Yeah," I answered.

"I can help," Teri interjected.

"No, you're on lookout," Jose said. Teri opened her mouth to object, but Jose shut her down immediately. "My cemetery, my rules," he said firmly.

Teri said nothing, but I felt the need to speak up. "Don't underestimate her," I said. "She saved my life last night."

"I'm not underestimating anybody," he replied. "We're a team, and everybody on a team is important. Even the lookout. What if some of those flower people show up and try to stop us?"

That was a sobering thought. There were no laws governing how we battled a demon, but what if a person intervened? What if one attacked us and we had to defend ourselves? We'd have a hard time explaining that to the police.

Father Mubita emerged from the sanctuary wearing an ornate scapular around his shoulders and a large cross around his neck. As he walked toward us, he raised up a bottle of water. "Holy water," he said.

"Good idea," Jose said.

Father Mubita patted his shirt pocket. "I've got a consecrated host, too," he said. "I want to put it in the coffin when we're done. It should prevent her return."

"I like your style, padre," Jose answered with a smile.

Chapter Forty-Two: The Army

We left through the rear of the church. Jose grabbed the shotgun seat while Father Mubita got behind the wheel. I was happy to sit in the back with Teri.

The twilight quickly surrendered to night as we drove toward the cemetery. I could smell the putrid stench before I could see it. Teri coughed, then held her hand over her mouth.

"You smell that?" Jose asked.

"Yeah," I answered.

"Imagine working there every day," he said.

"I'm surprised you didn't quit," I replied.

"And abandon my crew?" he answered, a little insulted by implication. "No way."

The Buick crested a hill, and Eternal Faith came into sight. In the gathering darkness, the grounds appeared to be an empty, black void. The outline of the trees, like the familiar willows near my family plot, could only be detected if you knew where there were. The only lights came from the "eternal flames," small electric lights, placed on the vaults on the outside of the mausoleum. No light came out of the building itself. The glass doors weren't even visible from the road.

The main gate was closed and locked. Father Mubita stopped in front of it. Jose jumped out and unlocked the gate. Pulling the iron door open, he motioned for Father Mubita to drive in. However, the car sputtered out when Father Mubita put his foot on the gas.

"Wait a second," he said.

He tried starting the car again. The engine turned over but stalled out immediately. Jose impatiently hurried over to his window as Father Mubita tried again. This time all he got was an ugly grinding sound. "It's never done this before," he said, turning to Jose.

"Well, we're not waiting around for Triple-A," Jose answered. "Pop the trunk, Padre. We're walking."

We piled out of the car and went to the trunk. Jose stuck the screwdrivers and two of the flares in his pockets and took one of the five-gallon gas cans. I grabbed the remaining flares and other five-gallon gas can. Teri and Father Mubita grabbed the buckets, hammers, and the crowbar. After we stepped inside the cemetery, Jose closed and locked the gate. Turning toward the blackness between us and the mausoleum, Jose sighed. "I wish we would've brought some flashlights."

"Want to use one of the flares?" I asked.

"Nah," he answered. "People would see it from the road and wonder what the hell we're doing in here."

He was right, as usual, but I would have been happy to light a flare if only for the heat. It was probably still almost eighty degrees and humid in the church parking lot. Here, it was cold enough to mist our breath before us. It was ridiculous. Since this thing began, the cemetery had gotten colder and colder, yet none of us thought to wear appropriate clothing.

Oh well, I thought, *soon we'll be warming ourselves over a fire.*

Rather than follow the roads, Jose stepped onto grass in the most direct route to the mausoleum. We followed behind as he took point. I normally drove around the cemetery in a car. Only now, walking in the darkness and carrying five gallons of gasoline, did I appreciate the size of the grounds. The mausoleum, located at the far corner of the property, was probably at least a half a mile away. Maybe more. Before long, the four of us were breathing heavily, although I would credit the poisonous atmosphere rather than our exertions for the difficulty. I felt particularly bad for Father Mubita as he limped unevenly alongside us.

"Are you going to be okay, Father?" I asked after he nearly tripped over one of the low grave markers.

"I'm fine," he answered. "I don't feel any pain, unless I have to run."

I nodded and turned to Teri. She scanned the cemetery like a hawk for trouble with a hammer in one hand and the crowbar in the other as she walked. I couldn't help but be proud of her resolve. She was a brave woman. Braver than me.

As we walked, I couldn't resist turning toward the willow tree. I expected to see my mother and brother standing at the family plot, but they were not there. Their absence surprised me. Perhaps Betty realized the apparitions had lost their effectiveness now that I knew they were only her masks. On the other hand, I feared she might be conserving her powers for an all-out defense of her crypt. She knew we were coming. She had to know what we were planning. When was she going to show her hand?

I heard the distant noise of an engine. I turned back to the road to see a tractor-trailer truck driving past the gate. I found it strangely unsettling. It took me a moment to figure out why: the sound. We were only about seventy yards from the front of the cemetery, but the truck sounded as if it was miles away. Somehow, Betty was muffling the sound. As the truck moved away, I listened intently, but I couldn't hear anything but breathing and footsteps. Not a single bird or cricket. There was no sound at all until the first crack.

It sounded like a thick branch snapping somewhere in the distance. Instinctively, I turned to the willow tree on the hill, but I didn't see any movement. I turned to the others. They all heard the sound as well, and they were looking in different directions. Then there was another crack to our right. It was a little louder but still muffled. Jose raised a hand in the air to stop us.

"What was that?" Teri asked.

There was another crack to our left. Although it wasn't loud, in the unnatural stillness, it sounded like thunder. We all turned toward it. Father Mubita took out his cellphone and shined the light in that direction. The small circle of light revealed nothing of the enemy. Jose reached over and lowered his hand. Another crack rolled down the hill to us from the willow tree. I didn't know what the hell it was, but I didn't like it. Now I was scared.

"Oh, no," Jose said softly.

"What?" I asked.

"It's the coffins," he said.

"The coffins?" Teri said, her voice cracking.

"At the first cemetery where I worked, this lazy funeral director backed his big ass hearse over a bunch of graves and that's what I heard: crack, crack, crack, as the coffins broke under the weight," Jose said contemptuously. "I could have killed that guy."

Suddenly, there was a loud crack nearby. Now we could tell for sure that the sound was definitely coming from underground. Jose put down his can of gasoline and took Father Mubita's cellphone. Using the light to guide him, he wandered slowly in the direction of the sound. We followed. He stopped near a fresh grave.

"Mr. Holloway," he said softly. "We buried him last week."

Ignoring a growing chorus of cracks around us, Jose bent down at his knees near the exposed patch of dirt and clay. Another crack came from beneath it, startling him. Father Mubita started saying a prayer under his breath. I couldn't make out the words.

"It's just an illusion," I said. "A trick."

Jose ran the light from the cellphone over the grave. He stopped over a small hole. While we watched, the hole slowly expanded as the dirt fell inward like a whirlpool to fill some void below the surface. Jose leaned closer to get a better look. As he did, a low moan rose up through the hole.

Jose jumped to his feet. He crossed himself as Father Mubita's prayer skidded to a stop mid-word. The four of us watched in horror as the dirt rose up as if something had slammed against it from underground. An angry grunt followed as the dirt whirlpool widened. There was no denying that the late Mr. Holloway was trying to get out.

"Richard!" shouted a voice that cut across the deadly still of the cemetery like a knife.

I don't know if the word was clear to everyone. The articulation was imprecise, as if someone whose mouth and throat were eaten away by decay shouted it. I recognized both the word and the voice. It was my mother. I turned to the family plot on the hill. I could see the silhouettes of two figures rising up from the ground. I knew it was her and Lenny. Who else could it be?

"Do you see them?" I asked, pointing toward the hill. I was hoping the answer would be no. I was hoping they were simply illusions designed to torment me alone.

Teri, Jose, and Father Mubita turned to the hill. "Yeah," Teri said.

"That's my mother and my brother," I said softly.

"Look!" Father Mubita shouted, pointing to the left of the hill. Another figure rose from the earth between the gate and us. Then another. And then another. There was no going back now. No escape.

"She's raising an army," Father Mubita said in utter astonishment.

I froze, less in fear than amazement. Now I understood why those ancient pagans worshipped Betty as a God in my vision. Who else but a God could raise the dead? Such power was incomprehensible. I had expected countermeasures from Betty, but nothing on this scale. How could we expect to beat her, even if we had God on our side?

This was suicide.

"We're going to die," Teri said softly.

Before anyone could respond to her, another loud thud echoed from the Holloway grave. More dirt poured into the whirlpool as the ground rose and fell in conjunction with subterranean movement. I stood transfixed. I fully expected to see Mr. Holloway's head break through the surface. Instead, his white, bony hand pushed through the soil of his grave. His fingers extended into the air as if they were sucking in the oxygen after a long absence.

"Start moving, now!" Jose said, with a battle-hardened calm.

We didn't need to be asked twice. Jose took point again, but he walked considerably faster this time. We quickly followed him. As the cracking continued in all directions, Jose picked up his pace to a quick trot. Teri and I kept up with him, but Father Mubita, his limp exaggerated by the pace, fell steadily behind.

"Are you okay, Father?" I asked, looking over my shoulder.

"Don't worry about me," he answered. "I'll be fine."

Teri and Jose stopped while I went back to assist Father Mubita. He put his big arm around my shoulder and laid his considerable weight from his bad leg on me.

"This is good," I said. "You balance out the gas can."

"I'll take that," Teri said as she traded her crowbar for the heavy, plastic container of gasoline.

"Are you sure you can handle that?" I asked.

Before Teri could reply, Jose shouted, "Come on! Now, now!"

As we started moving again, I looked over my shoulder to see dozens of shadows shambling toward us in the darkness. They were not particularly fast, but they made steady progress. My eyes instinctively drifted to the hilltop, but I could no longer see my brother or mother. They must have gotten lost in the crowd on the left trying to get between the mausoleum and us.

Father Mubita and I quickly found a rhythm, but we still fell behind. Jose trotted about thirty yards ahead of us. His head darted right and left, gauging the growing threat as the dead rose on all sides of us. Teri, awkwardly carrying the gasoline container in front of her with both hands, hurried about fifteen yards behind him.

"Have you ever seen anything like this before?" I asked Father Mubita.

"No, nothing."

Suddenly, Teri took a spill ahead of us, falling face first onto the ground. The gas container rolled and tumbled ahead of her. Releasing Father Mubita, I raced forward as Teri began kicking and screaming. As I neared her, I saw that an emerging corpse had grabbed a hold of her ankle. It was using its grip on her to pull itself to the surface. The back of its head and one of its shoulders were now fully exposed. From the full head of long, gray hair, I assumed it was a woman. I think it was trying to speak, but there was too much soft tissue gone to succeed. It emitted a husky, almost-canine barking instead.

I raised the crowbar and brought it down on the corpse's head as I passed. The woman must have been dead a long time because the crowbar collapsed her entire skull right down the shoulders. Dried brain matter sprayed into the sky. The end of the crowbar must have hooked some bone near the shoulder. It yanked me backwards. Thrown off balance, I released the weapon as I rolled to the ground. Teri was still screaming. Despite losing nearly its entire head, the corpse maintained a firm grip on Teri's ankle and continued pulling itself up to the surface.

Dumbfounded, I crawled back to save Teri. I was used to zombies in the movies and on television dying when you destroyed their brains so I had no idea how to stop this one. Jose and Father Mubita arrived as I yanked the crowbar out of the corpse. Rising up, I pounded again and again on the corpse's forearm with the crowbar until I finally broke the bones. Only then did her dead fingers release their grip on Teri's ankle.

Jose helped Teri to her feet as I stood up slowly. My shoulder hurt like hell where it had hit the ground, but the pain seemed insignificant as I looked back. The vanguard of the dead army was nearly upon us, only twenty or thirty yards away. They were close enough now to see the details of their dirty faces. None of them had eyes anymore, just hollow sockets. Their jaws hung open, moving wordlessly. Their clothing, cut in back and laid on them by their funeral directors, hung loosely in front of them. Others were completely naked, having lost their clothes during their climbs through the earth. One of the fresher corpses lumbered forward revealing an ugly autopsy scar, an ill-stitched Y down from his chest to his pubic bone.

Jose saw them, too. Turning to us, he shouted, "Run!"

He turned and picked up his gas can and started running. He snatched up the can Teri had been carrying as he passed it. Teri and I exchanged a glance. "Go," I said.

It was obvious she didn't want to leave Father Mubita and me.

"Run!" I shouted.

She did. Father Mubita grabbed my shoulder, and we hurried along as quickly as we could. A quick glance over my shoulder revealed that we were getting ahead of the dead, but they were still too close for comfort. The mausoleum loomed just ahead of us. I watched as Jose set the containers of gasoline in front of the door. Teri arrived as he started fumbling with the keys to the door.

"Come on, come on," I muttered under my breath.

Jose finally managed to open the large glass doors of the mausoleum just as Father Mubita and I arrived.

Chapter Forty-Three: Betty

Jose closed the glass doors behind Father Mubita and myself as we entered the mausoleum. He grabbed the crowbar out of my hand and put it through the loops of the ornate door handles.

"Aren't you going to lock the door?" I asked.

"There's no lock on the inside," he explained. "Cemetery doors are designed to keep the dead in, not the living out."

Then he walked over and turned on the lights. After the complete darkness, the overhead lights had us blinded for a second. "Do we have everything?" Jose asked.

We laid out our tools: two five-gallon containers of gasoline, two bucket, two hammers, three flares, and two screwdrivers. We lost one of the flares outside. Jose turned to the door and said, "We're going to need that crowbar."

"How are we going to hold the door shut?" Teri asked.

"Wait a minute," Jose said, before he ran toward a utility closet in the corner of the mausoleum.

I joined Teri at the door. Her hands tightly gripped the handles. I looked outside, but the light inside the mausoleum completely ruined my night vision. Neither of us could see Betty's army of the dead, but we knew they were quickly approaching. Forget about the lock and the crowbar; I doubted the glass itself would hold them back for long.

"I want you to go," I said, turning to Teri. "Jose's truck is parked in front of the office. If you leave now, you can get to it." Turning back into the building, I shouted, "Jose, where are your keys?"

"I'm not leaving," she said.

"Please," I begged. "I can't watch another person I love die."

Her soft, blue eyes widened with surprise at my declaration. In a perfect world, she would have responded by telling me that she loved me, too, but this wasn't a perfect world. This was the mirror opposite of a perfect world. Before she could respond, we heard moans outside. We both gasped when we turned to see the first of the zombies stepping into the pool of light outside the door. Much to my horror, Lenny and my mother led the way.

Lenny wore a torn hospital gown. I guess the funeral director decided not to dress him in the clothes my mother carefully picked out for him after we opted against an open casket. His eyes were gone, and his nose had collapsed in upon itself. Most of his flesh was gone, leaving some cartilage and bone. Still, the general contours of his face remained recognizable. Even more recognizable was the wound to his skull, which I remembered clearly from the vision Betty foisted upon me. Neither the coroner nor the funeral director made any real attempt to repair the damage prior to burial. His skull had been wrapped with a long bandage. It still made a few loops around his forehead, but the bulk of it trailed behind him. Dirt and tufts of grass from the climb filled the cavity, which should have housed his brain.

My mother, despite being dead for nearly as long, was obviously the recipient of more careful preparation. Her nose remained, as did most of the flesh on her face. It was discolored, and some gaping holes were opening up on it, but she was easily recognizable. She wore the formal blue dress I had picked out for her. It was torn away from her right shoulder during the climb, revealing a sagging, hollowed-out breast. Her eyes were gone, but I could tell she was looking directly at Teri.

"That's my mother," I said to Teri, pointing to the corpse. "And that's my brother Lenny."

Teri took the little silver cross out from under her shirt and held it up to the dead, but it had no discernable effect on them. Groaning, they slammed against the door like a putrid tidal wave. Releasing the cross, she grabbed the door handles and the crowbar. So did I. Father Mubita, who had been quietly praying since our arrival, rushed to our assistance. The glass doors swung on a hinge that could either be pushed in or pulled open.

My mother and Lenny grabbed the handles and tried to pull the doors open. The panes opened enough for some of the other zombies to get their fingers between them. They pulled back on the door, too, but the other dead, further from the opening, counteracted them by pressing against the doors.

It was an appalling sight to behold. Some of the dead banged against the doors with bony fists. The decaying skin of others ripped away as they rubbed their faces against the glass. I didn't know how many of them there were, maybe two hundred, but more continued to join them. My mother was the one who scared me most. Her eyes were long gone, but her shadowy sockets remained glued on Teri. Despite the decay, her rage and hatred was easy to discern. She still wasn't about to let another woman get between her and her family.

"Why you need my keys?" Jose shouted as he hurried back.

"Never mind," I said as I turned to him. He was carrying a broom and a mop. "Where'd you get those?"

"The broom closet," Jose said as he moved alongside Teri. He slid the broomstick and then the mop between the two handles of the door. Then he reached for the crowbar.

"No," Teri said, grabbing it. "They'll get in without it."

"We need it to break through the sealant on the vault," he said. "We'll worry about them after we burn the witch."

Teri released the crowbar. Jose yanked it out.

"Hold them as long as you can," Jose said to her, before he turned to Father Mubita and me. "Let's do this." Jose motioned to the gasoline containers and the buckets. "Padre, fill the buckets up to the brim with gas; then come on down," he said. Then he scooped up the hammers, screwdrivers, and flares and headed toward the vault. As I walked alongside him, he handed me a screwdriver. "You ready?" he said.

"Hell, yeah," I said.

I looked ahead at the vault to see Betty's ceramic photograph again. Her smile had gone from smug to positively jubilant. She obviously felt she was still in charge. However, the anxiety I previously felt when I walked toward her grave no longer plagued me. Betty had pushed me too far. It was fight or flight now, and she cut off all escape routes. I had no choice. I had to fight, and, frankly, I preferred fighting one of her than the two hundred zombies pounding on the door.

As we neared the vault, Jose raised the hammer to smash the picture but I grabbed his hand. "No, let me," I said.

Despite his own desire for revenge, Jose handed me the hammer. I kicked the idolatrous flowers aside as I walked the final few feet to the vault. I smiled as I gave Betty's photograph one final look. If Emile was correct, this was the physical last image of Betty that remained on planet Earth. When we were done, no one would be able to use Betty Kostek to call the demon Azardon into our realm again.

"Bye, bye, Betty," I said.

I raised the hammer and brought it down on the ceramic photograph. The broken pieces tinkled to the floor in a strange silence. Even the zombies at the door froze.

It was as if the mausoleum itself had exhaled the evil. With the evil gone, we gained more than silence. The building felt clean. The heavy, poisonous aura of Betty was gone, but only briefly. The mausoleum inhaled the evil again after a few seconds, but now, it was worse. New allies within the mausoleum joined the dead outside, who now slammed against the glass doors with renewed vigor. All around us, movement and banging came from within the sealed vaults.

Jose's eyes darted around the building before turning to me. "Don't worry, they can't get out," he said. "The vaults are too low to open the lids and too narrow to break out the sides."

"I got the gas," Father Mubita shouted.

"Good, leave it there for now, and go back and help Teri with the door," Jose replied. Then he turned to me. "Let's roast this pig."

Jose worked the crowbar into the seam between the marble covering of Betty's vault and her neighbor. After a moment, he turned to me. "Get back."

I stepped back. Jose used the crowbar to pop the thick marble front of the vault away from the wall. It hit the ground with a loud crash and cracked into a number of pieces.

"That's gonna cost me a paycheck," Jose said to me with a smile.

A metal barrier secured by screws and a sealant now stood between us and Betty's coffin. I started undoing the two screws on my side while Jose did the ones on his side. While we worked, I noticed there was no noise coming from Betty's vault. She wasn't struggling to get out. Why? Wasn't she afraid? What did she know that we didn't?

"Done," I said as I finished my screws. I stepped back. Jose picked up the crowbar. He dug away at the sealant surrounding the edges of the metal barrier.

"Hurry!" Teri shouted.

I looked back at the glass doors. They heaved inward at the weight of the dead pressing against them. Teri and Father Mubita pushed back with all of their might, but it looked like a losing battle.

"Step back," Jose said.

I stepped back. Jose worked the end of the crowbar along the edge of the metal and then popped it forward. The heavy metal plate landed on the broken marble with a dull thud, cracking it even further. Looking up, I saw Betty's grey, metal coffin sitting in the dark vault.

"Okay, let's lower this end to the ground," Jose said.

We both grabbed the handle on the end of the casket and pulled it out of the vault. The metal scraping against the marble resulted in a high-pitched screech. The activity in the other vaults intensified with the sound. When we had the coffin about halfway out, it was clear we weren't going to be able to lower the end to the ground.

"Move to the side and we'll lower it down," Jose said. We moved our hands from the rear handle to the sides ones.

"Got it," I said.

"Lift," Jose said.

We lifted the casket up. It was actually lighter than I expected. We managed to carry it beyond the broken marble and set it down on the floor. "Father, bring down the bucket," Jose said.

Father Mubita left the heaving doors and carried the bucket of gasoline down to us. Now only Teri stood between the army of the dead and us.

"I'm going to unlock the coffin and open it," he said to Father Mubita. "As soon as I'm clear, throw the gas on her."

Father Mubita nodded.

"Throw, not pour," Jose reiterated. "We're only going to get one chance at this."

"I understand," Father Mubita said.

Jose grabbed me and pulled me a few steps behind and to the left of Father Mubita. Once he positioned me exactly where he wanted me, he took out a flare and lit it up. "Be careful with this. Keep it pointed down until after Father Mubita throws the gas," he said. "I don't want you lighting him up by mistake."

Jose handed me the flare. Thanks to his warning, I was now actually more nervous about accidently catching Father Mubita on fire than Betty's reaction.

"Hurry, I can't hold them alone," Teri shouted.

I gave her a quick glance. She was definitely hard-pressed. The wooden broom and mop handles were creaking under the pressure. How the hell were we going to stop them after we dealt with Betty?

"In a minute," I said to Teri before I turned back to Jose as he neared the coffin.

"There's two locks," Jose said aloud.

He undid the first lock along the edge of coffin below the lid. I gulped. I couldn't believe this was actually happening. I was also a little relieved to see Jose wasn't immune to the fear either. His gait slowed considerably as he neared the head of the coffin. He turned back to us.

"Are you ready?" he asked. I nodded. Father Mubita lifted the bucket into position. "Give me a chance to jump back," Jose added.

"I will," Father Mubita said.

Slowly Jose bent down at the head of the coffin. His hand reached under the lid of the coffin. He nodded to us when his finger found the lock. He closed his eyes and muttered something under his breath before we heard the soft click of the lock.

Both sections of the lid suddenly flew open without any assistance from Jose. Betty rose from her prone position in the coffin into a standing position on her own power as if she were on a hinge. She wore a black dress and pearls, and her hands were crossed over her chest. Her face, under the thick makeup applied by the mortician, looked just like her picture, only about twenty years older. She showed no sign of decay. The demon Azardon obviously worked overtime to preserve her body and maintain his presence in our world.

Nothing could prepare me for the terror I felt when she opened her eyes. They were dark brown and filled with inhuman malevolence. She turned to me and gave me the same smug smile from the photograph.

"Die!" Jose shouted.

Jose's machismo got the best of him. Instead of jumping out of the way and letting Father Mubita douse her with the gasoline, he took the opportunity to smash her in the back of the head with the crowbar. The blow had no effect on her. Unperturbed, Betty turned her head slightly toward him. Then she grabbed him. Her hand was so fast that I wondered if she actually moved it physically or if she somehow miracled it into position around his neck. Showing no exertion whatsoever, Betty lifted Jose off his feet and threw him back against marble vaults. He hit them with such force that I doubted he could survive. One down.

With Jose out of range, Father Mubita finally threw the bucket full of gasoline on Betty. Turning toward him, she simply raised her hand in his direction, and he went flying back against the marble vaults on his side. He fell to the floor in an unconscious heap afterwards. Two down.

Betty turned to me. Although I raised the flare, her expression indicated complete confidence. She displayed no fear of me at all.

I'll show you, I thought.

It was now or never. Mustering my courage, I prepared to throw the flare when I heard the cracking of wood behind me followed by a long scream from Teri. Instinctively, I turned to see the dead flooding into the mausoleum. One of them had Teri by the neck.

"No!" I shouted.

Forgetting Betty, I raced to Teri's rescue. A corpse had both of its hands wrapped around her neck, squeezing hard. Teri desperately fought back. Her hands ripped away at the flesh of the monster's wrists, but she was unable to break the grip. I had to do something. My eyes went from Teri to her attacker, and my heart sank. It was my mother. She was now doing to Teri what, under Betty's pernicious influence, she had longed to do to Gina. I couldn't let it happen.

"Stop!" I shouted.

I charged toward them, lowering my flare in the process. When I reached my mother, I thrust the burning tube ahead of me into her empty right eye socket. The impact didn't kill her, but it jolted her enough to release her grip on Teri's neck. Teri gasped for breath as I pulled her away from my mother. Her neck was bruised and flaked with dead skin.

I protectively pulled Teri close as the dead turned to us. All of them. We backed up as they steadily moved forward. Lenny led them, his hands extended toward me. My mother walked right behind him, unconcerned about the flare sticking out of her right eye that emitted an uneven stream of sputtering flames out of her eye socket.

"Ricky," Lenny groaned.

I heard no rancor or hostility in what remained of his voice. Nor was there any hostility in the way he reached for me. His palms were up, and he moved his fingers in a welcoming gesture, as if he wanted to hug me. But I knew the truth. If I let down my guard, he would tear me to pieces. They all would.

"What are we going to do, Rick?" Teri asked, still coughing. "There's too many of them."

Before I could reply, I heard that little voice again.
There is only one.

Only one, God? Really? *What game are you watching?* I thought. *We're down twelve-to-three in the ninth with two outs.*

Only one, the voice said again.

Betty began to laugh. As we continued backing away from the advancing dead, I looked at her over my shoulder. She was smiling broadly, and her hands were extended before her. Her fingertips danced up and down as if she was a puppet master.

There is only one, I thought.

There was only Betty.

But what could I do about it? I had blown my chance. Betty played me perfectly. She knew I would waste my opportunity to destroy her in order to save Teri. Maybe that was why she brought us together in the first place. She manipulated me into falling in love with Teri in order to save herself. It was all a ploy. A trap. And I fell for it.

I deserved to die.

No! I refused to believe that. Betty had not brought Teri and me together for our destruction. God brought us together to destroy her. And we would. Tonight, it would end.

I turned from Betty to my mother. The flare stuck in her eye seemed to be sputtering out, but I only needed a little spark. Releasing Teri, I grabbed the flare and yanked it from my mother's skull with a squishy, sizzling sound. Turning to Betty, I threw the dying flare. It flew across the room end over end, spitting fire and sparks.

I watched the flare in agonizing slow motion. It wasn't a pretty sight. I soon realized why I was always the ninth inning substitute right fielder in Little League. The flare drifted to the left of Betty. I couldn't believe it. I was only twenty-feet away, and I was going to miss! This was really the end. I grabbed Teri and pulled her close. I prepared to say goodbye as the dead stepped within grasping range. Then the flare suddenly sputtered again. Sparks showered Betty, igniting the gasoline on the lower half of her body.

The dead stopped in their tracks when Betty burst into flames. She looked down at the flames climbing up her clothes. Her expression reflected surprise but not panic as she calmly began ripping her clothes off.

"More gas!" Teri shouted.

I charged over to the second bucket of gasoline Father Mubita had filled up. As I lifted it, I saw that Betty nearly had the burning dress completely removed. I had to act immediately, but I saw Jose lying on the ground not too far beyond her. I didn't want the gas to spill in his direction. I shifted my angle as Teri shouted, "Hurry!"

I tossed the bucket of gasoline at Betty, aiming at her head and shoulders with the hoping that the residue would land in the coffin. She gave out a cackling shriek as her hair burned away in an instant. Flames engulfed her completely. She crumbled crookedly, her mouth moving wordlessly, before she fell backwards straight into the coffin.

Not taking any chances, I refilled the bucket completely with gasoline again. As I did, I saw Father Mubita stirring alongside the vaults. "We got her," I said as his eyes opened.

Taking the bucket, I walked over to the coffin where Betty's blackening body jittered and shook convulsively. After exchanging a glance with Teri, I tossed the bucket of gasoline onto our nemesis. The ensuing fireball scorched the ceiling and knocked Teri and me from our feet. When the flames receded, we both worked our way back to the metal coffin. The badly burned corpse no longer moved. More importantly, the army of the dead was gone as if it never existed.

It was only Betty the whole time.

Chapter Forty-Four: Sunrise

Jose wasn't dead, but it took us quite a while to revive him.

Certain he had suffered a concussion, we all begged him to go to the hospital. He refused. He wouldn't leave the job half-finished. I am glad he stayed. Much work remained.

Jose wasn't kidding when he told me earlier that it wasn't easy to burn a body completely to ashes. Although Betty barely seemed decayed at all, her flesh was dry and burned easily with the help of the gasoline. Her bones proved more of a problem. The fire darkened but failed to consume them. Every time the fire went out, Jose and I used the hammers and pounded on them, shattering them and making them easier to burn. Afterwards, we poured more gasoline into the coffin and lit her up again. We repeated this process many times throughout the night.

Teri said little as the night progressed. She just sat quietly alongside the coffin with me watching the fire. She leaned gently against me, often resting her head on my shoulder. She took my hand whenever I set it down near her, but she never said anything about my ill-timed declaration of love. She just watched the pile of bones get smaller and smaller with each succeeding fire.

Father Mubita sat a couple of feet further back from the foot of the coffin, his palms up, his face skyward, with his eyes closed. He prayed and sang hymns of thanksgiving throughout the long hours of the night. Sometimes Teri joined him when she was familiar with the tune. She possessed a wonderful voice that blended beautifully with his lilting baritone, especially as it echoed off the hard marble walls. I was both captivated and inspired. I wished I could have joined them, but I didn't know any of the songs. I hoped I would one day.

As the orange glow of sunrise illuminated the glass doors, Jose and I were nearly finished with our gruesome work. The only recognizable bits of the Betty that remained now were her teeth. A couple hammer blows broke them into tiny pieces. Using the broom, we swept all of the ashes in the metal coffin into a small pile and poured on some more gasoline and lit a match. There wasn't enough organic material left to feed the fire; even the coffin lining was long gone. Once the gasoline burned off, the fire quickly died out. Nothing remotely human-looking remained.

Father Mubita got to his feet and examined our work. He had us stand with him and hold hands as he offered a prayer before sprinkling the inside of the casket with holy water. Then he placed the consecrated host and a crucifix upon the ashes. After Jose closed and locked the coffin lid, Father Mubita offered a final prayer and sprinkled holy water on the lid. All four of us lifted the coffin and placed it back into the vault. Jose and I screwed the metal plate back into place but didn't bother with the marble front. It was too broken to use.

The mausoleum was a complete mess. No denying that. Everything, from the marble walls to the white painted ceiling, was covered with a thick layer of grime from the oily smoke. The heat of the fire in the coffin also discolored the marble floor beneath it. Jose wasn't worried. They had pre-cut marble slabs in storage. Betty's vault would get a new marble front, but Jose said he wasn't planning to replace the bronze nameplate, unless there was a complaint from her family. I told him not to worry about that.

As we prepared to leave, I helped Jose take a large, folding partition out of the broom closet and position it in front of the glass doors. He and his team had to clean the mausoleum thoroughly before visitors could enter again. Jose didn't think the temporary closing would be much of a hardship. Aside from the people making their floral offerings, the number of visitors to the mausoleum had declined dramatically since they moved Betty inside. Now the other families would feel comfortable visiting their loved ones again.

When we left the building, Jose locked the glass doors behind us. With the partition in place, the damage inside was invisible. "You gotta fix it today?" I asked.

"No. I'm going home and going to sleep," Jose said. "And, hopefully, I won't have any more bad dreams."

"According to my aunt, you might still hear her a little," Teri said. "But she won't have the same power."

Jose nodded before motioning to his truck parked in front of the office. "I'll give you guys a ride up to the gate and get your car started," he said.

"That'd be great," Father Mubita said. "Thanks."

"If you don't mind, I'm going to walk on up," I said.

"That's cool," Jose said.

"Can I go with you?" Teri asked.

"Sure," I said.

We crossed the road onto the grass, which glistened with the morning dew. I knew the sun would burn it off soon. I could tell it was going to be a scorcher. The air was already thick with humidity. Teri didn't walk directly alongside me. She stayed about a half a step behind. I think she knew where I was going, and she wanted me to lead the way.

I didn't walk toward the gate. I headed instead for the willow tree on the hill and the little family resting near it. Teri and I walked in silence. There was no need to remark that none of the graves were disturbed. When the dead disappeared, I knew all evidence of them would disappear as well. They were simply manifestations that Betty conjured. Our eyes and senses couldn't be trusted. That didn't mean, of course, that they were not real. The bruises around Teri's throat attested to that. They were real enough to kill. They just weren't really real.

After climbing the rolling hill, Teri and I passed the willow tree and stood at the graves of my mother, father and brother. Thanks to Jose, the graves were well maintained. No weeds, just lush, trimmed grass. Still, the graves didn't look loved. No one took the time to clean and polish the bronze nameplates. Nor was there a hint of flowers. My mother used to visit the graves every month, and she kept them spic and span. She said it was actually common to find a beer or a joint on Lenny's grave. Once she even found a condom, fortunately unused. I wondered if Lenny's friends still visited. I knew Janet visited the graves on everyone's birthdays. She'd send me a text and ask me if I wanted to come. I never did.

"This is the first time I've been here since my mother's funeral," I said.

"Really?" Teri asked as she moved a little closer and put a hand at the small of my back.

"It was too painful. No matter how hard I tried, I could never convince myself they were resting in peace," I explained. "But Father Mubita gave me hope that I might see them again one day."

"You will," Teri said softly.

I turned to her and met her eyes. "But will I be seeing you?"

"I certainly hope so," she replied.

"Well, what I mean is..." I stammered, "I don't think I can go on with our original friends-only agreement."

"Richard Bakos!" she exclaimed, mock offended. "That agreement ended Thursday night when I kissed you."

"Really?"

"You really don't know anything about women, do you?" she asked, taking my hand.

"I guess I need a teacher," I said.

"And a teacher you shall have," she answered.

Teri leaned forward and gave me a kiss on the lips. Her lips were sweet and gentle, and the kiss lingered for what seemed an eternity. The perfect antidote for a life spent in sorrow and doubt. When she finished, she met my eyes and said, "I love you, too."

I wish the moment could have lasted forever, but the beeping of a car horn cut it short. We turned to see Father Mubita and Jose waving to us from the front gate. They had gotten his car started. Father Mubita may have known a lot about battling demons, but he had zero sense of timing when it came to romance. Didn't he know you never interrupt a couple kissing on a grave?

Hand-in-hand, Teri and I walked toward them. I was the happiest I had ever been in my life. Teri's smile told me she felt the same way. I really thought I had loved Gina, but it was nothing like this. Teri was right. I was waiting for the right person all along.

Her.

CPSIA information can be obtained
at www.ICGtesting.com
Printed in the USA
LVHW031041200322
713908LV00006B/979